FUNAKOSHI ON

A Portrait of Life on a Ryukyuan Island in the 19th Century, with Special Reference to Karate

OTHER BOOKS BY CLIVE LAYTON

Conversations with Karate Masters
Unmasking the Martial Artist
Mysteries of the Martial Arts
Mind Training for the Martial Arts
Training with Funakoshi
Karate Master: The Life & Times of Mitsusuke Harada
Shotokan Dawn: Vol. I
Shotokan Dawn: Vol. II
A Shotokan Karate Book of Facts: Vol. I
A Shotokan Karate Book of Facts: Vol. II
A Shotokan Karate Book of Facts: Vol. III
The Kanazawa Years
Reminiscences by Master Mitsusuke Harada
A Shotokan Karate Book of Dates
The Shotokan Karate Book of Quotes
Kanazawa, 10th Dan
The Shotokan Dawn Supplement (in press)
James Starts Karate (in press)

FUNAKOSHI ON OKINAWA

A Portrait of Life on a Ryukyuan Island in the 19th Century, with Special Reference to Karate

BY

DR. CLIVE LAYTON

KIRBY PUBLISHING
PO BOX 26397
LONDON, N8 8ZS, ENGLAND

First Published in 2004
by **Kirby Publishing**, PO Box 26397
London, N8 8ZS, ENGLAND
www.shoto.org

**British Library Cataloguing-in-
Publication Data.
A catalogue record for this book is
available from the British Library.**

**Hardback Edition   ISBN 0 9539338 5 7
Paperback Edition   ISBN 0 9539338 4 9**

DEDICATION

TO

CEDAR

We walked ten thousand miles together

ACKNOWLEDGEMENTS

The author and publisher would like to thank the following people for their assistance in the preparation of this book: Rachel Layton; Pandora Layton; Frank Riley 5th Dan; Dr. Kanishka Samarasingh 3rd Dan; Mitsusuke Harada 5th Dan, Chief Instructor to Karate-Do Shotokai; Morio Higaonna 9th Dan, Chief Instructor to the International Okinawa Goju-ryu Karate-Do Federation; Harry Cook 4th Dan, Chief Instructor to the Seijinkai Karate-Do Association; Stephen Bellamy; David and Teresa Kirby; Marcella Kirby; Susan Chalk 4th Dan; Marty Randall; Nicholas Bernard Adamou 8th Dan, Chief Instructor International Association of Shotokan Karate; Mark Hooper 4th Dan; Francis Carpenter 2nd Dan; Bamber Wrasse; Fujiko Kobayashi, Japan/Korea Librarian, The School of Oriental and African Studies, University of London; unknown staff of the British Library and the numerous staff of libraries up and down the country for their invaluable assistance in tracking down long-forgotten books and papers.

Front cover: Guillemard, F.H.H. (1886) *The Cruise of the Marchesa to Kamschatka and New Guinea with Notices of Formosa, Liu-Kiu, and Various Islands of the Malay Archipelago* (John Murray, London, Vol. I), p. 54. Engraving by Edward Whymper.

Back cover: Chief magistrate of Naha (1856). Hawks, F.L. (1856) *Narrative of the Expedition of an American Squadron to the China Seas and Japan, Performed in the Years 1852, 1853, and 1854, Under the Command of Commodore M.G. Perry, United States Navy, by Order of the Government of the United States.* Plate facing p. 155. Credited to Brown.

Photo credits: Rachel Layton, 245.
                   Kirby Publishing, 246.

CONTENTS

INTRODUCTION

Just what was it like to live on Okinawa during the nineteenth century? This has been the burning question at the heart of the author's research, for, once established, it can provide students of karate, and the limited number of other traditional martial arts taught sporadically throughout the world that can genuinely lay claim to Okinawan origins, with an invaluable reference point. Master Gichin Funakoshi, for example, the man credited with introducing karate to Japan and the founder of the Shotokan style, and, for that matter, the initial inspiration behind the Shotokai style, was born in Shuri, the island's ancient capital, in 1868, and began practising karate some ten years thereafter. Shotokan is considered the most widely taught form of karate in the world today, due, primarily, to the expansionist policy of the Japan Karate Association from the late 1950s, and throughout the 1960s and 1970s, in particular. From the late 1970s, the enormous following to Hirokazu Kanazawa's Shotokan Karate International organization, with over one hundred member countries, has added significantly to the practising numbers, as have the students of students of the JKA and SKI.

In the nineteenth century, Yasutsune Azato and Yasutsune Itosu (to use the Japanese renditions of their names), Funakoshi's principal teachers, whom Funakoshi made famous in his writings, were also born (in 1827/28 and 1830/32 {the exact dates are not known}, respectively), as was the legendary Sokon Matsumura (varied dates are also given as to his birth, but probably 1809), from whom Funakoshi also received instruction. Founders of other styles of karate, such as Goju-ryu, Shito-ryu and Uechi-ryu were also born on Okinawa and received instruction at this time. For hundreds of years surrounded in secrecy, it was during the last decade of the nineteenth century that karate ceased being such a clandestine activity, and began to be practised more openly, with even demonstrations being given.

However, the notion of being able to imagine life on a small Pacific island during a feudal, and then a much neglected period, is about as obscure and esoteric for the average western mind of the twenty-first century to grasp as one can sensibly get, separated, as it is, not only by

distance, language and culture, but made far more remote by the passing of so many years, which is further amplified by the enormous
changes in social conditions and lifestyle that took place, particularly
throughout the twentieth century. A link was considered so important
though, that a means of connection had to be found, and found it was.

During the last years of the eighteenth century, and on some thirty
occasions during the first half of the nineteenth century, western ships
called, normally briefly, for one reason or another, on the islands of the
Ryukyu chain, of which Okinawa is the largest. Some crews were
English speaking, and a few officers recorded their adventures. During
the second half of the nineteenth century, more western ships docked,
including those of Commodore Perry on their way to an historic
encounter with the Japanese (as distinct from the Okinawans), and
again officers and missionaries added to the literature. These accounts
proved to be an absolute gold mine of information, both factual and
descriptive, that acted as a backbone for the composition of the present
work. An Okinawa long past, and difficult to access, suddenly became
more approachable.

Before continuing further with this theme however, in order to
avoid confusion, an important note is in order at this juncture. The
island of Okinawa was so named by the Japanese; prior to this it was
widely known, and spelt, as Luchu or Loo-Choo. The first recorded
use of the name comes from the Chinese during the Sui dynasty. The
Emperor Yang-ti, in 610 A.D., demanded homage from the Luchuan
king, and when this was refused, the emperor sent a fleet, killed the
king, and took five thousand prisoners.

The Ryukyuan islands were first made known to Europeans from
information gained through the Chinese, but it wasn't until 1584 that
Francisco Gali, a Spanish pilot, sailing from China, came near, but not
in sight of the 'Lequios,' and was informed by a Chinese mariner that
the islands contained a number of good harbours. The islands were
visited by the English in the early seventeenth century (see later), then
by Capt. Broughton in 1796–97, and shortly afterwards the principal
island was touched by Capt. Torry of the *Frederick of Calcutta*, of
whom nothing else of pertinence is known. It wasn't until the publication in 1818 of Capt. Basil Hall's account of his voyage to the islands
in 1816 that the educated public, in Britain at least, had the opportunity to become aware of the unique nature of the Ryukyus and their
inhabitants.

In his readings into the subject, the author has found Luchu
variously written in a number of European languages – most notably

English, German, Dutch and French – for example: Lekayo, Lekeyo, Le-kyo, Lequeos, Lequeyo, Lequio, Lewkew, Licou Kicou, Lieoo-kieoo, Lieou-Kieou, Lieu-chew, Lieuchieux, Lieukieu, Likeo, Lioe-Kioe, Liou-Kiou, Liow-tcheow, Liquea, Liquejo, Liqueo, Liquieux, Liquijo, Liquio, Liu-chiu, Liu Kiu, Loqueo, Low-Kow and Lutschu. According to McLeod,[3] 'Lew Chew' conveyed the true tone and accent of the word(s). The lower-class natives, especially the less educated, apparently referred to the island as 'Doo-choo.' The earliest of these forms, as has been noted, comes from the Chinese annals of the seventh century and means, literally, 'a floating hornless dragon,' which is a representation of the shape of the islands in the group. The Japanese name was 'Ryu-gu' (Dragon Palace). The Okinawans, as I will, with some regret, refer to them in the main text (readers, so inclined, will need to consult the original reference to determine which variant was used when 'Okinawa' appears in a quote) strangely made scant use of the name Luchu (with all its various European spellings) in the nineteenth century, the name by which the world at large knew them, referring to the main island as Uchina, from which 'Okinawa' – used originally to denote the whole archipelago, with the exception of the northern-most islands – preserves a more archaic form, meaning 'sea-rope,' a representation of what the islands supposedly resemble – rope floating on the ocean. Another ancient Japanese name for the archipelago is 'Urama.'

It is, perhaps, interesting to note, that the Chinese also made reference to a Little Luchu, and this referred to Formosa (Taiwan), or parts of it, and the island of Lambray. Formosa, although considerably larger than Okinawa, was apparently named Little Luchu as a consequence of the few inhabitants who lived upon it.

Naha, the principal harbour of Okinawa and later capital, likewise had a number of spellings in the literature of the time. In British writings and charts of the eighteenth and nineteenth centuries, Nafwa, Napa, Napachan, Napa ching (city of Napa), Napafoo (district of Napa), and Napakiang (or Napa keang – meaning 'inlet of Napa') are most frequently given, yet Okinawans referred to the town as Nafa or Napa. The Japanese called the city Naba or Naha during this period, and as Naha has now become standard, it is the spelling used in this book (and so, once again, readers so inclined will need to consult the original reference to determine which variant was used when Naha appears in a quote).

Shuri, the old capital, was variously written too, with a number of variations recorded, including: Cheudi, Samar, Scheudi, Sheni,

Sheudi, Shiuri, Shoody, Shoolee, Shoomi, Showlee, Shui, Shuy, Soomar, Tchoole and Tseuli. Sometimes, Shuri was referred to as Kin ching (meaning 'golden city'), alluding to the palace within the walls, or Kin-tching, or Kint-ching. Similarly, Tomari, a village opposite Naha, and some two miles from Shuri, and, like its two neighbours, also important in the history of karate, was also variously written as Tonau, Tumai, or Tume. The last of the four main towns, Kume, was sometimes written as Kumei.

Captain Bax, writing in 1875, noted that the Okinawans had "altered little in manner and customs since his [Basil Hall's] time,"[19] and Admiral Sir John Hay, a visitor to the Ryukyus in the 1840's noted, in 1895: "I should like to point out how little change has taken place in the Luchu islands since Captain Basil Hall . . . visited them to the present time."[4b] Writing as late as 1899, Dr. William Furness, again using Hall's account as a marker, commented on the Okinawans so: ". . . [Hall's] accounts of the people agree in every particular with what Dr. H.M. Hiller and myself observed in 1896 . . . albeit during these four-score years the independent rule of the king has been abolished, and the islands are now entirely under the government of Japan. In view of this fact, the conclusion seems warranted that all changes in manners and customs in this small country are slow, compared with the rapid advance which is going on all around them. What was true in 1816 was probably true a hundred years before."[27]

Strange as it may seem therefore, despite the downfall of the Ryukyuan monarchy, and an alteration to the existence of the *shizoku*, or privileged class, life continued much as it had always done. When the islands came under direct Japanese control after the king's abdication, the new owners largely neglected their acquisition for some twenty years, allowing old ideas and habits to die out naturally along with their proponents, before gradually integrating a populace whose affiliation, certainly in intellectual circles, appeared to have been more at one with China.

As little changed throughout the nineteenth century then, the author was able to make the most of contemporary publications covering some one hundred years. It took more than a year to locate and secure all the necessary references, and, it should be noted, that virtually every known publication written in the English language during the nineteenth century that related to Okinawa, however fleeting, was read – about one hundred books and journal papers. The few exceptions (mentioned later) were unobtainable due to the fragile condition of the originals, with university libraries quite understandably not wishing to lend or photocopy. It was felt, however, that these texts would add little of value, otherwise the author would certainly have made arrangements to consult them *in situ*, as it were. A few references proved to be untraceable.

Throughout this book, quotes are taken from a number of such nineteenth century works and are written in italics to show their origin – due credit thus being given. Each quote has been taken from the original for scholarly purposes, though instead of being expressed objectively, in the third person, they are expressed subjectively, in the first person. It is hoped that the italicised text, rather than possibly interfering with the flow of the book, will add considerably to readers' appreciation. It should be noted however, that the author was often obliged to change the tense of such material from the present to the past, for obvious reasons, and these changes are marked with an asterisk in the text after the reference number. Due to computer problems, some minor inaccuracies may be noted in references 1 to 16 as to whether some quotes should, or should not take an asterix, but this should not be of concern to any but the hardened academic. If a reader finds this troublesome, they are advised to think of all such quotes with an asterisk, then the asterix, rather than the quote, may be incorrect.

Similarly, in such quotes, the personal pronoun 'they' is altered to read 'we', 'their' to 'our', and so on. On rare occasions, the exact opposite occurs. Being strictly accurate therefore, it is often the spirit that is imparted in relation to the quoted references, rather than the exact wording, with such minimal, but well-intentioned alterations, hopefully, causing but little offence and injustice to the original. American spellings have been kept where they obviously differed from the English, and spellings such as 'inclosure' for 'enclosure,' 'staid' for 'stayed,' 'shewy' for 'showy,' and so on, where obvious, were left unchanged, as they provide a sense of temporal distance. In the nineteenth century, 'which' was often written where 'that' is now correct – the original is retained here. The liquor, *sake*, sometimes spelt '*sackee*' in quoted work, has been standardised to the former, now established spelling.

This book could, of course, have been written a number of different ways without calling directly upon such nineteenth century material. However, it was felt early on, that by making strong reference to the writings of educated western men who were actually on Okinawa at that time, would not only impart a certain freshness, but enhance historical accuracy and a feeling of the period beyond all measure.

The earliest such reference quoted in the text in this regard comes from Book II of Captain William Robert Broughton's, *A Voyage of Discovery to the North Pacific Ocean . . . in the Years 1795, 1796, 1797, and 1798*, published in 1804 by T. Cadell and W. Davies.[i] Broughton's ship, *Providence*, struck a reef in the treacherous waters off Typinsan (Miyako Island) in 1797, and after a call at Maco, on the South China coast, re-visited the Ryukyu islands, making a three day stop at Naha. In truth, there is not much contained in Broughton's work that is of direct interest to the text of this book, for the material was superseded by later works, though a few references to Broughton are made in the current text, mainly because they contain a certain charm reminiscent of the writing from that period.

Whilst Broughton is the earliest text directly referred to, it was not the earliest consulted. That distinction lay with Sir George Staunton and his, *An Authentic Account of an Embassy from the King of Great Britain to the Emperor of China . . .* [etc.], published in London in 1797. Only brief mention is made to Okinawa however.[ii]

Captain Basil Hall's, *Account of a Voyage of Discovery to the West Coast of Corea and the Great Loo-Choo Island* (John Murray, 1818) is an astonishingly readable day by day account and provides a truly marvellous insight into Okinawan life of the time as seen through the eyes of a Royal Navy officer. Hall's arrival on Okinawa aboard the *Lyra* took place in 1816, and it is perhaps a sobering thought that only fifteen months had passed since Napoleon had been defeated at Waterloo. It was the second European book on Okinawa by an eye-witness of its customs, and contained much more detail than Broughton's work. A particularly noteworthy feature of Hall's book, was that it contained more than one thousand Okinawan words and phrases as used at the time (Broughton's contained a mere twenty-one words). This contribution was compiled by Herbert John Clifford, a lieutenant in the Royal Navy, who accompanied the voyage on half-pay, with a view solely to acquire knowledge. Captain Beechey, who visited the island eleven years later, found the 'dictionary' to be "very correct."

Okinawan, which is said to originate from a common proto-Japanese language, at the time, was described as musical, "rather soft and harmonious,"[3] and in most cases easy to pronounce. Bishop Smith described the Okinawan dialect as "the most regular and euphonic contrivance of speech that ever fell under my observation"[17] and com-mented that the "rich vocabulary" was "unlike the monosyllabic and indeclinable words of the Chinese language . . . Lewchewan is capable of great variety and flexibility."[17] As Basil Hall Chamberlain, a notable descendant of Basil Hall wrote: "Suffice it to say that the Luchuan language proves to be related to Japanese in about the same degree as Italian is to French. Though mutually quite unintelligible, and though there are considerable divergences both in the phonetic system and in the details of grammar, the structure of the sentence is practically identical, as in the case of French and Italian, and a study of each language throws vivid light on the other."[4b] Regional dialects on Okinawa were sufficient to be mutually intelligible, and speech differences could be so great that even neighbouring villages had noticeable dialectical variations. Furness wrote of the Okinawans and their dialect, that: "One of the most striking indications to me that they are of Japanese parentage rather than Chinese is the fact that they cannot pronounce the letter 'L,' and substitute therefore the sound 'R.' For example, they do not call the archipelago on which they live the 'Luchu' Islands, but 'Riu Kiu,' and in their language there is no word with 'l' in it; hence the name Luchu or Liu Kiu (as it is sometimes called) can hardly have been other than of a purely Chinese origin."[27]

For the present author, the discovery of Clifford's vocabulary was a wonderful moment, and, very occasionally, Okinawan words and phrases, written phonetically, exactly as Clifford recorded them, are integrated into the current work and dotted throughout the text.

At the same time as Clifford was composing an English-Okinawan vocabulary, the Okinawans took the opportunity to collect an Okinawan-English counterpart, the contents of which was later added to courtesy of the ships crews of *Brothers*, under Captain Eddis, *HMS Blossom*, under Captain Beechey, and the *Partridge*, under Captain Stavers, who visited Naha in 1818, 1827 and 1832, respectively, amongst other, later callers.

The people of Okinawa left a lasting impression on Clifford, as they did on many, and in 1843, twenty-seven years after his visit, he launched an appeal from his home in Dingle, County Kerry, Ireland, for funds for what became the Loo-Choo Naval Mission. The public response was considerable, and Clifford, acting as honorary secretary, sat alongside a number of Admirals and senior officers on the committee, with the Duke of Manchester, Commander of the Royal Navy, the patron. Unfortunately, Clifford's acquisition of Christian zealousness gave rise to an awkward and unintended problem for the Okinawans in the shape of Dr. Bettelheim (see shortly). Fortunately for the present author however, Bettelheim was an avid writer.

Captain Hall was, perhaps, responsible more than any other

traveller, for drawing the West's attention to Okinawa in the nineteenth century, and his book remained the chief reference for the 1800s. Certainly, the present author drew heavily from Hall's inspiration, and indeed, it is true to say that it laid a solid foundation for the current work. As Hall is quoted often then, it seems pertinent to say something of his life.

Basil Hall was born in Edinburgh in 1788, the son of geologist, Sir James Hall of Dunglass. He entered the navy at thirteen, and it was after his accompaniment of Lord Amherst's embassy to China aboard the sloop *Lyra* that Hall sailed for Okinawa. He was made a Fellow of the Royal Society the same year. Not long after, Hall met with the exiled Napoleon on St. Helena, and they spoke at length on Okinawa and the Okinawan people. Napoleon was greatly interested in what Hall had to say, asking many questions, and was particularly incredulous to Hall's comments that the happy Okinawans carried no weapons and had seemingly engaged in no wars (see Hall, *Narrative of a Voyage to Java, China, and the Great Loo-Choo Island . . . and of an Interview with Napoleon Buonaparte at St. Helena*). In fact, Hall, despite visiting the islands, was incorrect, and Napoleon's disbelief was justified, for the Okinawans had engaged in wars and did have access to weapons. This point is of considerable importance, and is discussed as a separate note following this introduction. It is most interesting to mention that Gichin Funakoshi knew of Napoleon's views on the subject and referred to them both in *Karate-Do Nyumon* and his autobiography, *Karate-Do Ichiro* (*Karate-Do: My Way of Life*), books in which he propagated the myth, in karate circles at least, that the Okinawans had no weapons. Master Itosu also knew of both Napoleon and Wellington, and mentioned them in his *Ten Teachings*. After travelling throughout Europe, Hall wrote of his travels to both South America and North America. Also writing a number of novels and short stories, he died in Haslar naval hospital, near Portsmouth, in 1844.

On his famous voyage to Okinawa, Capt. Hall accompanied Capt. Sir Murray Maxwell, who commanded the mission aboard the *Alceste*. Aboard this ship was a surgeon, Dr. John M'Leod, who wrote of his experiences in, *Voyage of His Majesty's Ship Alceste to China, Corea and the Island of Lewchew, With an Account of her Shipwreck* (John Murray, 1820). This book too, is very readable, and a fine supplementary work to Hall's account. A number of M'Leod's descriptions are also given in the text of the present volume. On many occasions during this project, the author was able to secure the original leather-bound, or part leather-bound copies of books by Hall, M'Leod and others, which added much to the pure delight of the research.

Interestingly, Hall's grandson, Basil Hall Chamberlain, who, astonishing as it might seem, was Professor of Japanese and Philology at Tokyo Imperial University towards the end of the nineteenth century, has considerable bearing on the present work. He visited Okinawa in 1892 and 1894 and published, *An Essay in Aid of a Grammar and Dictionary of the Luchuan Language* in 1896. He also wrote a number of extremely interesting essays, of which, *The Luchu Islands and Their Inhabitants*, which appeared in three parts in the *Geographical Journal* of 1895, is especially relevant to the present work. As extracts, often of considerable length, have been integrated into the present text, each part is credited separately.

Another major inspiration for this book was the, *Narrative of the Expedition of an American Squadron to the China Seas and Japan, Performed in the Years 1852, 1853, and 1854, Under the Command of Commodore M.G. Perry, United States Navy, by Order of the Government of the United States*, by Rev. Francis Lister Hawks (1856), the title normally being abbreviated to, *United States Naval Expedition to Japan, 1852–1854,* and published by order of the Congress of the United States. This is a very extensive work, and, once again, numerous quotes are to be found throughout the present text.

Quoted in the *Narrative . . .* are some truly lovely descriptions by Victorian traveller, Bayard Taylor, who joined Perry's squadron in Shanghai, and due credit was given in the *Narrative . . .* at Perry's insistence, to Taylor's contributions. Portions of some of Taylor's descriptions are, likewise, quoted in this book, and given separate acknowledgement.

Details were also extracted from the associated Volume II, relating to subjects as diverse as birds and fish found on Okinawa at the time, to the island's agriculture, botany and geology. Reports were made to Commodore Perry by a number of officers, and where extracts are taken for inclusion in the present work, reference is made to the actual author of the report, so: Dr. J. Morrow, *The Agriculture of Lew Chew*; Dr. D.S. Green, *Medical Topography and Agriculture of the Island of Great Lew Chew*; Dr. C.F. Fahs, *The Botany, Enthography, Etc, of the Island of Great Lew Chew*; and two reports by the Rev. G. Jones: *A Geological Exploration, Etc, of the Island of Great Lew Chew*; and, *An Exploration of Great Lew Chew*.

Matthew Galbraith Perry – the younger brother of Oliver Hazard Perry, another naval officer of note, who defeated a British squadron on Lake Erie in 1813, but who died of yellow fever six years later – was born in 1794, and took command of the first US naval steamship, *Fulton II*, in 1837. He was involved in the suppression of the slave trade on the Africa coast in 1843, and took an active part in the Mexican War of 1846–1848, including being present at the siege of Vera Cruz. It was his intention to use the Ryukyu Islands as a point of rendezvous for American ships from which to launch his expedition to Japan. To this end, he set-up a coal depot at Tomari to fuel his ships. Perry was a very capable individual, and his humourless and stern character, coupled with his pomposity, was presumably what was ordained to be required on this venture. Bettelheim (see below), in his diary, described Perry as "many sided and gifted with an abundance of talent." Perry must have always had in his mind an unfortunate incident that had happened to Commodore Biddle, who was struck by a common Japanese soldier and was unable to retaliate. This was seen as a weakness by the Japanese and news of the episode spread quickly. Perry's uncompromising approach served his mission and his country well, but his use of violent threats and a contemptuous disregard of all international laws of courtesy, marked him out in the eyes of the Okinawans - a people noted for their propriety. Somewhere along the way, Perry seemed to have forgotten President Millard Fillmore's instruction to act only with the consent of the natives, for he forced his way into Naha, "paraded the island, insisted on being received by the king, and terrified the inhabitants generally."[4] Privately, he may have been sympathetic to the Okinawans, but he had a job to do, and used the island as a pawn, and was prepared to seize it.

As the *Narrative* . . . notes, "It was a judicious determination on the part of the Commodore to make . . . [his uninvited trip to the palace at Shuri] and, having announced such determination to the Lew Chewans, it was especially wise to carry it through to the letter. The moral influence produced by such a steadfast adherence to his avowed purposes very soon exhibited itself. It was part of the Commodore's deliberately formed plan, in all his intercourse with these Orientals, to consider carefully before he announced his resolution to do any act; but, having announced it, he soon taught them to know that he would do precisely what he said he would. To this single circumstance much of his success is to be attributed. He never deceived them with any falsehood, nor ever gave them reason to suppose that his purposes could be altered by their lies and stratagems. They, of course, saw at once that he was resolute, and that it was dangerous to trifle with him. His whole diplomatic policy was simply to stick to the truth in everything – to mean just what he said, and to do just what he promised. Of course, it triumphed over a system which admitted of no truth, but for purposes of deception."[5]

It was during Perry's absence in 1854 – he sailed to Japan and then returned - that several ugly incidents occurred on Okinawa involving three seamen left behind to guard US instillations. Two of the seamen were set upon after a quarrel at a butcher's (it was the general view by other crew members that the seamen got what they deserved), and one, whose name was Board, was stoned and subsequently drowned after committing rape (it was generally felt that he too had received his just dessert). These were noteworthy incidents, for even in a land where violence was almost unheard of, the patience of even the most courteous could be stretched to breaking point.

The islanders were indeed famed for their propriety. Ever since the first western ships called during the early seventeenth century, virtually every traveller commented upon their fine manners and eagerness to please. Richard Wickam, in a letter of 1614 to Capt. Richard Cocks, noted that the Okinawans were a "very gentle and courteous people,"[iii] and William Adams, in his logbook[iv], wrote that, "We found marvellous great friendship [on Okinawa]." These quotes are historically interesting, because they were made before the doors were shut tight on Okinawa to westerners for two hundred years, due to the interventions of Portuguese and Spanish missionaries, in Japan, into political affairs. When Capt. Broughton landed in 1797, he too commented upon the "singular humanity of the natives."[1] Nineteen years later, M'Leod wrote that, "They all seemed to be gifted with a sort of politeness which had the fairest claim to be natural; for there was nothing constrained – nothing stiff or studied in it."[3]

As an indication of how gentle and law abiding the Okinawans were in the nineteenth century, Basil Hall wrote: "We never saw any punishment inflicted at Loo-choo; a tap with a fan, or an angry look, was the severest chastisement ever resorted to, as far as we could discover. In giving orders, the chiefs were mild though firm, and the people always obeyed with cheerfulness. There seemed to be great respect and confidence on the one hand, and much consideration and kind feeling on the other. In this particular, more than any other that fell under our notice, Loo-choo differs from China, for in the latter country we saw none of the generous and friendly understanding between the upper and lower classes."

This feeling of good-naturedness shown to westerns was typical. Satow noted that according to Japanese accounts, the Ryukyuan people were "of a calm and reflective temperament, not given to losing their presence of mind even on the most trying occasions."[14]

Such gentleness was not always in such evidence however, as the Reverend Jones noted, when in the town of Nugah: ". . . as the populace, in their curiosity to see the strangers, crowded a little beyond the limits allowed them by Lew Chew etiquette, the island officials, by sound blows upon the backs of the intruders, soon restored them to their places," though he continued, "the blows . . . [were] received with a patience and equanimity very wonderful to Americans." As S. Wells Williams found in 1837, "On approaching the boats, an underling made himself conspicuous in clearing the way, by applying the bamboo rod of office to the half-clad natives, who appeared to receive his castigations very submissively . . ."[13]

Sir Edward Belcher, in 1845, noted that shortly after landing on Okinawa he had spotted a friend, and wrote: "He was manifestly afraid to speak, but the distress in his eye was too evident. I stepped out from my party, and shook him by the hand, but one of the police in the most brutal manner, raised his arm to strike him, thinking, possibly, that the act was his own. My upraised arm prevented this taking effect, but the poor fellow was huddled away amongst the crowd, and I could not see him again."[11]

The missionary, Dr. Bettelheim also encountered this beating when people stopped to listen to him preaching. He wrote, "and on they came, bearing long and heavy bamboos, striking upon the naked bodies of the people as if they were a mass of cattle."[24]

The lower classes, even on-board a foreign property, could seemingly not avoid the stick. In May, 1827, Captain Beechey of *HMS Blossom*, a twenty-six gun, one hundred man ship, noted that: "The mandarin, however, fearful we might experience some annoyance from having so many people on-board without any person to control them, sent off a trusty little man with a disproportionably long bamboo cane to keep order, and who was in consequence named Master of Arms by the seamen. This little man took care that the importance of his office should not escape notice, and occasionally exercised his baton of authority, in a manner which seemed to me much too severe for the occasion; and sometimes even drew forth severe though ineffectual animadversions from his peaceful countrymen . . ."[24]

Basil Hall's account of life on Okinawa was, in truth, a romantic one, based, as it was, on limited knowledge. The happy and innocent picture of the people that his work conjured up, denied what lay beneath - a stagnant and highly suppressive system, dominated by spying and officialdom. As Bishop Smith noted: "The first impressions of a newly arrived visitor will generally be favourable rather than the reverse; and it requires a lengthened residence to obtain the intimate acquaintance with the darker features of the native character . . . the common people owe the unamiable traits of their disposition to the oppressive system of their government. The latter presents the degrading moral spectacle usually observable in oriental despotisms, alternately cringing in abject submission before the dreaded power of foreign nations, and wreaking all the worst passions of a vindictive, cunning, feeble oligarchy, on the awe-stricken and unresisting peasantry."[17]

The extent of the spying, a sense that Big Brother was watching, at least when foreigners were afoot, was truly formidable, as Bayard Taylor wrote: "The perfection to which the system of espionage is carried in Loo Choo . . . is almost incredible . . . We were surrounded with a secret power, the tokens of which were invisible, yet which we could not move a step without feeling. We tried every means to elude it, but in vain."[5b] A number of writers commented upon just how capable these spies were, as Bettelheim remarked: "They appear and disappear like ghosts on the stage . . . One would often be tempted to think they can pass through walls, so sudden is their disappearance and reappearance."[25]

Speaking of such officials of the government that operated on Okinawa at the time and their relationship with the common man, the *Narrative* . . . noted: "These [spies] infest every corner and every threshold. If the officers walked the streets, these fellows might be seen preceding or following them, directing all doors to be closed, and the women to keep out of sight. The people, indeed, whenever they were sure of not being seen by some of these vermin, manifested no indisposition to communication and intercourse, and gladly received from the strangers little gratuities and presents, which were taken with a trembling hand and instantly concealed, while their eyes glanced rapidly and furtively from side to side to see that they were unobserved. The Commodore was deeply moved, as indeed were all the gentlemen of the expedition, by the tyranny exercised toward the mass of the people. 'God pity these poor creatures!' says the . . . [Commodore] in his journal: 'I have seen much of the world, have observed savage life in many of its conditions; but *never*, unless I may except the miserable peons in Mexico, have I looked upon such an apparent wretchedness as these squalid slaves would seem to suffer. The poor, naked creatures, who toil from morning till night, know not the relaxation of the Sabbath, nor the rest of an occasional holiday, generally granted by even the most cruel taskmasters. The wages of the field laborer is from three to eight cents per diem; the mechanic may receive ten. Out of this, he has to provide food, clothing, and shelter for a family, with which most common people are burdened, and it is surprising to see how soon the boys, for we see but little of the girls, are made to labor. In looking into a blacksmith's shop at Napha, I observed a father and two sons making nails; the elder son, probably ten years old, was using the hammer, while the younger, not more than five, was blowing the bellows, or rather moving the piston of a sort of air pump, which required some amount of physical exertion. When we entered the shop, neither of the three took the slightest notice of us, but went on with their labor; even the little boy scarcely lifted his eyes; and this seeming indifference, it may be remarked, was the case with laborers and all others whom we met, when they supposed the eye of the spy was upon them. Whatever progress we may make in conciliating the higher classes, and we have made considerable, the lower orders of the people dare not, even by a look, evince the slightest emotion; their stolid and impassive features express nothing but toil and care, and are a sufficient index of their abject condition. I can conceive of no greater act of humanity than it would be to rescue, if possible, these miserable beings from the oppression of their tyrannical rulers.' "5

Belcher, who had actually been to Okinawa eighteen years previously, in 1827, aboard *HMS Blossom*, before his voyage on *HMS Samarang*, noted that: "The working-classes are invariably in such a tattered, filthy state, that one naturally avoids them, fearing the effects of contact."[11] Additionally, and quite surprisingly, comparing the Koreans, Japanese, Okinawans, etc, with the Chinese, he wrote: "I am not disposed to accord to any of them the characters of neatness, cleanliness, or purity of morals. I believe them to be less cleanly than the Chinese, who may be generally noticed at the doors of their houses, after sun-set, making every effort to wash off the accumulation of the day. I never witnessed any such attempt at extensive ablutions amongst any of the island races, and when they have by chance exposed the skin, it presented a coarseness which indicated frequent, if not complete, exposure [to the sun]."[11]

Whilst quiet and mild in manner, it would be incorrect to believe that the Okinawans were meek, however. The author does not wish to discuss karate at this point in the proceedings, that will come later, but reference should be made at this point to a quote by Basil Hall, who described a most interesting incident on pages 168 and 169 of his work, and it is the earliest and nearest descriptive evidence of an Okinawan fighting spirit the author has found in the nineteenth century western literature. Some chiefs had been invited onto the *Alceste*, and all was going well, then an incident occurred, meant in friendly terms, that points to an Okinawan martial spirit, otherwise hidden. "On returning to the cabin for tea," Hall wrote, "they were all in high spirits, and while amusing themselves with a sort of wrestling game, Ookooma, who had seen us placing ourselves in sparring attitudes, threw himself suddenly into a boxer's position of defence, assuming at the same time a fierceness of look which we had never before seen in any of them. The gentleman to whom he addressed himself, thinking that Ookooma wished to spar, prepared to indulge him; but Madera's quick eye saw what was going on, and by a word or two made him instantly resume his wonted sedateness. We tried in vain to make Madera explain what were the magical words which he had used on Ookooma. He appeared anxious to turn our thoughts from the subject, by saying, 'Loo-choo man no fight; Loo-choo man write – no fight, no good, no, no. Ingerish [English] very good, yes, yes, yes; Loo-choo man no fight.' "[2]

It is pertinent at this stage, proceeding from the above quote, to draw the reader's attention to Ernest Satow's famous paper of 1872, which relies upon the work of Tomioka Shiuko, entitled, *Chiuzan-koku Shiriaku*, or, *Short Account of the Loochooan Embassy*, in 1850, on the last occasion when an embassy visited Yedo. An extremely important quote is contained therein: "Their [Okinawan] skill in boxing is such that a well-trained fighter can smash a large earthen water-jar, or kill a man with a single blow of his fist."[14] It would seem that there is little doubt that the boxing referred to by Satow was, in fact, karate.

The only other quote from western literature of the time that the author has uncovered that refers to 'boxing,' comes from Furness in 1899: "We were told that the young men occasionally engage in boxing bouts, with bare knuckles; all blows are struck with the right hand, while the left is used solely as a guard. Clinching and wrestling for a fall are considered legitimate features of the sport."[27] What, exactly, Furness is describing is hard to determine – but the two sentences are certainly fascinating.

Funakoshi, in his autobiography, makes a number of references to violence, however. It is true that these are likely to fall beyond the final date of this book – 1892 – but they are worthy of note nonetheless, if for no other reason than as examples of a potential increase in lawlessness and a decline in exacting standards when Japan took over the Ryukyus and inflicted a policy of lack of interest. Fist fights between neighbours, fist fights following tugs-of-war where "many an Okinawan has been injured," a mugging, an attack upon a karate master, the need for Funakoshi to act as an intermediary in a dispute that was getting out of hand, and, when Itosu and his students were stopped in the road by a gang, are little anecdotes that are very far from the pictures painted by nineteenth century visitors. Funakoshi wrote in his *Karate-Do Nyumon* of the "rowdy violence among the youths of Azato village." Azato lay between Shuri and Naha, and the chief was Master Azato, famed for his prowess in various martial arts. It may simply be Funakoshi's story-telling, though if the youths of Azato were having altercations, rest assured that it would not bode well for other villages. No doubt these stories reflect the depressed and uncertain times that underpinned Okinawa then, which Okinawan men, irrespective of social class, found themselves confronting.

Many of the punishments inflicted by the government upon the rare wrong-doer on Okinawa, certainly beyond the first quarter of the nineteenth century, and one imagines into the 1850s and 1860s – and certainly within living memory of people known to Funakoshi – were anything but mild, and appeared to exhibit the refined cruelty of the Chinese of that time. Captain Beechey had purchased a book of punishments in China and showed it to Okinawan people in 1827. He wrote: "Those which they acknowledged were death by strangulation upon a cross, and sometimes under the most cruel torture; and minor punishments, such as loading the body with iron chains; or locking the neck into a heavy wooden frame; enclosing a person in a case, with only his head out, shaved, and exposed to a scorching sun; and binding the hands and feet, and throwing quicklime into the eyes. I was further assured that confession was sometimes extorted by the unheard-of cruelty of dividing the joints of the fingers alternately, and clipping the muscles of the legs and arms with scissors. Isaacha Sando [an Okinawan] took pains to explain the manner in which this cruelty was performed, putting his fingers to the muscles in imitation of a pair of sheers, so I could not be mistaken: besides, other persons at Potsoong told me in answer to my inquiry, for I was rather sceptical myself, that it was quite true, and that they had seen a person expire under this species of torture. However, lest it should be thought I may have erred in attaching such cruelties to a people apparently so mild and humane, I shall insert some questions that were put to the Loo Chooans out of Dr. Morrison's Dictionary, and their answers to them respectively: 'Do the Loo Choo people torture and interrogate with the lash?' 'Yes.' – 'Do they examine by torture?' 'Yes.' – 'Do they give false evidence through fear of torture?' 'Yes.' 'Are great officers of the third degree of rank and upwards, who are degraded and seized to be tried, subjected to torture?' 'No.' – 'Is torture inflicted in an illegal and extreme degree?' 'Not illegal.' – 'Do you torture to death the real offender?' 'Yes, sometimes.' – 'What punishment do you inflict for murder?' 'Kill, by hanging or strangulation.' – 'For robbery?' 'The same.' – 'For adultery?' 'Banish to Patanjan . . . [probably an island]; – 'For seduction?' 'The same.' Minor offences we were told were punished with a bambooing or a flagellation with a rod."[24]

Spies would, as we have seen, inflict immediate punishment upon those found willingly talking to westerners – or at least certainly in the case of Bettelheim, who wrote: "A native gentleman once accompanied me for some distance on my way, not minding the threats and shouts of the spies; he was dragged from my side, dragged away by the beard, and cruelly beaten for no other sin than that he walked a few steps in friendly conversation with the English barbarian. Another Lewchewan, whose heart was attracted by the excellence of our faith, betrayed by his partiality to a foreigner, who he was not afraid to call 'father,' was dragged from our neighborhood, and we have never learned what became of him."[25]

Whilst the Okinawans throughout the nineteenth century seemed a notably polite and law-abiding people, crimes directed at westerners, as has been noted, were not unknown. Bettelheim wrote in a letter to the Rev. Dr. Peter Parker, that he had upwards of several hundred dollars stolen in 1848. The authorities caught the thieves, but Bettelheim, in reply to his request to know the punishment of the wrongdoers, was refused. The letter, written by the superintendent of affairs in Chungshan, a certain Shang Tingchu, noted that, "the crime of these two prisoners may be said not to be a capital offence according to the laws."[25] Perhaps the superintendent did not wish to offend the missionary (Bettelheim was relieved to hear the news that executions were unlikely to be the judgement), then again, assuming the letter was truthful, theft against an unwanted westerner, might not carry the usual loss of life.

Due to the exclusion laws, Okinawans and other members of the Ryukyus were not permitted any social intercourse with foreigners. As Smith noted: "Political fears were at the bottom of the whole policy . . . they [the Okinawans] dreaded the vengeance of their Japanese masters, who would view the residence of a European in Lewchew as the first step towards breaking down the exclusiveness of Japan itself."[17] The Okinawans, on the other hand, did not wish to incur the displeasure of western visitors with their formidable armament, despite knowing the intentions of both the Europeans and Americans. Hence, Smith's note that an "odd mixture of outward respect and unwillingness to enter into conversation was the kind of reception universally experienced."[17] Doctor Fahs noted in 1854 that, "Numerous spies were always about to report any infraction of the laws. When we first arrived, the people ran away as soon as we came near them; and if any one walked through the streets of the city, they were cleared in a minute, and all the doors locked. Several thousand persons selling and buying in the markets would desert their stores merely at the sight of anyone. Their custom, formerly, was to supply vessels coming in with everything they required, but they would take no remuneration, and would tell them to leave."[8] William Upton Eddis (see shortly), noted that during his very brief stay in the port of Naha, in November, 1818, on enquiring whether it was possible to discuss trading, he was told by the Okinawans that had come aboard the brig, *Brothers*, that such intercourse was "impossible, as the King would put any person who should even mention the circumstance, to death." Similarly, when Eddis offered a Chinese New Testament, it was said that the king would "cut their heads off if they accepted it."

The spying and the oppressive regime operating on Okinawa spoilt the visit of many a western visitor. Bettelheim, for example, noted: "Whole troops of these wretched hirelings"[25] would follow him, and "march in files before and behind me, like soldiers; every side lane being guarded on both openings, and their shouting and hooting [was] almost deafening."[25] Beechey, likewise afflicted, wrote: "The day of departure was consequently near at hand. This event, after which many anxious inquiries were made by the natives, was, I believe, generally contemplated with pleasure on both sides; not that we felt careless about parting with our friends, but we could not enjoy their society with so many restrictions, and we were daily exposed to the temptation of a beautiful country without the liberty of exploring it, that our situation very soon became irksome. The day of our departure, therefore, was hailed with pleasure, not only by ourselves, but by those to whom the troublesome and fatiguing duty had been assigned of attending upon our motions."[24]

Perry, likewise, was pleased to be away from the island, though he left nine men buried there. A treaty was signed in 1854 with Okinawa on behalf of the United States, but it was never ratified. In 1856 and

1859, similar treaties were signed between Okinawa and France, and Okinawa and Holland, respectively. The *Narrative* . . . notes: "All seemed very well satisfied to get away from Lewchew. The picturesque interests of the island were, for the time being, thoroughly exhausted, and the dull realities of life began to weigh heavily on the visitors."[5] It was also written that: "Either Captain Basil Hall was mistaken, or the national traits [of the Okinawans] have changed since the time of his visit. He represents them as without arms, ignorant even of money, docile, tractable and honest, scrupulously obedient to their rulers and their laws, and, in fact, as loving one another too well wilfully to harm or wrong each other. Many of the officers of the squadron went to the island, expecting to find these beautiful traits of character; but gradually and painfully undeceived in many particulars, they were constrained to acknowledge that human nature in Lew Chew was very much the same as it is elsewhere."[5] Though in conclusion it was noted: "[the Okinawans] . . . have, on the whole, many excellent natural traits, and their worst vices are probably the result, in a great measure, of the wretched system of government under which they live."[5] Perry died four years later in New York, his name recorded to history.

This, 'other side of the coin' is, perhaps, best expressed by Gubbins. He wrote: "The division of the people [of Okinawa] into two classes of *shizoku* and *heimin* has been attended with the worst consequences; it has had the effect of enervating the one class and degrading the other. The samurai of Japan formed a vast standing army; they were the product of a military system, which had for one of its objects the independence of the country; and though the privileges of their class were only maintained at the expense of the rest of the nation, there is no doubt that the military spirit thus fostered elevated the national character, and gave it a tone of independence which it otherwise would have lacked, and which can be traced in the Japanese farmer of the present day [1881]. In Loochoo the same class distinction exists, with all its faults and none of its advantages. The *shizoku* of Loochoo has no spirit, no pride of country, and his pride even of self does not rise beyond the empty pharisaical [*sic*] boast that he is not a *heimin*. The *heimin* is an ignorant serf, who knowing that he is working for others and not for himself, has no heart in his labour, and lives from hand to mouth; and whose highest sentiment is a feeling of stupid respect for the privileged classes. The Loochooan samurai is thus infinitely below his counterpart in Japan, while the peasant in Loochoo is even more immeasurably inferior to the Japanese farmer.

Both classes live and think in the same grooves as centuries ago."[10]

In the text of the Introduction to date, and considerable italicised text in the work that follows, after each quote a number in superscript is given. Such quotes cover an enormous diversity of material, factual and descriptive, from General Grant's role over the 'Lu-chu problem' to a young English naval officer's encounter with a deadly snake, for example. Reference numbers are attributable as follows, with some additional information given where appropriate:

1   Broughton, W.R. (1804) *A Voyage of Discovery to the North Pacific Ocean . . . in the Years 1795, 1796, 1797, and1798*, Book II, (T. Cadell and W. Davies).

2   Hall, B. (1818) *Account of a Voyage of Discovery to the West Coast of Corea and the Great Loo-Choo Island* (John Murray).

3   M'Leod, J. (1820) *Voyage of His Majesty's Ship Alceste to China, Corea and the Island of Lewchew, With an Account of her Shipwreck* (John Murray).

4   Chamberlain, B.H. (1895) *The Luchu Islands and Their Inhabitants* (*Geographical Journal*, Vol. V, pp. 289–319).

4a   Chamberlain, B.H. (1895) *The Luchu Islands and Their Inhabitants* (*Geographical Journal*, Vol. V, pp. 446–462).

4b   Chamberlain, B.H. (1895) *The Luchu Islands and Their Inhabitants* (*Geographical Journal*, Vol. V, pp. 534–545).

5   Hawks, F.L. (1856) *Narrative of the Expedition of an American Squadron to the China Seas and Japan, Performed in the Years 1852, 1853, and 1854, Under the Command of Commodore M.G. Perry, United States Navy, by Order of the Government of the United States.*

5a   Taylor, B. (1856) From Vol. I of *Narrative of the Expedition of an American Squadron . . .* (see Hawks).

5b   Taylor, B. (1864) *A Visit to India, China and Japan in the Year 1853* (G.P. Putnam, New York, pages 365–388 and 444–456).

6   Morrow, J. (1856) *The Agriculture of Lew Chew*. From Vol. II of *Narrative of the Expedition of an American Squadron . . .* (see Hawks)

7   Green, D.S. (1856) *Medical Topography and Agriculture of the Island of Great Lew Chew*. From Vol. II of *Narrative of the Expedition of an American Squadron . . .* (see Hawks).

8   Fahs, C.F. (1856) *The Botany, Enthography, Etc, of the Island of Great Lew Chew*. From Vol. II of *Narrative of the Expedition of an American Squadron . . .* (see Hawks).

9   Jones, G. *(1856) A Geological Exploration, Etc, of the Island of Great Lew Chew*. From Vol. II of *Narrative of the Expedition of an American Squadron . . .* (see Hawks).

9a   Jones, G. (1856) *An Exploration of Great Lew Chew*. From Vol. II of *Narrative of the Expedition of an American Squadron . . .* (see Hawks).

10   Gubbins, J.A. (1881) *Notes Regarding the Principality of LooChoo*

{*Journal of the Society of Arts*, June, pages, 598-608}). John Gubbins worked for the Consular Service.

11   Belcher, E. (1848) *Narrative of the Voyage of H.M.S. Samarang, During the Years 1843-1846 . . . Vol. II.*

11a Adams, A. (1848) *Notes From a Journal of Research into the Natural History of the Countries Visited During the Voyage of H.M.S. Samarang.* A substantial work forming the latter part of Volume II of Sir Edward Belcher's book. The *Samarang* was engaged in surveying the islands of the eastern archipelago – the Okinawans objected to their islands being so surveyed – and Arthur Adams was assistant surgeon on the voyage.

12   Gutzlaff. C. (1834) *Journal of Three Voyages along the Coast of China in 1831, 1832 & 1833 . . . with Notices of Siam, Corea, and the Loo-Choo Islands* (Frederick Westley and A.H. Davis, London, pages 357-368). Charles Gutzlaff describes five days on Okinawa in the month of August, six months after a visit made by Captain Stevens of the *Partridge*.

13   Williams, S.W. (1838) *Narrative of a Voyage of the Ship Morrison . . .* (*Chinese Repository* ({Canton}, Vol. VI, pages 209–229; 353–380; 400–406. {Also see pages 114–118 for a review of Chow Hwang's work on his visit as envoy to Okinawa in 1757}). Samuel Wells Williams was a naturalist aboard the American ship *Morrison*, under the command of Capt. David Ingersoll, who visited Okinawa in the summer of 1837. Ingersoll died three months after visiting Okinawa, aboard ship, in the Straits of Gaspar.

13a Williams, S.W. (1838) *Notices of Some of the Specimens of Natural History, Which Were Collected During the Voyage of the Morrison to Lew-chew and Japan.* (*Chinese Repository* {Canton}, Vol. VI, January, pages 406–417). This is actually an uncredited work, almost certainly S.W. Williams (or possibly Ingersoll).

14   Satow's, E. (1872) *Notes on Loochoo* (*Transactions of the Asiatic Society of Japan*, Vol. I, pages 1-9).

15   Clutterbuck, W.J. (1910) *The Lu-Chu Islands* (*Travel and Exploration*, Vol. IV, No. 20, pages 81–88). This article, whilst published in 1910, refers to the fact that Walter Clutterbuck's six week stay was four years after Basil Hall Chamberlain's, so the date of the visit is likely to be either the last couple of years of the nineteenth century or the beginning of the twentieth century. The article is also important because it contains three photographs of everyday Okinawan scenes.

16   Young J.R. (1879) *Around the World with General Grant . . . in 1877, 1878, 1879 . . .* (The American News Company, pages 415–416, 433, 545–546, 558–562). Grant undertook his travels after being denied a third term of office as President of the United States, and became involved in the Lu-chu question in 1879. Substantial quotes are taken from Volume II of John Russell Young's work, as they provide a 'reader friendly' view of that particular political situation.

17   Smith, G. (1853) *Lewchew and the Lewchewans: Being a Narrative of a Visit to Lewchew or Loo Choo, in October, 1850* (T. Hatchard, London). Doctor George Smith was Lord Bishop of Victoria, Hong Kong.

18   Halloran, A.L. (1856) *Wae Yang Jin: Eight Months' Journal Kept on Board One of Her Majesty's Sloops of War during Visits to Loochoo, Japan and Pootoo* (Longman, London, pages 16–35). Alfred Laurence Halloran visited Okinawa in March, 1849.

19   Bax, B.W. (1875) *The Eastern Seas: Being a Narrative of a Voyage of H.M.S. Dwarf in China, Japan and Formosa* (John Murray, London, pages 95–103).

20   Bettelheim, B. (1852) *LooChoo Naval Mission: Extract From the Reports From 1850–51* (*North China Herald*, No. 78, January, Shanghai, pages 102–103).

21   Balfour, F. H. (1876) *Waifs and Strays From the Far East . . .* (Chapter VI. *The Kingdom of Liuchiu*, pages 55–62, Trubner, London).

22   Habersham, A.W. (1857) *The North Pacific Surveying and Exploring Expedition: or My Last Cruise, Where We Went and What We Saw: Being an Account of Visits to the Malay and Loo-Choo Islands, the Coasts of China, Formosa, Japan, Kamtschatka, Siberia and the Mouth of the Amoor River* (J.B. Lippincott, Philadelphia, Chapter XI, pages 180-199). Habersham was a naval lieutenant.

23   Guillemard, F.H.H. (1886) *The Cruise of the Marchesa to Kamschatka and New Guinea with Notices of Formosa, Liu-Kiu, and Various Islands of the Malay Archipelago* [in the years 1882-1883] (John Murray, London, Vol. I, Chapters II and III, pages 26–63).

24   Beechey, F. W. (1831) *Narrative of a Voyage to the Pacific and Beerings Strait to Co-operate with the Polar Expeditions: Performed in His Majesty's Ship Blossom under the Command of Captain F. W. Beechey R.N., F.R.S., etc, in the Years 1825, 26, 27, 28* (Henry Colburn and Richard Bentley, Vol. II, pages 139-226). Beechey describes a two week stay on Okinawa in May, 1827.

25   Bettelheim, B. J. (1850) *Letter from B.J. Bettelheim, M.D., giving an account of his residence and missionary labors in Lewchew during the last three years.* (*Chinese Repository* (Vol. XIX, pages 17–49, 57–90). This article refers to an exceptionally long letter sent to the Rev. Parker by Dr. Bettelheim (see below).

26   Farre, F.J. (1853) *Medicine in Lewchew* (*Medical Times and Gazette* {London}, Vol. VII, pages 136–138, 164–166, 188–190). Frederic Farre's paper was drawn up from information supplied by Dr. Bettelheim, and proved to be a valuable source.

27   Furness, W.H. (1899) *Life in the Luchu Islands* (*Bulletin of the Free Museum of Science and Art of the University of Pennsylvania*, Vol.II, Pt.1, pages 1–28, 44–49).

28   Brunton, R.H. (1876) *Notes taken during a visit to Okinawa Shima – Loochoo Islands* (*Transactions of the Asiatic Society of Japan*, Vol. IV, pages 66–77).

Please note that the references above are ordered as they were generally integrated into the text. If there was repetition in relevant factual material, the earlier reference work normally took precedence. In the case of descriptive material, that which the author considered the finest took precedence. Quotes from further afield were simply not possible, given the project's remit, but in truth, authors tended to repeat information and all salient material was considered extracted from the major sources represented above.

Many other nineteenth century texts were also consulted in the preparation of this book, which are not directly alluded to, and information indirectly integrated into the text. Among the more important, arranged chronologically, are:

Captain James Burney's, *A Chronological History of the Voyages and Discoveries in the South Sea or Pacific Ocean* (Luke Hansard, London, 1813, Vol. III, pages 431–433).

William Upton Eddis's, *Short visit to Loo-Choo in November, 1818* (*Indo-Chinese Gleaner*, No.7 {1819}, pages 1-4).

David Abeel's, *Journal of a Residence in China and the Neighbouring Countries from 1829 to 1833* (James Nisbet, London, 1835, Chapter XVII, pages 330–336).

H.H. Lindsay's, *Reports of Proceedings on a Voyage to the Northern Ports of China in the Ship Lord Amherst*; J.J.B Bowman's, *Account of the Wreck of the Indian Oak* (*The Nautical Magazine and Naval Chronical for 1841*, pages 299–308, 385–394). This paper includes an encounter with hostile and heavily armed Japanese soldiers from Tokara. *Loss of the Transport Indian Oak (Captain Grainger) on Lew Chew, Aug. 14, 1840* (*Chinese Repository*, Volume 12, {1843}, Number 2, Art. IV, pages 81–82), gives another account of the ill-fated vessel.

Ernest W. Satow's, *Notes on Loo-Choo* (*Phoenix*, Vol. III, Pages 174–177, 1872–1873 – the reference to karate is referred to identically in this article as in 14 above); *Cruise of the U.S. Sloop-of-War Preble, Commander James Glynn, to Napa and Nangasacki* (*U.S. Senate Documents: 32nd Congress, 1st Session (1851–1852)*, Vol. 9.

John R. Black's, *Young Japan: Yokohama and Yedo 1858–1879*, Vol.II (1883), Trubner, London (reprinted in 1968 by Oxford University Press), pages 399–405.

Japan's (a pseudonym), *Coronation of the King of Loochoo* (*China Review*, Vol. VII, pages 283–284 {1878});

Herbert J. Allen's, *The Lew Chew Islands* (*China Review*, Vol. VIII, 1879, pages 140–143).

H. T. Whitney's, *Protestant Mission Work in the Loochoo Islands* (*China Recorder*, Shanghai, Vol. 18, No. 2, pages 468–472 – December, 1887).

Albrecht Wirth's, *The Aborigines of Formosa and the Liu-Kiu Islands* (*The American Anthropologist*, Vol. X, No. 11, 1897, pages 357–370).

S.W. Williams, *A Journal of the Perry Expedition to Japan* (*Transactions – Asiatic Society of Japan*, Volume 37, Part 2, 1910) provided additional insights. This reference was included in this section due to the late nature of publication.

Basil Hall Chamberlain, *Contributions to a Bibliography of Luchu* (*Transactions –Asiatic Society of Japan*, Volume 24, 1896).

A few of the writers from whom quotes are taken, such as the Reverend Dr. Karl Friederich Gutzlaff, under the guise of missionary work, apparently imposed themselves on the obliging Okinawans to an objectionable degree, as did associates Dr. Peter Parker and Samuel Wells Williams. To the author's mind these men operated under a very strange code and, despite their supposed pious intentions, were not, apparently, averse to dealing in opium, for example.

Unwelcome catholic missionaries also felt the need to 'spread the word.' French priests like Forcade (who resided in a single room and cabin in Tomari), Leturde and Adnet, made little progress however, and either died or were shipped back from whence they had come after a few years. The Okinawans attempted to restrict the liberty of these people. Of one French priest, Capt. Belcher wrote in Volume I of his work, that he had been confined "within the walls of his garden . . . and that on several occasions they had *forcibly* [Belcher's italics] carried him home when he straggled."[11] Adams noted a more conciliatory approach regarding this catholic priest, for he "informed me that he had not succeeded in making a single convert, and though his tenets were smiled at as being too absurd for credence, yet he was treated with the greatest respect, mingled, however, with a little jealousy."[11a] The Okinawans just wanted rid of him, and those like him. Writing in 1895, Basil Hall Chamberlain noted that on his visit to the islands the year before, "the only European in the whole archipelago was Abbe Ferrie, a French Catholic missionary, who . . . lived in the northern island of Oshima."[4]

The most intrusive, and without doubt the most troublesome of these missionaries (at least from the Okinawans perspective) was Bettelheim. As with Hall and Perry, it would be neglectant not to say a few words about Bettelheim, for his contribution to this book is notable.

Born in Pressburg, Hungary, in 1811, Bernard Jean Bettelheim showed a marked ability in languages in his youth, and went on to read medicine, obtaining his M.D. at Padua in 1836. He became a cholera specialist, and worked as a surgeon for both the Egyptian and Turkish navies before moving to London, where he married Rose Barwick. By this stage he was proficient in an astonishing ten languages. His wife and two small children, by way of a ruse, landed at Naha from the *Starling* (sometimes the *Marling* is recorded, yet Bettelheim refers to the former), on the 2nd May, 1846, after an appointment made by the Loo-Choo Naval Mission. Bettelheim had had, shall we say, an eventful career to this date, but this shrewd, academically brilliant, and some might argue, mentally deranged individual, proved to be unbelievably disagreeable to his burdened hosts the entire eight inglorious years he was on Okinawa. Amongst the first things he did was to occupy the ancient Gokoku-ji (temple), refusing all entreaties to leave. The local people were unable to worship there the entire time he was on the island. His rudeness, arrogance and self-importance, coupled with the propensity for occasional sycophantic ingratiation (such as to Perry), seemed to know no bounds, and he could be downright hostile at times. Samuel Wells Williams, in a later paper, commenting on the Protestant missionary at the time of a meeting with the Okinawan Regent, wrote: "[Bettelheim] talked a great deal, and his way of making signs and motioning with his face was very much disliked and wrongly interpreted. I hardly know what to think of the man, for he whisks about in his opinion like a weathercock . . ." and that he and his fellow officers had visited Bettelheim, "more as a mark of respect than goodwill ... [and that] he had contrived to get the suspicion or active dislike of almost everybody." In the entire time he was on Okinawa, Bettelheim made two converts [some say only one], and that one was, according to Bettelheim,[20] murdered.

Bettelheim was a highly-strung insomniac, who, to all intents and purposes, had a distorted view, not to say disturbed mind. He was fortunate that the Japanese did not oblige him with the martyrdom he no doubt craved. He was quite aware, and it was "no secret, that foreigners arriving in Japanese territory are . . . guilty of a breach of law, and considered prisoners of state."[20] As he wrote: "I am a missionary, a soldier that beareth hardship, and to whom life is not more dear than the end for which it is to be endured . . . A single moment of forgetfulness, the least act of rashness, might cut the thread on which our lives hang"[25] – "our lives" referring, of course, to his own and those of his wife and children. The Okinawans even used physical force against him, as Dr. H.T. Whitney noted: "On the 6th of January, 1850, he was seized by a company of six to eight policeman, while in a private house, and thrown into the street and badly injured. He was unconscious for a time, and laid in the street some two hours before Mrs. Bettelheim knew of it. He was then taken home and kept his bed for

Plate 1. The Reverend Doctor Bernard Jean Bettelheim (1811–1870)

several days in consequence of the injuries and shock received." Just what provoked the peace-loving Okinawans to this act is not known exactly, but some of Bettelheim's methods for saving souls were quite extraordinary. For example, when doors leading to properties were shut, he would, in his own words, find "my way in through the deep gaps in dilapidated back walls."[25] He would then burst in upon the unsuspecting family. Again, in his own words: "I was little moved with the cries of the women, or frightened at the screams of the children, but seated myself in the first room I could gain access to."[25]

What seems remarkable today, was that the Bettelheim problem, as it became, went to the very highest offices in England, with Lord Palmerston, the Prime Minister, becoming involved, and writing a letter to the Okinawan government stating the British Government would view with displeasure any attempt to repel the missionary from

Okinawa through annoyance or persecution. A copy of this letter, delivered by Capt. Shadwell, commander of *H.M.S. Sphinx,* a British man-of-war, in February (6th–17th), 1852, may be found in the appendix of Dr. George Smith's book, the net result being that, "The Foreign Secretary of State has, in the name of the Queen of Great Britain, thrown the shield of British protection around the missionary, Dr. Bettelheim."[17] Indeed, it was specifically to check on Bettelheim that gave rise to Smith travelling to Okinawa aboard the H.M steam-sloop, *Reynard* (Capt. Cracroft commanding), which resulted in a ten day visit to the island in 1850 (4th–14th October), on his way from Hong Kong to Shanghai, and a number of quotes are taken from this book in the present work. Smith's visit much improved Bettelheim's position, to the extent that "his medical labours were eminently successful during the prevalence of the small-pox" (written by George Rochfort Clarke, London, 1851, in the appendix to 17), but the real purpose of the mission was to open up the possibility of launching a Christian assault on Japan, as Clarke noted: "Dark Japan maintains its sullen separation from the rest of the family of Adam, with eyes averted from Christ, and ears stopped against the sound of the Gospel. In one solitary spot of her dreary dominions, the Lord has set before us an open door: towards that door let us press with increasing strength."

A view of what at least some other people thought of Bettelheim is given in an abstract by Ella Embree in Goncharov's *Fregat Pallada*[v]: "A thinnish man with a Semitic face, not pale but 'faded,' and with hands that looked somewhat like a bird's claws, and a voluble talker. There was nothing attractive about the man; in his conversation, in his tone, in the stories he told, in his greeting, there is a sort of dryness – a slyness – something that made me feel unsympathetic . . . I began to get suspicious of this all-embracing criticism of the Ryukyuan people. Our crew told me later that when they asked the inhabitants 'Where does the missionary live?' they [the Okinawans] showed obvious dislike for him, and one of them said, in English, 'Bad man! Very bad man!'" (taken from Kerr – see below). Indeed, as the *Narrative* . . . also pointed out, on the Commodore's arrival, Bettelheim "and the inhabitants were living in a condition of undisguised hostility towards each other."[5]

During the stay of the *In Gan-cho,* or Bespectacled Dog-doctor, as Bettelheim was derisively known among the locals, a number of European and American ships docked at Naha. Among the British ships were *HMS Sphynx* and *HMS Reynard,* already alluded to, *HMS Riley, HMS Contest, HMS Mariner,* under Capt. Matheson, the sloop

Plate 2. Doctor Bettelheim's residence on Okinawa

Preble, under Commander Glynn, and the yacht, *Nancy Dawson*, under the command of Capt. Shedden. A number of other European ships also paid visits, including the French brig, *Pacifique*. Uninvited guests were beginning to frequent the islands a little too often. Bettelheim left Okinawa in July, 1854, only to be replaced by another unwanted missionary named Moreton, though he left after two years leaving the Loo Choo Naval Mission abandoned. Bettelheim amassed a considerable sum of money from his Okinawan experience in unspent money, but in fairness he and his family had suffered much hardship and deprivation. He certainly seems to have felt an affinity with the island for he named his second daughter, Lucy Fanny Loochoo. After additional controversial adventures that included acting as a surgeon in the American Civil War, Bettelheim, an extra-ordinary fellow, died in Missouri of pneumonia on the 9th February, 1870, aged fifty-eight, followed by his wife, two years later.

Bettelheim's journals were destroyed in a fire at Brookfield, Missouri, and whilst a manuscript copy supposedly exists, it was not consulted in the preparation of this book, mainly because it could not be traced. However, a few papers by Bettelheim that appear in learned journals and diary extracts[vi] were read, and relevant information is quoted in this book, with credit numbers given previously. The attitude of such missionaries seems to have been, if I may quote from S. W. Williams: "Along with their [the Okinawans] simplicity, and, as some would say, happy ignorance, they are debased by idolatry, and besotted in sin; and until this incubus is removed, whatever stimuli to enterprise are presented, they will never rise in the scale of civilization. Let the vivifying influences of our holy religion be felt, their comforts, their pleasures, their rank among their fellow-men, and their condition in this life, will be enhanced a thousand fold; and in the train of these will follow joy and peace beyond the grave."[13] Nevertheless, for all his possible 'faults,' Dr. Bettelheim was an important figure in the history of nineteenth century Okinawa and her relationships with the West. A highly complex character, he was the epitome of Victorian religious fervour who, in his own words saw "a harvest ripening for the Christian Church in Loochoo."[20] In response to the troublesome Bettelheim, the Okinawan government made life pretty miserable for the missionary. Bettelheim wrote: "The means used by government to rid themselves of us are all directed against the animal man; they beat, they pelt, they starve us, when they please; they send us bad provisions, and abridge our locomotion, and knowing we possess a modicum of human feeling, they harass and vex us in endless methods."[25] Bettelheim continued: "In this land, where every prospect pleases, and only man in vile, the difficulty is not to live and work as a missionary, but to live at all, to live and move about as a man."[25]

Why, the reader might rightly enquire, didn't the missionary, encountering such overwhelming difficulties, simply depart the island? Well, it was the notion that he might surmount the problems that made him stay. Because he met such great opposition, he felt an enormous burden of responsibility. As he wrote: "One of the great reasons that forbid my leaving, believe me, is to prevent or at least retard, shame and reproach to fall on Christianity."[25] Bettelheim was acutely aware of not being able to overcome the Okinawan resistance, and yet he battled on in true missionary spirit. This was, perhaps, made even more impressive, when one considers that, no doubt due to all the trials and tribulations he faced on Okinawa, he knew all was not well with him, for he wrote: "I know also that my present state of mind is in no respect bright, perhaps not even right."[25] In many ways, for all his eccentricities, he must be regarded as quite a man. Certainly, the present volume would have been the poorer if it had not been for Bettelheim and his writings.

But, perhaps Dr. Whitney (*ibid*) conveyed the best view, when he wrote some thirty-five years after Bettelheim's departure from Okinawa: "If I may be allowed a kindly word of criticism, there is no question about Dr. Bettelheim being an earnest, zealous, devoted and defatigable laborer for the cause of Christ. But from his own sayings and doings I am led to believe that he did not always exercise practical wisdom. Many of the ways and means employed to further his cause seemed only to aggravate and hinder, and were often of such a nature as to demean himself and lose respect for Christianity. His course certainly does not present to us a model to be followed now in opening up new stations. And yet we can pass over many things when we consider that it was in the early days of mission work, before missionaries had learned wisdom from experience. And when we remember that he was a nervous, impetuous man, isolated from friends and deprived of the privilege of mutual counsel and encouragement from associate missionaries." According to Whitney, in his professional duties as a doctor, Bettelheim treated some two hundred people during his six-year stay on the island.

In the quest for authenticity, 19th century literature dominates the present work. However, numerous references were consulted that are of the twentieth century, and odd snippets of information gleaned from such works, here and there, relating, or thought to relate, to the period in question, are inserted into the text. In a few cases, descriptive material is actually quoted, and the name of the author is given, rather than a superscripted number.

The span of twentieth century papers and books was considerable – from Charles S. Leavenworth's, *A visit to the Loochoo Islands* (*North China Herald*, Vol. 73, Oct. 1904, pages 807–809) and, *The History of the Loochoo Islands* (*Journal of the China Branch of the Royal Asiatic Society*, Vol: 36, 1905), through such works as Charlotte M. Salwey's very readable, *The Loo Choo, or Ryu Kyu Islands* (*Asiatic Quarterly Review* (London), 3rd series, Vol. XXXIII, 1912, *Japanese Monographs*, No. XVI, pages 313–327), to *Taira: An Okinawan Village,* written by husband and wife team, Thomas and Hatsumi Maretzki (Wiley, 1966), who researched the village, sited on the northeast coast of the island, in 1954.[vii] Needless to say, many books containing factual material, such as Kodansha's *Encyclopedia of Japan* (1983), were consulted.

Okinawa: The History of an Island People, by George H. Kerr (Tuttle, 1958) rises above all twentieth century works on Okinawa, as an authoritative work. The origins of this book are interesting in that it was felt by the American Civil Administrator for the Ryukyu Islands, Brigadier-General James Lewis, seven years after the Pacific War was over, that "Okinawan youth, uprooted by the war and cut off from Japan, knew very little of its past history and virtually nothing of the circumstances which had drawn the United States to the western

Pacific frontier and into Okinawa for a second time within one hundred years," and thus asked the Pacific Science Board of the National Research Council to produce an historical summary with the view to translation into Japanese for distribution on the islands. This book was completed in 1956 and entitled, *Ryukyu Rekishi*. That work was a forerunner of *Okinawa: The History of an Island People*. The present author would recommend this work wholeheartedly to anyone with an interest on Okinawan history, and there is a very extensive bibliography, many books and articles of which the present author consulted in the preparation of this work and that are not mentioned above due to their numbers.

Additionally, a fair number of highly esoteric articles were read from the nineteenth and twentieth centuries, and the necessary facts integrated into the text. Works ranged from to Jan La Roe's, *Native Music of Okinawa* (*Music Quarterly Journal*, Vol. 32, 2, 157–170), through Harold Fink's, *The Distribution of Blood Groups in Ryukyuans* (*American Journal of Physical Anthropology*, Vol. Vol. 2, {June, 1947}, 159–163), to Professor Basil Hall Chamberlain's, *A Quinary System of Notation Employed in Luchu on the Wooden Tallies Termed Sho-chu-ma* (*Journal of the Anthropological Institute of Great Britain and Ireland*, Vol. XXVII, 383–395).

Of all the references obtained for this book, only six texts sought remained unread. James Burney's, *A Chronological History of the Voyages and Discoveries in the South Sea or Pacific Ocean* (London {1803–1813}, Vol. XV, 260–268; Vol. III, 431–432) lies in the library of the University of Glasgow and was apparently too fragile to lend or photocopy, as was, J. Willet Spalding's, *The Japan Expedition: Japan and Around the World, An Account of Three Visits to the Japanese Empire, with Sketches of Madeira, St. Helena, Cape of Good Hope, Mauritius, Ceylon, Singapore, China and Loo-Choo* (New York, 1885, Ch. VII, 100–131; Ch. IX, 173-175; Ch. XI, 205-210, Ch. XIV, 334–344), which resides in the University of Edinburgh library. Peter Parker's, *A Journal of An Expedition From Sincapore to Japan with a Visit to LooChoo, etc* (revised by Rev. Andrew Reed), London, 1838, was only available on microfilm. Henry B. Schwartz describes an Okinawan wedding on pages 405–408 of Volume I of *Japan Magazine* (June, 1910), and, *In Togo's Country: Some Studies of Satsuma and other Little Known Parts of Japan*, (New York, 1908), Schwartz writes, on pages 117–163, on *Loo-Choo: a Forgotten Kingdom*, but both references proved to be untraceable in Great Britain, as was Malcolm Bingay's, *Life in Loochoo*, that appeared in *Forum* (Vol. V,

No. 1, 44–45), the date being unknown. For the above untraceable references, the information given is presumed correct, the material probably being available in the USA.

So, with all the necessary facts, figures and descriptions of a far off land, in a bygone age, elicited and recorded, it was then time to consider what was known about nineteenth century Okinawan karate. With the exception of Satow's and Furness's brief comments on Okinawan boxing however, and Hall's reference to an unexpected unarmed fighting spirit from which inferences may be drawn, no quotes written in English for that entire century have been unearthed.

Okinawan and Japanese sources are nearly as bereft. Harry Cook[viii], in his, *Shotokan Karate: A Precise History*, notes three references. The first comes from Sagenta Nagoshi's, *Nanto Zatsuwa*, published in 1850. A Satsuma samurai, Nagoshi had been exiled to the north-eastern Ryukyuan island of Amami Oshima, and, writing on his observations, noted a fighting form called '*tsukunesu*'. What is of paramount importance concerning this work however, is that it confirms that training on the *makiwara* (see Chapter IV) was practised at that time, for there is a line drawing to that effect which is reproduced in the present book.

Shiuko's, *Chiuzan-koku Shiriaku*, referred to earlier, quoted by Satow, was published in 1852. Cook notes two further quotes from this work that involved Shiuko's interviewing of members of an Okinawan embassy: "A person well-trained in kempo is able to kill with only his fist – even two men," and, "An enemy in front can be beaten with the fist; and enemy to the rear with the foot."

Perhaps the most unexpected reference though, comes from the celebrations forming part of King Sho Tai's enthronement on the 27th July 1866. As part of these extended celebrations, Cook[ix], an authoritative source, notes that ten martial arts demonstrations were given at the Ochayagoten of Shuri Castle's East Garden in Sakiyama village on the 24th March 1867. These displays involved *sai*, staff, rattan shield and *tode* (the early name for karate). Karate was featured in the form of two performances of *kata* – *Seisan* by Tsuji Aragaki, and *Suparinpei* by Chikudon Tomura, plus two pre-arranged sparring demonstrations – the first showing staff and karate by Chiku Maeda and Aragaki, the second, karate only, by the same practitioners.

There is no documentary evidence that has yet come to light to show specifically what karate was like on Okinawa during the century in question. It is not a case of the material having been lost, for it appears never to have existed in the first place. The central reason for this being that practice in all forms of martial arts was believed banned, so training was conducted in great secrecy. The author uses the cautionary word 'believed', because the demonstrations given before Sho Tai seem not only to contradict that long held assertion, but give such arts the highest acknowledgement and prominence. However, Funakoshi was adamant about the need for secrecy, so the notion has been adhered to in the present work. For martial art historians, the fact that nothing revealing any real technical aspects of karate have been discovered before the twentieth century may be calamitous, but for the writer it leaves greater freedom for informed guesswork, extrapolation and imagination, and what might have been is what this book is all about.

In the last decade of the nineteenth century though, as mentioned earlier, karate began to come out into the open after centuries in the shadows. Funakoshi reported that a karate demonstration by an unmentioned teacher was given at the Shuri Jinjo Koto Shogakko around 1891/1892. By 1901/02, Funakoshi had given a demonstration at his school for Shintaro Ogawa, commissioner of schools for Kagoshima Prefecture. Concurrently, according to Funakoshi, physicians, seeing the benefit of training in its practitioners, recommend karate practice as a form of health promotion. This trend led, probably within a year, to Funakoshi introducing karate to the Men's Normal School in Shuri and the Prefectural Daiichi Middle School. Within a short time, karate became successfully integrated into the Okinawan school curriculum, and this gained momentum, with numerous demonstrations, some highly prestigious, being given by Funakoshi, and other masters like Mabuni, Motobu, Kyan, Gusukuma, Ogusuku, Tokumura, Ishikawa and Yahiku in the first two decades of the twentieth century. In 1917, Funakoshi led a karate display to the Butokuden in Kyoto, and, at the request of the Okinawan Educational Affairs Office, and as President of the Okinawan Association for the Spirit of the Martial Arts, he led a karate demonstration at the First National Athletic Exhibition held at the Kishi Gymnasium, Ochanomizu, Tokyo, on the 1st April, 1922. Realizing that there was considerable interest in karate from learned circles, he never returned to live in Okinawa, devoting the remaining thirty-five years of his life to the promotion of his beloved art.

It is recorded that karate, at least in some quarters, underwent certain revisions when the art was introduced to children on Okinawa. It is known, for example, that there were alterations made to at least some *kata* (forms – set movements performed in set sequences), the principal means of practice, in terms of the removal of dangerous techniques, as at least some forms were diluted of martial content. But the extent of this dilution is unknown. It may have been considerable, as the first downward trend to the gymnastic, so obvious today, became evident. On the other hand, it may have been minimal, with the established *kata* hardly being touched at all, for they were seen as living reference works, containing the legacies of great masters past, in a culture where respect for tradition was highly valued. It is widely believed that the first, so-called basic *kata,* were devised at this time, essentially with the school curriculum in mind, with techniques and movements drawn from the established *kata.* The *Pinan* (later referred to as '*Heian*') *kata* of Shotokan, said to have been created by Itosu, are considered a fine example of this sideward step.

It wasn't really until November, 1922, and the publication of Gichin Funakoshi's, *Ryukyu Kempo: Tode*, by Bukyosha, that we have something tangible to grasp, something from which comparisons with twenty-first century Shotokan can be made. This, the first book on karate ever published[xi], provides little real insight into the art's history, and subsequent works by Funakoshi and a few others who trained on Okinawa during the years in question, throw but little light on the issue. No one really knows, examining the crude figures of a *karateka* (a student of karate) drawn by Hoan Kosugi in that first book, to what extent the techniques accurately reflect practice at that time, let alone how accurately they reflect karate practice on Okinawa as little as twenty years or so earlier, before any alterations may have taken place. A number of minor discrepancies are evident in technique between the publication of *Ryukyu Kempo: Tode* and Funakoshi's second book, *Renten Goshin Tode-Jutsu*, published by Kobundo, three years later. Perhaps the original drawings were not as accurate as they might have been, and the *kata* techniques of the time were more accurately portrayed in the photographs in the second book. Certainly, Kosugi had only been training in karate a few months under Funakoshi when the figures were drawn[xii], but Funakoshi must surely have passed them for publication. Funakoshi, in his autobiography, wrote of the 1922 book that "to its composition I devoted every ounce of effort that I had, and so among my various publications it remains a favorite." He also noted that the book was "beautifully designed by Hoan Kosugi" (*ibid*). If the book was a favourite and he liked the design, by which he presumably included the drawings (though a few are placed in the wrong order), for no other reference is made to them, then it seems reasonable to assume that he was happy, and that the techniques represented corresponded with his practice. And this leads to the question, of course, as to whether the minor discrepancies were in fact minor changes. The techniques and movements of *kata* were certainly not seen as sacrosanct, with each master entitled to his own opinions and mode of practice.

Funakoshi, having been a schoolmaster for over thirty years[xiii], would have acquired a most critical eye. When this fact is combined with the knowledge that he would have been conscious of the gravity of being the author of the first karate book ever published, given the respect he had for his karate instructors, it seems hard to believe that the minor differences were not accepted by the master. Similarly, in a culture that greatly respected neatness and precision, it does seem unlikely that minor inconsistencies or slight changes in form were deemed as unimportant.

Funakoshi had a mission, for his ambition was to introduce karate to the Japanese educational system. To this end, he was following in the footsteps of Jigaro Kano, the founder of judo, who had introduced his art into the Japanese school curriculum. Certainly, Funakoshi was on good terms with Kano, and respected him greatly. Funakoshi believed that he needed to be eclectic and then standardise karate to a single art. This necessitated change.

The recently discovered film of Funakoshi performing *kata* at Keio University in 1932, reveals the type of change that occurred over the intervening time span. Whilst the techniques and movements of the *kata Tekki Shodan*, for example, essentially remained the same, the lower stances were a revelation, as was Funakoshi's hip and knee flexibility at the age of sixty-four, when his previous books gave no indication whatsoever of such ability. Similarly, the timing and emphasis within the *kata* was, in places, somewhat different from that practised some twenty years later.

In 1935 came the publication of *Karate-Do Kyohan,* arguably Funakoshi's most important work, and the trend for change continued. The most important element of this work however, was that the master attempted to raise the *jutsu* of karate to an art form, to a *Do,* a Way of life, with a sound philosophical, moral and spiritual underpinning. Over the next ten years, significant developments continued with the master's third son, Yoshitaka, who became a legendary figure before his premature death in 1945. Then, after the destruction of the Shotokan *dojo* and the ending of the Pacific War, the Japan Karate Association was formed on the 1st May, 1949, with a view to preserve karate in the Funakoshi tradition. Shotokan became the domain of the universities. Funakoshi was in his eighties, and whilst held in great reverence by his students, his influence, technically, was minimal. Many spirited young men practised, essentially, what they wanted to practise and what they thought they should practise, with only real guidance occasionally being given. As Master Kanazawa noted: "for with most of the seniors it was just a case of repetition – techniques again, and again, and again, hundreds of times, and nothing was ever really explained. That's all I wanted to do at that stage as well. Young men you see, we didn't understand karate at all."[x]

What Shotokan *karateka* generally practise today has remained largely unchanged since the 1950s. Through the considerable and well-intentioned efforts of the late Chief Instructor to the JKA, Masatoshi Nakayama, and through the administrative abilities of Masatomo Takagi, their Shotokan karate was introduced to the world via the likes of Hidetaka Nishiyama, Teruyuki Okazaki, Taiji Kase, Osamu Ozawa, Masataka Mori, Hirokazu Kanazawa, Takayuki Mikami, Tetsuhiko Asai, Yutaka Yaguchi, Toru Iwaizumi, Kenosuke Enoeda, Hiroshi Shirai, and so on. One thing seems highly likely however, and that is that if Yoshitaka had not died, the Shotokan of the last half of the twentieth century would have been noticeably different; his passing, in some quarters, has been seen as a catastrophic disaster, for he was Funakoshi's natural successor.

What should be appreciated is that differences exist between what is practised today in Shotokan and what was practised by Funakoshi when he first introduced karate to Japan, and this brings us back to the question of what karate training was like on Okinawa at the end of the nineteenth century and its relation to *Ryukyu Kempo: Tode*. The time from when *Ryukyu Kempo: Tode* was published, and the time of the formation of the JKA, twenty-seven years had elapsed. From the publication of *Ryukyu Kempo: Tode,* and the end of the story contained in this present book, thirty years elapsed. The changes that took place in Japan with regard to form and emphasis are thought to far exceed the changes that took place on Okinawa in the thirty preceding years in the traditional *kata*. Yet, when we look at the *kata Tekki Shodan* or *Kanku-dai* today, for example, we can actually see little real difference between them and what is shown in *Ryukyu Kempo: Tode*. With this in mind then, and bearing in mind the former technical director of the JKA, Master Hidetaka Nishiyama comment's that "the outside movements [of *kata*] . . . are irrelevant,"[xiv] and, "only an outside symbol that represents the inside,"[xv] the author of the present work has drawn on Funakoshi's first book as the basis of form during the latter part of the nineteenth century. Kanazawa noted in his *Shotokan Karate International Kata – Vol. II* (SKI, 1982) that, "We definitely know that *Tekki Shodan* was practised in Shuri since ancient times," and that, "*Tekki Nidan* and [*Tekki*] *Sandan* were created by Master Itosu from Shuri-te using *Tekki Shodan* as [the] model." Where obvious complications arise therefore, such as precisely when *Tekki Nidan* and *Tekki Sandan* were created by Itosu, detailed analysis of these forms have been omitted from the text, as no one knows whether they existed before 1892 or not.

Before closing on the point about changes in form, one final issue should be addressed with regard to the relevance of extrapolating back in time from *Ryukyu Kempo: Tode*. Funakoshi was an educated man who displayed clarity of thinking, order, purpose, and high principles. His personality was often referred to in the most respected terms in the highest of circles. Given what is known about the mores of the culture in the time under investigation, it may be tentatively possible, and to some extent, to place brakes on the number of changes that may have taken place in Funakoshi's karate with the advent of its introduction into Okinawan schools.

Whilst *kata* were not seen as inviolate, with very senior masters changing moves in forms and creating new ones, Funakoshi had enormous respect for his teachers, and although he was, no doubt, independent of them, it seems unlikely that he would have had the effrontery to change moves, at least in their lifetime. Master Itosu had died just six or seven years before *Ryukyu Kempo: Tode* was written, so it is very likely that any Itosu *kata* were minimally affected at this time. Funakoshi's favourite *kata*, *Kanku-dai*, represented in that first book, would almost certainly have been approved by Itosu.

It is unknown whether Funakoshi actually changed any *kata* to accommodate the Okinawan school curriculum. It is likely that he would have left that to his seniors, such as Itosu. And that begs the question of how much Itosu changed technique, movement, timing and so on. Itosu was about seventy years of age at the turn of the twentieth century, and in his mid eighties when he died, and, generally, old men are apt to be loathed to change, and this would have been more marked at the time, given the culture, and the fact that *kata* were seen as a living heritage. Also, of course, as has been noted before, Itosu created basic *kata* for inclusion in schools, and may well have left the remainder untouched.

This book tells a story of karate training on Okinawa during a period of only five years, 1880–1885, before possible changes to the art were brought to bear. Notable references to technique in *kata* are made from Chapter II, mainly to draw the reader's attention to any difference between form at that time, taken from *Ryukyu Kempo: Tode*, and JKA karate of the early 1960s, when this book was 'written.' The author would like to thank Master Mitsusuke Harada, Chief Instructor to Karate-Do Shotokai, for translating relevant sections of *Ryukyu Kempo: Tode*, and, given his enviable association with Gichin Funakoshi in the 1940s and 1950s, for his comment and opinion. The author would also like to thank Master Harada for eliciting certain information on his behalf, including such useful data as the names of Funakoshi's uncles, on his father's side. In Chapter III, the differences in *Tekki Shodan* between 'then' and 'now' are noted in some depth, and in Chapter V the differences in *Kanku-dai*. For reader reference, it was decided, where appropriate, to include reference numbers in brackets of *kata* moves, so: {56/9a}. The first number refers to the *kata* move number in *Ryukyu Kempo: Tode*, the second, to the *kata* move number in Hirokazu Kanazawa's, *Shotokan Karate International Kata: Vol. I*. The latter book was chosen because Master Kanazawa was taught by Master Funakoshi; it is a first-rate book; and, it is widely available. Where '{—/14a}' is recorded, only the second book is referred to. Differences in techniques and moves between *Ryukyu Kempo: Tode*, and *Renten Goshin Tode-Jutsu*, are given in the notes for each chapter in the References at the end of this work. In Chapter V, two quotes are taken from the author's book, *Kanazawa, 10th Dan,* as Kanazawa saw the master perform *Kanku-dai*, and these quotes are designated with a superscripted 'e.' The single superscripted 'f' refers to a quote from page 70 of Randall G. Hassell's book, *Conversations with the Master: Masatoshi Nakayama* (Focus Publications, 1983). Chapter V is especially technical in one section, and as such information occurs very near to the end of the book, it is strongly recommended that readers merely read the text without getting 'hung-up' on the details, and then return to them once the book is completed.

It cannot be over emphasised that the intentions of the author with regard to this work go far deeper than merely relating what may be reasonably taken as karate technique in the Funakoshi tradition more than a century ago. The purpose, as the sub-title of this work clearly states, is to paint a picture, provide a backdrop, from which the fictitious aspects of karate – if one wanted to be totally accurate – could be acted out. It is hoped then, that the text will conjure up an image in the reader's mind's eye, and in so doing will hopefully enrich the reader's life of karate. The actual technical practice of karate is far down the list in the author's priorities in the scheme of this book, and, indeed, perhaps as a reflection of this, the name 'Funakoshi' and the word 'karate' do not even appear in the text until the second chapter.

Direct quotes relating to karate have been kept to a minimum, and come from three principal sources, all by Gichin Funakoshi, and are also acknowledged in the text. *Karate-Do Kyohan: The Master Text* (Kodansha, 1973), *Karate-Do Nyumon* (Kodansha, 1988), and *Karate-Do: My Way of Life* (Kodansha, 1975), are recorded and superscripted as *a, b* and *c*, respectively. It was decided to attribute alphabetical referencing for the karate references for the benefit of readers, so that confusion between nineteenth century western and Funakoshi's historical or autobiographical text is not confused. The original *Karate-Do Kyohan* appeared in 1935, as has been noted, the above version being the third edition. *Karate-Do Nyumon* was first published in 1943, and *Karate-Do: My way of Life*, in 1956. The above are the first English translations. Funakoshi's other works await translation, but it is felt that nothing of unusual historical merit lies within them in relation to the remit of the present work. There are also four short quotes taken from the present author's book, *Reminiscences by Master Mitsusuke Harada* (1999, KDS Publishing), and these are superscripted 'g'. Additionally, literally hundreds of articles on karate have been consulted, but no useful technical information was forthcoming, for reasons already given. Such articles were helpful however, for providing the names of relevant *karateka* living at the time, their dates of birth, places of birth, and so on. These have not been cited independently, otherwise the book would have been weighted with references in the text, or footnotes, distracting the reader and making the book, in places, a chore to read for all but the most austere enthusiast. It should be noted however, that the list of Okinawan kings and there dates of accession in Chapter II are taken, with permission of Master Morio Higaonna, from his, *Traditional Karate-Do – Okinawan Goju-ryu: Vol. I – The Fundamental Techniques* (1985, Minato Research and Publ. Co.).

Once all the historical and karate material had been collected then, the next question was how best to present it. In the preliminaries to the author's 1992 book, *Training with Funakoshi*, which was, essentially, a simple and unobtrusive, but one hopes engaging story, based around a synthesis of information about Funakoshi's life from 1922, as known in the West, and his introduction of karate to Japan, it was noted: "Written purely as a factual account, the result would have been a fairly dry historical piece, not overly readable, and therefore not very acceptable." With the success of that book in mind, the author was prompted to adopt a similar format for *Funakoshi on Okinawa*, in that, "The author therefore opted for another, softer approach, and this involved him taking the liberty of writing the text as though he actually trained with Master Funakoshi . . . The book thus reads rather like a partial autobiography, albeit false. This method of presentation has allowed the author to elaborate in a more informal manner than would have otherwise been possible, and to discuss in more intimate terms his interpretation of events . . ." (*ibid*).

Of course, the two books contain completely different material. The present work tells a story about a specific period in Funakoshi's life, 1879 to 1885, on Okinawa, though brief mention is made of Funakoshi's wedding in 1888 and another subsequent meeting in 1892, whilst the former book focuses, essentially, on a different subject, a thousand miles away, starting thirty-four years later. In *Training with Funakoshi*, the author was a student of the master's, in the present book, the author is a contemporary – or senior by one year to be precise – learning with the master to be. It is in this spirit that the text of the present work is thus presented, and what follows is a curious blend of fact and fiction, where the plot may invariably be fictitious, but where the props are always real.

Given that no real technical information on karate exists from the nineteenth century on Okinawa, it should come as no surprise to learn that not a single photograph of karate practice on the island during that time has emerged. There is a single photograph known to the author of Master Funakoshi as a teacher that is likely to come from the late nineteenth/early twentieth centuries. As it is the earliest known photograph of Funakoshi, it was decided that it should be included.

Fairly frequently, interesting additional (sometimes contradictory) information that could not appropriately be placed directly into the mouth of the 'author' in the text is located by superscripted Roman numerals, and the notes they refer to are to be found, by chapter, in the References section. Roman numerals are also the means of reference for noted technical differences in *kata* referred to earlier. There are one hundred and twenty such notes in the book. It is hoped that any distraction caused in the text will be greatly outweighed by the benefits of the material so imparted. Also, there are a further fifteen references, again using superscripted Roman numerals, that appear in the Reference section for this Introduction. This was necessary so that important information that would have appeared awkward in the text could be included. No doubt the reader will have identified these already.

Most readers will, or course, be established *karateka*, and will be familiar with most of the karate terms used throughout this book, for many are widely referred to in the *dojo* on a daily basis. However, a significant minority of readers will, no doubt, have only limited karate experience, and a few may have no experience at all, so for these, a glossary has been included at the end of the text. Providing such a glossary enabled the author to detract from placing translations in parentheses throughout the work, which can get tiresome for the reader, and when there are many such brackets, downright cumbersome, not to say irritating. All Japanese words not generally found in English concise dictionaries, excluding personal names, place names and names of martial arts, of course, are italicised for easy reference. Needless to say, if errors of any sort are found throughout the text of this work, they are made in good faith.

In keeping with the 'temporal distance' previously noted, imperial measurement and pre-decimal coinage have been retained and used. For those readers too young to remember, and to refresh the memories of those who are not, in coinage, there were twelve pennies in a shilling and twenty shillings in a pound. Ten shillings was equivalent to 50 pence. Halfpennies were also in use. In distance, there were twelve inches in a foot, and three feet in a yard. An inch is equivalent to 25.4 millimetres. In area, one acre equals 0.405 hectares. In capacity, eight pints is one gallon, which is 4.546 litres. In weight, one pound is equivalent to 0.453 kilograms; one hundredweight, 50.80 kilograms.

Okinawa in the nineteenth century was a very tranquil backwater, and the author has tried to capture, within the limitations of the remit of this book, the spirit not only of the Okinawan people, their island, and other islands in the Ryukyu chain, but of the time. This, hopefully, has been achieved by using quotes from the period to form a narrative mosaic, with the author weaving a tale like fresh mortar that locks the *tessellae*, so that the mosaic may be made permanent and appreciated for what it is. Running parallel to this theme has been the objective of integrating as much factual and historical material as possible, so that western readers may be made familiar not only with a way of life, but a history, that becomes more incomprehensible with the passing of every year. In keeping with the *zeitgeist* then, there are no cheap scuffles or confrontations in this book, no sensations for readers' titillation. The book might best be described as 'quiet,' because that is what it was like on Okinawa more than a century ago, when Funakoshi was a young man, and, therein, can be said to lie whatever charm the book may possess.

To practise karate techniques for their own sake is a hollow exercise. We are fortunate in both Shotokan and Shotokai to have a fine heritage, and the purpose of this book has been to tap this rich vein. If we have an understanding of the past, then the present becomes clearer. If the present lacks clarity, how are we to advance with certainty?

September, 2002

CLIVE LAYTON, M.A., Ph.D (Lond.)

AN IMPORTANT NOTE

Were There Really Weapons on Okinawa During the Nineteenth Century?

There has been a long-held belief, already alluded to in the Introduction, that the Okinawans, being forbidden weapons, developed karate as a consequence of this denial. Historically, there were indeed edicts from Japan requiring the populace to disarm, for weapons to be collected, for the production of weapons to cease, and the forbidding of ownership of arms, and these are referred to in Chapter II of this book, but were these edicts always strictly adhered to? So ingrained and widespread is the belief that there were no weapons on Okinawa, and Gichin Funakoshi makes reference to it in his highly influential books, that few writers on karate have ever really questioned it. In fact, there is good contemporary, first-hand evidence from the nineteenth century to suggest that, within certain circles at least, individuals may indeed have had access to weapons.

As we have seen, Basil Hall's book was the essential reference work for westerners interested in Okinawa throughout the nineteenth century, and it was he who propagated the myth. It is almost certain that Hall and his fellow sailors on that voyage indeed saw no weapons on Okinawa, and were convinced, after questioning local people, that weapons did not exist. Adams, reinforcing this point noted that: "Both Hall and M'Leod . . . aver that these people are totally unacquainted with the use of arms."[11a] Samuel Wells Williams wrote in 1837, "Arms we saw none, neither swords, matchlocks, nor knives,"[13] and Taylor commented that, "during our journey we never saw a single weapon of any kind."[5a] Habersham noted in 1857: "As far as my observation went, they have no arms of any description.[22] Fahs wrote of "no arms or ammunition . . . not even spears nor bows and arrows."[8] It must be said that this myth continued for more than eighty years, for a number of visitors to the Ryukyus as late as 1899 were reporting that "there is no native hostile weapon of any kind or sort whatsoever to be found in the islands."[27]

Yet there was evidence, despite the fact that concealment was near-ly total, and it was more a matter of good fortune if clues could be spotted, that there were indeed weapons of various sorts on Okinawa at the time. Adams continued: "Thinking to throw a little light on the subject [of weaponry], I enquired casually of A-sung, our Chinese interpreter, who was much among them, what they would do if they were attacked by an enemy, when he informed me that they had large stores of arms which he had seen, shields, spears, and bows and arrows, but that they wished to keep the knowledge of their existence in the island a secret, even from their own people."[11a]

Careful observation could sometimes pay off, as Capt. Beechey discovered. For example, inside the house where Capt. Basil Hall vis-ited, was a screen. Beechey recalled: "It was made of canvas stretched upon a frame forming two panels, in each of which was a figure; one representing a mandarin with a yellow robe and *hatchee-matchee* seat-ed upon a bow and quiver of arrows, and a broad sword; the other, a commoner of Loo Choo dressed in blue, and likewise seated upon a bow and arrows. The weapons immediately attracted my attention, and I inquired of my attendant what they were, for the purpose of learning whether he was acquainted with the use of them, and found that he was by putting his arms in a position of drawing the bow, and by pointing to the sword and striking his arm forward; but he implied that the weapon belonged to the mandarins only."[24] Perhaps the screen, which protected three idols, had been removed at the time of Hall's visit, or maybe it had been acquired in the eleven intervening years?

Beechey continued: "The supposition that the inhabitants of Loo Choo possessed no weapons, offensive or otherwise, naturally excited surprise in England, and the circumstance became one of our chief objects of inquiry. I cannot say the result of the investigation was as satisfactory as I could have wished, as we never saw any weapon whatever in use, or otherwise, in the island; and the supposition of their existence rests entirely upon the authority of the natives, and upon circumstantial evidence. The mandarin Ching-oong-choo, and several other persons, declared there were both cannon and musket in the island; and An-yah distinctly stated there were twenty-six of the former distributed amongst the junks. We were disposed to believe this statement, for seeing the fishermen, and all classes in Napa, so famil-iar with the use and exercise of our cannon, and particularly so from their appreciating the improvement of the flint-lock upon that of the match-lock, which I understand from the natives to be in use in Loo Choo; and unless they possessed these locks it is difficult to imagine from whence they could have derived their knowledge. The figures drawn upon the panels of the joshouse, seated upon broadswords and bows and arrows, may be adduced as further evidence of their possessing weapons; and this is materially strengthened by the fact of their harbour being defended by three square stone forts, one on each side of the entrance, and the other upon a small island, so situated within the harbour, that it would present a raking fire to a vessel entering the port; and these forts have a number of loop-holes in them, and a platform and parapet formed above with stone steps leading up to it in several places. This platform would not have been wide enough for our cannon, it is true, but unless it were built for the reception of these weapons, there is apparently no other use for which it could have been designed. I presented the mandarin with a pair of pistols, which he thankfully accepted, and they were taken charge of by his domestics without exciting any unusual degree of curiosity. Upon questioning An-yah where his government procured its powder, he immediately replied from Fochien."[24]

As early as 1818, when aboard William Upton Eddis's brig, despite the Captain's stay in the Napachan roads for only forty-four hours, Okinawans had come aboard after being invited, and measured and sketched just about everything, including the small arms. When guns were fired by westerners, the peasantry were frequently startled. This was often cited, and Taylor noted, for example, "Mr. Heine . . . astonished the natives [of Pino], some forty or fifty of whom had collected . . . by firing at a mark with his rifle,"[5a] but people of the senior classes were not so affected, for they had seen firearms before. What seemed to interest the Okinawans, apart from Mr. Heine's aim, "was the fact of the piece [gun] exploding without the application of fire (nothing but Japanese matchlocks ever having been seen on the island), and its being loaded at the breech. They were familiar with the nature of gunpowder . . ."[5a]

Beechey was "disposed to believe that the Loo Chooans have weapons, and that they are similar to those in use in China. And with regard to the objection which none of them having ever been seen in Loo Choo would offer, I can only say, that while I was in China, with the exception of the cannon in the forts, I did not see a weapon of any kind, though that the people are well known to possess them."[24] Taylor noted that the Okinawans "were familiar with . . . arms,"[5b] and Gutzlaff wrote that "they possessed arms . . . but were averse to use them"[12] [this statement is also recorded by Morrow[6] and Abeel].

Hawks wrote that, "the Lew Chewans pretended ignorance of

offensive weapons, and of such no open display is was made by the people, but Dr. Bettelheim has said that he has seen fire-arms in their possession, though they seeked to conceal them from strangers; and they are doubtless, by nature, a pacific people."[5]

Bishop Smith wrote: "Dr. B(ettelheim) states the circumstances which led to his discovery of Japanese soldiers engaged in cleaning and polishing their fire-arms; and dwells on this fact as an instance of the wrong impressions which formerly existed in the minds of Europeans as to the total absence of military armour and accoutrements among the Lewchewan people."[17] Of course, Japanese were Japanese at the time, and Okinawans were Okinawans, so not too much should be inferred from this, for it would be rather like a less than accurate observer recording that there were arms on the island when one of Perry's explorative parties "armed with cutlasses and carbines, and ten rounds of ball cartridges each"[5] were seen.

Indeed, not only is it highly likely that the Okinawan populace, or at least certain quarters of it, were aware of weaponry; that there were likely to be stores of weapons on the island for dire emergencies; that ownership, even of firearms, by some, almost certainly the higher or highest ranks seems probable; but it possible that the Okinawan people actually manufactured weapons. Beechey noted that, "Supao-Koang mentions among the manufactures of his country [Okinawa] are . . . arms,"[24] and it was commented by the Chinese that the Okinawans had weapons, and indeed they "were manufactured in the island."[24]

When one of Commodore Perry's parties explored the island, taking notes on botany, geology, and so on, a certain Lieutenant Whiting came across what he reported was a gunpowder factory at Vicoo. A subsequent trip to Vicoo by the Reverend Jones's party found nothing, and "the natives professed entire ignorance of the existence of any such thing."[9a] Was Whiting incorrect in his observation, or were the Okinawans being deceitful? Certainly, it is well known that the Ryukuan island of Io-Jima, a fearful, god-forsaken place shown on western charts at the time as Sulphur Island, was a major source of sulphur – a necessary component of gunpowder – over which the Okinawans had tight control. Approaching the island was an experience in itself, for even at a great distance smoke could be seen bellowing from the volcano's crater. The island, no greater than "four or five miles in circumference, rises precipitous from the sea, except in one or two spots; and its height must be considerable, judging from the distance . . . perhaps twelve hundred feet. The sulphurous smell emitted,

Plate 3. Perry's men firing a salute

even when two or three miles off, was very strong."[3] According to
M'Leod, a "few families . . . [were placed there] at certain periods of
the year to collect the sulphur emitted by this volcano, which forms a
considerable branch of revenue to the king of the Lewchew islands."[3]
The area was also rich in mercury.

The highest, privileged echelons of society were likely to be privy
to weaponry then. If other, lower members of society were aware of
the existence of arms, then the subject was likely to be viewed as taboo
and certainly not open to debate with strangers. What form, exactly,
these weapons took is questionable. High-ranking individuals, such as
Azato, almost certainly possessed a sword at their house and maybe
even a firearm. Regarding the inhabitants of Kumi, Adams, quoting La
Perouse, noted that "each had a dagger, the hilt of which was gold,"[11a]
so the practice may have been much more widespread than thought. It
seems quite possible that there were hordes of arms secreted away, but
whether firearms were included is unknown. Satow, in 1872, quoting
from Shiuko, twenty-two years earlier, wrote that, "As regards more
manly accomplishments, they [the Okinawans] are expert archers on
horseback and good marksmen with the matchlock,"[14] and, clearly, in
order to be a fine archer or marksman, it was necessary to practise.

Master Funakoshi recorded in his writings that his first, and most influential teacher, Master Azato, was an expert, amongst other things, with the sword and bow, and this should alert readers immediately to a certain discrepancy. Indeed, Funakoshi reported that Azato defeated the famed swordsman, Master Yorin Kanna, in a contest. Such contests had also been banned. Funakoshi also noted that his father, Gizu, was an expert with the *bo* (staff), and, once again, it is not only necessary to have a weapon to become a master of a martial art, but to practise assiduously with it. Yet these very obvious admissions, assuming them to be true – and there is no reason to doubt them – have, seemingly, been overlooked by writers of karate with regard to this context. This incongruity has, at least to the author's knowledge, never been seriously addressed.

One will never know if Funakoshi knew of the existence of weapons on the island beyond the sword, bow, staff, and so on, though the master was born into the lower echelons of the *shizoku*, and it is very doubtful whether he would have been in a position to have known officially. This is largely academic however, for his description as to the origins of karate on Okinawa – that the art arose chiefly due to the denial of weapons – is almost certainly true. The purpose of this note has been to show that quite sophisticated weapons probably existed on the island at the time, and that when reference is made to them in the text to follow, their existence has been based on evidence.

It is now time to enter into the spirit of this book.

'AUTHOR'S' NOTE

Eighty-five years have passed since I first learned the art of karate on Okinawa, secretly, under Ankoh Shishu [Itosu]. After two years, I met Gichin Funakoshi, and we remained firm friends for the next five years before I left Shuri to study in Tokyo.

Mister Funakoshi's commitment to karate was total. Even as a young man his perseverance and dedication to the art were second to none, and I am sure it was because of his determination that he was able to introduce karate to Japan in 1922. He also had education, great refinement, and a full sense of propriety, for which Okinawans are justly famous. These characteristics unquestionably allowed him to associate with the influential people necessary to enable him to fulfil the tasks he had set himself – to establish the art of karate in Japan, to raise it to a Way, and to secure its recognition as a martial art.

The karate that Funakoshi and I learned all those years ago was somewhat different from that which is taught today. Recently, I was invited to a university demonstration that featured displays of karate from various schools, and I can say that whilst there may have been some technical changes, there seems to be a worrying trend for praising gymnastic ability and competition far beyond their proper position. I fear that something indescribable may be on the brink of being lost. I know that Mr. Funakoshi felt the same way, and was genuinely troubled about the direction the art was taking.

Three years after Funakoshi's death in 1957, and following on from a chance introduction and subsequent lengthy conversation with historian, Nobuo Sakuma, I was asked by a representative of a publishing company if I would be prepared to record my memories of my early life on Okinawa and my training with Gichin Funakoshi. It was anticipated that, due to the increasing popularity of the art (for I now understand that karate is being practised as far afield as America and Europe), students would be likely to wish to have access to further information on the art's more distant history, and that I might be able to make a contribution in this regard.

With a specific, yet culturally diverse readership in mind therefore, I have attempted to write the text to this work with people from many nations in mind, and have made much reference to historical events and environmental settings that are unlikely to be known outside Okinawa. I have concentrated on these points because, if I may use a metaphor, a play without scenery is too isolationary, too clinical, too mean on the senses, too pseudo-intellectual. Actors seen solely performing against a white backdrop are totally unfulfilling and unsatisfactory in my opinion. I perceive that one day, through the efforts initiated by Mr. Funakoshi, the benefits of karate will be available to all, and might, perhaps, genuinely touch a few. With this notion in mind therefore, I have attempted to provide a background for modern karate, and tried to recreate the world of Matsumura, Azato and Itosu, amongst others, and what it was really like to live on Okinawa in the nineteenth century.

I sincerely hope that readers will find something of value in the varied, and sometimes disconnected recollections of an old man, who was fortunate to have been born on a small, but rather special Pacific island, a very long time ago.

Kyoto August, 1962.

I

THE END OF A KINGDOM

A solemn and respectful silence hung over the multitude of subjects that cool early evening of the 30th March, 1879, as King Sho Tai and his procession passed westward through the *Kokugaku-mon* [Gate of National Learning] and forever into exile. The king's rounded face, whilst regal and detached in its countenance, nevertheless could not hide the deep sadness that lay within, and the procession took on the dark and laboured appearance of a cortège in the fading light. Even the brightness of His Majesty's white silk robes, a colour worn by the king alone, seemed dulled, and I recall that his two large, jewel encrusted golden topknot pins, that normally shone so brightly, reflected only shadow, as the deep foliage above absorbed the last rays of that day's sun, setting over a calm East China Sea. The *richly flowered silk, stripped with gold and purple*[18] of the highest officers, likewise seemed faded, as did the pearl garments of the king's attendants, which had taken on a premature yellow hue reminiscent of ancient ivory – an effect that was made more striking by the servants' crimson turbans and richly worked Chinese silk girdles. Prince Shoten, Sho Tai's eldest son, sat erect, unmoving, staring forward, in a royal palanquin following his father. The blinds of the *kagu* had not been lowered; there was no shame, no hiding. The horses, *used to carry loads*,[2] were unnaturally subdued too, as if in tune with the king's thoughts, and, as the weight of centuries lay upon him, so his earthly goods now burdened them. A strange, heavy atmosphere, unlike any other I have known, pressed down over the unhappy scene, which seemed further laden by the castle's massive grey, weather-worn walls, that, upwards of sixty feet, dominated the citadel. For five hundred years, the ancient castle of Shuri had been the seat of the Ryukyuan kings, a symbol of nationhood to thirty-six[i] tiny, and often so desperate islands, spread out thinly over countless miles of desolate ocean. Surely, never had such a gathering of people been seen before on Okinawa? Perhaps the entire population of the one hundred thousand or so people living in the four inter-connected towns of Shuri, Naha, Tomari and Kume were there, outside the castle's main gates and lining the roads. I know that many people came from the countryside around to witness His Majesty's departure. Within minutes of Sho Tai's leaving, the castle and its beautifully kept grounds were swarming with some two hundred Japanese troops from the Kumamoto Garrison. It was a poignant moment, an historic moment, an era had come to an end.

I remember walking home with my father on a soft carpet of pine needles, amongst the hustle and bustle, along *the broad, well-paved, and beautifully clean streets, which were kept constantly* swept,[18*] the amber light catching the red tiled roofs of the buildings below, as we descended the steep hill, some three to four hundred feet high, on which the castle stood. Okinawan roads were built straight up and down hills in those days, and one always had to be mindful on the descent, especially if one's attention was captivated by the justly honoured Okinawan pine, *a tree which the artist would prize much more highly than the lumberman.*[5b] The village of Shuri, embosomed by the thick leafy covering of trees so suggestive of shady retreats, the houses half buried in deep-green foliage stretching over an extent of a mile on the southwest slope of a group of hills, spread before us. *The fields of upland rice . . . gracefully bending like waves before the wind,*[5] continued as far as the eye could see. *The harbour lay like a map beyond,*[23] calm in the dimming light, *and away westwards, against the horizon, rose the dim outlines of the Kerama Islands. It was, in its quiet unobtrusive beauty, as charming a view as one could wish for.*[23]

My father and I did not return straight home, but took a rather reflective, meandering stroll, first through a nice part of town. In those times *there were no carts or wheeled carriages of any kind,*[2] and the roads, which were between six and ten feet wide, were devoid of ruts and kept in excellent condition, so walking was very pleasant. *Each house had a courtyard with a wall round it, which had a hedge of the banyan tree cleverly trained along the top. Farther in the country the courtyards had no wall, but only a hedge of evergreen around them, which had the opening before the door so arranged by a short piece of evergreen planted inside the opening and overlapping it, that no one passing on the road could see into the courtyard or house. The houses were raised off the ground, and were fitted with sliding panels instead of walls, so that if there were many visitors all the partitions could be made to slide back, the house becoming one large room, with only one little apartment left for the women.*[19*] I remember meeting *a school of young Buddhist priests on the road, wearing long yellow dresses, and carrying books under their arms.*[19] A strong smell of camphor hung in the air, which was very unusual, and, subconsciously, I think it was this very warm, dense aroma that prompted my father to impress upon his twelve year old son the gravity of what we had just witnessed. The camphor trees were very large, with huge trunks, and looked quite grand in the forest, but they were *gradually diminishing, on account of the wasteful manner in which the camphor was obtained.*[19*] My father, more in a form of thinking aloud than instructing me, spoke of the most ancient of Okinawan origin myths, and after, he fell silent.

Once, he said, there had been two deities, one male, Shiniriku, the other female, Amamiku, who had created Okinawa out of chaos and confusion. With the help of a typhoon, they were blessed with three sons and two daughters. The eldest son, Tinsunshi, became the first ruler of the islands; the second son, Anshi, became the first nobleman; whilst the third son became the first commoner. The first daughter became the first patron of all females of noble birth; and the second, patron to peasant-women. So, mythology had set the scene for the social order of Okinawa for who knows how many centuries. Now it was all gone. The three comma crest, revolving in a clockwise fashion, that had graced the royal house for more than four hundred years – since the reign of Sho Toku, the last king of the first Sho dynasty, to be exact – would be seen no more. The analogy with the predicted fate of the camphor tree was fairly obvious in retrospect. My father's grey expression and slow amble brought some reality to the events that were to shortly unfold, as we entered the less salubrious eastern sub-urb of the capital, which was *composed principally of bamboo huts, thatched with straw.*[5] The blinds of split bamboo that covered the doors were all open and everyone was out and about discussing the momentous events that had befallen us. As though in a world of his own, I recall my father mused on Sho Tai's crowning some thirteen years before, by Tieu Sing, the Chinese Special Ambassador. The Imperial junk had sailed from Fuchu where there was a sizeable Okinawan community, and where a large number of Okinawan graves, some of envoys past, dotted the hills.

The morning following the abdication, men, women, boys and girls of all social classes, were to be found on the open land, rectangles *some two hundred yards long, and some twenty to thirty wide, and, being perfectly level, were well adapted to racing, whether on horse or foot, wrestling, etc, and to ball-playing.*[7*] I recall *Hama nage* [a game similar to hockey] being played that day as though nothing had happened. Sure enough, life went on much as it always had done for many people. Whilst chaos was about to descend upon those of rank, the *heimin* or *nya* [commoners] saw vulgar opportunity.

Prince Nakijin[ii] had been handed a letter on the 28th March, 1879, by Chief Secretary Matsuda, stating, in no uncertain terms, that due to non compliance with an imperial decree four years earlier, ordering the feudal system operating on the islands to be abolished, the deposed king was expected to report immediately to Tokyo. Sho Tai, however, did not board the *Meiji-maru* as intended, but rather, stayed in Naha. The official reason for this delay was given as ill health, but I doubt whether this was really true, for such an excuse was a common ploy used by members of the royal family against foreign demands they did not wish to comply with. One might believe that it was some kind of noble defiance, for I was later told that the king was hoping that China or perhaps even America might exercise some influence. If this was so, then his waiting was, like Minamoto Tametomo's wife before him, in vain.

Allow me to explain this tale for those unfamiliar with it. Tametomo is a legendary figure from the 12th century, famous for his great strength and skill as an archer[iii], who landed at Un-ten and took a Ryukyuan wife, a younger sister of an *anzu* [chieftan] with whom he had a son, Shunten. Tametomo set sail for Japan with his family, but was obliged to return to land after encounters with typhoons at sea. The superstitious Japanese sailors believed that a woman on-board was the cause of the Dragon God sending the tempests. Tametomo was obliged to leave both her and Shunten behind at Makiminate so that he might follow his destiny, and they lived in a humble dwelling in Urazeye forever awaiting his return, though he never did. Shunten became the founder of the Okinawan kingdom and ruled successfully for fifty years.

Despite Okinawa and the other islands under her control being of immense advantage to a great country in time of conflict, China was not prepared to wage war for the Ryukyu kingdom and America was not swayed, and two months later the thirty-seven year old king and a retinue of nearly one hundred courtiers set sail for Japan. Two weeks thereafter, on the 10th June, Sho Tai was presented to Emperor Mutsuhito.

Two days after Sho Tai's audience with the Emperor, my father told me that General Ulysses Grant, the former eighteenth president of the United States, who was in Tientsin as part of his world trip, was pressed by the Viceroy, Li Hung Chang, who laid upon him *the desire of the Chinese government that he should act as arbitrator between Japan and China on the Okinawa question. Li Hung Chang repeated the arguments of Prince Kung, and added to them many others, especially one argument to the effect that the possession of the Okinawa Islands by Japan would block the channel of Chinese commerce to the Pacific, and that China could not permit this. General Grant repeated to the Viceroy the assurances he gave Prince Kung. He was afraid, he said, that the Chinese overrated his power, but not his wish, to preserve peace, and especially to prevent such a deplorable thing as a war between China and Japan. He would study the Japanese case as carefully as he proposed to study the Chinese case. He would confer with the Japanese authorities, if possible, on reaching Japan. If the question took such a shape that he could advise or aid in a peaceful solution he would be happy; and, as he remarked to Prince Kung, his happiness would not be diminished if the advice he gave did not disappoint the Chinese government.*[16] I know the Viceroy again raised the Okinawa question with General Grant before the latter's departure, and begged that he *would speak to the Japanese Emperor, and in securing justice remove a cloud from Asia, which threw an ominous shadow over the East.*[16]

The Emperor met the fifty-seven year old Grant informally, in a summer-house situated on the banks of a palace lake in the early afternoon of an unusually warm day. They spoke on a number of issues including the possibility of granting an assembly to the people, and of the potential legislative functions thereof. This was the single political question the Japanese people had much feeling towards at the time. European influence in Asia was discussed, and General Grant raised the problem of the crippling nature of the Japanese land-tax – where farmers were obliged to surrender half their crops – which he saw as a blockage to economic advancement. National indebtedness was also mentioned and *General Grant said that there was nothing which Japan should avoid more strenuously than incurring debts to European nations ... The General spoke to the Emperor on this question with great earnestness. When he had concluded he said there was another matter about which he had an equal concern. When he was in China he had been requested by the Prince Regent and the Viceroy of Tientsin to use his good offices with the Japanese government on the question of Okinawa. The matter was one about which he would rather not have troubled himself, as it belonged to diplomacy and governments, and he was not a diplomatist and not in government.*[iv] At the *same time he could not ignore a request made in the interest of peace. The General said he had read with great care and had heard with attention all the arguments on the Okinawa question from the Chinese and Japanese sides. As to the merits of the controversy, it would be hardly becoming in him to express an opinion. He recognized the difficulties that surrounded Japan. But China evidently felt hurt and sore. She felt that she had not received the consideration due to her. It seemed to the General that his Majesty should strive to remove that feeling, even if in doing so it was necessary to make sacrifices. The General was thoroughly satisfied that China and Japan should make such sacrifices as would settle all questions between them, and become friends and allies, without consultation with foreign powers . . . The* [Japanese] *Prime Minister said that Japan felt the most friendly feelings toward China, and valued the friendship of that nation very highly, and would do what she could, without yielding her dignity, to preserve the best relations . . . General Grant said he could not speak too earnestly to the Emperor on this subject, because he felt earnestly. He knew of nothing that would give him greater pleasure than to be able to leave Japan, as he would in a very short time, feeling that between China and Japan there was entire friendship. Other counsels would be given to his Majesty, because there were powerful influences in the East fanning trouble between China and Japan. One could not fail to see these influences, and the General said he was profoundly convinced that any concession to them that would bring about war would bring unspeakable calamities to China and Japan. Such a war would bring in foreign nations, who would end it to suit themselves. The history of European diplomacy in the East was unmistakable on this point. What China and Japan should do was to come together without foreign intervention, talk over Okinawa and other subjects, and come to a complete and friendly understanding.*[16*] The meeting lasted two hours, concluding with Grant's views on the educational institutions he had seen, commenting particularly on the Tokyo School of Engineering.

But this was not the end of the matter, for on the 22nd July that year [1879] Grant met Mr. Ito, Minister of the Interior, and General Saigo, Minister of War, at Nikko. *Mister Ito presented the case of Japan at length, contending that Japan's rights of sovereignty over Okinawa were immemorial, and going over the whole question. When Ito had finished, General Grant said that he had been anxious to have this conversation with the Japanese government, because it enabled him to fulfill a promise he had made to Prince Kung and the Viceroy, Li Hung*

Chang. He had read the Chinese case and studied it. He had heard with great interest the case of Japan. As to the merits of the controversy he had no opinion to express. There were many points, the General said, in both cases, which were historical and could only be determined by research. His entire interest arose from his kind feeling toward both Japan and China, in whose continued prosperity America and the entire world were interested. Japan, the General said, had done wonders in the last few years. She was, in point of war materials, army and navy, stronger than China. Against Japan, China, he might say, was defenseless, and it was impossible for China to injure Japan. Consequently, Japan could look at the question from a high point of view. At the same time, China was a country of wonderful resources, and although he had seen nothing there to equal the progress of Japan, there had nevertheless been great progress.

General Grant continued by saying that there were other reasons why Japan should, if possible, have a complete and amicable understanding with China. The only powers who would derive any benefit from a war would be foreign powers. The policy of some of the European powers was to reduce Japan and China into dependence which had been forced upon other nations. He had seen indications of this policy during his travels in the East which made his blood boil. He saw it in Siam and China and Japan. In Siam the king was unable, as he had told the General, to protect his people from opium. In China opium had been forced upon the people. That was as great a crime against civilization as slavery . . . If war should ensue between China and Japan, European powers would end it in their own way and to their own advantage, and to the disadvantage of the two nations. 'Your weakness and your quarrels are their opportunity,' said the General. 'Such a question as Okinawa offers a tempting opportunity for the interference of unfriendly diplomacy.' Minister Ito said that these were all grave considerations; but Japan, standing on her immemorial rights, had simply carried out an act of sovereign power over her own dominions. General Grant answered that he could not see how Japan, having gone so far, could recede. But that there might be a way to meet the susceptibilities of China, and at the same time not infringe any of the rights of Japan . . . Mr. Ito said that what had been communicated by General Grant would be submitted to the cabinet and be considered very carefully.[16]

Readers may enquire, quite rightly, how I know so much about what was confided, and this is because I later had the opportunity to discuss the matter at some length with Mr. Yoshida, who had actually attended both meetings, on a professional matter. What a great shame that Grant, who was so eloquent a speaker, should have died of cancer of the tongue and throat six years after leaving Japan.

In fact, behind the scenes, I know the problem of the Ryukyu dispute went on for a further sixteen years. At one point, it was decided at a conference held in Peking, that the Ryukyus should be effectively equally divided between the two parties. Plenipotentiaries of the two empires signed an agreement to that effect. The Chinese, however, refused to ratify this compromise, and in doing so lost the entire archipelago. China ceased disputing the islands in 1895. It was clear however, that whilst the islands were from 1879 under the auspices of Japan, traditional and sentimental ties of the majority of Ryukyuans I knew were undoubtedly with China. However, I walked in rarefied circles and this view may be biased.

True, the Okinawans *had kept up commerce with Japan, but our sympathies had always been on the side of China, and our respect for her was unbounded. At the same time there had never been any agreement between our rulers and the Emperor who overflowed so copiously with tender compassion for us, which would have justified us in expecting any energetic action in our favour, should occasion have arisen. The overtures of friendship had always come from Okinawa.*[21]*

However, *the Japanese were to be found in numbers in Okinawa, and strolled about as uninterruptedly as the natives; they intermarried with the Okinawans, cultivated lands, built houses in Naha, and, in short, seemed to be perfectly at home. But a Chinaman was much hunted and spied after, and pelted, and insulted as any other foreigner . . .* [The Okinawans] *were evidently quite as much opposed to intercourse with China as with all other nations, notwithstanding the similarity, if not the identity, of our religion, literature, and many of our manners and customs. Indeed, we were de facto and de jure a part of Japan, and our motto was 'uncompromising non-intercourse with all the world.'*[5]*

In actual fact, in Japan, *the public feeling appeared to be against . . .* [the annexation of the islands]; *that is, if we* [now] *can form any idea of that feeling from the native newspapers. The Hochi Shimbun devoted a very ably written and somewhat amusing article to the consideration of the matter, deprecating in the strongest terms the unprofitable expenditure then incurred. The arguments of the writer are tersely put. He asked what benefit to Japan would ever accrue from possession of the islands; what diminution of taxes it was likely to be brought about; what the Japanese would gain by garrisoning the* *islands for their protection against invaders; and, whether they, the Japanese, would be more feared by England, Russia, France or Prussia in consequence? To this last question we thought we might safely hazard a negative reply. The condition of the Imperial treasury, urged the native paper, was not such as to justify the Japanese in spending large sums of money on people who disliked them, who treated their benefits with ingratitude, who flouted their ambassadors, and whose only true loyalty was given entirely to China. 'And what has hitherto been the result of Japan's beneficence?' asked our writer, here rising almost to eloquence. 'Nothing more than this: that last July, when a terrible disease fell upon the Okinawan pigs and killed numbers of them, the enterprising natives salted the poisonous meat, and exported it by junk-loads to Japan! Is it not hopeless,' he asked, working to the climax of his argument in a tone of reproachful indignation, 'to expect a reproductive outlay from a country whose highest ambition is to export diseased pork, from which doubtless many of the people have died? Look at the present condition of Japan. There is no surplus in the treasury, and there is a multitude of reforms which we ought at first to make in this country before seeking other places in which to bring them. We therefore say to the Government and our countrymen that useful and precious treasure ought not to be lavished to maintain showy but useless honours.' Such appeared to be the opinion of many of the Japanese*[21]* at the time.

My father, a privileged government official, held a very senior rank. The higher nobility was split, such as the *Oji, Anzu*, and *Sanzukwan*, who wore gold hairpins in their topknots to denote their position and to clearly distinguish them from other levels. I believe that the practice of wearing hairpins to denote rank came from Japan, and stretched back more than one thousand years. The *Oji*, denoted First Rank, First Grade, were close relatives of the king, whilst the *Anzu*, who were denoted First Rank, Second Grade, were relatives of the king. Then came the Second Rank. My family was *Sanzukwan*, and was thus held in high regard and treated with much respect. My father would wear the purple *hatchee matchee* [turban] of a state councillor. The turban *originally consisted of a long piece of cloth wound round the top of the head . . . [at the time] is was formed of sheets of paper pasted together, covered with silk damask in overlapping layers, seven in front and twelve behind, and the rank of the wearer was indicted by the colour.*[14]

In 1879, there were seventy-two families of noble rank. The *Wekata*[v], or lesser nobility also formed this group. Such individuals were entitled to wear silver hairpins in their topknots ornamented with gold flowers. These men were mostly the younger sons of chiefs, but also included those who had performed with meritorious service to the state. Because of their social position and responsibilities, in reality the *Sanzukwan/Oyakata* held a rank alongside the *Anzu*.

Then came the gentry classes, classified as *Pechin, Satunushi*, and *Chikudung*, who wore silver hairpins. These men were descendents of senior soldiers, retainers, scholars and priests, though sometimes commoners who had risen due to exceptional service. *Shizoku* was the generic term for the privileged classes. Following on from the gentry in the Okinawan social order were the commoners, who generally wore brass hairpins, and consisted of farmers, fisherman and labourers, with butchers, beggars, prostitutes, and so on, at the lowest end of the social ladder. In theory, it was possible to move between certain ranks by one's endeavour and service, but in practice the hope of promotion was fairly remote. In all, there were nine ranks, each with two grades, and the last, which held no rank, were called the *Zashiki*. So, if one included the king, who occupied the first level, there were twenty levels in the Okinawan social hierarchy, and my family was on the fourth level.

It must be said however, that many Okinawans, largely irrespective of class, *displayed a spirit of intelligence and genius, which seemed the more extraordinary, considering the confined circle in which they lived; such confinement being almost universally found to be productive of narrowness of mind.*[3] When, for example, a foreign ship landed in the past, it would take certain individuals only a few weeks to be sufficiently proficient in the visitors' language to be tolerably understood.

My father worked within the *Moshikuehi-ho*, or Department of Foreign Affairs. The duties of the Foreign Office were twofold – to conduct relations with foreign powers, and, strange as it might seem, to oversee distribution of rewards and punishments. My father was involved exclusively with the former. His main preoccupation seems to have been to balance *owning one lord and paying homage to another . . .* [which was] *a task calculated to call into play the very highest diplomatic accomplishments, and the attempt was one which could hardly fail to result in fiasco,*[21]* which, of course, it did. In the past, skilful diplomacy, or the art of procrastination and evasion to be exact, had worked, reaching its zenith in the seventeenth century, but events in the 1870s became quite uncontrollable and both Japan and China could not be accommodated. I believe it true to say that the *Sessei*, or Prime Minister, who presided over the *Hiojo-sho*, or Council of State, along with the *Sandzukwan*, were responsible for running the country, with the king having only a nominal role.

I remember when my father accompanied the brother of Sho Tai, when he *presented a formal petition to Sanjio, the Prime Minister of Japan, expostulating in the most earnest manner against* . . . [Japan's insistence that Okinawa should no longer pay a tribute to China]. *'It is now five hundred years,' said the Prince, 'that we have enjoyed the kindly protection of China, and were we now to discontinue our connection with that Empire it would be at once ungrateful and unjust. It is known to all nations that we pay tribute alike to China and Japan, and if we continued our tribute to China it would not involve us in any new tributary relation. Now, if His Majesty the Mikado would graciously permit the continuance of our connection with China, it would reflect lustre upon the virtues of His Majesty, and the world would not say that this is unreasonable . . . Being a small territory . . . and dependent as tributaries on two empires, we have enjoyed protection and quiet for five hundred years. But if we now suddenly discontinue our connection with China, without a sufficient reason, it would cause us great inconvenience, and seriously affect our Chinese trade.'*[21]* It may interest readers to learn – it is just one of those facts that I have retained in my mind, I know not why – that *a tax of eight thousand two hundred kokus of rice was levied by the Japanese Government* . . . [on Okinawa, which was paid] *in sugar; that being the most valuable produce of the island*[28]* in 1876.

The Prince continued that the Japanese Minister for Foreign Affairs had decided – in 1873 I believe it was – that neither the Okinawan *nationality nor mode of their Administration should be altered, and in 1874, when the supervision of Okinawan affairs was transferred from the Guaimusho to the Naimusho, a verbal order was received from Hayashi Gako to similar effect. Such were the principal arguments put forward by the King's brother.*[21]

Looking back, the Okinawan request to continue to pay a tribute to China, despite being a Japanese *Han* was totally unreasonable, but the thought of not continuing the tributary tradition was *an order which we appeared to have taken most grievously to heart.*[21]*

The Japanese Han no longer existed in the Empire itself. They were all converted into Ken in 1871 or 1872. They were what can best be realized under the English word 'clan,' but did not quite correspond to that. Their names connoted the district in which the class lived as well as the members of the class themselves. They were mostly under Daimios, and after the abolition of these latter the Han were also abol-

ished and their liabilities, &c., taken over by the Imperial Govern-
ment. The . . . Han organisation, which resembled a corporation, gave
way to . . . [a] system which was more allied to the French system of
Prefectures. [21]*

For men of senior rank, these were harrowing times. I remember
my father returning home from work early one afternoon, a few days
after the king's abdication, and quietly announcing that he no longer
had a position, and that a much younger Japanese had taken his job.
There had been a fair number of Japanese residing on Okinawa at the
time, as I've noted, and they would stroll *about as unconcernedly*[17] as
the locals, and, in particular, *settle in Naha.*[17] [vi]

Because of my father's position, he knew the abdication was likely
to happen of course, but when it came it was still un-nerving, not to
say a shock – somehow, it wasn't sufficient for the intellect to simply
reason it. My people knew *but little of the stirring world beyond, with*
all its ceaseless energy, its ambition unsatisfied, its labour unending by
reason of the competition [Salwey] that the end of the nineteenth century aroused. My father was later seized by Japanese police carrying
sai, and subjected to lengthy lectures about the virtues of the new
imposed system, re-training I believed they called it, but he was also
threatened with physical violence, as many were. He may have been
taken to the Japanese garrison in Naha where arms were kept, though
I'm not sure. As a family however, we were lucky, for my father had
had the foresight to invest wisely, and he was offered a post teaching
the mandarin dialect of Chinese, which he was only too pleased to
accept during those difficult days. There were, after all, six thousand
households in Naha at the time and some twenty-four thousand people,
and suitable local jobs were few and far between. Teachers commanded great respect in a then largely illiterate community, where literacy
was seen as an essential means to advancement and power. Indeed,
paper on which anything had been written was held in great respect,
and small stone erections in the shape of boxes were to be seen by the
roadside. These were provided with cavities in which any old scrapes
of paper on which [Chinese] *characters had been traced were placed*
and burnt. It was considered highly improper to throw such pieces of
paper away.[10]* The reason for this respect for odd bits of paper was
lest the name of any deity which may happen to have been inscribed
on these [scraps] *should have been exposed to the dishonour of being*
trodden in the dirt.[23]* Despite this fascination and respect for the written word though, not a single bookshop was to be found on Okinawa
in those days.

Similarly, at that time, *the principal superstition which met the eye in passing through the streets* [of both Naha and Shuri] *was the great number of little images placed on a little opening or chimney in the tiled roofs of the houses, which was intended as charms and preservatives from conflagration. Sometimes . . .* [people] *made a model of a house, and solemnly consumed it by fire, in order to appease the divinity supposed to preside over that element, and to avert a domestic* calamity.[17]*

Schools appear to have been established in Okinawa as far back as the reign of Chun-tien, about the year 1317, when [written] *characters were introduced into the country, and the inhabitants began to read and write. These characters were said to be the same as those of the Japanese alphabet yrofa. In the year 1372 other schools were established, and the Chinese character was substituted for that of the Japanese; and about the middle of the seventeenth century, when the Mantchur dynasty became fixed upon the throne of China, the Emperor Kang-hi built a college in Okinawa for the instruction of youth, and for making them familiar with the Chinese character.*[24] There were only some thirty schools on Okinawa in 1879, eighteen of which were situated in Shuri, and my father took over from a man who had died during the year of uncertainty when all schools had remained closed. My father instructed in language and literature through the Chinese classics, on which he was something of an authority. The study of Chinese literature was based on the commentaries of Kuotzu, a learned scholar of more modern times. Classics were read according to the modern Chinese pronunciation and calligraphy of Chinese characters was practised, though the majority learned the Japanese *hiragana, and copied the handwriting of the Japanese calligraphists Ohashi and Tamaki.*[14]*

So, as I a say, we were fortunate. A fair number of my father's friends and acquaintances were forced to move to other towns and neighbouring islands within the archipelago to seek employment, usually in quite menial, not to say degrading work. For many, this was a very humbling experience, having had both rank and money under the old regime. In fact, less than a month after the king's abdication, an edict from Tokyo stated that bar the exception of three main Okinawan families, all Okinawan nobles and gentry would become commoners and would be entirely dependant on their own resourcefulness. I remember the utter consternation of my father and others like him, and indeed, such was the outcry that Tokyo rescinded the edict eight months later. A large number of families, three-hundred and eighty to be precise, received pensions and stipends, of which ours was one, but such was the general inexperience of management and simple lack of opportunity that many a family verged on bankruptcy. Times were both difficult and painful as members of the upper classes were thrown into a world, the harshness of which they had been protected for generations. Many became depressed, and a few, overwhelmed and unable to adapt, committed suicide. As a result of increasing poverty, intermarriage with families of lesser rank was forced upon them, a practice that had been, but a few years before, extremely rare. There was simply no way of contesting the strong current of events, and it became obvious that a realistic appraisal was necessary. Some members of the elite families formed the *Kai-ka To*, an association whose aim was to act as a kindly moderating force, reconciling the old, comfortable world of Okinawa, with the new realities. My father was a founding member of that group, and devoted much time to it. I believe that members did quite a lot of useful benevolent work during this transitional period.

Also, the *moai* system continued to operate for about thirty years after the king's abdication. This system was a kind of collective, whereby members would contribute according to their output and benefit those in the group who were less fortunate than themselves through no fault of their own. No one knew, in the future, who would be forced to draw from the holdings. Fear and a community spirit kept the *moai* in operation. It was this kind of deep sense of social obligation and group responsibility in maintaining the welfare of community members that characterised the Okinawan spirit. Strange as it may seem, it was probably a clever tax system based on mutual obligation levied by the Japanese centuries before, which made individuals aware of their personal and group responsibilities.

I remember once going with my father to one of his colleagues to attend such a meeting. This colleague worked in the *Yobutsu-za* or Chinese Tribute Department, and was very rich, though *there could not be said to be anything approaching to grandeur or magnificence perceptible anywhere among the wealthiest*[17*] in those times, and this was true of this gentleman also. We met some of my father's friends on the way, and it must have been cold, so it was probably January, when temperatures are about fifteen degrees centigrade, for they all wore cloaks or great coats made of a thick blue material like woollen cloth, buttoned up the front. Customarily, on Okinawa in those days, when the weather changed, one added or subtracted layers of clothing depending on conditions; these cloaks were tight fitting, so it must have been very cold. Things were so ordered on Okinawa that the first day of the tenth month was official winter clothing day, and this was followed by a festival for planting the new rice crop.

It was the custom for a man of rank to be *attended by a boy, generally his son, whose business it was to carry a little square box* [called a *chow-chow*], *in which there were several little draws, divided into compartments, filled with rice, sliced eggs, small squares of smoked pork, cakes, and fish; and in one corner a small metal pot of sake, besides cups and chopsticks. By having this always with us* . . . [it was possible to] *dine when and where we chose*.[2]* As you can imagine, I fulfilled this attendant role for my father.

I recall passing fine examples of acacia, areca and cyas on our way, and some of the tallest bamboo I ever saw. The gentleman's house *was situated in an elevated position at some distance from the sea, environed by a square wall of stones twelve feet high, leaving a gateway to enter by, over which was a guard-house. The rooms were spacious, opening on the sides, with projecting balconies*.[1] I remember a large pond filled with golden carp. The house was raised three or four feet from the ground, Japanese fashion, being traditionally one story on account of the fierce winds. The roof tiles that, as I have noted before, were red, were also very thick. Their shape was quite different from Japanese tiles. *Over the joint between two concave tiles, a convex one was laid, and these were all semi-circular in cross section. The tiles were made at Naha*[28]* and were of good quality.

Our host possessed what was, in many ways, a fine example of an Okinawan face. His eyes, *which were black, had a placid expression*, [and his] *teeth were regular and beautifully white*.[2]* He *received us with the greatest civility, in a . . . house well adapted to the country: the floors were well matted, and everything relating to the furniture extremely neat. On these mats we sat in the Oriental custom, and partook of refreshments . . . Several venerable old men encircled . . .* [us], *and dressed in large loose gowns of fine manufacture, similar to tiffany, of various colours and different patterns. These flowing garments were tied round the middle with a sash; and they also wore trousers and sandals. The crown of their heads were shaved, and the* [glossy black] *hair from behind brought up to a knot on the top, and securely fastened by metal pins*[1], a practice that *dated back only two centuries*.[14]* *They made use of fans universally; and some wore neat straw hats tied under the chin. The aged men had most respectable beards*[1], which *were kept neat and smooth*.[2]* We all *squatted down*[2] [in the Turkish fashion]. We ate *painted eggs, smoked salt pork, and*

Plate 4. Going on a visit

various preparations of eggs and fish, with sweet cakes in numberless forms, besides tea . . . [and, for my elders] *pipes, and sake . . .* [served] *hot.*[2] I recall the guests saying, *"Masa! Masa!"* [Good! Good!] on sipping this beverage, and on toasts the assembled men would stand, and, with full Okinawan honours, would drain *the tea-spoonful of sake at one gulp, and* [then] *turn the cup bottom upwards.*[5b*] I remember the *thin slices of pork* [were] *broiled and cut into the shape of a horseshoe with the outer edge indented . . . Pig's liver appeared in many different forms, fried, grilled, roasted, stewed etc. Broiled ground-nuts and roasted cocoas were also provided in plenty.*[18] *When any subject was discussed, one at a time rose to speak, but not in order of rank* [which was the order they sat down in], *and they never attempted to interrupt one another.*[2]

The tobacco grown on Okinawa – which was mostly cultivated in the southern part of the island – ended up as a rather poor product. The large, fine leaves, after being cut were dried in the sun by stringing them on poles, *where they were allowed to remain for days exposed to the dew and rain; so that by the time the process was terminated, all the volatile principles to which it* [the leaf] *owes its virtues were dissipated, and thereby rendered almost useless.*[8] Having said this though, *some specimens could be found which were very good.*[7] Enough tobacco was grown *for the consumption of all classes, and the people, from the highest to the lowest, seemed equally to use it, and to be equally unable to do without it.*[7] The best tobacco, however, was imported.

Ironically, some might say, given what had happened to the upper-class families of Okinawa, the first Japanese governors to the island, Nabeshima Naoakira of Saga, and Uesugi Shigenori of Yonezawa, were members of well-established feudal families in Japan. They were sensitive of our position, and were helpful during this awkward time. Uesugi, whose appointment as governor was regrettably cut short by Tokyo because of his disapproval of unequal tax demands made on the prefecture, and his subsequent reforms, was important to me personally, for I was, later, the recipient of a substantial grant award from a foundation that he set up, which allowed me to study academically in Tokyo.

As I am getting underway with this book now, perhaps it would be pertinent at this stage to mention the robes worn by Okinawans when I was a boy, and the footwear common to all but the lowest classes. The clothing was very different from that worn today. The *loose robes were generally made of cotton, and of a great variety of colours. The robe of . . .* [an adult] *was never flowered or printed over with figures,*

Plate 5. A quiet smoke in the afternoon on Okinawa

being generally of a uniform colour, though instances occurred of striped cloths being worn by the chiefs. This robe opened in front, but the edges overlapped, and were concealed by the folds, so as to render it difficult to say whether or not the robe continued all the way round; the sleeves were about three feet wide; round the middle was bound a belt or girdle about four or five inches wide[vii], always of a different colour from the dress, and in general richly ornamented with wrought silk and gold flowers. The folds of the robe overhung the belt, but not so much as to hide it. The whole dress folded easily, and had a graceful and picturesque appearance . . . Under the robe was worn a short garment of silk or fine hempen cloth.[14]

The garments worn by the children were often gaudily printed with flowers. In rainy or cold weather [as I have just mentioned], *a sort of greatcoat was worn by the chiefs only . . . This cloth resembled the coarse cloth used in China . . . and may possibly have been originally brought from England. The sandals worn by all ranks were exactly the same; they were formed of straw wrought into a firm mat to fit the sole of the foot, smooth towards the foot, and ragged underneath: a stiff smooth band of straw, about as thick as one's little finger, passed from that part of the sandal immediately under the ankle and over the lower part of the instep, so as to join the sandal at the opposite side; this was connected with the foremost part of the sandal by a short small straw cord which came between the great toe and the next one. The upper classes wore stockings of white cotton . . . that buttoned on the outside, and had a place like the finger of a glove for the great toe.*[2]* The labouring classes always went barefooted, and whilst all other classes wore the straw sandals, in wet weather wooden clogs were naturally preferred.

As I cast my mind back more than eighty years, I recall another meeting where I accompanied my father to a house much closer to home, where the garden was an effusion of colour with hibiscus, prince's feather, and, above all cockscombe, *with its brilliant shining bracts glittering in the sun.*[11a] I believe that I am correct in saying that this gentleman had been the *poo-ching ta-foo*, or local governor of Naha, and known as the third officer in power, after, in order of seniority, the *tsung-li ta-chin*, or vice-governor-general of the country, ostensibly the prime minister of the King of Okinawa, and the former, similarly named, *poo-ching ta-foo*, whose authority extended over the southern portion of the country. However, I recall the day of this meeting mainly for another reason, which still haunts me.

From an ornithological point of view, owing to the migration of *birds that find the Ryukyus the first station across the eastern Pacific, the migration is on a very great scale . . . After the breeding season is over, feathers of all colours and hues were collected, and exported for many purposes to foreign countries. The trade in feathers was enormous. Flocks of birds literally darkened the sky as they sought refuge or rest for awhile. They were permitted a certain amount of time to enjoy the soft warm air, ere the slaughter and desecration was organised for the sake of pampering fashion, in supplying the cravings of passing fancies.*[14]* As my father and I walked home, we saw mules laden under so many feathers as to make their going difficult, for their high-packed loads were caught by gusts of wind that seemed eager to reclaim that which had ridden and sung with them. It was the booty from a terrible massacre, and, in its own quiet way, a truly dreadful scene.

I'm afraid this reflected the normal sad state of affairs on the island, where any bird seen was hunted for one reason or another. Not surprisingly therefore, few birds were seen on Okinawa outside of migration.

The room . . . [the above meeting was held in] *was open at first on two sides only, but afterwards the partitions on the other two sides were taken down, being contrived to slide into grooves; thus the rooms were enlarged or diminished at pleasure* [much as they are in traditional homes in Japan today]. *When the partition behind us was removed, several strange looking figures made their appearance . . .* [and they] *were Bodezes or priests. Their heads and faces were shaven, their feet bare, and their dress different from that worn by the rest of the people, being somewhat shorter, and much less free and flowing, without any belt around the waist, the robe being merely tightened a little by a drawing string tied at the side; over . . .* [their] *shoulders hung an embroidered band or belt, like that used by drummers; the colour of their dress was not uniform, some wearing black, others, yellow, and some deep purple. They had a timorous, patient, subdued sort of look, with a languid smile, and ghastly expression of countenance. They were low in stature, and generally looked unhealthy; they all stooped more or less, and their manners were without grace, so that a more contemptible class of people cannot easily be imagined . . . Bodezes were strictly confined to a life of celibacy . . .* [I] *felt at first disposed to treat these Bodezes with attention, but this was looked upon as ridiculous by ...* [the others]. *Instead of being the class most respected . . .* [the *Bodezes*] *were considered the lowest, and if not held in contempt, were at least neglected by all other ranks.*[2]*

However, the *priests held a higher position than they did in China,* *and consequently were treated with more respect, and were not looked upon as* [completely] *worthless and degraded as soon as they left the precincts of the temples. Though their social position was . . . better than in China, it was by no means enviable, and they were the same bald-headed mendicants that they are there.*[8]*

Confucianism, the oldest established religion on the islands, was the domain of the upper classes, whilst the lower classes, if they were pressed, would express an interest in Confucianism, Buddhism or Shintoism, but in truth lacked all knowledge of them. I was once *told, and fully believe, the presents sent to China were not so much viewed as tribute, as intended for sacrifices and thank-offerings for the blessing of Confucianism received of old and continued to be received from China. And hence a great part of this tribute, if such it was, was really offered upon sainted shrines in the original home of that capricious system . . .* [and that it is said that Okinawa] *would never have become a nation, and would long ago have ceased to be a country, were it not for this intercourse with China.*[17]* However, without doubt, as we shall see later, it was ancestor worship that guided Okinawa life in the nineteenth century.

I will note here, an aside. The Japanese had for centuries, looked down upon Okinawans as poor rustic cousins. This was the case at the time of my youth, and was a legacy that was to last well into the twentieth century – and, indeed, such attitudes may be said to linger to this very day in some quarters. This was the chief reason, I believe, for my family not moving to Japan at the time, which we could easily have done. I'd go as far as to note that *the Japanese regarded . . .* [Okinawans] *with utmost contempt as an effeminate race*[6] and of *timorous*[24] disposition.[viii] This view was not a fancy just of the Japanese, for I remember reading an account of a westerner who wrote that *to a newcomer both sexes of the natives looked exactly the same . . .* [though] *after three or four days amongst . . .* [us] *considerable difference . . .* [could] *be detected. The young men in spite of their feminine faces . . .* [could] *in a moment be distinguished by the way their hair was done.*[15]*

In their turn, it must be said, that the inhabitants of Okinawa generally felt considerable condescension when dealing with the people of the northern province of Kunchan and the surrounding islands in the archipelago. These natives were invariably despised for their poverty, rough speech and manners, by Okinawans from the heavily populated central and southern provinces. To a certain extent, one may be protected from such feelings when near the top of such a system. I found some prejudice in Japan, despite what I have sometimes read, and whilst very proud of my birth and heritage, when I went to the Imperial University, I never advertised the fact that I was Okinawan. Indeed, and I am ashamed now to say it, but I was at very great pains to conceal any accent that might betray me, as I tried to fit into the Tokyo way of life. I even searched out a tutor to assist me in diction, and, especially, pronunciation. As it turned out, my conversion proved to be quite a challenge. *The sound of the F in Okinawan is peculiar. It is pronounced as if it was written Fw . . .* [but] *there is another peculiarity in the language which distinguishes it from any other known tongue. This is the extraordinary pronunciation given to vowels in certain words . . . It is a long drawl of the vowel, the tone of the voice of the person who speaks rising higher as the sound is uttered. The pronunciation cannot be rendered into words, and no system of trans-literation would convey it; it must be heard to be understood.*[10] Nevertheless, the spoken language has been described as most pleasing to the ear, and is reminiscent of the Korean accent.

For young men of my social rank, it had been the custom for centuries to reside in China for two or three years to study, though some stayed longer, under grants from the Chinese, to return to prestigious positions in Okinawan government. *Almost yearly . . . youths of the best families* [were sent] *to be educated in Foochow,* [which was] *known as an emporium of learning. Others proceeded to Peking, and yearly some returned fully imbued with Chinese manners and lore, and by them the latter was perpetuated . . .*[17]* The Okinawans at that time *looked upon the principles of Chinese government as a model of rectitude and enlightenment, and taught the ethics of Confucius in all their schools.*[21] It has also been said, and I am sure there is some truth in this also, that the two-yearly tribute ship to China was nothing but a barter between the two parties, in that *the amount of the copper* [which was *of a superior quality*[18]], *sulphur, and native brandy sent, being the joint contribution of government and of the parents or relatives of the* scholars.[17] Because of the change in political events, scholars now went to Japan, though some, I believe, still journeyed to China. I am reminded here that in earlier times *a castle on an island in the harbour* [of Naha] *was reserved for the use of the Chinese traders. The castle was still standing* [on my last visit], *but was used as a rather ultra-fashionable and exclusive 'tea-house.'*[27]

I encountered some difficult situations at university that make me laugh now. I suppose I lived a kind of double life, but if I wanted to be successful in my chosen career, which was medicine, I had to play my

Plate 6. Departure of an Okinawan junk with tribute to Peking

cards close to my chest. It was a case of self-protection and advancement through mimicry; adapt or fall by the wayside. Okinawans are generally a diminutive people, though better proportioned than the Japanese, and many of my countrymen, when they went to Japan, wore shoes with thicker under soles and slightly raised heels, and walked in a very upright fashion. Okinawans from the higher classes were generally taller [see later], and closely resemble the Japanese, unlike the lower classes, and I therefore believed that I passed quite easily for a Japanese in this department. Also, my skin was relatively pale, as was noticeable in other people of my class, so I felt confident in that department too. However, I had an Okinawan friend studying engineering whose skin was a deep copper complexion. Okinawan skin colouration can differ markedly, from dark to almost white, which was highly prized, with a dusky olive perhaps best describing the general prevalence, and whilst one might have been able to get away with that, copper was more obvious. He used to treat the rare reference to it as a joke and say that his grandfather had been very rich, and that as a child he had let him play with all his gold and silver, and the mixture of their colours had, quite literally, rubbed off on him, and permanently stained his skin. He said that he couldn't help playing as a child, and he couldn't help what his grandfather had given him to play with, so his colour wasn't his fault, but at least it showed that he was from a wealthy family, and that he would have taken great offence if someone had said that he had acquired his colour from copper coins! Said in a light-hearted manner, it seemed to work. There were no medical reasons known in the nineteenth century that could have accounted for his supposed condition, and I don't think there are today, though I am no dermatologist. Looking back, these little ploys we used seem very foolish, but at the time I felt that if I, at least, had not taken this route, then I would probably have found myself practising medicine in a very rural part of Japan, if not back on the Ryukyu islands themselves. My view was that, in a sense, my class had been knocked off its pedestal, but I believed a man should be given a fighting chance. I didn't want to face prejudice. I wasn't going to play a game against the loaded dice of discrimination.

There were few doctors operating in the Ryukyus at that time, and those that did practice had only rudimentary medical knowledge. Armed with plaster, pill and *moxa*, anyone who enjoyed a little early success could be raised to the rank of professional doctor. I had been properly trained and did not wish to be associated with these people. I also had little in common with them. It was a question of adaptation for a purpose, and it was pretty ruthless now I come to think about it, but life moves on, and there was little point wallowing in the past as, to be honest, my father did. It was a young man's world, and one had to adapt if one wanted to carve out a name in such drastically changing times. A few student physicians, it is true, studied in China or Kagoshima, and it was only these individuals who were allowed to carry the *inro* [medicine case], which was the distinguishing feature of a properly trained physician; those 'doctors' who were native trained, could not. The only benefit of being Okinawan in the last quarter of the nineteenth century, having been annexed by Japan, was that one was not conscripted into the armed forces!

Most Okinawas were *extremely superstitious, and invoked their deities upon every occasion, sometimes praying to the good spirit, and at others to the evil.*[24]* However, the vast majority of Okinawans were atheists. Disease was thought to be caused by malevolent supernatural forces. These spirits essentially fell into two groups – natural and ancestral. Patients were more likely to visit the *yuta*, or shamen, than a doctor, the former attempting to treat afflictions with spells and incarnations. My people were *not without the vices natural to mankind*,[24] and venereal disease was rife. Tuberculosis was the second most common communicable disease. Skin conditions plagued the population – nearly all the children had impetigo, for example. Intestinal parasites, such as hookworm and tapeworm were highly prevalent. It is not that surprising then, that the appeals of the *yuta* to the spirit world, via rice oracles, went unheard. However, despite achieving very little, the *yuta* managed to hold an influential position in social life, and although their standing was compromised and their activities initially restricted by the government, and then, in 1884, their practices were finally forbidden, the habits of centuries do not fade so easily. The *yuta* invariably blamed neglect of ancestor worship as a cause for the evil maladies that struck, but when this answer was found wanting, the deceased from other villages were blamed.

Okinawans at that time had many strange customs. When a woman was pregnant for example, she occasionally ate dog flesh, and was exposed to a hell in miniature. *Immediately after delivery* [of the baby] *a fire was lighted in the room, however hot . . . the weather, and both mother and infant were placed as close as possible to it for the space of a week . . . The friends and relations assembled, and made loud music all night and every night with drums and other instruments, so that the poor creatures could not get a wink of sleep till daylight came.*[4b] I am told, that the barbarous custom of 'mother and infant roasting' continues to this very day in the more remote areas of the archipelago, but the practice, which I am at a loss to explain, unless it is so that malevolent spirits do not attach themselves, had come to an end in Southern Okinawa by the time I left for university. Women were also exposed to *earthenware warming pans pressed close to the body, behind and before, and woman and pans covered over with the whole stock of clothing the family and friends could muster. The frequent supervention of haemorrhage, mostly fatal under this treatment, is not surprising . . . The population of Okinawa was literally decimated while being born.*[26]*

In a certain village near the sea, we were told, quite a contrary practice prevailed, by which mother and child, immediately after the act of parturition, were immersed in the sea.[26]* Certainly, only a short distance across the waters, it was the custom of some of the natives of Formosa to plunge a newborn child into a tub of cold water, as was, I believe, the custom of ancient Germany.

Every infant was supposed to be infected at its birth with hereditary poison, te duku, which was [seen as] *the source of the pus in small-pox, and of other critical matters, and which required to be eliminated. Hence every child, as soon as it was born, was immediately doctored, to get rid of the te duku. After certain disorders, the remaining . . . yu duku was still liable to produce tumours and other swellings, and also required to be removed from the system, for which there were various processes.*[26]*

Local 'medics' were very fond of bloodletting and *moxa* cautery was a universal remedy. *Moxa* weeds, for example, would be burned on the skin to cure nephritic conditions. Other weeds, such as *mogusa*, would also be burnt. They used to blood-let for eczema, and just about everything else. There was *no Okinawan of any rank who had not dozens of burn-marks on his body . . .* [The process was considered] a *counter-stimulus of the highest medical virtue. The internal disease . . .* [it was said] *would thereby be dragged out upon the surface of the skin. Even infants were moxa'd on the four limbs. It was applied to the forehead, eyelid, behind the ear, on the neck, belly, back, etc; no part of the body was too delicate for it . . .* [The practice] *constantly had recourse to induce hard tumours, especially syphilitic ones, to suppurate.*[26]*

Next to the moxa, the chief remedy in all disorders was eating, or, rather, high feeding . . . [food was literally forced] *down the throat, notwithstanding all the protestations of the patient. Children, especially, suffered from this ill usage, and were said to have died sometimes with the food in their mouths, probably even choked by the violence* *employed . . .* [It was maintained] *that, as it is impossible to live without eating, the more one eats the better life is preserved; and that, in illness, man has more than at other times of recruiting his strength . . .* [The term for medicine was] *kutturi,* [which] *signified properly anything taken inwardly to benefit the body, in addition to the daily food; so that feasting was, according to their view, quite within the scope of medicine. The same idea – the more the better – was connected with medical remedies.*[26*]

Another strange cure involved the exclusion of light and air. *Though, when in health, impatient of heat, and delighting to sleep with open doors, or exposed to the cool air of the summer nights, in sickness . . .* [the Okinawans] *went to the other extreme, and slept under the catcha (mosquito curtains, mostly of thick texture, or among the poor, of paper, and impervious to the air), while every means was employed to increase the heat, and produce perspiration. The doors were closed; and even in the height of summer, a portable coal fire – sometimes two or three – were kept burning in the room, and tea, warm water, and soups were always at the ready. The patient laid with his head on a level with, or even lower than, the fire, which, for want of air, was always in a mouldering condition; and it was far from improbable that death was sometimes caused by the carbonic acid emitted from it.*[26*]

The smacking cure was said to be a substitute for bleeding. In inflammatory disorders, the upper arm, near the elbow, was tied; the part between the ligature and the shoulder was wetted, or wrapped in a wet cloth, and briskly smacked.[26*]

Trampling and kneading the belly was a more serious method of cure. It was employed in cases of colic, and other forms of enteralgia. The patient was laid on his back, and his friends, in succession kneeling on his belly, trampled and pounded him with knees and fists into an agonising perspiration, until he swooned into sleep.[26*]

Perhaps the most far-fetched operation was to cut open the belly in a kind of Caesarean operation as a cure to hypochondriasis, or *shuku* as we used to call it, which was prevalent, especially among the higher classes. *The section was made across the epigastrium . . . It was a genuine Okinawan invention, introduced by a renowned physician of high antiquity, who slit open a man's belly, introduced a dish to serve as a second covering to the intestines, or a kind of lining to the natural walls, and healed up the wound to the perfect satisfaction of all parties. This was far from being a joke,*[26*] and many a patient's intestines fell out when the edges of the wound would not heal.

I remember the traditional cure for a cold was goat soup! My grandfather suffered from various aches and pains and was treated with *hot cataplasms, made of the recent aromatic leaves of the sansjo[ix], and, as he informed me, with considerable* benefit,[11a] so perhaps not all such practice was to be found wanting. Tattooing, which I shall refer to, in-depth, in the next chapter, was also thought to act as a counter-irritant to rheumatism. It was not that uncommon to see men and women, with criss-cross tattoos on their arms, shoulders and legs. Tattooing was also used as a counter to evil forces. On the small fishing village of Itoman, for example, the fisherman and their sons would have a *trident design tattooed on their right upper arms; in some, the trident was replaced by a slanting line, with three short, straight projections on one side of it, directed downward, like the teeth of a saw.*[27]

Okinawans at the end of the nineteenth century, despite putting on a brave face, and swearing to the restorative qualities of ginseng, did not enjoy particularly good health, though they faired better than many other people of that region. The native plague was the itch, scabies, which, the reader may know, is caused by a mite. The female burrows into the skin, especially on the front of the wrist, between the fingers, the buttocks, genitals, and feet, and lays her eggs. The larvae hatch and their movement causes the severe itching. The itch was cured with sulphur ointment.

Dysentery was a constant threat; pleurisy, sometimes linked to tuberculosis, was unfortunately rather too common; and, then, there were the occasional epidemics, including Japanese encephalitis.[x] Occasionally one saw a person marked with the smallpox. For immunization purposes, I recall that up until the mid nineteenth century, *the powered scab was almost always introduced to an individual as a snuff into the nose.*[26][xi] Okinawans did, and still do, take great care of people who are ill.

The entire absence of marshes, together with the pure air constantly wafted over the land in the breezes of the surrounding sea, must exempt the island of all miasmal diseases, such as intermittent fever and neualgias, remittent and yellow fevers etc; possible mild intermittents may arise about the time of the maturing rice, when water is drawn off from the land for a brief period. Situated near the tropics, intense heat might be expected . . . [on Okinawa]; *but this is so tempered by sea winds and the elevation of the land, as not to be excessive or severe; hence, diseases thence arising, as bilious disorders, diarrhoea, cholera morbus, etc, are not to be apprehended. Nor do the cold northwest winds from the continent of Asia reach this favored isle with their chilling blasts, being mellowed by traversing a lengthened sea, through which is flowing a current of warm water from the south. Thus softened in their long course, we did not bear . . . inflammatory affections, such as pneumonia, pleurisy, rheumatism, and the like.*[7]

It wasn't just the mighty that fell from grace in 1879. When the ninety-five thousand members of the privileged gentry classes, about one-third of the population, lost their positions in the various departments and boards, their retainers also lost their jobs as the old system collapsed. Looking back, some people had astonishing responsibilities in equally astonishing offices. For example, entire buildings were devoted to the control of lacquer and vegetable wax. Former retainers spread throughout the archipelago when the upheaval came, becoming mostly farmers, fisherman and craftsmen of various descriptions. Indeed, many of their previous employers also attempted to earn a living in exactly the same way, and became traders, slowly sinking to subsistence level.

The next twenty years, to the turn of the twentieth century, were filled with hardship on Okinawa, as the annexed islands, of absolutely no economic value to Japan, were left largely unattended. What was of intrinsic value was spirited away, and, if I may use Iha Fuyu's words, "We were like cormorants of the Nagara River, made to catch fish but not allowed to swallow." The government's strategy was, I am sure, to let time pass; to let the thoughts of resistance and reinstatement of the old *han* fade, become a distant memory, as the older Okinawans died. In my youth, I recall comparing the situation with Ch'in Shih Huang Ti's policy [in the 3rd Century BC] of burning all records of the past so that a new beginning could be made without reference to that which had gone before. The First Emperor was more obvious, the nineteenth century Japanese version was more subtle, but the ends were the same – the Okinawan people were to begin history anew.

And the old system certainly did break down. In 1884, Sho Tai was permitted to return to Okinawa for one hundred days. I saw him. He conducted himself with his usual bearing and formality, but there was no disguising the fact that he looked defeated. The affairs and torment of those five intervening years had clearly taken their toll. His pencil line moustache, goatee beard, and thinning jet black hair, combed back to reveal a low forehead characteristic of the Sho family, seemed to just add to his aged, resigned expression. This was the last time Sho Tai visited his former kingdom. Like Gihon[xii] before him, he seemed to have accepted responsibility for events and entered the forest alone, never to be seen again.

Plate 7. King Sho Tai (1841–1901)

I do not know whether he ventured, or was allowed to return to the family seat, but had he done so, he would have found the castle stripped and dilapidated, left to the elements, like so many Buddhist buildings no longer under patronage. The castle, so much enclosed by trees to screen if from the common herd, was now obscured for another reason – there were no longer *flags flying upon tall staffs*.[24] In 1881, my father and I visited the palace and *a more dismal sight could hardly . . .* [have been] *imagined. We wandered through room after room, through corridors, reception-halls, women's apartments, through servants' quarters, through a perfect labyrinth of buildings, which were in a state of indescribable dilapidation . . . Every article of ornament had been removed; the paintings on the frieze – a favourite decoration with the Japanese and Okinawans – had been torn down or were invisible from dust and age. A few half-rotten mats laid here and there, but the floors were for the most part bare, and full of holes, which, combined with the rottenness of the planks, rendered our exploration a rather perilous proceeding. In all directions the woodwork had been torn away for firewood, and an occasional ray of light from above showed that the roof was in no better condition than the rest of the building.*[23] To my father it was a depressing experience of the first-order. He no doubt reflected back to a time the palace shone in all its magnificence, when my grandfather was present at the time the officers of the steamer Sphinx [in February, 1852] were the first westerners ever to be received at the castle.

From these damp and dismal memorials of past Okinawan great-ness, it was a relief to emerge on an open terrace on the summit of one of the great walls, from which we got a splendid view of the islands.[23] We walked home in silence amid the heavy, reassuring scent of pine.

Some of the *matesee kee* [pine trees] in Shuri and Naha, with their limbless trunks and flat, broad speading tops, were magnificent, reaching in excess of one hundred feet in height, with girths of more than four feet. Shikina-en, a royal country residence, in Mawashi, sur-rounded by such trees was not, however, left to decay, and members of the Sho family lived there until the modest residence and lovely gar-dens, along with so many ancient buildings, were totally destroyed in 1945. I remember reading an account of how the Shuri Castle, under Lieutenant-General Ushijima, had withstood the American heavy bombardment for sixty days, before succumbing to the guns of the USS Mississippi. Ushijima committed suicide overlooking the sea shortly afterwards, and it was felt, if I can put it metaphorically, that Amaterasu, the Sun Goddess, had returned to a great cave at Kumayanon, on Iheya Island. As so many times before in the history of Okinawa, the inhabitants of the Land of the Happy Immortals were far from happy. It had been believed for at least fifteen hundred years that the secret of immortality lay with the inhabitants of islands to the east of China. These islands were generally assumed to be of the Ryukyuan chain. Several Chinese emperors sent out expeditions to the islands in a search of the secret.

Ushijima was, of course, Japanese, but Okinawans also occasionally committed *seppuku* [*hara-kiri*]. I write this because I know the practice is of some fascination to western readers. A man about to be executed on Okinawa in days past, a very rare happening among a peaceful, law abiding people, even during the tempestuous days of Okinawan history, was often offered a knife and left to contemplate his lot. To many on Okinawa, especially those with Chinese affinities, *seppuku* was seen as *i-jin*, as barbaric.

In contrast to all this sadness and destruction, I recall with warm satisfaction a visit I made to Shuri Castle when it was flourishing. I had the opportunity to wonder at the splendour of the beautiful gardens, parks and ancient buildings without any attendent strain being placed upon me. One afternoon, before the abdication, my father returned from work and said that he had to visit the castle and asked whether I'd go with him. With the aid of an old plan, I should like to describe what I saw, all those years ago.

The massive earthworks that formed the walls of Shuri Castle were said to have been constructed by a master mason from Yaeyama in the sixteenth century. They were of Cyclopean proportions, *and the blocks of stone were joined with wonderful accuracy*[23]* and were of enormous thickness – *some of which were sixty to eighty feet high and fourteen to fifteen feet thick . . . Cactus in profusion grew along the tops of the walls and they were covered on the outside with various creepers.*[28]* *They were built in the form of a series of inverted arches, which, doubtless, helped them greatly in sustaining the tremendous pressure from the earth behind them . . . In the old days of bow and arrow and hand-to-hand fighting, they might justly have been considered impregnable.*[23]* I remember that *at the foot of one of these walls, and close to the second gate . . . a spring of water gushed from a cleft in the solid rock, over which was carved in Chinese characters, 'This water is good' – a naive remark that a Chinese envoy on a visit to the island had caused to be committed to posterity.*[23]* Other, similar inscriptions, were to be found close by, and were attributed to the same author.

A well-kept road encircled the castle, and lush vegetation grew to one side. An occasional overhanging bough provided brief shelter from the sun. My father and I did not enter the castle grounds by means of the famous *Shurei-no-mon* [ceremonial arch], though we could have done, but rather took the road to one of the subsidiary outside gates which we entered east of the Dragon Pool, whose *still, black waters, were dotted with lotus plants. The rich green leaves and*

Plate 8. Sonohyan Utaki Gate, Shuri

delicate pink flowers were mirrored on its surface with marvellous clearness, and on the opposite banks it was hard to trace the limits of water, so merged was the reflection in the reality.[23] [xiii] Between the Buddhist Enkaku-ji [temple] and the Shinto Sonohyan Utaki, a hearth shrine so important to the Okinawan tradition, stood. The Sonohyan Utaki gate, erected in 1519, was designed to enclose the sacred hearth and grove of the Chief High Priestess of Okinawa.

But let me mention the two tier ceremonial arch of Shuri Castle for the original is gone, having been destroyed in the Pacific War. It was built in 1554 to display a tablet inscribed 'Land of Propriety' by a Chinese Emperor, upon four wooden rectangular columns providing three entrances, and was regarded as a national treasure. *Under this arch the common people were not allowed to pass.*[5] Commodore Perry, in the summer of 1854, imposed himself upon the palace and regent, entering through this arch accompanied by a retinue of some two hundred, including a company of marines, and displaying artillery, to the band of the *Susquehanna* playing *Hail Columbia*. Ninety-one years later, the Americans returned.

The gate my father and I entered the castle by lead to the treasury and associated administrative buildings, and it was to these that my father had to make his short visit. After he re-appeared, he took me through the *Zuisen-mon*, or second gate, ever ascending, then through

Plate 9. Commodore Perry's visit to Shuri

the *Ryukoku-mon* and *Kofuku-mon* [third and fourth gates], and to an open area, a courtyard, *some sixty yards by thirty yards, paved with red tiles, placed closely together, and laid so as not to cover the whole space enclosed, but to form a series of walks.*[10][xiv] To my right, was the Hall of the Royal Ancestors, where all the genealogical records of the royal household were kept. Both the first and second gates were guarded by fierce lion sentinels, *rudely sculptured . . .* [and] *nearly the size of life.*[5b]

To my left, was the *Hojin-mon,* or fifth gate. Beyond that lay the *Sho-in* [*Seiden* – Audience Hall], guarded by dragon-pillars which flanked its approach. It was in this hall that the king met envoys. *This building resembled in shape the large gateways built at the entrance of Japanese temples; the front walls were painted red and blue, and the roof was tiled in the ordinary manner. Anything more ugly* [one imagines] *can hardly have been conceived* [to the modern eye]. *To the left were the offices of the Council of State, the principal hall of which was used as a guest-chamber. The ceiling and panels of this room were ornamented with roughly painted representations of tigers, cranes, and deer. To the right of the entrance was a low building, containing, a suite of rooms occupied by members of the royal household, and through these a passage led back to the king's apartments, which were at the back of the audience-hall.*[10]

The *iseki,* a variety of cedar, provided the material for the construction of many a grand building, especially the columns, and the Audience Hall was no exception. The *iseki* came from the northern islands of Tatao [Amami-Oshima] and Ki-ki-ai.[xv] Other shrines were also to be found in this vicinity of the palace. There were truly beautiful gardens. It was very rare for outsiders to venture beyond the fifth gate.

The *large reception-hall* [was] *hung round with tablets . . . They were of red lacquer, of a peculiarly deep, rich colour, emblazoned in gold with the names of the Okinawan kings. They dated back for about two hundred years, but though history records the dates and reigns of the sovereigns of the islands for many centuries, this present custom appeared to have been of recent adoption . . .* [I recall] *that no tablet commemorated the name of him who had closed the list forever.*[23*]

I will always remember that day. If I close my eyes, I can see it all so clearly. My father, long dead, is calling me. The fawn-coloured, cellular, granular limestone walls, covered in algae and fresh blue lichens – which are quite unusual on Okinawa – and the greenest of mosses are all around. It was my father's position that allowed us to penetrate

Plate 10. The palace at Shuri

so deeply into the royal residence. How sad we were then, two years after the king's abdication, when *from the ramparts of the castle we looked out on a succession of bright green hills, sloping down to the sea, or uplands rich with barley and sugar-cane, and valleys filled with rice; and when we turned from this charming prospect and observed the marks of decay everywhere – the untrimmed walks and shrubberies of tropical luxuriance choked with weeds – we could not help thinking that where nature had done so much, man might do a little more.*[10]

Later, the Shuri Castle grounds – immediately outside the palace itself, in fact – became the *dojo* of Shimpan Gusukama[xvi], before it became a museum. Today, where the castle once stood, the Ryukyu University campus is sited.

I also remember seeing His Majesty a number of times in my childhood, but the incident that stands out most clearly was when he was being carried on a camp-chair with a red cover over the top. His pipe bearer was in attendance. The king was wearing a cap that we called a *ben, made according to a pattern worn in the time of the Ming dynasty. It was of black gauze, and consisted of a spherical piece which sat close to the head, with a low crown rising above it. On each side rose a long piece of gauze . . .* [which the writer likened to asses' ears].[14]*

The party stopped close to where I was situated, under some aforementioned giant pines that were actually more reminiscent of cedar of Lebanon, and a servant carrying the king's fan, fanned not just his face and neck, but also Sho Tai's arms, which became exposed when he lifted them, the large sleeves of his over garment falling back. I believe there were six servants in attendance. The senior members of the party, advisors, wore loose, flowing dress. All wore identical short stockings and shoes, though their *hatchee matchee* were coloured differently. Their fans were tucked into their broad silk belts, and a short tobacco pipe kept in a small bag, along with a pouch, hung from their girdles.

I recall seeing the One-Leg Pavilion, so-named because of a very strange story from the 16th century. I must have entered the castle grounds on another occasion, but my memory fails me here. I remember the nine steps leading up to the palace for some obscure reason, so perhaps I was nine years old? A princess threw herself from a pavilion in the Shuri Castle grounds after her love, Chobin Heshikiya, had been beheaded for treason – this was a merciful form of execution, for many were lingering. It is said that in the early days of execution on Okinawa, an iron awl was used. The year was 1734, and at the sight of the white flag fluttering in the wind in the distance, a sign that the king's will had been done and the execution carried-through, the young woman is said to have launched herself from the pavilion's heights, but on recovering her body, only a leg was found. I have always remembered this tale, as I am sure readers now will, and, having been familiar with Conan Doyle's detective, Sherlock Holmes, consider that a like story might have made a famous inclusion in the Holmesian canon. After this incident, the pavilion was thereafter known as *Kunra Gushiku* [One-Leg Pavilion].

With the collapse of the old system, Shuri lost its importance as the old capital with many a grand house likewise falling into decay, and the administrative centre at Naha became the new focal point. On his return to Tokyo, Sho Tai[xvii] was created a marquis under the new peerage of Japan. He remained a state prisoner for more than twenty years, living at *Ryukyu Yashiki* [Ryukyu Mansion], and died in 1901. But the loss of his kingdom, for generations in his family, must have weighed heavily upon him. He no doubt felt 'like an unmated bird shut up in a cage, [who] had lost all hope of returning home.' I have taken this quote from the King's Oath of Sho Nei (1611) following the Satsuma expedition and subsequent control of the islands in 1609. Sho Nei was allowed home to resume a puppet-like position, but degraded, this sorry man gave orders that upon his death, he was not to be buried in the royal tombs, but in a cave high in the hills near Urasoe, with a mask placed upon his face, to forever hide his identity in the spirit world.

Well, I suppose I should mention at this late stage that I was born on the 13th February, 1867, the very day that Crown Prince Mutsuhito, then aged fifteen, succeeded as Emperor, but I don't think that this was an omen for good or bad! It might interest western readers to learn, that one of my very first recollections was of being taken down to the harbour at Naha, to see the British ship *HMS Dwarf*. This ship was under the command of a Capt. Bax, and I recall seeing for the very first time, Europeans. They had been granted permission to land, and I was immediately struck by their height. The Okinawan body shape is small, as I have said, with about five feet tall being the norm for men in those days. Women were, of course, on the whole generally a little smaller. But these Englishmen looked a good foot taller, an impression heightened by their broad muscular shoulders and lithe build, which was in contrast to the Okinawans rather stout, stocky predisposition. As the seamen strolled down the streets of Naha wearing their blue and white striped shirts, straw senet hats, and carrying their canvas lined jackets slung over their shoulders, the shopkeepers hid themselves from the 'giant' strangers, and refused to trade, just as they had done when Commodore Perry's men had come ashore nineteen years earlier. Strange as it may seem to readers today, but many people considered these sailors to be of great age, for it was common on Okinawa then, to judge age by height.

The officers were the most striking members of the ship's company in their blue uniforms, wide white lapels and cuffs laced with gold. The foreigners appeared to me, then, like figures out of a storybook come to life. Some of the sailors were so striking with their blond hair. I recall one most imposing figure in particular, whose hair was a blaze of flaming red, and who had a great bushy beard to match. That man left a lasting impression that is still fresh in my mind. I remember asking my mother about their blue eyes, for I had only ever seen brown before that time. I recall seeing an officer, buttons in threes on his single-breasted coatee, who had a scarlet stripe on his cuff and anchor and serpent badges on his collar. I believe I remember this because of the snake, for I was always being told to watch out for the treacherous *habu* that invests the islands. Having later researched this point of uniform, I found that the man's insignia was that of a naval surgeon. Investigations have shown that the date of this incident was September, 1871, so I was four years old.

When the ship left harbour, many boats went out to sea, and I was in one of them. The canoes were made of pine, and varied in length from about twelve to twenty feet, with a width of two to four feet. Up to ten people could get into the boats of the largest size. These canoes were mostly made from one piece of wood. They had two sails and moved more quickly, that day, when paddled, assisted by an oar over the stern. Each boat had a rudder, and anchors were made of wood. The low seats, one for each person, were made from rattans.

Only three months after this incident, an Okinawan junk became stranded on the southern coast of Formosa [Taiwan]. Of the sixty-six men aboard, the Botan savages killed fifty-four. This incident is famous in the annals of Okinawan history, and I mention it not only because of its infamy, but also in the hope that it gives a sense of temporal distance.[xviii]

I recall my great-grandfather[xix] telling me about the occasion when Capt. Maxwell and Capt. Hall of the *Alceste* and *Lyra*, respectively, in 1816, fired a farewell salute in Naha harbour to Okinawa and the Okinawan people. All the locals waved a fond goodbye with their fans till the ships could no longer be seen. He said that both the *Englelees* [English] sailors and Okinawan people were in tears at the parting, so well had things gone.

My great-grandfather and my grandfather both saw Captain Beechey of the *HMS Blossom* depart from Naha in 1827, when again the people waved goodbye with fans and umbrellas, many of which were white. There were a number of such visits from western ships over the next fifty years, but few were encouraged to set foot on the islands.

Maxwell, Hall and Beechey had respected Okinawan customs, and that was why they were remembered with affection. Later, other western visitors to our shores failed to show such consideration.

I also recall being told about the officers and men of three Russian ships, under Vice-Admiral Putyatin, who drilled for ten days in Tomari in 1854. These were big occasions, and the arrival of any western ship was heralded with both enormous interest and impending dread, though it must be said that such interest was always restrained, because the intent of the visitors was unknown. Ships from England, America, France and Holland, I recollect made short stays. In the summer of 1873, the German schooner, *R. J. Robertson*, on route from China to Australia, was driven onto the coral reefs off Miyako by a storm, not far, in fact, from where Captain Broughton's ship, *The Providence*, had been wrecked seventy-six years earlier. The men of the *R. J. Robertson* stayed on Miyako for over a month, and were finally rescued by the British ship, *Curlew*. I mention these incidents because they may appeal to western readers unfamiliar with our history, and to show that our connections go back a long time.

My grandfather told a story when I was a child that I remember well, and this was in regard to the use of handkerchiefs. My grandfather said that he had told a group of ship's officers that it *was a disagreeable practice to use a handkerchief and carry it about all day, and thought it would be better for them to adopt our custom of having a number of square pieces of paper in our pockets for this purpose, any one of which could be thrown away when it had been used.*24* The captain of the ship had sent for some handkerchiefs, but my grandfather and others, *declined using them, saying paper was much better.*24 My family would often raise the issue about what westerners did and how different their customs were from our own. We wondered what had surprised them about our little ways.

II

MEETING GICHIN FUNAKOSHI

A s a boy, I suffered from ill health. I wouldn't have said that I was weak exactly, but I was fairly frail, and I did seem to get illnesses twice as badly as everyone else. So, in order to help me build a strong constitution, as my father put it, he suggested one day that I learn the art of *bushi no te*, which is now known as karate, and took me to a good friend of his named Ankoh Shishu, or, Yasutsune Itosu, as he is more commonly known, thanks to Funakoshi's writings. I was ten years old at the time. Readers will note that karate was taught primarily for health promotion and for training the spirit in those days, the self-defence elements, although important, were of a secondary consideration.

I vaguely knew of some form of self-defence or fighting system for, *as children, we often heard our elders speak of To-de and Okinawa-te,*[b] but had never given it any real attention. The art was also referred to simply as *te*. When the term 'karate' was used, which was far less frequently, it would have been written with the *kanji* meaning 'Chinese-hand,' and not 'Empty-hand.' It was Funakoshi who, popularly, changed the *kanji* to its present form after he introduced karate to Japan, but Chomo Hanashiro [1869–1945], a senior pupil of Itosu's, used the new *kanji* in the first decade of the twentieth century. Presumably Funakoshi would have known of this.

I was taken to Itosu's house in the evening. I remember that distinctly, for my father disturbed me, his candle, made from unrefined wax and with a paper wick, giving off an excellent light. I recall him brushing aside the mosquito net as I lay, resting, in the heat of an Okinawan summer night, which, believe me, can be humid. It is strange the things one remembers from one's childhood, is it not, but I recall, on the way to Itosu's house, walking alongside hibiscus hedges, under a large *fukugi* tree, an evergreen, with a narrow, upright trunk and a crown of very dark green leaves, and past a *very singular banyan tree with contorted branches.*[13] *Fire-flies illuminated the air in all directions, and made the sky glitter with sparks of light. Under our feet glow-worms lay so thick that scarcely a square yard of ground was unoccupied by these glittering insects.*[17]

Trees on Okinawa were generally small, and wood was not plentiful. *A hard timber named Komon, and a soft wood named Fuchitsuba, were grown on the island*[28*] and were used in the construction of temples and the like, *but a great part of the wood used was the ordinary Japanese wood which was imported from Kagoshima. Owing to the scarcity of wood, stone had entered much more extensively into the building operations . . . than it had in Japan. The execution of the mason work was also infinitely superior to anything to be seen in Japan.*[28*] The Okinawans had grasped the principle of giving strength to masonry work by friction between the beds of adjacent stones. *The joints were therefore made with truth, and although the stones were generally of the most diverse shapes, they fitted into each other with perfect accuracy, unlike Japanese masonry, the stones in which were only kept in place by a bearing on each other of a few inches wide on their outer edge.*[28*]

My father, on the journey to Itosu's house, told me that my great-great-grandfather had also studied karate because of ill health, and had trained under Master Ason at Naha. He also spoke of his training friends, Gushi, Sakiyama and Tomoyori. Another relative had trained with Iwah in Shuri, and had such experts as Matsumura, Maesato and Kogusuku as contemporaries. He also spoke of Master Waishinzan, who taught in Kunenboya and Uemonden. My father seemed to know quite a bit about karate, refering to Isei Kojo [1832–1891], who trained in China for twenty years under Iwah; Taitei Kojo [1837–1917], who studied under Ryu Ryuko, a teacher of Shaolin kempo of the Southern School in Fuzhou, Fukien Province, as did Norisato Nakaima and Kitoku Sakiyama. In particular, I remember my father saying that he had been greatly impressed by a demonstration of the *kata Suparinpei* given by Seisho Aragaki [1840–1918] at Shuri Castle the year I was born. My father had been one of the dignitaries present when a Chinese delegation had visited. My father was an expert with the sword and in *rokshaku . . . a manly sport of the order of the single stick, with a staff about six feet long.*[27]

Master Itosu was born in Yamagawa-muri, Shuri, the birthplace of one of his teachers, Sokon Matsumura. Itosu was warm and friendly in manner and of average height for an Okinawan, but he had two very distinguishing features. Firstly, he was barrel-chested, and secondly, he had a long moustache and flowing beard, both of which were completely grey, and of which he was justifiably proud. He was approaching fifty years of age when I first met him. He acted as the king's private secretary, and thus had a very professional air about him. It was through his official duties that my father had come to know him.

When we arrived at Itosu's house, the master greeted us with a hearty smile. *The customary salutations were exchanged, which consisted in clasping the hands together before the chest as in prayer, then lifting them as high as the face, and immediately advancing them still clasped towards the breast of the person saluted, bowing the head forward, and repeating several times the words Chin-Chin.*[18] I recall the grounds around the house were quite spacious by Okinawan standards, and the enclosing stone walls, ten to twelve feet in height, whilst maintaining privacy, did not give the usual claustrophobic, prison-like appearance, so familiar with Okinawan properties at that time.

Itosu and my father spoke for a short while, and I was introduced to another, slightly older boy, whose name was Kentsu Yabu.[i] Much later, Yabu *Sempai* became Itosu's chief assistant after karate came out of the shadows and became integrated into the Okinawan school system. He taught, along with Itosu's other senior grade, Hanashiro, at Naha Middle School and at the teachers' training college. Yabu had an eventful career, and killed a soldier with a single blow, palm-heel I believe it was, when he served in the army. He died of tuberculosis in 1937. Amongst Itosu *Sensei's* later top pupils were Chosin Chibana, Shinban Jyoma, Kenwa Mabuni [the founder of Shito-ryu], Anbun Tokuda and Choyo Yamakawa.

I recall that Itosu told me that he too had taken up the art to improve his physical health, as he had been very weak in childhood as well, but I have no memory of that first evening's training. I must have stripped down to my loincloth, for we did not have *gi* in those days, and I suppose he must have shown me how to make *seiken*, how to make a stance, *shiko-dachi* perhaps, and so on.

What are the origins of karate? No one knows for sure. Funakoshi researched the subject much deeper than I, and his books are to be recommend in this regard, but he was unable to elicit much information other than that based on what his teachers had told him and in the form of legend via Chinese texts, as no written records were ever kept.[ii] I would, however, like to briefly relate what I do know.

My personal view is that karate came to Okinawa from southern China, and Fukien Province in particular, and blended with a relatively crude indigenous fighting art. Chinese boxing reached its zenith during the Tang [AD 618–917] and Sung [AD 960–1279] dynasties. Perhaps karate's roots lie in the culture of the Yellow River Basin? Certainly, the five thousand years of history is sufficient time to have made even the clearest of waters murky. Funakoshi gave a brief, but informative account of these early times in his *Karate-Do Nyumon.*

Whether karate was developed in China or whether it was introduced from India, via, perhaps, the Middle-East, is pure conjecture. No one knows, and no one is ever likely to know. If one looks hard enough, one can find karate-like postures in many places, especially on artwork, which, with the passage of time, becomes poorly understood. I have seen figures on ancient Greek vases, for example, that picture warriors in postures remarkably like those practised in karate.[iii] I have heard it said that karate came from Siam, but I do not think that this is correct

There are a number of theories as to how Chinese methods came to Okinawa. All are based on historical fact and all have a case to put. But first let me make an important point. Whilst Chinese invasions of Okinawa may be traced back as far as A.D. 605, China never actually annexed any of the Ryukyu Islands. A certain benevolence based more on the passing of years than anything else developed between Okinawa and China, and even when the Japanese seized control in 1609 (see below), Okinawa still, as I noted earlier, paid friendly tribute to China as well as to Japan. But let us return to the possible historical basis for karate on Okinawa.

Firstly, during the last decade of the fourteenth century, a group of Okinawans were shipwrecked near Swatow, China, and the Emperor directed that they should be sent home from Foochow accompanied by thirty-six Chinese carpenters and their families, to aid the Okinawans in building sturdy junks. The thirty-six families emigrated to Okinawa in 1392 and are thought to have introduced a fighting system. It is said that *the descendents of . . .* [these Chinese families] *became generally the schoolmasters of the country, and amalgamated with the people.*[17*] The story is well known, as are the descendants of the families who arrived on our shores during the Ming dynasty. This tale provides a possible beginning in my view.

Secondly, during the fifteenth century – the most prosperous period in Okinawan history – known as the Unified Three Kingdoms period, all chieftains were ordered to deposit their weapons at Shuri, and later (*c.* 1470), in order to minimise friction among Okinawan families whose rivalry was almost traditional, the lords were obliged to reside in the capital where an eye could be kept upon them. Interclan marriages were encouraged to blur the old rivalries. But there was always mistrust, and it is believed that it was during this period that the notion of acquiring empty-hand techniques was first entertained more generally and with greater seriousness. I recall one of the first points that Itosu ever told me, indeed, it may have been the very first metaphorical point of importance for karate training. He said that Okinawa was split into three warring factions in the 14th and 15th centuries; that Hokuzan was the northern territory with its castle at Nakijin; Nanzen was the southern territory with its castle at Ozato; and, Chuzan, wedged between the two, had its castle at Urasoe. The great Hashi of Chuzan won over the other principalities unifying the country in 1429, and bringing to an end one hundred and fifteen years of feuding. Hashi later became Sho Hashi. The corresponding names given to the divisions were Shang Peh [Northern Mountain], Shang Nan [Southern Mountain] and Chung Shan [Middle Mountain]. Itosu asked me to think deeply on why Chuzan had prevailed?[iv]

Thirdly, in 1609, the Shimazu, the daimyo of Satsuma, after a forty-day campaign, invaded the Ryukyu Islands with three thousand samurai under Kabayama Hisataka, as a result of the Okinawan king's refusal to assist Japan against Korea. In order to avoid a reprisal, it was declared that no swords should be worn as personal arms. It is generally believed that it was following this declaration that the art of karate underwent tremendous development, as did the forms of self-defence and counter using everyday objects, such as *sai*, sticks, harvest threshing implements, *kama* [rice sickles], flails and horse bridles, *nunchaku*, grindstone handles, *tonfa*, fish spears [as short swords], and so on. There was at least one *kata* developed using solely turtle-shells as shields. Indeed, many of these practices almost certainly date from around this period. The surrender of weapons as a way of maintaining the peace on Okinawa pre-dates the sword edicts of Toyotomi Hideyoshi by eighty years.

Incidentally, for those readers interested in associated historical matters, I believe that the first important correspondence between Okinawa and China was 1372, when King Satto sent envoys and tribute. Likewise, I understand the first official dealing with Japan was in 1451, when a delegation from Okinawa brought a present of a thousand strings of cash to Ashikaga Yoshimasa, the ruling Shogun, and is mentioned as the first intercourse between the two nations in a manuscript called, *Riukiu Jiriaku*, written by Arai Hakuseki.

The *shizoku* were clearly the most disadvantaged by these edicts banning weapons – they had most to lose – and so the art that was to become karate, developed, but strict secrecy was enforced, so that the authorities were unaware that the Okinawan privileged classes did have something to fight back with should the need ever arise. I must agree with Funakoshi when he wrote, *these bans cannot but have played an important role in the development of karate.*[b]

Around 1611, Article 11 of the Ordinance of Shimazu Iehisa, Prince of Satsuma, noted that quarrels and personal encounters were prohibited on Okinawa and in 1669 Satsuma declared that the government swordsmiths at Shuri should close, putting an end to the manufacture for ceremonial use. Thirty years later, it was forbidden to import weapons of any kind, although, ironically, firearms first entered Japan through the trading post on Tane-ga-shima, a northern island in the Ryukyu chain. Jana, the leader of pro-China factions, who, with the king at his side, refused to sign documents placing Okinawa in an untenable position with Satsuma, was taken aside by samurai and beheaded on the spot. That act inclined the Okinawans to play the Japanese game, but unless there was some form of weaponry, there was no hope. It must have been like living with the nuclear bomb, the taking of one's life must have seen as beyond one's personal control, and so the Okinawans did something about it, but to all intents and purposes, when the inspectors came to see if the prohibition of weapons was being observed, they could hardly take away hands, arms, feet and legs, or the seemingly innocuous instruments of everyday existence – though decapitation was not unknown.

The earliest reference to karate I have ever found comes from the late seventeenth/early eighteenth century, when Tei Junsoku [1663–1734], one of Okinawa's greatest [Confucian] scholars, who became chief of Nago in 1728, and was famous for his *Rikuyu Engi*, refers, fleetingly, in one of his poems to 'the art of *te*.'

When Kusanku[v] arrived on the shores of Okinawa from China in 1756 and taught Chinese boxing, introducing *kata* perhaps, it is almost impossible to believe, given what has been already noted, that there was not in existence some form, if surely not various forms, of self-defence. This was no doubt found by those Chinese who arrived in the wake of Kusanku, such as Anan, Ason, Iwah and Wan Shin Zan, and all but Anan were military attachés. Anan taught Kosaku Matsumura and Kokan Oyadomori, founders of Tomari-te. It is known that a number of Okinawans at this time travelled to China, and the earliest I am familiar with is Ko Sai. Kushanku, of course, is said to have taught the *kata Kusanku* in Shuri, which became *Kanku-dai* in Shotokan.

Funakoshi made some interesting historical observations, providing 'family trees,' and later pressed a number of points home most forcibly to me. I'd like to echo some of his thoughts if I may, for I am sure he was as close to the truth as one is likely to get on Okinawan karate.[vi] Funakoshi noted that two styles were practised on Okinawa in the nineteenth century – *Shurite* and *Nahate*[vii], the styles being specific to Shuri and Naha. These were based on Chinese systems called Wutang, named after a mountain and accredited to Chang San-feng, and Shorinji kempo, supposedly founded by Bodhidharma, who is said to have taught the system to monks of the Shaolin Temple, though beyond legend there is no evidence, I believe, to support this.

Both Azato and Itosu told Funakoshi and I that the two styles of karate – Shorin and Shorei, came from China, and each had its own merits.[viii] I think that Funakoshi expressed it very well when he wrote that Shorei, *emphasizes primarily development of physical strength and muscular power and is impressive in its forcefulness. In contrast, the Shorin-ryu . . . is very light and quick, with rapid motions to the front and back, which may be likened to the swift flight of the falcon.*[a] It was well known that both systems had strengths and weaknesses. During our youth we never enquired any further. Our teachers were instructing us in the time-honoured manner. If they knew anything else, they would have passed it on. This applies not so much to myself, as I left for Japan, but to Funakoshi, and that is why I advocate his history. It was first-hand knowledge, as it were. However, I must be honest and say that the history of karate is, because it was confined to human memory and the vagaries of instructor whim, very poorly recorded.[ix]

One point I am sure about however, and this may be said to be historical, hence its inclusion here, is that it is impossible to discuss karate fully in Japanese, only Okinawan has the words and phrases for the more profound concepts.

One night, or early morning, to be precise, three years into my practice [1880], just as karate training was finishing, Itosu had two visitors. A fellow trainee, whose family name was Azato, and I, were being encouraged by Itosu with his usual, '*kakatte koi*' [come on], when we heard a muffled knock upon the old wooden door that led into the Itosu residence. It was raining; there had been a heavy shower, leaving the ground slippery. We usually trained in the garden, with lanterns on the ground to light the perimeter of the training area, but were inside Itosu's house that night. We heard Itosu invite the unexpected guests in. This was very unusual, strange. I looked at my comrade, as much as to say, "We'll be found out!" but he just smiled, and in walked a tall, broad shouldered man, aged about fifty, with bright, penetrating eyes, and golden hair pins, accompanied by a small boy, aged about twelve, who wore a single silver hairpin. As I noted previously, it was the custom at that time to wear two hairpins. *At the age of ten years boys were entitled to wear the usisashee, and at fifteen they wore both*,[3] the other being called *camesashee*, which had a small star or narcissus-flower at the end of it, which pointed forward. The ceremony of manhood was called *gembuku*, and occurred *between the ages of sixteen and nineteen*.[14*] My fellow trainee walked over and greeted them both. Evidently, the man was his father, and the boy a brother or good friend. Itosu came over and introduced the two newcomers to me. We bowed, and I was introduced to Azato's father, Ankoh [Yasutsune] Azato, and his pupil, Gichin Funakoshi, who eyed my single gold hairpin, revealing an acknowledgement that I outranked him in the social order. I learned that Funakoshi attended the same school as Azato's son, his eldest son actually, two years my senior, and that Azato taught him karate. In those days, it was not considered best to teach one's own children karate, so that was why Master Azato's son studied with Master Itosu.

As I was later to discover, Azato was a truly formidable *karateka*, though I was only fortunate enough to train under him on two or three occasions. He would sit very upright, very proper, and by today's standards, very stiffly, on his wooden balcony over-looking his well-kept garden, and watch by the light of a lamp. Amazingly, like my great-grandfather, myself, Funakoshi and Itosu, Azato too had started karate to improve his health because of frailty in his childhood. He was a pupil of Sokon Matsumura and kept that lineage, whereas Itosu kept the lineage of Gusukuma, who, like, *Kanagusuku, Matsumura, Oyatomari, Yamada, Nakazato, Yamazato, and Toguchi, all of Tomari*,[a] were students of a southern Chinese who landed on the shores of Okinawa in the late eighteenth, early nineteenth century. As Funakoshi noted, and he knew Azato much better than I did, he excelled in archery, which he learned from Sekiguchi; horsemanship, which he was taught by Mekata, tutor to the Meiji Emperor; and, *bojitsu*. But Azato was best known for his skill with the sword, and he was famed for defeating Yorin Kanna. Azato was a master of the Jigen School, and studied under Ishuin Yashichiro. Funakoshi wrote that Azato's martial skills were *without equal in all of Okinawa*,[b] and having seen him demonstrating, I would have to say, my very limited knowledge of karate accepted, that Itosu and Azato were on a par, though very different. Their philosophies of karate were also very different. I believe that Azato's favourite maxim, as Funakoshi recorded, *"When you practise karate, think of your arms and legs as swords,"* sums up his very mental approach to his art, which seemed at odds with Itosu's maxim, which was to condition the body to accept all blows. One was also very much encouraged to think as others' fists and feet as live blades too. Azato's karate strongly emphasised the skill of visualisation. Part of his reasoning was, that if you imagined an opponent so armed, when faced with such a foe with an actual sword, one would not be afraid. He is said to have defended himself in such a way. He was a member of the *literati* and a brilliant scholar, writing under the pseudonym, *Rinkaku-sai*, from whom Funakoshi learned much about Confucian philosophy. I found Azato a very friendly man in all matters, but when it came to karate instruction, he was hard and terse, and praise was infrequent and short. For Azato, like Itosu, karate training was a deadly serious business. Good humour was reserved for after training. Azato later moved to the Kojimachi district of Tokyo, and acted as *military attaché and adviser to the House of Sho.*[b]

An important point that I was alerted to quite early on, was that karate was very much an individual search. What does a beginner do when told two seemingly opposite points of view? Which one does he opt for? Is one correct, the other incorrect, or are they both correct or incorrect? These points puzzled both Funakoshi and I when we began training.

The very next day, as fate would have it, I saw Funakoshi in the busy market square in Naha, which was in direct contrast to the nearby streets, which were very quiet. The usual street scene in town was of men sitting, contemplatively, smoking Lilliputian clay pipes in the shade of a large tree, some playing *go*. A man would pass wearing a straw sombrero, having visited the local well, carrying two full water buckets that hung by short ropes, one each end, on a shoulder pole. By a wall, a stone edifice, about four or five feet in height and resembling the shape of the large stone lanterns so common in Japan stood, *full of little rolls of human hair*[23] which were burnt by priests on certain occasions. Street traders, with brightly coloured fans, carrying umbrellas – though at one time it was decreed that commoners could not use umbrellas as sun shades, but could use them in the rain – walked quietly on their way to the square and to customers. The higher-ranking were being carried along in a *kagu* by two bearers wearing, like many, broad-rimmed hats; lush vegetation, a myriad of greens under a brilliant blue sky, trailed over property walls.

Plate 11. A street in Naha

Now, having travelled the world, I see that *the streets had a most peculiar appearance, owing to the houses being built in little compounds, and separated from the street and one another by massive walls from eight to fourteen feet in height. These walls were of great thickness, and sloped outwards at the base in the manner as those of the old feudal castles of Japan. They were composed of large blocks of coralline limestone, and were most beautifully built . . . They were no doubt originally constructed for purposes of defence, most probably on account of defending the town as a whole; and, in the days of the infancy of artillery, the enemy would have gained but little had they entered the city, while they would in every direction have been exposed to a cross fire which must have speedily decimated them. Every man's house was literally his castle, the entrance to which was through a narrow and easily-defended door in the high wall . . .* [The houses inside each compound were] *built entirely of wood, and dark brown with age, displayed their interior with the inviting hospitality so characteristic of Japan . . .* [There were no tables and chairs, and people] *reclined peacefully on the thick oblong mats neatly plaited of rice straw . . . Outside was the familiar garden that all of us, whether from books or from actual experience, know so well – the pebbly paths leading to miniature bridges over embryonic lakes, the little stone lanterns,* [and] *the quaintly-clipped trees.*[23]*

Within the gardens one could hear, and along the streets, by the walls, one could see, children playing the various Tip-cat variations known as *Gicho* and *Teng*, using two sticks, and whip-top, the whip being made of bamboo with lashes of cotton, and the tops being of white coral or wood.

In *Gicho*, a *short piece of wood, known as the cat, was cut off obliquely at one end . . . In starting the play, the cat was laid upon the ground with the oblique surface downward and then with a quick rap of the bat it was tilted up and caught in the left hand; this required more knack than appeared at first sight, and failure to make this catch lost the turn of the batsman. The bat was then laid down and the cat passed over to the right hand and thrown into the air about three feet; while it was in the air the bat was snatched up and the cat struck before it fell. The fielder tried to catch the cat on the fly, whereby the batsman forfeited his turn; failing to catch it, the fielder picked it up and threw it towards the batsman, who again struck it and then measured off the distance to where it had fallen, in so many lengths of the bat; this constituted the score. The fielder had the right to confuse the batsman by throwing in to him two pieces of wood like the cat, and the* *batsman had to distinguish between the right and the wrong piece; if he struck the wrong he lost his turn.*[27]*

Teng was played in the district near Kumamoto and was known as *in ten*, the small stick being called *ko*, 'son,' and the longer *oya*, 'parent.' A *small stick was first placed in an inclined position in a hole dug in the earth, the projecting end being struck. Afterwards the cat was laid across the hole and tossed in the air by means of the bat placed beneath it, and then struck. The object of the game was to knock the cat as far as possible, the distance back to the hole being measured with the long stick, the lengths counting. The players sometimes caught the cat in aprons when it was knocked in the air, and then threw it back to the batsman, who endeavored to strike it again.*[27]*

But back to the market! One *came suddenly upon the square in which were congregated many hundred women, each with a small basket, bargaining for rice and other necessaries, and laughing, chattering, and cheapening in the most discordant and emphatic manner ... All these lively and energetic females belonged to the lower orders, and rejoiced in countenances by no means attractive.*[11a] It was hard to imagine that, when western foreigners walked into such a place, they found *the damsels scampering in every direction, leaving their goods to the mercy of the males ... Many of the elders not gifted with charms, quietly sat still, with their backs towards ...* [the visitors] *pretending to be engaged in other matters, and generally screened by some well-meaning male.*[11]

The plaza probably covered a space of two acres, and it was crowded with country-people, their packhorses, truck-carts, and articles which they had brought in for sale. The citizens of all ages ... were there also, making their purchases in their usual ... manner, and apparently wrapped up in their bargains[22] *... The market* [was] *crowded, and a brisk trade* [was] *going on in vegetables, cheese, pork, earthenware, paper, plain cotton goods, and other articles in common use.*[5b]

To outsiders, *the variety of colour and pattern in the dresses of the people ...* [was no doubt] *remarkable ... Blue, in all its shades, was the prevalent colour, though there were many dresses resembling in every respect Highland tartans.*[2] The town women, who I have not yet had recourse to mention, wore dress *like that of the men, though somewhat shorter, and without any girdle around the waist.*[2] The country women's *outer dress differed from that of the men, it was open in front, and they had no girdle; they had an under dress, or sack, which was also loose, but not open; in some ...* [it could be seen] *that this came

Plate 12. An Okinawan girl, Naha

nearly to the feet, in others just to the knee, and . . . [it was to be] *imagined that those who worked in the fields had the short dresses: most of
them allowed their upper garment to flow out with the wind behind
them. Every person had one of the girdles before described, which
was, in general, richly ornamented with flowers in embossed silk, and
sometimes with gold and silver threads. The dress was naturally so
graceful, that even the lowest boatmen had a picturesque appearance.*
[Although] . . . *rather low in stature,* [my countrymen] *were well
formed, and had an easy graceful carriage, which suited well with
their flowing dress* . . . *In deportment they were modest, polite, timid,
and respectful, and in short, appeared to be a most interesting and
amiable people.*[2]*

   *There are some harmless snakes besides the poisonous
Trimeresurus. The latter, called habu by the* . . . [local people], *is four
or five feet long by two inches in diameter, and is an object of universal fear and hatred. In Okinawa, indeed, one rarely meets with it
except in the forests to the north, and the islands of Kerama, Oki-no-
Erabu-shima, and Kikai-ga-shima are said to be quite free of it; but in
Oshima and Toku-no-shima it is ubiquitous. Not only does this dreaded reptile spring out at passers-by from the hedges, where its habits
lead it to lie in wait for birds; it actually enters houses, making it
perilous during the warm season to walk about the house at night
except with a lantern* . . . *No antidote* . . . [was known]. *The general*

result of such cases . . . [that did] not end in death was lifelong crippling. Pecuniary rewards were offered by the authorities for the bodies of these snakes, dead or alive, and the villagers [would] go out into the woods to secure them. Even so, the number of the habu did not seem to diminish perceptibly, and there was at least one case . . . [at that time] of a village having to be abandoned by its inhabitants because they could not cope with their dire reptilian foes. This species . . . is, I believe, peculiar to the Okinawan archipelago. Several of the Ryukyu Islands also produce sea snakes, locally known as Erabu-unagi, literally, Erabu eels, and which, though all lumped together . . . [by the locals] really belong to at least three different species. Most are harmless, but of one species the bite is poisonous. Of the commonest species the females are about four feet long and nine or ten inches round; the males about two and a half feet long; the females having a white belly and rings on the back, while the males have reddish bellies. A second and less common sort is somewhat larger, sometimes as much as five feet long; the belly reddish, with white, green, and black bands. All these can be easily caught in a depth of about seven fathoms. The poisonous species is still larger, running to as much as eight feet. Like vipers in some of the rural districts of Japan, these Okinawan sea-snakes were highly prized, being consumed as food by the rich, and in smaller quantities as medicine by the poor. They were smoked alive by being tied round and round a stick and placed at a suitable distance above a fire. They become nearly black in the process of smoking, and at first sight looked like short black sticks to one viewing them in the Naha market, where they were commonly exposed for sale.[4]*

Funakoshi, who was small for his age even by Okinawan standards, was standing by a stall selling such delicacies, listening to an overweight man not much taller than my new acquaintance, whose nose had been caved in so that it was flat with his face. Okinawans are noted for their strong hair growth, and this man's beard was long and plaited, and brought to a sharp point by means of some adhesive. The man's expression was gentle and pleasing despite his disfigurement, though somewhat melancholy. He was speaking to a tall, handsome gentleman who, I later discovered, was Funakoshi's father, Gisu, an expert at *bojitsu* [stick fighting]. It was an extremely rare sight on Okinawan soil to see obesity, and I believe that, along with the fact that this fat fellow, as Funakoshi and I later recalled with much hilarity, rushed off to the new public toilets in the Tsuji quarters, was why, all these years on, I remember the scene so vividly. All three wore the silver pins of the *shizoku*. A woman with a hare-lip, which was quite common on the islands, from Yonakuni, walked by carrying an infant on her back, Japanese style, in a sort of sling called *tsikumya*, peculiar to that island. A singularly unattractive woman stall-keeper was sitting by her collection of *common crockery, apparently imitated from Japanese designs, and not of particularly good shape . . . the chief articles being cups and small tea-pots.*[23] Her hair was kept in position by a single pin, similar in design to the *usisashi*, but much larger, hexagonal in shape, and *constructed of alternate pieces of black and transparent horn, neatly joined by glue.*[23]

How different this scene, the daily one of the market square, was from the scene I remember my father telling me about. He was witness, as boy, when an American ship docked at Naha, a few years after Commodore Perry, and some of their officers and crew entered the market square unannounced. "Suddenly," my father had said, "*a confused feeling of alarm pervaded the whole square: strangers had appeared . . . Those who were near the opening of the street down which . . .* [the Americans had] *come, rushed pellmell from . . .* [them] *on either side, just as a crowd makes a passage for a mad bull . . .* [the people] *left most of their things behind, though there was one fellow who took time to sling a pig over his shoulders, and one tall, finely-formed woman who gathered up her bundle of rice and walked off in majestic dignity. Those who were more distant from . . .* [the Americans] *mostly disappeared down neighboring streets or into friendly houses, though there were some who had the courage to remain to pack their wares hurriedly before flight.*"[22] The umbrellas that covered the primitive market stalls were large and fixed into the ground. When it rained, which was frequently, sheets of oilpaper were secured to act as a makeshift defence against the elements. These sheets were hurriedly thrown over the trays and baskets containing edibles, toys and so on, before the owners fled. *The cattle, too, became alarmed at the general commotion, and added their antics to the confusion of the scene.*[22]

But that wasn't the end of the story for our family, and I should like to quote from Lieutenant Habersham's 1857 work, a copy of which is now in the family library. He wrote: '*Finally we emerged from the city into the outskirts, then into the by-paths of the fields, where we met with a Okinawan gentleman and his servant upon their way, as we subsequently inferred, to spend the day with a friend. The boy carried his master's "chowchow-box" which contained his dinner, saki, etc, as it is the fashion in Okinawa for the guests to carry their meals along.*

This gentleman directed us by the shortest cut to the high-road to the capital of Shuri, which we were in search of.' [22] I am sure that the 'boy' was my father, the 'master' by grandfather, for my father told me that his first spoken encounter with a westerner was as Habersham described, shortly after the market-square incident.

The market seemed to have been particularly busy the day I saw Funakoshi. Stalls abounded selling everything an Okinawan might require, and I remember a man, whose name I forget, who had come down in the world, and now earned a comfortable living selling food-stuffs and herbs; well, his wife actually did the selling on a series of stalls. Sage, cat-mint, horehound, garlic, onion, black pepper, pig-weed, spinach, beet, cymlings, water-cress, black mustard, radish, Jerusalem artichoke, common artichoke, lettuce, common wood-sorrel, yellow wood-sorrel, fennel, egg-plants, water-melon, pumpkin, cucumber, timothy, millet, rice, kidney-bean, pea, peaches, pears, figs, brinjoles, sweet potato, orange, lemon, and gourds of an enormous size – you name it, she sold it. She sold six types of rice and six sorts of beans. He supplied our house with goods and my father would often chat to him. The shops were few, selling *chiefly paper, rice, tea, sweet-meats, and clothing.*[5] The rice was very fine, and when boiled became as white as snow. In the absence of gold and silver, Japanese copper coins of the early seventeenth century were used, but because Japan refused Okinawa any further coinage, rice became the measure of value. Tea was a favourite beverage of the Okinawans, and it was drunk anytime of the day or night, and *much attention was bestowed on its appearance, bouquet and 'feeling'* . . . [Its price varied tremen-dously] *and while it was possible for the poorer classes to obtain it for as little as twopence per pound* [in 1883] . . . [those] *of high rank would set before his guests a carefully-selected leaf which had perhaps cost him from eighteen to twenty-shillings, or even more.*[23*] We pro-nounced tea as *tsha* . . . *and drank* [it] *without milk or sugar.*[24] x

Exchange of money and trust were problems. The first bank was set up on Okinawa by Kimbara Meizen in 1879. He had come from Shizuoka Prefecture. It took about three years before there was confi-dence in the general population in the yen and *sen*. Many Okinawans, distrustful, would issue IOU notes to one other, should events transpire that the Japanese currency would somehow become invalid. I remem-ber that I visited the police station in Naha with my father over a prob-lem associated with an IOU note. The station was a house, entirely built of wood, *situated in a little compound, the entrance to which was overhung by a magnificent Ficus with a quaintly gnarled and twisted*

Plate 13. An Okinawan merchant

trunk . . . The rooms were open at the sides, the sliding, paper-covered panels having been drawn back, but the beautifully clean mats that would in Japan have covered the floors were replaced by a red and green carpet that could only have owed its origin to English or German taste.[23] The police made regular inspections of the bath-houses and the brothels.

The market-place, which was the centre of life at Naha, was entirely in the hands of the women, who showed no timidity whatever, exposing not only their faces, but their arms and even their legs. This made the seclusion of their social superiors all the more remarkable by contrast.[4a] Women had been in charge of the market place for centuries. I remember reading that Su-poa-koang, an ambassador or teacher to Okinawa, noted that they were in charge of all *interior commerce or marketing*[3] in 1719.

I could see that the aforementioned unattractive woman stall keeper was from the island of Miyako-jima, and I tell you how I knew this. *All Ryukyuan women tattooed their hands . . . The women of Oshima gave free rein to individual fancy.*[4a*] I can never forget a wretched and most hideous creature, inflicted with elephantiasis, who had had herself literally covered in tatooes. *Those of Miyako-jima likewise had a great variety of patterns, and continued tattooing a long way up the arm. In Yaeyama, on the contrary, it was restricted to the hands.*[4a*] These tattooes were often coloured blue, *and a square on the wrist . . .* [was] *a sign of the married state.*[13] Tattooing was common on all the local islands, including Formosa, for example, where some of the natives, both men and women, would have their faces, and other parts tattooed, in blue and red. These savages were black-teethed, head-hunting cannibals, who would have an additional tattoo for each head they brought home! This woman had tattoos up her arm, which were partly exposed, so I knew her origins. However, even if I hadn't seen her arms I would have known she was from Miyako-jima, as the designs on her hands were quite distinctive, as were, for a matter of interest, the patterns used on the island of Oshima. As with all Ryukyuan women, she wore a single instead of a double hairpin in her topknot, which was positioned on the right[xi] of her head and slightly forward.

Tattooing was a *custom* [that] *prevailed equally in high life,*[24] as well as on the hands of the peasantry. *The female children were tattooed on the arms, from the fingers up to the elbows, with small black dots.*[14][xii] Each finger and thumb was patterned with a long, thin, arrowhead-like tattoo, pointed at the fingertips, just short of the nail, widening slightly down to where the fingers and thumbs meet the hand. At this point, the finely angled barbs were shown, and the whole arrowhead coloured in. On the knuckles where the fingers join the hands, the striking point in *seiken,* there were either circles or flattened X shapes, with the two sides of the X edged and filled in with tattoo colouring. On the middle of the back of the hands were circles, like the ones on the knuckles, and once again coloured in. On the back of the hand just where the hand joins the wrist, there was a large circle or a square, tilted on its side, with four equilateral triangles on either side.[xiii] Tattooing was still *universal among women*[27] on Okinawa in 1896 despite being banned by the Japanese government, and was still prevalent in 1912 [Salwey], though dying out. On young children one could often see the beginnings or outlines of designs.

The *tattooing implements of Oshima and Okinawa, comprised of needles,* [a] *stick for tracing patterns, ink slab and ink. The needle used in Oshima consisted of three needles stuck together with wax or a gum and set in a handle of paper bound over and over with thread until it was pear-shaped and easy to hold. The needle used in Okinawa was made up of twelve needles stuck together in a row between two slips of bamboo which were set in a handle of paper similar to that of Oshima. The ink was ordinary Japanese (India) ink and the slab was an inverted top of a glazed pottery jar. It was provided with a wooden cover. The needles were jabbed into the skin straight up and down, after the pattern had been painted on with a thick solution of the ink*[27*] moistened with *shoju.*

Tattooing was always done by women, who made a regular business of it during the months of July and August, when the hard manual work in the fields was over for a time. The operation made the hands so sore that hard work was impossible . . . The whole of the pattern was not worked in at one sitting, but a part of the hand was tattooed in successive years, beginning when a child was four or five years old, and continued until the whole was finished.[27*]

The reader may reasonably enquire how such universal tattooing had come about in the first place. *In Okinawa the origin of the custom is traced to the earliest time in the following legend: The first woman who wove cloth on the island was exceedingly beautiful, and when commerce began to spring up between Okinawa and Japan, the Japanese were so much pleased with the peculiar beauty of the cloth made in Okinawa, that they insisted that the weaver should be sent to Japan to instruct the people in the art. The Okinawan Council, fearing that the beautiful weaver would be claimed as a bride by some of the* *wealthy samurai of 'Dai Nippon,' and the art to be thereby lost, determined to make her less attractive, and to put on her a mark whereby she would always be recognized and reclaimed from the Japanese, in case of treachery. Her hands were accordingly freely tattooed, and she was allowed to go. The scheme proved a success; the black tattooing so cheapened her that she returned to Okinawa unmarried, and lived to a good and weaving old age. After her death she was elevated to the skies, made a goddess, and was still worshipped . . . in the city of Naha*[27] until at least the end of the nineteenth century. It would seem that indeed the tattooing had something to do with weaving, and on Myako-Jima, to the south of Okinawa, may be found something approaching the original intent. Men, for taxation purposes, would be assessed as a proportion to the amount of millet or rice they could produce; women by the quality of the cloth they could weave. *There were about twenty grades or more of cloth, determined by the difficulty of the pattern, and when a woman became proficient in weaving any one of the patterns, that pattern was tattooed as an enduring proof of skill.*[27]*

This woman storekeeper left a lasting impression on me, and I know not why. Perhaps it was for her unhappy countenance, but this was a common characteristic of Okinawan women, as a result of a *slight downward curve at the corners* [of the mouth] . . . *giving the whole face a somewhat sad expression.*[27] *The women of the lower classes rolled their hair round and round in a twist on the top of the head, and then stuck hairpins through it . . . gold, silver, pewter (sometimes wood), much less often tortoise-shell on specially auspicious occasions. The silver-pinned ones also wore silver rings; the pewter dames wore pewter rings. There being nothing to keep the roll of hair with its hairpins in place, it was apt to lop over on one side, making the wearer look as if she had taken a drop too much. . . . The appearance of the Okinawan women was* [a] . . . *little prepossessing, especially to one fresh from Japan, the land of graceful femininity. They fastened their dress over from the right side as often as from the left* [for example], *which was a dreadful slip of manners in Far-Eastern eyes.*[4a]* Their gait too, must have been seen as masculine and striding.

The small obese man opposite Funakoshi, quite literally as round as he was tall, was certainly less than five feet in height, and his roundness merely seemed to exaggerate his diminutive stature. He really was a most curious sight. He was also clean shaven, suggesting that he was under *the age of four-and-twenty*[14][xiv], for on Okinawa at that time it was the custom to shave one's face until that age and then to grow a moustache, and a beard *six years later*,[14] though shaving the cheeks.

Height, in fact, is an interesting issue. I remember a western writer commenting that *while the men belonging to the heimin classes were almost dwarfish in their stature, physical development, and the shape of their limbs, the shizoku were, as a rule, fine big men, and were undeniably well made. Moreover, while the former in physiognomy resembled the Chinese, the latter had all the features of the higher classes in Japan. It may be that the degraded condition of the heimin during many hundreds of years was sufficient to account for this distinction of feature and physical development, but the existence of this clearly-marked difference led one to suppose that a fusion of races had taken place at some remote time.*[10]*

Azato was a fine example of a tall *shizoku*, with bearing. Height, on Okinawa at least, was a sign of descendency from a noble family from Shuri.[xv] He did not, however, have the slightly curved nasal ridge, which was also characteristic. Sure enough though, he held the very senior rank of *anzu* and was hereditary chief of the village of Azato, that lay between Shuri and Naha. He acted as a military advisor to the king, a position he was privileged to hold for at least the two years I knew him prior to the forced abdication.

Generally though, Okinawans were, and still are, a short and stocky people – *the average height of the men* [for the time] *not exceeding five foot two inches at the utmost.*[3] [xvi] So, Funakoshi, being *shizoku*, was, as I say, small, at five foot at best, when fully grown. I think he was always conscious of his height.

Before rushing off, our obese man was in the process of buying something or other from the stall, and as he talked away, a high-pitched scream of a suckling pig, tied on a cushion of straw, with its legs sticking out fore and aft, was being carried on the top of the head of a shoeless, heavy-boned woman. The Okinawan women at that time plastered their hair with pigs' fat, so that it shone brightly in the light. Goats would also be carried this way. A peasant woman would carry as much as two hundred pound on her head. Some of them carried immense empty earthenware jars capable of holding thirty-six gallons when full. The sudden scream took everybody's attention away from what they were doing, and quite startled a street vendor sitting beside his piles of coarse cheesecakes. A high-class woman, who would travel to the market, was so taken aback that she dropped her piece of cloth, which was about a foot long, that she carried. It was the custom in those days for the better class of woman to carry such cloth to distinguish her from her social inferiors.

Funakoshi glanced up, and in so doing saw me standing there, looking at him. I remember a young boy walking past with a *toy drum, painted red; decorated with* [a] *picture of* [a] *Chinese lion and* [a] *ball.*[27] Funakoshi acknowledged me and, joining his hands and placing them on his breast,[xvii] bent his torso and legs profoundly, in the most approved manner, and I reciprocated with a similar *kow-tow*, which, as I have noted before, was the custom. Funakoshi was very sincere, one could tell this from his demeanour, and I hoped, even then, at our second encounter, that, despite the social gap between us, we might be friends. Readers will, I hope, appreciate, that whilst we were both of the *shizoku*, much like being officer status in the armed services, the gap between us was considerable in rank, in that Funakoshi's family had, for generations, been associated with a lower-ranking official, and my family were nobles. This point is made not out of any snobbery, I am merely trying to impress upon the reader what times were like then, and how Funakoshi and I felt.

Unlike virtually all people from my social rank, I actually liked walking, though sometimes I rode my sturdy, shaggy horse, despite the most uncomfortable wooden saddle, *the heavy uncouth stirrups,*[11a] and grass-rope bridle. The horses were small, pony size, *ten to ten-and-a-half hands high,*[28] but hardy, active and strong. Horses were *chiefly used for riding by the rich* . . . [though some carried] *burdens to market, etc, but almost all such labor was done by men and women.*[7] *My rides about the southern half of Okinawa were extremely pleasant. The openness of the country, which in many places allows the ocean to be seen on either side, with colours deliciously varying according to the depth of the water above the coral reefs; the fresh sea-breezes; the alternation of hill and dale; the marvellous cultivation; the picturesque blocks of coral, standing up like ruined castles that bear witness to a former less settled state of society; the happy-looking groups of labourers in the fields, all diligent and all most courteous when addressed; – these things made up a scene which it would be hard to match for quiet charm.*[4]

The northern part of the island abounded with marshy thickets and hills overgrown with dense woodland, infested with wild boars, but the southern portion was one vast garden.[5b]* *While at labour in the summer* [the peasants. . .] *were nearly naked, merely wearing a rag a few inches square*[17] that hardly passed even for a loin-cloth; at other times, they were decently clothed. *In rains they did not abandon their work, but, donning a broad-brimmed conical hat, and a loose, shaggy, short cape, both rudely made of the leaves of sugar-cane or banana, they*

Plate 14. An Okinawan peasant

labored on without intermission.[7] It was customary in those days for
the *heimin* not to wear clogs, and they would wander the fields bare-

footed as they hoed, *and their feet seemed to have attained the hardness of a horse's hoof, if we might judge from the rapidity and ease with which they ran over the hard coral* stones.[17] *The ha-koo-shoo, who were the peasants, or fieldworkers . . . farmed the country* [which, in times past had been] *at an exorbitant amount of rent, and paid to the government, as feudal lords of the soil.*[xviii] *The crops thus produced formed the principal revenue of the government, and the means of subsistence to the literary class in their indolent abstinence from labour.*[17*] There were some *oo-bang, or public slaves, who possessed no civil rights nor personal freedom, and were absolutely dependent on the commands, or even the mere beckoning of the literati,*[17*] working the fields as well. *Filial piety was the canonized virtue of Okinawa, as of China, and was the principle on which the government ground their claims to the obedience of the people.*[17*]

Looking back, *the lower orders were as free from distress as those of any country*[24] I ever visited. I recall thinking at the time that *if, to have few wants and . . .* [if] *easily satisfied, constitute riches . . .* [these workers could] *be considered a contented, cheerful people. While viewing their merry countenances, and listening to their light-hearted voices, I could not help reflecting on the universal law of compensation by which a wise and merciful Providence equalizes the conditions of mankind - causing the sons of luxury to pay the price of civilization in many sorrows and cares, from which these children of nature enjoyed an immunity and exemption. The sweets of civil liberty, of social refinement, or of personal ambition, possess no charm for the man whose chief happiness is to satisfy hunger and to repel want.*[17]

I remember well, that as a sign of respect to past Ryukyuan kings, the names of whom were inscribed on tablets within the sanctuary of the Sogen-ji main gate near Tomari, everybody would dismount and pass on foot. *By the side of the road a stone pillar was standing, green with moss of many a bygone year. Its inscription – 'Superiors and inferiors alike must here dismount and rest' – was still legible, written on the one side in ordinary square Chinese characters, and on the other in Japanese katakana.*[23]

I recall being required to learn, by heart, the Ryukyuan kings of the Sho Dynasties and their dates of accession. With a love of history, this was no great chore, and proved very useful, for they acted as markers back through time, from which a sense of temporal perspective, and much more, could be gained. I can remember them still to this day, and as they may be extremely difficult for the reader to access, and as they are useful in the history of karate, I would like to give them here: Sho

Tai (1866), Sho Iku (1838), Sho Ko (1803), Sho On (1800), Sho Boku (1756), Sho Kei (1719), Sho Tei (1683), Sho Shitsu (1663), Sho Ho (1633), Sho Nei (1606), Sho Ei (1579), Sho Gen (1561), Sho Shin (1534), Sho Shin(1479), Sho En (1473), Sho Toku (1463), Sho Taikyu (1456), Sho Kinfuku (1452), Sho Shiken (1447), Sho Chu (1443), Sho Hashi (1425). The first Sho Dynasty was founded in 1429, but fell in 1470, when a new Sho Dynasty was established.

I used to like to ride across the Madama Bridge, near Naha, which was built in the early sixteenth century [destroyed in 1945], not far from which a butterfly, *beautifully marbled with crimson, brown and yellow*[11a] was sometimes to be found. Other insects such as *grass-hoppers, dragon-flies . . . honey-bees, wasps, moskitos of a large size, spiders . . . mantis,*[24] and the like, filled the air, forest and floor. Around me, banana (of which there were two types – *one edible species, being comparatively scarce, while the . . .* [other] *was used to weave cloth out of, and was very abundant*[4*]), fig and orange trees. *Cultivation was added to the most enchanting beauties of nature. From a commanding height . . . the view was, in all directions, picturesque and delightful . . . To the south was the city of . . .* [Naha] *and in the inter-mediate space appeared numerous hamlets scattered about on the banks of the rivers, which meandered in the valley beneath; the eye being, in every direction, charged by the varied hues of the luxuriant foliage around . . .* [the] *habitations. Turning to the east, the houses of . . .* [Shuri], *built in their peculiar style, were observed, opening from among the lofty trees which surround and shaded them, rising one above another in a gentle ascent to the summit of a hill, which was crowned by the king's palace; the intervening grounds between . . .* [Naha and Shuri], *a distance of some miles, being ornamented by a continuation of villas and country houses. To the north, as far as the eye could reach, the higher land was covered with extensive forests.*[3*]

The scenery around Naha was *more pleasing to the eye than that of islands near the equator, where the vegetation is so profusely lux-uriant, as to overload the picture with foliage to the exclusion of everything else. Here there was much variety; the numerous groves of pine trees gave some parts of it an English air, but the style of landscape was what is called tropical.*[2*]

I used to ride and come across limestone *pinnacled ridges, so much like ruins of ancient buildings, as to deceive the eye at a distance of only a few hundred feet,*[9] and never far from view the white cliffs of Mae-jima, a striking feature in the view seaward from Naha and south-eastern Okinawa generally.

Plate 15. Bridge and Causeway (at Ma-chi-na-too) on Okinawa

Plate 16. Lotus Lake at T'skina

I often rode to the summer residence of the king, T'skina, two or three miles south-east of Naha. I recall there being a lovely level lawn with a border of bright flowers that seemed in direct contrast to the rest of the garden. *The large lotus-pond beyond . . . had a little island-temple in the centre, connected by two quaint stone bridges with the land,*[23] and behind rose the tall, dark pines.

Now, when I think back through the mists of time, I remember riding through the outskirts of Naha to Tomari, sheltered from the north winds by a row of trees, and behind a range of hills, the village lay at the juncture of the shore road and the main thoroughfare to Shuri. Out of interest, I should like to mention that my father saw Mr. Brown and Mr. Draper, from Commodore Perry's party, with a daguerreotype apparatus here in 1853. This early photographic process used iodine-sensitized silvered plate and mercury vapour. It was the first camera ever brought to Okinawa.

Near Tomari, I recall, by the sea, where the snipe would drum as they dived almost vertically from a great height, giving notice of their territory, salt was collected by the *Ha-koo-shoo. Large level fields were rolled or beat so as to have a hard surface. Over this was strewn a sort of sandy black earth, forming a coat about a quarter of an inch thick. Rakes and other implements were used to make it of uniform thickness, but it was not pressed down. During the heat of the day, men* *were employed to bring water in tubs from the sea, which was sprinkled over these fields by means of a short scoop. The heat of the sun, in a short time, evaporated the water, and the salt was left in the sand, which was scraped up and put in to raised receivers of masonry about six feet by four, and five deep. When the receiver was full of the sand, seawater was poured on the top, and this, in its own way down, carried with it the salt left by evaporation. When it ran out below at a small hole, it was a very strong brine; this was reduced to salt by being boiled in vessels about three feet wide and one deep. The cakes resulting from this operation were an inch and a half in thickness.*[2]*

I recall a time once riding, not long after an earth tremor, when a point of timing and application struck me concerning a particular *kata*. I had just crossed over a stream – which are numerous in that part of Okinawa, but are necessarily very short, the longest attaining a length of only about six miles – where, on the banks, numerous people were washing clothes in the same way as they do in India, by dipping them in water and beating them on stones. I continued, and having left this scene safely behind me, I came upon a little haven where there was a profusion of orchids and white lily, and then, by contrast, an unusually rough area were *the ground was strewed with . . . blocks of coral of all sizes, most overgrown with ivy; the pandanus and dwarf palm grew wherever there was soil; and the grasshoppers and other insects flew about . . . in great abundance.*[13] I jumped off my horse, threw off my straw sandals and there and then, on the path, in bare feet, put into practice my thought on the application of two techniques from *Naihanchi*,[xix] today, in Shotokan, known as *Tekki*. I soon learned that one of the distinguishing features of karate was that it could be practised at anytime, anywhere. We had been told that to master the *kata*, we had to perform it many thousands of times, and in the beginning I was always mindful of keeping my back straight and my shoulders down. Visualising an opponent was essential mind training. Now, as readers may be aware, *kiba-dachi* is the principal stance in that form. *Kiba-dachi* means 'horse-riding stance,' nowadays often referred to as 'straddle-legged stance.' The position of the legs is said to thus resemble the position taken when a horse is mounted, with legs astride. There is in fact only a superficial comparison, the main similarity being the feeling in the knees, thighs and abdomen, especially when riding bareback. I was always conscious of this of course, for Itosu constantly reminded us to think of everyday life as karate training. Unfortunately, when coming down into the stance performing *a fumi-komi*, I ripped the underside of my sole badly on a piece of coral that underlays these tracks. *The base of the island is . . . composed of gneiss, granite, and slate rocks; and upon this the zoophytes built their mountain masses of coral, which, being completed, were elevated by subterraneous upheaval,*[8] and it was upon this that my blood flowed freely. Readers might like to know that coral was burned in those days to make cement for building, and that the temples were *frequently ornamented with regularly cut pieces of madrepore.*[18] That little incident forbade training in stances for quite a few weeks, though I would, of course, practise the arm movements in a more inwardly directed stance, for as Itosu said, it was far better suited to what I was compensating for, than *hachiji-dachi.*

I remember a similar incident when I dismounted to see if I could lift a heavy stone. Amongst large bird's nest ferns, a ginger with fine yellow flowers and arum, I moved the rock by a *bora* [a large cactus] but a few inches, and in that instant, my attention was drawn to the movement of a large green tree frog, with a bright orange abdomen. I was watching this charming creature, neglecting the results of my efforts with the rock. Unfortunately, I had disturbed some scorpions that were underneath in the damp ground. There are two scorpions, as far as I am aware, that infest the islands, one quite small, the other larger and darker in colour. *Although held in great abhorrence by the . . .* [local people], *neither of these scorpions possesses much venom,*[11a] but being stung was not a pleasant experience, and the considerable irritation, swelling and soreness lasted some time.

My father, on the other hand, sometimes rode, but rarely walked. He invariably took a *kagu,* if he wished to travel locally. A *kagu* was *a closed chair borne on a pole by two coolies, and resembled the Chinese palanquin rather than the kago of Japan*[4a]*, but the *kagu,* which I have alluded to before, was *so small and shallow that the person carried had to sit huddled up with his head and neck turned to one side,*[9a]* and one had to hold on as best one could. As the *kagu* is no longer in use, I'd like to give a brief description of it if I may.

This little machine, being about two feet and a half in height, and slightly roofed at the top, was open at the sides, with the exception of a little loose blind used at option, and [as I say], *was borne on the shoulders of two men, one before and the other behind, who ran along with the weight suspended diagonally forward, at an uneasy, irregular pace of five miles an hour, resembling a jog-trot. The traveller entered at the side, and had to squat or sit in Turkish fashion on the bottom of the vehicle, occasionally grasping the pole above to prevent being shaken out into the road, and generally clasping his knees with his*

Plate 17. A typical Okinawan scene

hands close to his chin. A more primitive invention it was impossible to conceive. This was the only carriage known on Okinawa; and the only improvement in those used by the highest rulers consisted in a little additional width to the floor.[17]* These rather distressing conveyances were most beautifully made of plaited bamboo slips, coloured red, black and yellow in various patterns, and were furnished with little windows of wonderful neatness of construction.*[23] Needless to say, I found the ride uncomfortable in the extreme and the view always spoilt. Of course, I was fully cognizant that anything that could strengthened my legs would be helpful in my study of karate, and I would often tie weights of about two pounds around my ankles when I went for a walk. I sometimes made rather excessive leg movements to encourage muscular development, and I was once caught practising – walking, lifting my legs up, one at a time to my chest, as sprinters do – which greatly embarrassed me, for I knew only too well the owner of the quizzical look who appeared from behind a boxwood hedge. Itosu *Sensei* had advised me to train my body so that blows would simply bounce off. He trained his body in like manner and I concur wholeheartedly with Funakoshi when he wrote that *Itosu's body was forged and tempered to the point of seeming invulnerable.*[b] I wanted to be like that.

Itosu was a most formidable *karateka*, and there are a number of stories, recorded by Funakoshi, that confirm this – from his amazing grip, which I felt (and yes, he could crush thick bamboo stalks in one hand, most notably his right) to the time he punched through a door and grabbed the wrist of a would-be thief who was literally caught in the act of trying to pick a lock! But I remember, best of all, the story when Itosu punched through seven inches of solid wood. The passing of more than eighty years has not dampened my awe at the thought of this having being done. To this day, when I come across a thick wooden post, pillar, beam, wall, and so on, I estimate those seven inches and marvel every time. It never ceases to amaze me. How could he perform such a feat? And yet I am confident that he did, for the man who told me did not lie. It was said at the time that Itosu could kill with a single blow, and few doubted it.

Not only was I caught-out practising karate, I once came upon a young man practising what I later learned was the *kata Passai* [*Bassai*]. It may interest readers to know that *Passai* was the name of a cultured Chinese who lived on Okinawa teaching karate. I got chatting to this man, a nice fellow of good breeding, whose name was Chofu. We became good acquaintances, but deep friendship, alas, was never destined to blossom, as he caught cholera in the 1879 pandemic. The outbreak had first occurred in India and the spread, both east and west, was rapid. Naha, being a seaport, was exposed to many seamen and travellers, so the island was an easy target for this terrible disease. Those long months formed a dreadful, frightening episode, and many thousands died, especially children and the old. At the time of the equinoxes, owing to the heavy rains, the wells were usually contaminated with surface water that contained effluent due to poor sanitation. This was the primary source of infection, along with fly faeces on food, and great mortality was the result. The micro-organism *comma bacillus* could stay alive in water for several weeks, but thankfully was rapidly killed by drying.

But this is not the end of the story. When I enquired of Chofu, owing to his non-appearance at our meeting spot, I was told a most curious tale by a family member who witnessed a very strange and memorable event. After the sudden onset of the customary painless but copious diarrhoea and severe vomiting, followed by agonizing cramps and the skin turning bluish, I was told that Chofu had collapsed, and, as is sometimes the case in epidemics, this fit, powerful man was dead within a few short hours. It is true that the body of an individual who has died from cholera can remain warm for a long time after death, and, indeed, may be even warmer after death than at the time of death. This member of the family informed me that Chofu was pronounced dead, and he lay quite motionless on the floor, arms by his sides, and was left for a few short minutes under a mosquito net. When members of his family returned, soon afterwards, the corpse had partly opened its eyelids and moved its right arm and formed a right-handed fist – though the thumb had not entirely closed. What was most striking was that the arm was sticking up at a right angle to his body, the knuckles facing the ceiling. Muscular contractions do sometimes occur after death from cholera, and this is surely what happened. The man's spirit was strong; he trained assiduously – karate, even after death.

III

ICHIRAZICHI, WATER TRAINING, FUNERALS, AND OTHER STORIES

So, Funakoshi and I became good friends and training partners. Throughout the entire time I knew him before I left for university, he lived with his mother's parents. I don't actually know why this was, and he was never very forthcoming on this point. He wrote that being born prematurely, he was a sickly baby, which was true. The consensus was that he was not destined to live long and was thus *coddled and pampered by both pairs of grandparents.*[c] Where his parents were is something of a mystery. I have always considered this a very curious, not to say sad beginning, and I really wish he had confided in me. Anyway, Funakoshi attended primary school, which was quite a rare thing in those days. His paternal grandfather, Gifuku, was a Confucian scholar who had taught his grandson the Four Chinese Classics and the Five Chinese Classics of the Confucian tradition. Virtually all *shizoku* were familiar with these. They were tantamount to standard reading, like Shakespeare in the West, and Funakoshi knew them well. He had been properly taught, and, sure enough, Funakoshi later mentioned to me that his grandfather had instructed his *anzu's* family at the Kuntoku Daikun Goten.

We would get up very early in the morning, well before the sun rose, meet en route, and walk to Itosu's house in Shuri. I did not have far to travel of course, but my friend had a walk of some two and a half miles. At that hour, the large fruit bats were about, everywhere. I remember passing by a grove of banyan trees, which, on Okinawa, were not held sacred as in Buddhist countries, and a wonderfully mature ivory-nut tree. At that time, the Okinawan day, that is *between sunrise and sunset, was divided into six hours, as was also the night.*[2]*

One of those mornings I recall particularly well, for we encountered an earth tremor of considerable strength. *The island is subjected to frequent shocks of earthquake, showing further that it is not yet far removed from volcanic action.*[28]

After a full lesson in *Tekki*, Funakoshi and I would walk wearily home in our *hoba no geta*[i] which we used for leg strengthening, and each step seemed to get heavier than the one before. During the day, we'd often use heavy stone *geta*, hewn out of rock, to strengthen our legs, but as such practice was very obvious, we restricted ourselves and trained only in private. The bluish smoke rising through the thatched roofs of the *heimin* huts in the crisp dawn air revealed that life was beginning to stir, as the old women, always the first to rise, started their fires to boil the sweet potato and heat the soup that was to serve as breakfast. When we passed someone on the road at that hour in the morning, an exchange of suspicious glances always took place, followed by a courteous, "Good Morning." Such was the value that Okinawans attached to good manners and polished behaviour, that pillars inscribed 'Land of Propriety' were to be found on the corners of the streets of Shuri.

As the sun rose a little higher, the roughly made red and black, or red and white tiles of the roofs of the houses, made themselves discernible amongst the plantain trees.

In the half-light, I remember we passed an old man, over eighty, making rope bags and mats from the fibre of the fan palm. Coconut palm was the other species of palm on the island. Palms were under the superintendence of the government. He raised a hand in acknowledgement and continued with his work. He must have been working by feel, for the strain on his eyes in that light would have been considerable. As if to emphasise the point, we could see torches of dry reeds tied in long bundles being used, as movement in the village increased. And that reminds me of another incident concerning the eyes of an old man.

An unfortunate result of the political overshadowing of Okinawa by its two great neighbours, China and Japan, had been the habit of using the Chinese and Japanese languages for literary purposes, almost at the exclusion of the native tongue, which neither the Chinese ideographs nor the Japanese syllabary were well fitted to express. The Okinawans had no perfect written system of their own.[4b*] Funakoshi and I were walking one day south of Chimu, about twenty-five miles from Shuri on a path neither of us had travelled before, when we came across a venerable old man *with a snowy beard reaching nearly to his knees*,[5a] made blind by a severe case of trachoma, which is a chronic, persistent and severe form of conjunctivitis rampant in the tropics, and is the largest single cause of loss of sight in the Far East. The pale nodules, which have been likened to boiled sago grains, on the conjunctiva lining the eyelids were quite evident. Despite this not uncommon condition at the time, which invariably resulted in scarring, this was the worst case I had seen. Every time the old man blinked, his lashes rubbed against his cornea. Despite this dreadful condition, he sat there by the roadside alongside a large stack of dried millet stalks – each stalk of which can be six to ten feet in length, with a base of three-quarters of an inch, and was used for fuel – playing *Kagiyadefu*, a slow, solemn piece on the *samisen*. The forced, nasal voice, so peculiar to Okinawan song, seemed to just add to this poor man's plight. He had been *stamped as such by the sovereign hand of Nature*.[3] He stopped playing, and spoke to us in a low, soft voice, the dialect of which I could not fathom, and handed me something written in *Sho-chu-ma*, a form of writing then used in the more rural areas of Okinawa and on outlying islands. The man presented me with a fairly long stick – such sticks, which were quite crude in workmanship, ranged in length from about one to two and a half feet – with charcoal figures on the two flat sides, though some sticks allowed for writing on four sides, and pointed to some blackened figures, located at the top of the stick, and then to himself, and smiled an admirable cheeky smile for someone so affected. I could not make any sense of the writing and handed it to by friend. He too had no luck, and we bade the man farewell. Such sticks were generally kept out of sight, for the learned despised such a means of recording, but this man was blind and I felt no contempt. The symbols inscribed on the *Sho-chu-ma* tallies fell into two widely divergent categories – numerals, and signs for peoples' names. The numerals were arranged on a quinary basis and differed according to the material counted – rice, firewood and money being the three materials that occurred. Later, when describing the incident to another friend, I was informed that the old man was well known in the area and that he was over one hundred years old. I couldn't believe it, but have since come to the conclusion that there is something operating on the islands that can give extended life. Perhaps the ancients were right?[ii]

As an aside, readers might like to know the criteria for gaining upgraded status in the social hierarchy, for being a centurion was one such way. The reward of an increase in rank, an official appointment, presents of goods, and so on, could be had by those who *promoted the interests of agriculture in various ways . . . who had made themselves conspicuous by deeds of charity and benevolence; who gave assistance in cases of famine and shipwreck . . . [and] to officials who lessoned official expenditure; who improved the Government finances* *by inaugurating reforms of various kinds; to women who showed great respect to their husband's parents; to widows who remained single . . .* [and to those, as I say] *who attained the age of one hundred years.*[10]* So, presumably this poor fellow had missed out on his being granted increased social status, due to the fall of the system. The dignity that old man maintained, despite his great suffering, convinced me that my intended profession of physician was correct. That incident, and one other, which I shall briefly relate here, where nobody could help the sufferer, became etched into my memory.

In all my travels, *never have I seen a city or town exhibiting a greater degree of cleanliness* [than Shuri]*; not a particle of dirt, or even dust, could be seen.*[5] [iii] This cleanliness was highlighted one day when an old Chinaman had found his way up to the town and could go no further, and *it was very soon apparent that the old man's race was nearly run. He was the victim to the habit of opium smoking, which he was attempting to abandon . . .* [but had sunk] *into a state of nerveless-ness and emaciation painful to look upon . . . every joint in his skele-ton frame seemed to be in perpetual motion; his face was a ghastly yellow; his cheeks sunken on the bones; the eyes wild and glassy; and his mind in a state of semi-madness. Death, when it came, was a relief to the poor old man, as well as to those who saw him die . . . a more frightful example of the terrible effects of the use of opium it would be difficult to find. It exceeded in horror all the loathsome and repulsive results of the use of intoxicating drinks. Delirium tremens is horrible enough, but the last scene of this old opium smoker was more horrible still.*[5] But let us change the subject.

Funakoshi and I had been told that within certain forms of Okinawan dancing, different from the usual *maikata* dancing, were contained karate moves and techniques handed down from the past, and integrated into dance so as to avoid detection from the authorities. Whereas *kobudo* was the brother of karate, we were reliably informed that dancing was the sister. Funakoshi and I searched and searched for those secret moves, and I believe we found rhythm amongst other things. I recall we tried to find out something about the 'shield dance' and/or 'Wan dances' from the Chinese Chou dynasty, some two to three thousand years previous [1100 BC–250 BC]. We knew that we would be unlikely to find anything, and we were correct, but we pur-sued our interest with the vigour of youth.

If one looks closely, Okinawan dancing and *kata* share many simi-larities – muscular tension, concentration of energy, even the manner in which the feet pivot are the same. I remember that on one occasion we were advised to travel north to a small village to see a man who greatly disliked town life, but who was exceptionally skilled in a certain form called *Shishi*, and to watch out for the 'hard' and the 'soft.' I forget the name of the village now and his dance sequence, which is a very great shame, but I recall the man's name and a particular part of the journey well.

I used to like travelling to such villages, because it was in direct contrast to the life in a town. The population of the main island was, and still is, I imagine, very unequally distributed, with *more than half of the whole inhabitants being included in the four towns* [Naha, Shuri, Tomari, Kume], *which are also distinguished from the rest of the country by the fact that the population is composed almost entirely of shizoku.*[10] In fact, [by 1875 figures] half of Okinawa was composed of *shizoku* of the various grades.

The roads in and around the main towns were, I believe, quite good by nineteenth century standards, with the best road, paved, although this was uneven in places, running between Shuri and Naha, which compared very favourably with the best roads in Japan. The reason for the good state of repair of the roads, as I have said, is because there were no carts on the island. Once out of the towns, the roads swiftly became tracks. Unlike in Japan, the peasants were allowed to ride horses, and indeed were better horsemen than the *shizoku*.

The road struck out into the swampy rice fields, and we made for a green headland covered with pines. A village, almost entirely buried in bowers and arcades of bamboo, lay at its foot. As we were entering, we came upon two curious stones planted in the earth. The largest was about four feet high, and from its peculiar form struck me at once as a lingam, or emblem of the Phallic worship . . . It was a very hard, dark-colored stone, resembling porphyry, and the only thing we could learn from . . . [the local people] *was, that they called it 'ishee' . . . In the course of the afternoon we found two more, one of which was prostrate and broken. In conjunction with these remains, the face of the hill behind, for a distance of two miles, was almost entirely covered with excavated tombs . . .* [later, when we asked about them, the locals] *called them the 'houses of the devil's men.'*[5a] All this was very strange, and neither Funakoshi nor I could make anything of it. We fancied that we had ventured just a little too far north for comfort! It was a mystery that no one could unravel, though later I wondered whether there had once, in ancient times, been a settlement from Java.

We reached our destination, set amongst orange trees, with houses set in clusters of two's and three's, along a winding, but well-trodden

Plate 18. Naha from Bamboo Village

path. *The soil here was composed of a stiff marly clay, which the dew rendered exceedingly slippery, and much caution was necessary when walking.*[13] We passed a small cavernous rock, inside which had been placed an image of Kwan-yan, the Goddess of Mercy, a favourite deity of the island, though it must be said that Okinawans generally *disavowed practical idolatry because their reason disapproved the theory; yet they did in fact persevere in their unreasonable worship.*[12]* Each farm was obliged by law to retain four pigs or goats in those days as a precaution against famine, and so that their droppings could act as fertilizer for the fields for present and future generations. The motto was a form of 'live life as though you are going to die tomorrow, but tend the land as though you will live forever.' The scarcity of birds over this part of the island was rather singular, and the countryside was particularly silent here. Birds were very much appreciated by many of the islanders not engaged in their wholesale slaughter. I remember my father telling me that when we [the Okinawans] had *observed the effect of . . . fowling-pieces in the hands of some of the gentlemen* [officers who had landed from an English ship], *they begged they might not kill the birds, which they were always glad to see flying about their houses.*[3]

Among the many trees *was one fifteen feet high, covered with cream-colored blossoms, which exhaled the fragrance of nutmeg,*[5a] which was new to both of us. On arrival, we were directed to a particular hut close to an ebony tree of great age, set within a bamboo hedge, by the entrance of which *a large, red, hairy spider had woven innumerable webs.*[5a] *Most of the huts which we saw in this walk were surrounded with small wattled enclosures, in some of which were a few poor flowers, or a chicken, or a pig.*[13] In the gardens, oranges, bananas, pumelos and pomegranates grew. The middle-aged man we were to meet was standing outside a door, which was made simply of *a few bamboo branches knotted together with string straws, a loop of the same material being all the fastening required.*[25] He seemed to be just watching the world go by, sipping banana wine, which was made in some locations on the island. He stood and conducted himself as though of the highest breed, in spite of his surroundings. He wore no trappings of rank. His hair was shorn. Surely he was *shizoku* down on his luck? He invited us into what we mistakenly thought was his home, which was of the most humble design. The interior consisted *of a single room, smoke-blackened, and furnished with the rudest utensils . . .* [it had] *a grating of bamboo, raised, like a floor, about six inches above the ground, and the thick mats which served . . .* [the family] *as beds were spread upon this.*[5a]

Plate 19. Valley with rice houses

This house was a typical abode of the lower classes of the time, and of a *very primitive character. The roof was covered by a thick thatch, and was supported by four corner uprights about five feet high. The walls consisted of sheets of a species of netting made of small bamboo, which contained between them a thickness of about six inches of straw. This enclosed the whole sides of the house, a width of about two feet being left in one side as an entrance.*[28]* The *village was crawling with* [these animals], *and a very tedious and fatal illness was apt to follow the bites of . . .* [these animals], *to which . . .* [Okinawans] *were much exposed, from their habit of lying among vermin on the ground.*[26]*

Another man appeared of *shizoku* class, who I estimated to be in his seventies, then in came a commoner, and then another, and after a brief discussion, Funakoshi and I left for the man's residence. Apparently, there had been some problem of the paying of *zatsuzei*, or miscellaneous tax, by the village to the *Jito*, or lord of the manor, who, as it turned out, was our host, who had requested payment in an unusual format, which was his prerogative. Two taxes operated on Okinawa at the time – the *seizei* or regular tax paid to the government mainly in the form of crop produce, and the above *zatsuzei*. Our host was not a local man, but from Shuri, and had been appointed to the area by

Shuri. Times had changed, he had decided not to change with them, and had somehow managed to stay on in feudal triumph.

I remember that in the grounds of Ichirazichi's house was a small tree, the name of which I never discovered, but it was about the size of a cherry tree, which bore flowers that had a very peculiar quality attached to them, in that they *alternately, on the same day, assumed the tint of the rose or the lily, as they were exposed to the sunlight or the shade. The bark of this tree was of a deep green, and the flowers bore a resemblance to our common roses . . .* [it was said by some that] *by attentive watching, the change in hue from white to red, under the influence of the solar ray, was actually perceptible to the eye; – that they altered their colour, however, in the course of a few hours was very obvious.*[3]*

In the garden, two girls, Ichirazichi's daughters, were engaged in playing *Hajiki*, a game exclusive to girls, I believe. Merely to enquire about the health of a gentleman's wife and/or daughters at this time would have been seen as *rude and prying,*[27] and one never asked such things. Watching these two girls play was a delight. *Hajiki* was played with thirteen clay discs about half an inch in diameter, flat on one side and rounded on the other. *The game was started by each player throwing down three or four of these small checkers upon the ground, and the one to begin was selected by the 'counting-out' game which was called Mushi-ken, or the 'insect game,' in which the forefinger represents a snake, the thumb a frog, and the little finger a snail. If one player holds up a thumb and the other a little finger, the little finger loses because the frog can eat the snail, and the loser drops out of the contest; likewise the snake beats the frog, but the snake is beaten by the snail, because the snail can crawl into a hole where the snake cannot get at him. The winner in 'counting-out' started the play with the checkers by drawing a line with her thumbnail in the ground between two of the checkers; this was only to indicate which two are in play. With her thumb she snapped one checker at the other; if she hit, she took up the one that was hit, and again drew a line between her checker and another of the opponents, and kept on snapping until she lost her turn by a miss. The distance was never more than four or five inches, but unevenness in the ground often made the shots difficult.*[27]*

Shortly after our arrival at this far more substantial and permanent home, furnished in sumptuous Chinese style (the sign of a good family), some of the man's friends arrived – one of whom had been attached to the *Hiraho* [Judicial Department], who wore purple, and another who had been an official in the *So-yo-komi-sho* [the Board that

Plate 20. An Okinawan gentleman

supervised the customs and manners of the people], who wore yellow – and we all sat, crossed-legged, *in a circle, with a cup of live coals, a little box of fine cut tobacco, and a spittoon, in the centre. Thus seated, in dreamy indolence they drew forth their little pipes from their belts, unsheathed them, took a mere pinch of the tobacco from the box, and placed it in the little metallic bowl of the pipe, which was not more than half the size of a young girl's thimble, lit it, and after two or three long whiffs, they would retain the smoke for a minute or more, and then, with a strong impulse, send it through the nostrils, as the opium smoker does. This ended the enjoyment for that occasion. The pipes were then returned to their sheaths, when a little tea-pot, holding less than half a pint, with half a dozen cups, each of about the capacity of* *three teaspoons, was brought by a servant, and a general sipping took the place of smoking.*[5] Rain water used to be collected in jars, and abounding with infusoria, was boiled before it was used, thus cholera and other water-carried diseases could be minimised. *The tea disposed of, the pipes were again resorted to, and thus they did alternate between tobacco and tea.*[5] The pipes were deliberately made small so that they could often be *replenished, in order to enjoy the flavour of fresh tobacco, which was considered a luxury.*[24]* Funakoshi and I were invited to partake of course, but as neither of us smoked we just sat there and listened to the debate about dancing and karate, a subject spurred by our presence. *Boys were in attendance with fans to cool us, as well as drive away the flies.*[11]

I should just like to interject a curio at this stage. Both Funakoshi and I were advised not to smoke or drink by both Itosu and Azato, and, whilst I never saw either of them smoke, they both drank. I have never really known what to make of this, and I confess that it did worry me. Perhaps they meant don't drink to excess? I know Funakoshi wrote that he never drank, yet he was not averse to a cup of *sake* every now and then, and I saw him drink *mooroofacoo . . . , a dark coloured cordial possessing a bitter-sweet taste.*[24] I, likewise, never smoked, but must also confess to the odd drink. I think a little may do you good. Occasionally, it can elevate the mind; allow it to soar. Yes, I'm sure that is what Itosu and Azato meant, otherwise Funakoshi would never have touched a drop.

Before rising to separate, the sake was introduced and circulated, sometimes beyond the limits of prudence and discretion. These were the 'lords of creation;' the poor women, meanwhile, might be seen, half naked, delving with the hoe or the spade, in the adjacent gardens, under a scorching sun.[5] In fact, Ichirazichi had purchased a number of commoners for a term of some years, though on Okinawa, a man could sell his services to a rich man for life.[iv]

The meal set before us was very fine – indeed, one of the finest I have ever had – following *the Chinese custom of giving the sweets first, and reserving the substantial part of the dinner for the last.*[24] I cannot recall now how many courses were served, perhaps eight to ten, though twelve courses were served at royal dinners, with the *sweet palate*[24] of the Okinawan admirably catered for. I remember that the first courses were soups of various kinds, these were followed by *gingerbread; a salad made of bean-sprouts and tender onion-tops; a basket . . .* [full of] *balls, composed of a thin rind of unbaked dough, covering a sugary pulp; and a delicious mixture of beaten eggs, and the aromatic, fibrous roots of the ginger-plant. The gingerbread had a true home flavour. . .*[5b] *Among the dishes, besides some sweet cakes made very light, were different kinds of pastry, one of a circular form, called hannaburee, another tied in a knot, hard and disagreeable, called matzakai, and a third called kooming, which enclosed some kind of fish. There was also a mamalade, called tsheeptang, a dish of hard boiled eggs without shells, painted red, and a pickle which was used instead of salt, called dzeeseekedakoonee.*[24] We also tasted dog, which was *considered a delicacy.*[26] Funakoshi ate with restraint, as was his custom.

Ichirazichi's friends departed, the worst for a little too much *sake*, but this was the invariable result when, quite deliberately, *pickles, onions, leeks, and other pungent or salt vegetables were taken to provoke thirst.*[26*] Pork used to have the same effect. One must also remember that food, especially during the summer months, had to be dried and salted, otherwise it would not have kept in that very oppressive heat and in an atmosphere constantly charged with vapour. *Furniture, dress, stores, etc, felt damp and clammy; surgical instruments rusted.*[26*] The heat, rarely rising above ninety-five degrees Fahrenheit in the shade, or one hundred and eighteen degrees in the sun, made for great languor and drowsiness, so one can understand why Okinawans drank. Drunkenness was, I am afraid to say, *accordingly universal, in all ranks, at all ages, and in both sexes.*[26] One of the friends was bitten by a venomous centipede, *whose bite produces the same effect as that of the scorpion,*[26] before he left the garden. What was particularly distressing in this case was that this poor fellow had been bitten on one foot, the other already causing him great pain by virtue of an infected wound caused initially by a needle from some spikey shrub.

Being a medical man, I should just like to record that *disorders of the digestive organs were most frequent, as might be expected in a people who were continually eating and weakening their stomachs with tepid and spirituous drinks. Hence arose flatulent dyspepsia, vomiting, diarrhoea, and dysentery.*[26*]

When all was quiet, Ichirazichi showed us what we had journeyed so far to see. But first he told us of a story. Once, he said, more than fifty years before, he had been travelling north-east of Potsoong, at his master's request, to visit a certain priest. Evidently, Ichirazichi had studied karate from a young age, but he would not reveal his teacher to us. Ichirazichi *visited a temple of Buddha, situated in a romantic copse of trees. The approach to it was along a path paved with coral*

slabs, partly overgrown with grass, and under an archway in the for-
mation of which art had materially assisted the hand of nature. After
resting a short time in this romantic situation he descended the paved
way, passed some tall trees, among which was a species of erethrina
of large growth, and arrived at the house of [the said] *priest, who*
invited him to smoke and partake of tea and rice. Three young boys
were in the house, who, as well as the priest, had their heads shaved
according to the custom of the priesthood of China.[24] The two men
spoke about karate, and they spoke about dance. The priest, who
Ichirazichi also failed to name, knew the young man's master well, and
had been friends in childhood. After talking for many hours in the
shade, the old priest excused himself for a short while, and returned
with a heavy black box, inside of which were a set of fifteen exqui-
sitely carved ebony figures of ancient origin. The priest arranged the
figures in a certain sequence upon the floor, and sat back. Ichirazichi
said to us that he didn't know what he was being shown, and after a
while in thoughtful contemplation, bowed. The priest smiled, got up,
and, taking the position of the first figure, made the sequence of figures come alive in the form of a dance that wasn't just a dance.
Ichirazichi explained that he had never seen anything like it before.
The timing, the movements, the breathing, were those of dance, yet
they were also, strangely, those of karate. He said the form was like a
link between dance and karate *kata*. When the priest had finished, he
went to the carved figures, picked them up, and put them back in the
box in a jumbled fashion.

When he had finished his story, Ichirazichi stood up, asked us to be
patient, and walked out of the room. In a short while he returned
bringing with him a number of musicians carrying their instruments.
Funakoshi and I hadn't expected anything quite so grand as this! But
Ichirazichi explained that Masters Azato and Itosu must have had good
reason to send their pupils to him and out of respect for both of them
and their students, he wanted to give a proper account.

These were first-rate musicians with top quality instruments. The
sounding box of the *samtching* [*samisen*] player's instrument was
covered in python skin for example, the more usual and cheaper
alternative being goat's skin.[v]

Another musical instrument was the lengthy and heavy *kutu* [*koto*].
The instrument, over six feet in length and rectangular in shape, was
brought in by two men and laid carefully upon the floor. This was a
very fine instrument indeed, and extremely expensive. These were
professional musicians.[vi]

Another player had a *fuye*, a bamboo flute about fifteen inches in length, without keys, with ivory heads and ferrules, which was the only wind instrument on Okinawa. Whilst another had two drums – the *o daiko*, a large drum about eighteen inches in diameter, and the *ko daiko*, a small drum less than one foot in diameter, and a number of other percussion instruments. The drums were played with sticks.

Of all the music and song on Okinawa in my day, the human voice was the most important part to which the instruments formed a background. Our guest had had a singer booked as well, and was intent on doing us proud. I cannot remember now, what the music and song were called. But all the favourite ceremonial songs were about two hundred and fifty years old at the time. I seem to have a vague memory that it was like *Kajadifu*, and certainly not reminiscent of the more livelier songs, such as *Washinutui*.

We noted that the dance contained techniques we had seen our teachers refer to, such as *ippon-ken* and *keito*, but we, ourselves, had never yet practised. These techniques were performed slowly of course, and we asked Ichirazichi what his interpretation might be. We expected an historical or artistic definition, but instead, without a word, and in the most expert manner, he freely demonstrated their application upon us both. His speed was exceptional; the power, light, but truly penetrative. Funakoshi and I were speechless. We had never seen anything like it. When I close my eyes, I can see Ichirazichi's face quite clearly, smiling at our reaction, and I suppose it must have reminded him of his own, half a century before. We later found out that Ichirazichi had been a contemporary of Sokon Matsumura, and had trained in karate with him for many, many years. I am pleased that Funakoshi noted Okinawan folk dances in both his first book, *Ryukyu Kempo Karate*, and in *Karate-Do Ichiro*, for they must have had an effect on him too!

Another point that we were told was that karate-like moves and techniques had been integrated into theatre. It has been said that *Okinawan dramatic performances stand in the position of a rustic first cousin to those mediaeval Japanese lyrical dramas, called No no Utai and No Kyugen . . . Whereas the Japanese No theatre is patronized chiefly by the aristocracy, who alone can understand the obsolete poetic dialect in which the pieces are written, its Okinawan poor relation attracted the lower classes.*[4b*]

The theatre buildings were very ramshackle affairs, enclosed only as high as the eye-level of the passers-by in the street, and poorly *roofed in overhead. The rafters and supporting pillars were, however, elaborately decorated with dingy, painted dragons, snakes, phoenixes, and pink peonies, in accord with all things Japanese and Chinese.*[27]* *The spectators squatted on rather dirty matting, which was stretched anyhow on the uneven wooden boards, the back part being raised a little to enable those behind to see. People ate and smoked and came and went, and children played and cried, unmindful of the actors.*[4b]* *The audience squatted and indulged in tea and cakes, or sipped hot shoju* [an alcoholic beverage made from millet] *from little pewter cups no bigger than a thimble, all the while talking in a steady stream, apparently paying no attention whatever to the play.*[27]*

The first time I went I could not gather any definite impression from the mixture of much singing and dancing and little dialogue, except that the play was taken from the ancient native history, for the title was stuck up on a board on the stage . . . Part of each play was sung by an invisible chorus, and invariably there was dancing. Sometimes the dancing was itself the piece de resistance, and was very rhythmical and pretty, much of it posturing, none of it so rapid and violent as the ballet-dancing of Europe. As a rule, the dancers numbered four, or some multiple of four. The musical instruments played were the . . . jamising[vii]*, the flute, and the drum. These were really played, not deafeningly banged, as in the case of the Chinese stage; and the music seemed a degree nearer to that of Europe than either Chinese or Japanese music . . . It was, however, monotonous enough, certain short phrases being repeated to satiety. From the Okinawan jamising the better-known shamisen was derived in the seventeenth century. . .*[4b]* *The orchestra . . . struck up a rhythmical march at the entrance or exit of the principal actors.*[27]*

The actors, who *were a much despised class, on account of their dissolute habits,*[27] wore costumes peculiarly Okinawan, and performed short, concise plays, on incidents in Okinawan history. The 'T' shaped stage had a permanent scene upon it. The two arms of the transverse bar were used chiefly for entrances and exits of groups of actors. The right arm was *divided in the centre by a rustic bridge, which was supposed to pass over a rushing river; on the left there were a few genuine gnarled trees, which represented a grove. At the back* [of the stage] *hung a broad curtain, beneath which corpses rolled themselves when they had lain long enough on the stage to give the audience a realizing sense of their deadness, and from under this same curtain ghostly arms clad in black sleeves appeared and removed fallen hats, or broken spears, after an affray. On each side of this curtain were* *doorways also closed with curtains. Through these, the majority of the players had their exits and entrances, and they served as the doorway to a hut or a castle, without so much as the suggestion of a difference in the shade or color of the hangings.*[27]*

All lines were sung by the actors in a *monotonous, chanting tone, letting the voice drop at the end of each line, but there was not the stilted, squeaky tones of the Japanese actors nor the obtrusive din of gongs and drums, which accompanied all Chinese histrionic efforts; the voices were all mild and gentle.*[27]* Before I left for Japan, and up to the early 1890s, women took part in the plays, but with 'Japanization' they were prohibited. Readers might also like to know that *courtesans and the women who used formerly to act in the theatres were not allowed to be* [sufficiently] *tattooed; they were not supposed to work, hence they had to be distinguished from the workers, and they were allowed to put only two large dots on the first phalanx of the middle fingers of both* hands.[27]*

Funakoshi and I accepted the hospitality of our host and lodged the night, and the next day, the fifth day of the fifth month, as fate would have it, was the date for an inter-village tug-of-war, for which we also stayed. These were very popular at the time, especially in rural districts, as was a primitive type of horse-racing, and indeed, Funakoshi made mention of them in his autobiography. *For each of the opposing parties* [in the tug-of-war] *enormous grass ropes were twisted at least eighteen inches in diameter, with a large loop at one end and with side ropes that could be grasped. The opposing parties, fifty or more in number, camped opposite each other all day, stirring up rivalry and excitement by gibes and sneers. At midnight, the loops on the ends of the two ropes were brought together and interlocked with a stout pole. At a given signal the tug began. The point, marked by a flag, beyond which the people had to be dragged to constitute a victory, was only a few feet from the start, but those few feet were fought for with the zeal of desperation. The laggards and the lazy ones were kept up to their work by a force of exhorters, who, in addition to their sharp tongues, wielded flaming torches, wherewith they singed the legs of those whose sinews were not sufficiently strained. Women did not join in, but stood by and 'rained influence' with smiles and cheers, although from appearances I should have thought that the women could have pulled harder than the men. When the pole had passed the line, the victors, with a wild rush, invaded the territory of the vanquished, and the night ended in revelry at the expense of the defeated.*[27]* When it was time to leave, Ichirazichi called us into his private quarters. He bayed us sit.

We thanked him for all he had done and for what he had imparted. He held two short notes, one each for his good friends Azato and Itosu, and then placed them in our hands for safe delivery. Beside him was a stout wickerwork basket. He removed the lid and withdrew a black ebony box. He opened the box, and there, before us, were those mysterious figures of centuries past . . .

Whilst music and dance formed the distraction of many, the composition of verse was a favourite pastime of the upper classes on Okinawa. Okinawans had a stanza consisting of four lines, whereof the first three had eight syllables, and the fourth had six syllables, an arrangement differing from any adopted by the poets of China or Japan. Many a time, as children, my siblings and I we would be taken out for a picnic, and poems would be composed by the adults, but we, as children, were invited to have a go, in-between our kite-flying and games of *Chang koro*, which again was very popular in the nineteenth century. *Chang koro* was played with shells. *The object of the game was to turn the shells over on their concave side by throwing another shell down upon them. The shell which was thrown must, after accomplishing its object, also land with its concave side down.*[27]* In fact, *Chang koro* was a gambling game, with the shells representing copper *cash* or Japanese *sen*. If the thrown shell did not land concave side down, it was left until forfeited or redeemed.

I remember one such picnic my family had when I was a small child, overlooking the sea, where *the white beach-sand struck in our faces.*[5a] Brilliant white terns were flying, then diving into the shallows. The curlew and sea-snipe darted about by the waters' edge, and I caught a brilliant scarlet coloured fish, off a rock. The pectorals were tipped with orange and yellow and the tail had two clear white bars on it. My younger brother spent the afternoon catching *kohatatate* and *Nomigutsi*[viii], in the rockpools. I recall the curious stalactitic cave ten miles from Naha at Futemma.

Here the little pools teemed with life – *crabs, snails, star-fish, sea-prickles, and numbers of small fish of the intensest blue colour . . . The coral grew in rounded banks, with clear, deep spaces of water between, resembling, in miniature, ranges of hills covered with autumnal forests. The loveliest tints of blue, violet, pale green, yellow, and white gleamed through the waves, and all the varied forms of vegetable life were grouped together, along the edges of cliffs and precipices, hanging over the chasms worn by currents below. Through those paths, and between the stems of the coral groves, the blue fish shot hither and thither, like arrows of the purest lapis-lazuli; and others of a dazzling emerald colour, with tails and fins tipped with gold, eluded our chase . . . Far down below, in the dusky depth of the waters, we saw, now and then, some large brown fish, hovering stealthily about the entrances to the coral groves, as if lying in wait for their bright little inhabitants. The water was so clear that the eye was deceived as to its depth, and we seemed, now to rest on the branching tops of some climbing forest, now to hang suspended as in mid-air, between the crests of two opposing ones. Of all the wonders of the sea which have furnished food for poetry and fable this was assuredly the most beautiful.*[5a]

There is a land crab that inhabits the Ryukyu that used to be very numerous, so much so in fact that on occasions the sea shore seemed to move as they congregated in their thousands. I believe this to be especially true most notably for the southern group of islands, the Meia-co-shima. I remember my grandfather telling me about this. On one occasion, as a senior member of the Foreign Office, he had been asked to travel to China with the tribute party, and the captain had had to divert to the small island of Pa-tchung-san [Ishigaki Island], about eighteen miles in length and no more than six miles wide at the widest point, and secure the ship in a sheltered bay of emerald green water, to effect immediate repairs. Pa-tchung-san is famous for its black pearls, which are unique to the island.[ix] They were all sitting in a circle, along with the locals, around a large wood fire on a white, sandy beach, and *some young boys brought in several large crabs, having . . . their foot-claws covered in a very remarkable manner, with a quantity of coarse silky hair, so very dense and thick that they more resembled rabbits' feet than the claws of a crustaceous animal. These curious crabs . . . were immediately . . . thrown upon the embers alive, and when burnt to a crisp and brown, broken by the teeth of the assembled islanders, and consumed, with a few exceptions, shell and all. They appeared very much to relish this primitive, and somewhat savage type of feast.*[11a]

I remember the 'hidden-footed crab' that we used to track down. They were well concealed under their camouflaged shells. I recall too, the snake-tail starfish. *This singular animal inhabits the reefs near the shore, protruding its black scaly rays out of its retreat, ready to entrap the unwary prey, and draw it under to destruction. But if a powerful enemy seizes the exposed limb, it does not mind leaving it in the possession of the assailant, provided the safety of the remainder can be secured by the sacrifice, well knowing that the defect will shortly be supplied by a new growth. Their neighbours, the crabs, have a similar facility of repairing any mutilation of their limbs; and we might almost fancy that the two could attack and devour each other by turns, providing each other with a continual feast.*[13a]

As a child, I spent many happy hours collecting shellfish, which formed a principal article of food then, and studying the octopi that were washed up on the shore, some very large, with a spread of more than twelve feet. I used to delight in investigating sandy pools and under rocks for a curious looking shrimp-like animal, that when disturbed, and as an act of defence, would make a loud, sharp clicking sound, by snapping its foot-claws. I can still smell the almost insufferable stench of opened cuttle-fish, left to dry. If you were lucky, and you knew where to look, you could spend hours watching green turtles swimming in the tranquil bays, but you dare not enter the sea to join them, ever mindful of the sharks and sea snakes that infested the warm waters.

Sea snakes were numerous in the bays and creeks, and their bite is exceedingly venomous.[18]* As children, we were forbidden to enter the sea, and that, I fancy, was why many Okinawans failed to learn to swim, of which Funakoshi and myself are typical examples. The inland lakes and pools, where a bird of the dense reeds, the gallinule, could be encountered, were also highly dangerous because of our reptilian friends. There were no swimming pools in those days of course.

And what of the sea-devil, so grotesque, so hideous a creature, that once seen it is not easily forgotten. We used to find these fish amongst the seaweed. I am certainly no naturalist, but they must surely rank as one of the strangest of animals. They are able to live out of water for considerable periods by inflating their bellies with air. I have seen them on land, and I have heard it said that they have been found ascending branches of trees searching for food.

When I was older, I used to practise stances in the fast flowing streams where snakes were not a problem. I loved doing that; it was exciting and a real challenge. The strength it gave my legs was considerable, for the resistance of water is great. I liked practising movements from the *kata Tekki*. I used to practise *kiba-dachi* against the flow of the river. *Kiba-dachi, kosa-dachi, kiba-dachi* against the flow – yes, that was it. Wonderful, I can feel the pressure around my legs now, the water rising and splashing my forward leg, and having to drive off against the current and maintain good posture against the elements. The *kiba-dachi* of those times was much higher than I see today, about half a stance higher, and we did not employ the rigid toes in and knees out; indeed, the toes simply pointed forwards, but the knees were bent slightly outwards and the weight was forward, so the knees were squarely over the toes. Sideward-on technique, that was what *kiba-dachi* was designed for, was where the stance's strength lay. I soon learned that. However, I would often face the current face on and root my feet in the sand or shingle below, my toes burrowing as deep as they could go. This was difficult training, especially as the force of the incoming tide increased, but I considered such training, *hara* training really, *tanden* focus, was absolutely essential, for *Tekki* defends and counter-attacks with an opponent coming directly on of course, as if one is backed up against a wall with nowhere to go, and the shorter stance certainly aided this. I had been advised to practise wholeheartedly, to build not just strong technique, but a strong and courageous spirit. I remember that on one occasion, a great storm rose up, the water swelled in anger, hail fell from the heavens, and there was I, hip deep in water, secured by a thin hemp rope, battling the elements.

This training was dangerous though. I could not swim, as I have said, and risked being swept away by current and turbulence, so I would secure the rope around a large rock or tree trunk and then around my waist. This was, after all, training, but there was still risk. Many a time the rope saved me, when the pressure against the flat sur-face of my abdomen was just too great for my stance. Funakoshi had the same idea and used to face winds of great force, holding a large mat before him, which acted as a sail, trying to maintain the straddle-legged stance. Typhoons normally occurred during May to August. I recall that Funakoshi tried my method and I tried his; it was good, and Itosu would have approved.

Talking about increasing strength, I remember that Funakoshi and I would spend time engaged in *tegumi* to improve muscular power and spirit. These were serious affairs. It was mutually agreed beforehand that the usual patting of the opponent's body would signify submis-sion, but this rarely happened because we were after improving our driving force, rather like in sumo. He was smaller than I, so his centre of gravity was lower, and when we locked together it was essential for me to get as low as I could, otherwise I would really just use my arms and shoulders. Getting lower, of course, was excellent practise for karate. Sometimes, on the way to Itosu's house, by the dim lantern when the moon was not up, we'd stop, lock arms, and lean in on one another. Funakoshi's grip was notable, and, particularly he had a *formidable left hand.*[g] He was also *rather stubborn,*[g] and this made him a good opponent. I don't think we ever practised on the way back though, for we were always too tired.

Funakoshi also practised with the *bo*, and I trained a little with the *non-shaku*. *Non-shaku was played with a stick about three feet long to which was attached a rope. The object of the game was to disarm the opponent by whipping the stick out of his hands,*[27*]and Funakoshi and I used to engage with our weapons.

In those days, it was normal to train in a form for some three years before learning a new one, but in the six years I trained with Itosu *Sensei*, I learned only *Tekki*. I like to think that I got to know the *kata* quite well. I was advised then, and believe now, that there *is infinitely greater value in studying a single kata until one has digested it well than in possessing a shallow knowledge of thirty kata.*[b] I never graded, as gradings, as such, never existed in karate at the time. I believe this lack of external acknowledgement caused Funakoshi problems when he began teaching karate in Tokyo.

Tekki was Sacred Fists' [Itosu] favourite form, and, of course, he later created *Tekki Nidan* and *Tekki Sandan* from *Tekki Shodan*. I know that Funakoshi spent ten years under Itosu learning the three forms. *Tekki* is an important *kata* of Shuri-te, but Itosu, who had originally learned the *kata* from a Chinese who resided in Tomari, changed the original form. Funakoshi and I therefore learned the Itosu version and not the earlier one, and it is this later form that, through Funakoshi and [Kenwa] Mabuni, became well known in Japan.

It now seems opportune to get technical and to mention what seems to have changed from the Funakoshi *Tekki* of today [1962], compared to the Itosu *Tekki* eighty years before that I learned. I have practised the *kata* over all those years, alas not every single day as Itosu instructed, but I hope that my account is true. Unlike Motobu, who likewise knew only *Tekki*, it may not be said that I have mastered the form.

Tekki Shodan, and, later, *Tekki Nidan*, I understand, used to be practised in *naihanchi-dachi*, with the feet pointing inwards, concentrating the power inwards*; Tekki Sandan*, on the other hand, was originally practised in *hachiji-dachi*, with the feet pointing outwards. Funakoshi changed this so that all were practised in *kiba-dachi*, in what became known as Shotokan. Other schools that practise the *kata* may use other stances, at least one of which prefers an inverted form.

The first point to note is, I suppose, quite minor, yet it is one that I have observed. On the preparatory opening move of *Tekki Shodan* {47/*Yoi*} [see the Introduction, pages 44 and 45 for an explanation of bracketed numbers] – which is both a sign to opponents that one has no weapons, whilst at the same time guarding the groin – is that when we brought the feet together[x] to begin the form, the opened hands, left over right, palms down, were angled to form more of a 'X' shape, and not placed more as if left overlaid the right.[xi] Also, the thumbs were not bent, but left opened and free.[xii] This reminds me of the preparatory opening move in the *kata Wanshu* [*Enpi*]. Whereas today, the right fist and left open hand are brought to the left hip, in yesteryear they were brought to the solar plexus {—/*Yoi*}.[xiii]

There were no *fumikomi* {—/2a, 8a, 20a}[xiv], but there were *nami-ashi* {59, 62, 76, 79/10b, 11b, 22b, 23b}.

On the *koshi-gamae* {51/4}, we placed our hands in the same position as in the *Kushanku* [*Kanku-dai*] of the time, of which I will speak later, in other words, if the right fist was on the right hip, palm facing upwards, the left fist was on top, palm down.[xv] Today, I have seen the left palm, in that technique, facing the body.

The *kosa-uke* before the *uraken-uchi* {*ura-zuki* 56/9a} used to be more distinct and thorough.[xvi]

I should also like to say that *ura-zuki* seems to have replaced *uraken* in *Tekki* in some quarters. I must confess to always having practised *uraken*, and Funakoshi referred to the technique, when he refers to it specifically, in all three *Tekki*, as back-fist strikes. I am not sure what has happened here, for the former is a punch, the later, a strike, and their delivery and consequent feeling are very different. Also, the contact area is not the same, at least according to Funakoshi, for the *uraken* in the forms is focused on the philtrum, which is between the nose and upper lip, whilst the *ura-zuki* is generally focused on the chin.

In the *morote-zuki* {65/13}, sometimes the augmented arm took a greater forward role with the fist of that arm opposite the elbow of the punching arm[xvii]; sometimes it was less so, with the fist of the augmented arm opposite the armpit of the punching arm[xviii]

When I learned the *kata*, there were no *kiai*.[xix]

After the first *kiai* today, whilst maintaining the augmented right arm position, we did not, in my time, bring the left fist back below the right armpit {—/14a}, but commenced the *haishu-uke* immediately with the left hand, from the *morote-uke* position, whilst bringing the right fist back to the right hip. This move provided the most obvious difference in the changes in the *kata* I have seen.

Of course, *Tekki Shodan* duplicates the techniques and moves on the other side, and I shall not repeat the above differences.[xx] The second *morote-zuki* and *kiai* finish the active *kata*, as it were, and the last difference is not repeated, for one then comes to *yamae*.

When we came to *yamae* {83/*Yame* – B}, we used to bring the feet together in the same way, but the fists did not return to the open position already described, but were, rather, placed in the *yoi* position. The *enoi* was different therefore.[xxi]

At the end of the last active move on the *kata*, we used to keep our focus on the opponent for about two seconds, which is more than today. The *zanshin* of our day was more penetrating.

From the commencement of the opening technique to concluding the final technique, took Funakoshi and I about thirty-two seconds, much as it does today, though the timing within the form was notably different in places.[xxii] Funakoshi's timing was of the first-order, showing evidence of the effects of long and arduous practice, in that his movements and techniques were crisp and sharp. I would also like to recommend his suppleness in his hips and knees, which I understand was a feature of his karate into his seventies before he acquired an arthritic hip problem. As a youth, his hip use was excellent, and retained the Chinese feeling or flavour of the *kata*, something the Japanese that I have seen have been unable to readily imitate. *Tekki* is a Japanese form; *Naihanchi* is Okinawan.

Now, I must speak about the topknot incident that changed Funakoshi's life. *There was no variety in the fashion of dressing[2] the hair. The head-dress of the men . . . was quite different from the old-fashioned head-dress either of China or Japan.* [As I have previously noted] *the men and boys of all classes shaved a space on the top of the head about two and a half inches wide, extending from an inch and a half back of the margin of the hair, in front, to the crown of the head. In arranging the hair, the side, back, and front locks were combed together up to the crown of the head, and there tied, tight and close, to the scalp; the wisp of hair thus made was about sixteen inches long, and was stiffened with oil until it would almost stand alone; the oil used was exceedingly thick, and had not an altogether unpleasant odor of oranges . . . When this spike of hair had been sufficiently slicked, smoothed, and pulled – a stage in the proceedings proclaimed by the expression of abject agony on the face of the victim (often in the street entirely devoted to their trade we used to watch barbers at their work) - it was divided into two parts, whereof the larger was bent into a loop about three and a half inches high, and the smaller was wrapped around the base of the loop, making a stump at least an inch high, with a loop on the top. This loop was bent backward and down upon itself, until what was its upper curve encircled the base of the*

Plate 21. An Okinawan man

stump. To hold all this in place a [gold], *silver, nickel. . . brass* [copper or wood] *pin, with a head forming a five-petaled flower . . . was shoved from in front through the base of the stump and held down the curve of the loop at the back, while a second smaller pin, slightly scoop-shaped, held the loop down at the sides. This was the universal head-dress in Okinawa, and it was adopted by small children even of four or five years of age,*[27*] when I was a growing up. Our jet black hair was kept glossy by juice expressed from a leaf, and the time taken by a *shizoku*, each day, on its preservation and presentation, was up to one hour, which would, no doubt, seem grossly self-indulgent, not to say narcissistic, today.

Additionally, whereas the *hatchee-matchee* was worn by the higher ranks on special occasions, *the lower orders occasionally tied a coloured cloth or handkerchief round the head . . .* [which they called] *sadjee.*[2]

The topknot incident referred to by Funakoshi in his autobiography was actually a continuation of a problem amongst the Okinawan gentry that had gone back more than twenty years, when a fierce dichotomy had forced a wedge between the *shizoku*. The White Faction advocated closer ties with Japan, whilst the Black Faction advocated closer ties with China. Those who were for ending the top-knot were called Kaika-to, those who wished to keep it, Ganko-to. This dichotomy reached a zenith in the 1860's. Fierce debate raged not only between families, but also within families. To show the gravity of the debate, four people were executed.

The cutting off of the topknot was thus seen as a very tangible sign of one's allegiance towards what was happening in Japan. Cutting off the pride of manhood advocated support for the Meiji government; the keeping of the topknot was seen as support for the Tokugawa shogun. Fifteen years after the edict banning the topnot, many gentlemen had still not complied. Funakoshi could not escape the edict, and was caught out. He succeeded in changing his official date of birth, by changing his records, for only students born in or after 1870 could sit the medical examinations, but he kept his symbol of manhood a little too long. It is my personal view that he would have made a first-class doctor, but instead he became a first-class teacher. I am told his daughter[xxiii] married a doctor. Funakoshi shaved his topknot to the utter consternation of his family, and thus sided with Azato, who no doubt influenced him, and looked to the future. I, on the other hand, being better connected, sidestepped the edict.

In fact, the cutting off of the topknot backfired. The Japanese authorities cut off the topknots of criminals, and so, as no one wanted to be thought a jailbird, the topknot was kept!

Over the years following Sho Tai's abdication, the landscape began to change as rice fields were forsaken and sugar cane grown to satisfy Japanese interests. Sugar cane had been introduced to the islands by Gima Shinjo more than two hundred and fifty years earlier, and his contribution had always been appreciated by the Okinawan people. The village, not the individual, was taxed in sugar, and payment was shipped to Osaka. This had a disastrous effect on the villages, as they were dependant on foreign markets, and lost their self-sufficiency. I remember when riots broke out in 1882 and 1883 on Aguni Island due to corrupt tax collections methods, but I can not recall whether this involved sugar or not. In 1885, 1886, 1888 and 1889, riots also broke out in isolated spots throughout the islands as the result of the tax system. In those days, there were, essentially, four types of tax: land tax (the principal tax), special produce tax, miscellaneous tax, and poll tax.

When I used to go riding from Shuri, the patches of sweet potato met *the eye in every direction, cultivated in broad, flat beds, from eight to ten feet across, and seldom more than thirty feet in length . . . and separated from others like them by narrow and dry ditches and corresponding dikes. But few of these beds had entire possession of the soil, for, generally, they had growing in them at the same time a crop of the common kidney-bean, planted in rows two or two-and-a-half feet apart. . .*[6] The sweet potato came in two distinct varieties, white and red, and were often *watery, small and stringy.*[6] The beans on the other hand, were very prolific, and were *handsome, fat . . . with a black elevated ridge in the place of the eye.*[6]

Perhaps this would be a good time to very briefly mention some of the other crops we grew on the island too? Rice was the most important crop when I was a boy, and this was best grown in the central and eastern portions of Okinawa, and was cultivated everywhere with great care and attention. The fields, when ripe, were said to be beautiful beyond description. Everywhere was seen as potential for rice growing, even in mountain gorges. If the land could be ditched, diked and flooded, it was. Mountain terraces abounded, fed from the numerous fast flowing mountain streams. The water was *soft and almost entirely free from calcareous matter.*[8] There was no call for either the water-wheel or endless-chain pump to raise water to the higher levels. The rice, however, could not be called fine, *as the color was often reddish and striped; yet the plain was very good, and it was very nutritious.*[6]*

Tara was also grown in the low, wet land. Of the cereals, wheat, barely and millet, were the most common. Winter-greens were not widely cultivated, but I remember that they were grown near Tomari. Mustard, although it too thrived, was not extensively grown. The carrot and parsnip were small, long and well flavoured. Turnips were small too, and flat, and were pickled in salt and water. The abundant Okinawan radish was seen as a most remarkable vegetable by all who were not familiar with it, notably because of its size. *Many of these were between two and three feet long, and often more than twelve inches in circumference . . . it was difficult to distinguish their tops from those of the turnip. To raise so long and so large a vegetable, we subsoiled to a great depth, and forced our plants with night-soil and liquid manure.*[6]* Such enormous radishes were boiled, and were amongst the favourite items of diet.

My people, regardless of class, were not troubled by any religious mysteries there might be. They were practical, taking care of their dead in a way that befits someone who knows that they will join them one day – in other words, with the greatest reverence. *When an Okinawan died* [in those days], *a mosquito-net was hung over the body, and curtains were drawn all around, so that none might see in. The weeping relatives relieved guard, one by one, in the chamber of death. The funeral was attended not only by the family, but by other mourners, who, said to have been originally the servants of allied families, had in . . .* [those] *times developed into a professional class that earned a livelihood by simulating transports of grief . . . On one spring afternoon, while on my way to visit that little gem of beauty, the royal pleasure-grounds at Shikina, I suddenly came on such a procession hurrying along a country lane – the Buddhist priest in front, then the coffin, then a train of some thirty persons, of whom five or six were hired mourners, apparently females, though immense straw hats hide their faces from view. They were attired in coarse cloth made of banana fibre; they uttered the most dismal groans, and tottered so that they had to be supported on either side by assistants, who, as it were, bore them up and at the same time pulled them rapidly along. The portion of the professional mourner's art most difficult acquirement and most highly prized, was weeping copiously through the nose. In the production of those unpleasant tears – for so by courtesy let us call them – the professional mourners were said to attain extraordinary proficiency.*[4a*]

The women wept openly under their long white veils, while men remained openly calm, though some found it hard to restrain their emotions. The women wore *peculiar horn skewers* [in their hair] *about ten inches long, four sided in shape, with a pyramid point at one end, and a spoon bowl at the other. They were made in inch sections of yellow and black horn, and stood up on the women's heads in the most aggressive way. None of those pins kept the hair very steady; it slipped in every direction, and frequently hung over one ear in the most dissipated manner.*[15]

In the tomb, the priest said *a short prayer and rehearsed the many good qualities which the corpse was sure to have had during life, and the body was laid to rest in the family fault, with the head pointing toward the north.*[27*] The participants received a cup of *sake* before leaving the tomb area to cleanse them of the pollution of death. I recall seeing some mourners returning home to their village using a most circuitous route, in the hope of fooling the spirit of the recently departed

Plate 22. Okinawan sepulchre

not to follow them, though spirits of the dead were only considered harmful if the deceased was not from their village. New residents in the village would have to wait generations before they could bury their dead near the village, and the urns, in the meanwhile, were placed in caves. I mention this point because when Funakoshi's wife died in the late autumn of 1947 in Oita, the villagers, instead of relegating her body to the mortuary at Usuki, allowed her to be cremated in Oita. As Funakoshi noted, '*it was, I think, the first time in the history of the village that such an exception was made. It was a touching tribute to her memory, to her special human qualitites.*c'

The Okinawans had no cemeteries, but rather, each family built a vault on its own ground. *Nearly a quarter of the town* [of Naha] *was nameless, silent tombland.*[15]* Every man built a tomb wherever he had land. Such vaults are to be found on the island dating back centuries, and were introduced from China in the fourteenth century, or perhaps earlier. As many such tombs survived the bombardment of the Pacific War, I should like to speak of them in the present tense, for the visitor to my home may still see them.

Most vaults are horse-shoe shaped, but some are rectangular. The straight-roofed *ie-geta* tombs, reminiscent of a house, are an older type. Some tombs have *low pyramidical roofs – some tiled, some thatched.*[2] *The vault is sunk, so as to make it equal with the surrounding ground, generally coral rock; but the space in front being lower still (for vaults are mostly built on hillsides), the whole height of the front walls is seen. There is a metal door in front, and in the court there sometimes stands a stone screen about four feet high, six feet long, and one foot thick.*[27] [xiv] *The brilliant white colour comes from the plaster used*[4a], which was a mixture of shell lime and white-wash. *Formerly, the dimensions of the vault were fixed by law, according to the rank of the family owning it.*[4a] An average size might be: total height, about nine and a half feet; total breadth, about twenty two feet; length of court enclosed by walls, about twenty-five feet; height of opening in front, about three foot six inches; breadth of opening in front, about two foot six inches; with the stones being about one and a half feet thick.

In the past, *the coffin, having been brought to the vault, was left shut up for two years. In the third year the relations assembled again, and the nearest of kin washed the bones with the strong spirit called awamori.*[4a]* Women performed the cleaning because it was believed that they had greater powers to expel evil, *and then* [after wrapping them up in white cloth] *deposited them in earthenware urns called . . . jishi-kami . . . the urns were temple-shaped, and decorated with such Buddhist emblems as lotus-flowers and horned demons' heads (intended to scare away real demons). The colours – creamy white, blue-green, and yellowish brown – were harmonious and reposeful to the eye* [and weigh nearly two hundredweight]. *As a rule, the bones of the husband and wife were placed together in the same urn. For children, as also for adult bachelors and spinsters – but Oriental communities* [of the time] *harboured few such – there were urns of half-size. All the urns of a family were ranged round the interior of the vault on shelves, tier above tier, in order of precedence.*[4a]* If, in the act of washing the bones, a stranger ventured near the tomb, it was said that the spirit of the occupant of the bones would be frightened away, and never find rest. *Burning was never used at any stage of the proceedings, nor under any circumstances.*[2]*

I cannot forget once riding out. I passed through a grove of young trees, and found myself close to a hamlet which lay at the bottom of a highly cultivated glen. The rough houses were almost entirely hidden by trees and bamboo, the latter being the most conspicuous. This hamlet *was surrounded by a close hedge, and every separate house also had an inclosure: some of the houses had attached to them neat arbours, formed by a light frame of bamboo covered with a variety of creepers. The rice fields were divided by small banks of earth, made to retain the water, and along the top of each bank there was a foot-path*[2] that I rode upon. I came, quite unexpectedly, on a tomb from which emitted *sounds of the most violent grief.*[28] It was the time for disinterment, and the relatives had assembled to witness the last rite being performed upon the remains of the deceased, as described above.

Funakoshi and I reflected once that the Okinawan tombs *were so carefully constructed, that we said that the Okinawans bestowed more pains and expense upon these retreats from all pain, than would suffice to accommodate many of the living. As if in contrast, several miserable huts, containing inhabitants more squalid and wretched than I had before seen, were scattered among the graves.*[13] I recall, also, that we reflected upon the contrast between Okinawan custom and the savages of Formosa, who used to bury their dead inside their houses.

I was, of course, witness to many funerals, one of which I recall attending with Funakoshi. *One day, wandering over the rough country paths about a mile from Naha, we heard sounds in the distance as if coming from a number of children playing a game which required a great deal of shouting. The sounds approached nearer and nearer, till there appeared over the crest of a small hill a procession carrying in its midst a large red box which . . . was a coffin . . . First walked a rabble of blue-clad villagers, then the chief of the priests, dressed in red robes, followed by two men carrying the coffin, and surrounded by a crowd of mourners. About a dozen professional female mourners followed the coffin, their heads and bodies covered with sackcloth bags and bowed down; their eyes being in this way completely hidden; of course they could not walk alone, so were supported on either side by women, to whom they clung around the neck, all the time screaming and wailing to express the general woe of the company over the loss of the defunct. These ladies, who were smothering their feelings under sacks, were obliged to raise them before approaching the burying place, as there was not room to walk except in single file. They raised the coarse sacking, then dropped it again, peeping out in haste; and they did it furtively, as if it were a wrong mode of procedure. The unfortunate mourners had already walked about two miles, wailing all the while, before we entered the procession.*[15]

One point that should be recorded is that periodically, as one might expect, offerings to the spirits of departed ancestors were made. As in China, so in Okinawa, *offerings of eatables* [were offered], *and, when the materials of the feast had remained a certain time that the ghosts* *might consume the subtle ethereal portions of the meat, the grosser material particles were taken away, and were feasted upon by the living at their own homes.*[17]*

Another funeral I remember was one I came across when I was walking through *the dwelling part of Naha . . .* [and my attention] *was arrested by seeing a crowd of men all clad in the yellow banana-fibre clothes of mourners,* [as I have already mentioned], *and, hearing prolonged wailing in a house near by* [the owner of whom I knew] *. . . First came two men with flat drums and large brass cymbals, which they beat lustily, and following them were two children weeping and wailing in such an agony of grief that they had to be supported by an attendant on either side . . . Behind them came the hearse, or Gan, carried on poles on the shoulders of four men. The Gan was about four feet long by three feet wide, and had latticed sides and a roof like a temple or a Chinese pagoda, with bells at the four corners; it was the property of the town, and was loaned as occasion required. The dimensions may seem small, but then it must be remembered that, except in the upper classes, the usual position in which the bodies were buried was with the knees drawn up to the chin . . . Behind the Gan staggered four chief mourners, clad in the yellow of mourning and wearing on their heads flat straw hats about two feet in diameter. Each of these mourners, bent with woe, had two men to support and almost drag him along; genuine tears accompanied the woe-begone facial contortions . . .* [that] *not only coursed down the cheeks, but also* [as I noted previously] *flowed freely through the nasal ducts, producing a flow of mucus many inches in length, which, although a sight . . . most repulsively intolerable* [to westerners], *to the Okinawan mind was the very efflorescence of abysmal woe.*[27]*

The man who died was the very man who had caught me practising karate by the road, mentioned earlier, and his name was Ukuta. He was about fifty years of age, and had died, not from cholera, but from that other great disease of polluted waters and flies, dysentery. It must have been a severe case, with perforation of the intestine and severe haemorrhaging from the gut. His death came as a great shock to me, for the last time I had seen him, not long before, he was full of life.

It was the Okinawan custom, that when *death was near to hand, the eyes of the sufferer were closed, and so held until life departed.*[27]* Then, burial of the deceased took place *from twelve to twenty-four hours after death.*[27] I followed the cortege, as a mark of respect for a man I had liked, to the family tomb. *On the top of the coffin were placed the sandals last used; a small and prettily-made bag contain-*

Plate 23. Family tomb near Naha

ing all the teeth which had dropped out during life, and had been carefully preserved; also the parings of the nails just before death; in addition to these the body was provided with a pipe and tobacco-pouch, a teapot and some cakes, and a towel,[27]* so that he could enjoy Okinawan comforts in the afterlife. In those days, *in the burial of the better classes, thirteen kimonos of silk (a material worn in the Ryukyu Islands only at marriage and after death) similar in shape to those worn by the Japanese, except that they were a little shorter in the skirt, were put on the corpse, one over the other, varying in color from white, which was always the outermost, to red, blue, green, yellow, and purple. The peasantry put on only seven.*[27]*

A few days later, I rode past the tomb, and there, in the small enclosure immediately outside, in the thatched hut, Ukuta's wife was to be seen. She would live in that hut for seven days, eating hardly enough to sustain life, mourning. A more dreadful and pathetic sight would be hard to imagine. It was not uncommon for widows to die of grief during this period. Then, for the next fifty days, after leaving the tomb, the widow would return home and live in complete seclusion, only leaving the house in the early morning and after dark to visit the tomb. *On these occasions the mourner was draped from head to foot in a*

162

grayish-white cloth, and was attended by some near relative as a guide.[27]* For these fifty days, the widow would discard her metal hair-pin and wear pins made of bamboo. *Once the fifty-day period had elapsed, the bamboo pin was exchanged for a wooden one, and daily visits to the tomb were discontinued. After fifty days, a widower began to re-new social life, but a widow remained secluded for life. The wooden pin was worn for three years, by man or woman, and white cloth worn, until the ceremony of washing of the bones, when the tomb was opened. The hair-pins which were buried with the corpse at this time were removed and given to the younger members of the family, but a father's pin was the direct inheritance of his son.*[27]*

I remember a village, in the centre of which *stood a building like a temple, surrounded by a stone wall. It was filled with elegant vases of different shapes and sizes, closed up and ranged in rows on the floor; the verandah encircling the building was also covered in vases . . . Round the building bamboo poles were placed so as to lean against the thatched roof, having notches cut in them, to which bundles of flowers were hung, some fresh, others decayed . . . The elegant shape of the vases, and the tasteful way in which they were arranged, with the flow-ers hanging all around, gave to this cemetery an air of cheerfulness, which we are in the habit of thinking unsuitable to a depository of the dead.*[2]

Before concluding on the death rites of the Okinawans nearly a century ago, I would just like to add two postscripts. The first was that I recall visiting the graves of the Okinawan kings at the Buddhist tem-ple of Sogenji, in Shuri, a number of times. The funeral urns were truly magnificent. Secondly, and in direct contrast to the royal tombs, I remember investigating a cave I thought just a cave, but wasn't. I *dis-covered a corpse lying upon its back, half decayed and covered over with a mat.*[24] It was a *shocking spectacle . . .* [that] *much disgusted*[24] me at the time. If I close my eyes, despite all the illness and death I have been witness to, and the passing of so many years, the sight of that corpse still haunts me.[xv] But on to happier memories!

As boys, Funakoshi and I were shown where Capt. Maxwell and Capt. Basil Hall had kept their stores in 1816. Captain Hall's account of our island was very influential in alerting the West to our customs, and so I should like to provide an account of what I remember of the site. *It was an oblong inclosure, sixty yards by forty, surrounded by a wall twelve feet high, rather well built with squared coral: the entrance was by a large gate on the south side, from which there extended raised gravel walks, with clipped hedges, the intermediate* *spaces being laid out in beds, like a garden. The temple in which they feasted on the day of their first visit, occupied one corner of the inclosure; it was completely shaded by a grove of trees, which also overhung the wall. In that part of the garden directly opposite the gate, at the upper end of the walk there was a smaller temple, nearly hid by the branches of several large banyan trees; and before it, at the distance of ten or twelve paces, a square, awkward looking building, with a raised terrace round it. The temple first spoken of was divided by means of shifting partitions into four apartments, and a verandah running all around, having a row of carved wooden pillars on its outer edge to support the roof, which extended considerably beyond it. The floor of the verandah was two feet from the ground, the roof was sloping and covered with handsome tiles, those forming the eaves being ornamented with flowers and various figures in relief; there were also several out-houses, and a kitchen communicating with them by covered passages. In one of the inner apartments, at the upper end, there was a small recess containing a green shrub, in a high narrow flower-pot, having Chinese inscription on a tablet hanging above it on the wall. On the other side of the same room, there hung the picture of a man rescuing a bird from the paws of a cat; the bird seemed to have been just taken from a cage, which was tumbling over, with two other birds fluttering about in the inside: it was merely a sketch, but it was executed in a spirited manner. In one of the back apartments we found three gilt images, eighteen inches high, with a flower in a vase before them. The roof of the temple within was ten feet high, and all the cornices, pillars, etc, were neatly carved into flowers and the figures of various animals. The ground immediately round it was divided into a number of small beds, planted with different shrubs and flowers; and on a pedestal of artificial rock, in one of the walks close to it, was placed a clay vessel of an elegant form, full of water, with a wooden ladle swimming on the top. On a frame near one of the out-houses, hung a large bell, three feet high, of an inelegant shape, resembling a long bee-hive; the sides were two inches thick, and richly ornamented: its tone was uncommonly fine.*[2]*

That picture – the cage, birds, cat and man – what is one to make of it? Why has it stayed with me? Why do I recall it so vividly, now? I believe that Shuri-te may be out in the hands of the predator. Nahate and Tomari-te are safer. The man . . . who will save the karate of Itosu, through the Funakoshi line?

IV

HABU, JEEMA, A WEDDING, AND OTHER STORIES

Funakoshi wrote about an encounter with a *habu* at Sakashita, between Shuri and Naha, in the closing years of the nineteenth century, and like most people on the island, I too have a couple of tales to tell of meetings with this frightening creature. But before I progress, I should just like to say that, having read his account, and given his knowledge of the Way of karate, I have never really been able to grasp, despite what he wrote, why he pursued the snake into the potato field at night. It struck me as a very foolish thing to do, and most unlike the Funakoshi I knew.

Sugar was the principal industry on Okinawa, *and the process of manufacture was as primitive as could be imagined. A long pole, often a mere roughly-trimmed tree trunk, fastened at the top of an iron or wooden roller which turned two other rollers by means of cogs, was pulled round and round by a horse or bullock, urged to this work by one or two men with sticks, while two other men fed the mill with sugar-cane. The juice thus expressed was boiled on the spot, and then poured into tubs to solidify. The Okinawan sugar was a very dark colour and coarse quality. Most of it went to Osaka, in Japan. The manufacture of sugar in Okinawa dates from the seventeenth century, having been learnt from the Chinese.*[4a] The best sugar, and mats come to that, came from the Demon World, Kikai-ga-shima, a small timberless island where locals used cow and horse dung for fuel.

Anyway, rats liked the sugar of course. Two species of rats existed then – and undoubtedly still do – the house rat and another smelling strongly of musk. They outnumbered people on Okinawa in those days by at least three to one. These vermin, which are *of a very large size,*[7] provided the main diet of the *habu*, who would lie in wait for them.

I remember visiting a friend of my father's one afternoon, and coming upon his newly built farmhouse set in a sea of sugar cane. At that time, mainly because of the animistic beliefs of the people, when houses were built the natural spirits had to be informed what was going to happen and then pacified. Firstly, a *sanjinso* or *yekisha* [diviner] was consulted, who checked astronomical books and charts and gave his advice based on the birth date of the client. If all augured well, then the plot of land to be built on and the surrounding area had to be cleansed of evil spirits. Lumber, gravel from the beach, everything that had to be taken away from its natural setting, was believed to contain a spirit, and these spirits had to be approached in the proper way and then thanked for letting the builder use their 'homes' as part of the house he was building. A priestess presided over such ceremonies, and few people neglected them, for supernatural forces were seen as formidable adversaries, and life was hard enough without added burdens.

Considerable activity was going on outside, with attention drawn to the low farmhouse roof, which, despite its newness, had been damaged in a recent heavy storm. I sat on my horse for a while and then enquired what all the commotion was about. I was informed that a brown snake had been disturbed and had been seen slithering deeper into the thatch, where, no doubt, a number of rats spent the sunlit hours. This was in the summer, when the *habu* is at its most active and audacious.

A number of rough farmhands were banging the thatch with various long-armed farming implements, while a man of rank with an injured back, looked on. The fear was, of course, that the snake could literally drop into the home at any time, via construction work still to be completed. After I had introduced myself, against much protestation, I impetuously offered to help, as is the Okinawan way, and joined the labourers up a ladder. What possessed a man of my social rank, at the time, to do such a thing, I cannot imagine. I remember the flies thick near the pig pens and outhouses, and the mosquitoes whining incessantly around my sweating brow as I climbed up. I began to bang away with a stick, and, as fate would have it, the snake slithered out just by me, and I came, quite literally, face to face with death.

"*Haboo cootee sheenoong,*" [the sting {bite}of the *habu* will kill] someone cried.

In a split second I could see that it was angered and its snakeish temper very much aroused. I instantly let go of the stick I was holding, placed my hands either side of the coarse ladder, braced with my arms, kicked back my feet from under me, and slid down the ladder supports. Apart from painful friction burns and deep splinters embedded in my palms, I had escaped. I was indeed lucky, for the snake had, at the very moment of my sliding, struck over my head. I believe that karate had prepared me for acting the way I did. You see, I didn't have to raise myself up a little to take the weight from the rung and shift my balance before jumping backwards. I later told Itosu *Sensei* about the incident, and I remember him saying that self-defence could take many forms, and that the benefits of karate training were innumerable. The snake was eventually killed and my father's friend, grateful that I was alive, invited me to dine.

The meal was sumptuous: hard-boiled eggs cut into slices, fried fish in butter, sliced smoked pork, and sliced pigs liver. Tea, poured into cups of moderate size, had an infusion of hay. Pipe and tobacco were taken during the short intervals between courses. There was coarse, soft, black sugar, wrapped in unbaked dough, powdered over with rice flour, dyed yellow. Cakes like gingerbread nuts, and other cakes in many shapes including the shapes of wreaths. There was also cheese. We ate with the traditional chopsticks about a foot long and the thickness of a quill, which, in this case, were made of ivory (though they are normally made of wood), and always held in the right hand. Holding chopsticks in this manner caused me pain, as I was still very much feeling the effects of my wounds, despite the extraction of the splinters. The meal was all washed down with an ardent spirit called *samchew*, which I felt in need of after my experience. I don't recall my host's name now, but he was quite obviously *Ta-yin* [a Chinese title used by Okinawans to persons of rank], and I recall him constantly worrying aloud, "What would I have told your father should you have been bitten?"

The farm where the above incident took place was much larger than most, but typical nonetheless. It was about five *cho* [12.5 acres], and although this might not seem very much today, only about a handful of men owned that much land on Okinawa at that time [1880's]. The small, fat, well shaped black pigs, rarely going beyond one hundred and fifty pounds, were rooting about in pens. A number of dogs and cats wandered about in a state of domestication, as did a couple of goats, small wild boar and small wild deer. *The cattle too were small* [black and short-horned], *and the horses – or rather ponies* [which I have spoken of before] *– remarkably so, the majority being only from ten-and-a-half to eleven hands high, and some as little as ten hands; but they were wiry and extraordinarily sure-footed.*[4*]

The Okinawan pig, so ubiquitous on the island, was a stout fellow, though his meat was very superior in flavour. It was decided around the turn of the twentieth century to further improve the breed and the shape of the hams. Yorkshire and Berkshire pigs from England were imported with this goal in mind by the Okinawa Meat Preserving Company, who hoped to export meat to Hong Kong and Shanghai. I remember this because I had a friend who worked in the business, but I regret to say that I do not know the outcome of this experiment.

Okinawans used to make toothbrushes from pig bristles. I remember a gentleman coming from the Royal Brush Company in Osaka to determine whether this could be made worthwhile on a grand scale. However, the Okinawan pig was partial to scratching so much up against the sides of cottages that he reduced the silky length of his hirsute adornment, to the extent that the bristles could not be used for the finest brushes.

Pork was the principal meat of the islands, and once the flesh was eaten, the blood was a useful commodity, which, amongst other things, supplied a substance for a certain stage in the manufacture of the fine lacquer. *The lacquer industry of the Ryu Kyu employed many hands, owing to the amount of labour necessary to bring it to perfection. It had to go through thirteen or fourteen stages at least before a really good piece could be pronounced useful and perfect* [Salway*]. The rich brilliance of the scarlet lacquer of Okinawa was famous and highly sought after. At the family home we had some lovely pieces, covered in flowers, especially chrysanthemums, and of scenes, which were in duller hues, often purple, and raised from the brilliant background. It was, with much regret, on a later visit home from Tokyo, that I entered the best shop for lacquer in Naha and *found it filled with abortions in the shape of hideous large red lacquer breakfast cups, saucers, and even spoons, all of European shapes, perpetrated for export to America in connection with the Chicago Exhibition. How humiliating (is it not?) to see that in art, as in manners and in morals, the West cannot touch the East without corrupting and depraving it!*[4a] The pieces I saw were cheap and mass produced.

It may be worthy of note here that the *mammal most conspicuous in Okinawa by its absence was the monkey. This fact struck one the more on account of the wide distribution of the monkey in Japan, where it ranged as far north as the extreme north of the main island, despite months of snow and ice. Okinawa also has no foxes or badgers – a lucky deliverance in the opinion of far-Eastern Asiatics, by whom these animals were universally credited with supernatural powers of evil.*[4*]

If foxes and badgers were deemed evil, only the gods could have known what the *habu* was, and so I move on to my second encounter with this dreaded reptile.

It must have been just before I left for Tokyo that I was climbing a steep and arduous face of a mountain, for no particular reason other than to get to the top and, I suppose, to strengthen my legs. One does foolish things when one is young, and few Okinawans, for fear of snakes, would have placed their hands down in vegetation without looking first. When climbing however, this is not always possible. As any climber knows, ascent is easier than descent, and, having reached the peak of this particular climb and having admired the view, I was having difficulty finding footholds on the way down. At one point I was most precariously perched above a fissure, searching for a suitable grip amongst tuffs of grass that would easily give way, and having found some that would barely suffice in a fairly desperate situation, *I caught the sullen glare of two other eyes – sullen and leaden, and yet bright and sparkling, also alarmed with rage. They belonged to the flattened head of an ugly-looking snake, whose sinuous body and uplifted front indicated an active readiness for either flight or attack. I gazed and shuddered. I shudder now as the mind's eye returns to those flaming specks of rage which flashed their angry light within a foot of my nerveless hand . . . After a lifetime of hesitation and un-belief, I ceased to hesitate . . .* [and made a] *desperate leap.*

It was over. The very edge of the fissure [below me] *received me on its shelving side, bruised, panting, weak as an infant, and yet with whole bones and safety. It seemed as if the strength of a dozen men had rushed through my frame and thrown me bodily from the glaring eyes of that lifted crest, leaving me with cold drops upon my brow and a sickening feeling of overtaxed muscle throughout my limbs.*

Slowly, I regained my feet, rubbed my bruised side with half-numbed hands, looked back for the now absent snake, and at the friendly clump of grass, whose torn and drooping blades gave ample proof of the service they had rendered.[22]

Like my first encounter, it had been a truly desperate situation. If I hadn't leapt and the snake had struck, the *bite always put people to sleep*,[22] as the local people put it.

Where did such energy come from that allowed me to leap as I did? What gave my mind the perception that such a leap was feasible? What gave my muscles the strength to jump so far? To this day I am per-plexed by these questions. I believe, having read other such accounts of individuals exerting great strength in other desperate situations, that human beings have a great deal of power of which they are largely unaware. Perhaps to tap this energy is what real martial arts training is all about?

I know that attempts were made at the beginning of this century [before 1904] to eradicate the *habu*. A laboratory was set up at Naze, the chief port of Amami-Oshima – a northern island in the Ryukyu chain, which was infected with snakes – under the direction of an institution in Tokyo, under the able supervision of a Dr. Yamamoto, who was based at Naze, but the project was headed by the eminent biologist, Prof. Kitasato. A serum was eventually found, but to this day, snakes strike terror among my people. Around the turn of the century, about two hundred people were bitten by *habu* on Oshima Island. Most died, but of those who recovered, many were greatly disfigured as a result of the poison upon the nerves.

Rats, then, were a real problem, but a way was devised to keep granaries completely free of them. A granary consisted *of a section of a reversed pyramid, built of thin plank, and set in posts six or eight feet high, and carefully covered in thatch - usually rice straw. To prevent rats ascending the posts and working their way through the thin planks to the grain, a section of a small pyramid made of broad boards, and shaped very much like the body of a house, was fitted over the top of each post, so that when the rats ascended to this point, they found it impossible to go further; for, to do so, it would have been necessary* [to travel] *down the inside of the hollow pyramid – a feat utterly impracticable . . . Without these precautions, much of the grain would have been destroyed* [6], and starvation the result. Many who saw it described such a method of rat avoidance as ingenious.

I learned a great deal from animals in my study of karate. I loved to fish, and although this was poorly regarded for one of my social station, I knew a local fisherman, an employee of the family, who took me out and never said anything. We used to fish for dolphins, which, when I look back, I wish I hadn't done. It is one of the great regrets of my life. I am ashamed. They are intelligent creatures, and, of course, mammals like us. However, the gods will not let me forget my part in their destruction, and as I must be complete in this work, allow me to describe the method we used to capture them.

We'd venture out in a dug-out canoe, and we would use lines. The traces were made from wire and the *hooks, when properly baited, were quite concealed in the body of the flying-fish which had one side of the flesh cutaway. Several lines thus prepared were allowed to run out to the length of about ten fathoms, and when the dolphins were near, speed was given to the canoe, that the bait might have the appearance of a fish endeavouring to escape pursuit. In this manner . . .* [dolphins could be caught]. *If the fish happened to be large, the line was careful-*

ly drawn in, and they were harpooned with an instrument which every canoe carried for the purpose.[24]

I remember once, when further away than usual, this fisherman took me to a small group of islands for a reason I now forget. *On the centre island was only one hut, which, as there was no reason to believe it to be the actual abode of inhabitants, it may be allowable to describe. The walls were sunk under ground, so that only the roof appeared from without, and inside was fifteen feet by six. The walls of neatly squared stone stones, being two feet high, and the roof in the middle about six or seven high, formed of a ridge pole supported in the centre by a forked stick. The rafters of rough branches were covered with reeds, and thatched over with the leaf of the wild pine, which grows on all the coral islands. The fire-place was at one end of a raised part of the floor, and the other end appeared to be a sleeping place. It was conjectured, that this wretched place could only be meant as a temporary residence of fishermen, whose nets we saw lying about; but the number of water jars and cooking utensils which we found in and about it, gave it the appearance of a fixed habitation.*[2]

As we walked back down the tiny beach to our boat, fishermen came around the cove. My mentor knew these men, and chatted for a while. *Most of these people had eeo stitchee* [fish spears] *tatooed on their arms in the form of a trident, with rude barbs. When drawn on the right arm it was called oodeemaw, when on the left, tooga.*[2] Okinawan men wore no ornaments upon their person, and, unlike for women, tatooing was far from being a common practice. I recall, *the pools of water left by the tide were full of beautiful fish of a great variety of colours.*[2]

I enjoyed fishing very much in my youth. I liked the uncertainty, the excitement of anticipation; the temporal space between action and reaction – if, and when, the quarry would bite, and my strike. Is there Zen in this? I believe so. There is a deep oneness between creatures – the stalked and the stalker. Outward form, appearance, may differ, but the composing elements are the same. I felt it when I fished sometimes, and I felt it on the first occasion I faced a *habu*. I believe this awareness, in subtle form, affected my study of karate, by slightly changing the timing in my *kata*; giving me an immediacy of technique and movement that I would otherwise have lacked.

I remember another incident that occurred about a farm that involved Funakoshi and myself. I recall that, on route, we passed Nakagusuku Castle, near Shuri, which had been destroyed in centuries past, but when I was a youth I visited the ruins often, for they were

Plate 24. Ruins at Nakagusuku

very impressive. The site was *surrounded by a wall nearly a quarter of a mile square, from twenty to fifty feet high, and from ten to twenty feet in thickness. The stones used in its construction were sometimes large enough to weigh at least a ton, and must have required some more powerful means to elevate them than can at this time be discovered.*[8]*

I found Nakagusuku a strange place. *A flight of steep steps, cut in the rock, led downward on the northern side to a grotto under the foundation of the castle, at the bottom of which was a pool of cold, sweet water. The place was completely overhung by dense foliage, and inaccessible to the beams of the sun . . . The material* [of the fortress] *was limestone, and the masonry of admirable construction. The stones, some of which were cubes of four feet square, were so carefully hewn and jointed that the absence of any mortar or cement did not seem to impair the durability of the work. There were two remarkable points about the work. The arches were double, the lower course being formed of two stones hewn into almost a parabolic curve, and meeting in the centre, over which there was the regular Egyptian arch with its keystone . . . The other peculiarity was that in place of bastions there*

*were square projections of masonry, presenting a concave front which
would catch and concentrate the force of a cannon ball, rather than
ward it off.* But this fortress must have been erected many centuries
before the use of fire-arms of any kind could have been known to the
Okinawans.[5b*] So, like the phallic stones mentioned earlier, this was
another mystery.

I once paced the dimensions of the fortress out, and noted them
down in an archaeology and architecture book that I kept as a young
man, for they were interests of mine. As luck would have it, I kept that
little book and the dimensions were, for the interested reader: length,
two hundred and thirty-five paces; breadth, seventy paces; thickness of
walls at bottom, six to twelve feet; thickness of walls at top, twelve
feet; greatest height of outer wall, measuring along the slope, sixty-six
feet; height of wall from inside, twelve feet; and, angle of outer wall,
sixty degrees.[i]

Anyway, on our way across a valley further on in our travels,
Funakoshi and I were attracted by the appearance of a cottage, so
buried in *foliage as to be completely hid from our view till we were
within a few paces of the door. It was surrounded by a slight fence of
rods, about an inch apart, with a line of creepers along the top, and
hanging down on both sides. A wicker gate admitted us, and we
entered the house, which we found divided into two apartments, eight
feet square, besides a small verandah at one end. The floors, which
were made of slips of bamboo, were* [again] *raised about six inches
from the ground and covered with a straw mat. The walls were five feet
high, being neatly wattled with split bamboo, above which rose a
pointed thatched roof. It was occupied by an old man, whom we
appeared to have disturbed at breakfast, for cups and tea-things were
arranged on the floor . . . The little apartment we were in was as neat
as anything we had ever seen: on one side there was a set of shelves,
with cups, bowls, and cooking utensils; on the others were hung
various implements of husbandry, with hats and various dresses, all
clean and in order. Higher up was a sort of loft or garret, formed by
bamboo poles, laid horizontally from the top of the walls; on this were
placed various tools, nets, and baskets. The fire-place was in the middle of one side, and sunk below the level. On the outside, in the space
between the house and the fence, there was a pigeon house and a
poultry yard, and close to the little verandah . . . there stood two spin-
ning-wheels of a light and ingenious construction. All round on the
outside of the fence the trees were high and thick; and though the sun
was above the hills, the house was completely shaded except at one*

end, where a small opening admitted the rays into the verandah. We staid some time with the old farmer, trying to express our admiration of the simplicity and beauty of his cottage.[2]

I recall the old man not only because he was so clearly endowed with the personality that so epitomised the Okinawan people: gentle, unassuming, friendly, restrained, with a genteel self-denial, and displaying a great curiosity, though not rudely inquisitive to be obtrusive, but for a very special ability that I shall shortly relate. He had a strange, interesting accent, and we knew he wasn't Okinawan. We later found out that he was native to Yaku-no-shima, in the north-east of the archipelago, a circular island about fifteen miles in diameter. Heavily forested, supporting the *yaku-sugi*, highly prized for its timber, the old man had worked in the management of forestry in his youth, as befitted a *shizoku*, but this man's hair was long, white, and loose, which was virtually unheard of. What rank he actually held we were never to ascertain, for he wore no pins, and that, I fancy, had been his intention. *The inhabitants* [of Yaku-no-shima], *who numbered about nine thousand, enjoyed a reputation of an almost idyllic simplicity. Doors needed neither locks nor bolts in that happy land, where theft was unknown; and a man hanging up his coat on a bush would be sure to have found it untouched when next he passed by that way.*[4]* However, something had happened, and he was obliged to move to Sonai, the chief village on Iri-omote-jima, an island some fifteen miles long by twelve. It is a very mountainous island with dense forest. This island, in contrast, was quite different, with a quite odious climate of continual rain, and in those days, *fuchi*, malarial fever, was very common. The old man, on leaving Yaku-no-shima, had been employed on a mine on the island – I don't believe he was ever a miner – but the mine closed due to the intolerable loss of life, as a consequence of the appalling malaria.

Interpreting what the old man was saying was not always easy. At one point I had to confess, *"Sit'cheekarang"* [I cannot understand]. With a broad smile, he replied, *"Wang Doochoo cootooba yooshong"* [I am learning to speak Okinawan], and we all laughed heartily.

As the three of us conversed as best we could, the sweet song of an *aka-hige*, a ground bird peculiar to the islands, softly serenaded us, and a very large green tree-frog salamander, similar to that found in Japan, though the Okinawan variety has yellow on its belly rather than red, drew my attention to the trunk of an ancient tree, by which stood a tapered post, the top of which was covered with a bucket. Funakoshi and I knew exactly what this was – a *makiwara*. Close by lay a *tou*, used by many *karateka* for practising *tsumasaki mae-geri*. Somehow, this old man had been taught, but where and when we never discovered.

A *makiwara* was considered an essential piece of training equipment for *karateka* at that time, and I should like to say a few words about it.[ii]

A cuboid of resilient and springy wood measuring some six foot six inches to seven feet in length, three to four and a half inches in width, and three inches in depth, was sawn diagonally so that the ends tapered to about half an inch. Once cut, one therefore had two identical posts. A deep hole was then dug to the depth of at least one-third of the post, or better still, just under a half, and the previously thick charred end of the post was buried in the ground to the height of the chest of the intended user, and made secure. It was considered best to soak the earth at the base of the *makiwara*, and to pack large stones and earth firmly around it. The striking pad, the actual *makiwara*, was made from rice straw. One had to pack straw to the length of about fifteen inches, three to four inches in thickness, and then bind braided straw around it, leaving two or three inches at each end to allow for spread. Then one would soften the straw with a *chee-chee* [wooden mallet]. The *makiwara* was subsequently tied onto the top fifteen inches of the post ready for striking. Personally, I bound a strip of leather around it to minimise skin damage. After use, one covered the post with the *makiwara* still on it with a cover to stop the rain ruining it, and that's what the old man used the bucket for.

I also made a hanging *makiwara* [*sagemakiwara*] for kicking practice that hung like a child's swing from two hemp ropes. A large bundle of straw about twenty-eight inches in length and a foot or so in diameter was packed tightly and bound with braided straw as before, so that two inches were left free for movement each side. The weight was about two stone.

I have seen students at universities today hit the *makiwara* completely incorrectly, because in their search for hard hitting, they push through, and boast about their calluses. No, this is completely incorrect.

The first point we were told to remember when punching or striking the *makiwara* was to keep the shoulders down, for only by doing this could the *latissimus dorsi* muscles become properly engaged. If you were tense, the shoulders would rise, so a relaxed state was essential. We used to stand in *zenkutsu-dachi*, and, with our feet firmly rooted, keeping the body straight, and drawing power from the abdomen

Plate 25. *Makiwara* training in 1850

by keeping our hips low, we would twist our hips into *gyaku-zuki*, which would be locked-out as we focused our punches on the centre of the pad. Any injuries were treated by immersion in cold water. Of course, I would practise moves from *Tekki Shodan* such as *kagi-zuki*, *uraken-uchi*, and so on. For *kagi-zuki*, I would face the *makiwara* side-ward on. I suppose I used to perform about one to two hundred strikes a day, both sides, but Funakoshi and I never 'laid-in' to the *makiwara*, and so this gave the appearance that the techniques were light, though I can assure you the complete opposite was the case. We really used *makiwara* for mind training, for the mind was what we tried to project. Okinawan karate has never been about pushing power, it is about penetrative power, and that is why karate is an art.

The *makiwara* certainly needed a cover, for it rains about sixty percent of the year on Okinawa and this was August or September, which are the rainiest months – these are followed by the driest month, October (along with January). It was also quite hot, about thirty degrees centigrade, and the humidity was great. However, the *climate of Okinawa is a pleasant and salubrious one notwithstanding its moistness . . .* [for] *some of the other members of the archipelago . . . are less favoured in this respect, notably* [Amami-] *Oshima and Iriomote-jima, with their dampness prevalent throughout the year.*

Things are so bad on Iri-omote in this respect as to have given rise to a local proverb to the effect that it rains 'thirty-five days a month!' These are unhealthy places and in the summer, June and July, malarial fever is most prevalent.[4] I had been to Amami-Oshima but once, and not only was it extremely unhealthy, Naze was surely the dullest place in the entire Ryukyus. So, the old man had come to Okinawa many years before for his health.

It would have been difficult to have raised the subject of the *makiwara* with the old fellow, but when he knew we had recognised it for what it was, he bowed slightly, walked over to near where it stood, and bayed us, "*Eemeeshawdee*" [sit down on the ground], and the manner and ease with which he did so belied his years. Sitting there in the shade of small, but ancient, gnarled evergreens, that seemed to bend drowsily as if in tune with the midday heat, he enquired of us if we knew what the post was for, and when we answered that we did, he requested that we explain and demonstrate. Funakoshi enjoyed *makiwara* very much indeed, believing it to be essential to karate's practice, and after I suggested that he strike the pad – he was my junior, and this was protocol – he got up, took the cover off, placed it carefully beside the post, and proceeded to throw a number of punches that landed squarely.

The old man was, of course, seeing what we understood, and he called out, "*Choosa*" [strong]. But whether this was true, or just encouragement, I do not know, but from what was to follow, I fancy it was the latter. Then the old man gesticulated that it was my turn. I dislike demonstrating anything, always have done, but I reluctantly got up as it seemed only proper and fair. So, I too delivered a few punches, and received the praise of "*Gammacoo choorasa*" [good hips], which again I believe was well-intentioned encouragement. When we were both seated once more, the old man asked us who our teachers were, and we replied that we were not prepared to say. To this, he bowed low in understanding. Remember, the practice of karate was deemed illegal.

"I believe your teachers are different," the old man said. "You have different influences. You (pointing to myself), I think are a pupil of Itosu, and you (pointing to Funakoshi), are a pupil of Azato, but also Itosu?" He could tell from our faces that he was correct, and he laughed. Funakoshi and I found that astonishing, after all, the old man had seen but a few punches each, no more.

"Now I will give you something to take back to Azato and Itosu," the old man promised, and with that he rose, excused himself, and went into his cottage. Funakoshi and I thought it was some little gift and that we were to be the bearers, but we were wrong. The old man returned in a short while carrying a small, compact sheet of wood a good three inches thick, on which I thought some message had been inscribed, but he proceeded passed us and carefully fixed the wood over the straw pad by means of braided straw.

"You are students of great men," the old man announced, "and so I show you this, for I want them to know what I have discovered, for my time is short." He took up a high *zenkutsu-dachi*, and without any preparation hit the wood-covered *makiwara* once, a dull thud was heard, and he broke the attached wood with his fist. He then presented the two halves to us, one each. "Now you must go!" the old man ordered, and go we did.

Funakoshi and I were impressed with the man's demonstration, *tameshiwari* is easy to say, but always difficult to perform, but we knew our teachers could do the same, despite the thickness of the wood and the fact that it was 'sprung mounted.' We didn't feel that the man was pretentious; we didn't know what to think. When we next trained with Itosu *Sensei*, after the lesson, we produced the pieces of wood as requested.

"Now, tell me exactly what happened," Itosu said, "every detail," and we did. He sat quietly, and at length I ventured to break the silence.

"But is there anything very special in this *Sensei*?" I enquired, but Itosu did not answer. Instead, under his breath, he uttered, "*Koomoo teeda oosoo-ostang!*" [clouds obscure the sun], and we all sat in silence once again.

Eventually, Itosu jumped, "Yes! I know what he's done! By the gods, I know what's he done!" and turning to both of us he remarked, "Mark this day gentlemen, and mark it well!"

"But why *Sensei*?" I retorted, looking for support from my fellow trainee. "We don't understand." Itosu's reply literally raised the hairs on the back of my neck.

"Because the *makiwara* never moved," Itosu confided softly. "Jeema placed it on the *makiwara* so you could witness that very fact!"

Funakoshi and I turned to one another, our eyes revealing that we were replaying the event in our minds and looking for confirmation at the same time. Did it move, or didn't it? We weren't looking! The *makiwara* always moved when you hit it; we took that as obvious, as given.

Itosu sighed, stood up and shook his head, and muttered, "Eighty-five years old! A lifetime's focus. Would you believe it!"

It is true to say that Itosu, Funakoshi and I, were as astonished by the realization of what Jeema had shown as the natives of Tane-ga-shima, when they first witnessed a firearm being discharged by the Portuguese adventurer, Mendez Pinto, in 1542.[iii] It came down to education and effort, and back to this double-faced sword we shall now go, for back to Jeema we cannot go, as he died before we could return.

The Japanese enlarged the Okinawan school system with a view to indoctrinate and to assimilate. The Okinawan lifestyle was easy-going, almost casual and carefree, and many did not wish the rigorous discipline that their Japanese oppressors wished to force upon them in their pursuit for a colonial empire. It was really a question of language. The Japanese officials who ruled the island refused to speak in anything other than Japanese, so only the well educated among the people could communicate. In the early 1880's the two volume, *Okinawan-Japan Conversation Book* was published, a copy of which I still have on my shelves as I write. That little book served me well, if the truth be known. Within six years of my father taking a teaching post, the number of schools in the islands had nearly doubled, and within another six years, almost doubled again. I can still recall the first girls being allowed to attend school in 1885. But pupils were reluctant to go to school, and very few ever finished their course. Okinawans are stubborn by nature and distrustful of change, especially rapid enforced change. When my father started teaching, only about one in forty children attended school, quite a few of whom were married. They were very reluctant to abandon traditional dress and certainly did not wish to discard their topknots and pins. However, in March, 1888, a date I remember only too well, the pupils at the Shimajini Higher Primary School had their topknots removed and their hair cropped. Slowly, the sash, kimono and headband gave way to standard Japanese school uniform.

It was clear, as I have noted, what the purpose of these schools was. In each there was a portrait of the emperor and the empress. The Japanese students attached some special kind of reverence to these portraits, and treated them like sacred objects, which of course they were not. I can still recall the awe in which these pictures were held – here was a portrait of a living god – a feeling that the Japanese pupils tried to impart in the local children. The Okinawans, for the most part, would have nothing to do with it, seeing it for what it was. Gichin Funakoshi was an exception.

Whilst karate has spread far and wide, it may be of interest to readers to learn that English was taught at the Shuri Middle School, which had formerly been the Shuri Academy. In the latter part of the 1880's formal gymnastics were introduced into the school curriculum, which became the basis for military drill exercises. Later, I believe karate may be said to have fulfilled this role.

The Japanese language was taught as a subject during the first year of schooling. After that, it was used as the vehicle for instruction in other subjects. Many Okinawan officials at this time had only a rudimentary knowledge of Japanese. Funakoshi, working as a schoolteacher, was in a perfect position to export karate to Japan at that time. He had not been educated at a formal school initially, but rather had been taught by his grandfather, a knowledgeable and gifted teacher in the Chinese classics. This was quite normal for the time. All the books came from China. The Confucian classics were standard textbooks, and studies consisted *more in an apparently mechanical repetition of sounds than in any mental recreation from the sentiments contained in those literary monuments of a venerable* antiquity.[5] At the end of 1892, there were ten schools operating in Naha with twelve hundred and fifty-six children attending. In Shuri, there were two schools and seven hundred and ten pupils attending. The actual number of children of school age was much greater however, with less than one in five attending in Naha and Shuri; this attendance rate was however higher than for the rest of the island and the surrounding islands in the archipelago, where it was closer to one in seven children. At the Middle School and Normal School, which are not included in the above numbers, the young men were required to dress in Japanese style, which was European style.

The nineteenth century on the Ryukyu Islands had seen many thousands of people die of starvation. With the epidemics, storms and typhoons, *tsunami* and even droughts, the people were impoverished and exhausted. If it had not been for the *Kara-mmu* [Chinese potato – sweet potato], many more would have perished. I remember learning at school about Noguni Sokan who introduced the potato into Naha from Fukien in 1606. This changed the islands forever, in that the fear of famine was reduced due to the plant's yield of a cheap, nourishing food for man and beast alike – and of course, a fairly potent alcoholic drink can be distilled from it. *As many as five crops* [of sweet potato were] *raised in two years,*[4] whereas *three rice-crops were generally harvested every two years, the plan being to let the ground lie fallow during the fourth half-yearly period.*[4*]

When sweet potato was scarce in 1885 and 1886, the peasantry, who, like the *shizoku*, were remarkably fond of music, did not carry musical instruments into the fields to work by. Perhaps the gods had grown weary of not hearing the planting festival, traditionally held at

Plate 26. Okinawan country people

court each year to ensure a productive crop? People less fortunate than ourselves were close to starvation. I recall we used to climb the steep hillsides and search the waste places looking for the handsome *sotitsi* [*sotetsu* in Japanese], which was traditionally regarded as 'famine food' that would grow on the poor soil. I remember that I would ride out to a small village where, under a tree, there was *a blacksmith's anvil fixed in a block; the forge was of masonry, having an air hole, but the bellows was wanting.*[2] In bounteous years, the hillsides were ablaze with *sotitsi*, but in times of famine they were hard to find. A sort of sago can be got from the tree's pith. However, there were *number- less stories . . . concerning the unwholesomeness of this sago palm –*

181

that it gave bad breath, that it distended the stomach without feeding the system, that people sometimes fell down dead after eating it, etc.[4a*] Indeed, it is perhaps an ironic fact that the fronds of this palm were sent to Osaka and Yokohama and then all over the world, most notably Europe, for decoration in funeral wreaths! If there is any truth to these stories, it probably lies with faulty preparation and bad cooking on the part of the peasantry, who *made it into dumplings, sometimes pure, sometimes mixed with pounded sweet potatoes – a dish which could lie heavy on any but the stoutest stomach.*[4a*] The peasantry used to drink very inferior tea mixed with boiling mugwort, which was supposed to strengthen the digestion. I have personally eaten *sotitsi*, and if prepared properly *it is quite palatable and perfectly innocuous.*[4a] I recall there being an Office for Famine Prevention and the Planting of Cycads.

In 1888, on a trip back to Okinawa from Tokyo, I attended Gichin Funakoshi's wedding. Funakoshi was nearing twenty; his wife to be, was a mere thirteen or fourteen. This might appear extraordinarily young by today's standards, but was considered not uncommon at the time.[iv]

Funakoshi's intended came from a farming family in Mawashi (where, incidently, Tei Junsoku, mentioned earlier, was born), which was a village about two and a half miles from Naha, and it was in her family house that they lived after the marriage. In the old days, it was said that unrestrained courtship was possible, but in the last quarter of the nineteenth century this was not so. Young men would seek intimacies with girls from other villages, but in doing so ran the risk of evoking the wrath of the young men from these villages. For girls, such liaisons, if detected, led to ostracizism. Alternatives were the brothels of Naha. Many a young man learned the pleasures of womanhood this way, and although brothels were much more a part of ordinary life than they are today, the clients invariably paid an uncomfortable price, shall we say, for following their natural inclinations.

At the wedding I was introduced to Funakoshi's four uncles on his father's side, who were: Gishu, Gichki, Gika, Giji. I also met his grandfather, Gifku, and great-grandfather, Gitatsu.[v] All the first names of the Funakoshi family began with 'Gi' and Gichin Funakoshi named his sons in the same way. 'Gi' has connotations with a strong hero. One of them, I cannot remember who, was pox scarred. The year after I left for Tokyo [1886], smallpox, an horrific disease with its high mortality and hideous effects, had struck the island, and there had been five thousand reported cases. Cholera also struck again, and there were fifteen hundred cases. In all two thousand five hundred people died.

Perhaps readers might be interested to know what went on at such weddings?[vi] But let me first state that girls began to learn their home-bound duties at the age of four and five, which consisted in spinning and weaving cotton, hemp and silk. *Okinawa . . . produced woven fabrics of several kinds, which were highly prized in Japan, mostly for summer wear. Each island had its speciality: the tsumugi from Kume-jima, a silk fabric having light spots or stripes on a very dark background . . . the cotton kasuri – blue from Okinawa, brown from Yaeyama; the hempen hosojofu, in a blue and a white variety, from Miyako-jima;* [and] *the bashofu from Oshima, made of banana fibre . . . so exquisite was the care bestowed in former days on the manufacture of hosojofu, that a single piece of twenty-eight feet long sometimes occupied three years in the weaving, as the best work could only be done in dry weather. Such pieces would be sent as tribute to the Government of Okinawa.*[4a] Work was done largely on a cottage-industry basis before I left for Tokyo, with the backstrap-frame loom producing fairly plain weaved patterns, mostly geometric in design. This loom was shortly to be replaced by the treadle loom. Naha and Shuri were justly famous for their elegant *bingata*, which were made from stencilling resist paste on to fabric and colouring the unresisted area by hand. Patterns most commonly reflected natural scenes and creatures, such as birds, flowers, trees, rivers, clouds, and so on. Natural dyes were obtained from plants, such as blue from indigo; yellow, black and brown from tree bark; red from certain woods; and, brown and black from ferruginous mud. I remember seeing wonderful hand-spun silks from Kumejima Island.

Women's lives were seen as one of devotion to their husbands to be. Normally, *when a son had reached the age of six or seven, the parents looked around them, and from the children of their townsfolk selected a future bride suited to their son's station in life and worthy to become their daughter. Through some middleman the boy was offered to the parents of the girl as a suitor; if he proved acceptable, a day of good omen was selected, known as the kichi-nichi (lucky day), and on this day the contract was made and the boy's parents sent a present to the parents of the girl, but neither of the principals knew anything of all these arrangements for their future happiness.*[27]*

After the 'middleman' – the marriage broker, as he might be termed – had negotiated the preliminaries, and proper presents had been sent by the bridegroom to the bride's family, the proceedings were as follows:[vii] *The bride was escorted to the man's house at one or two o'clock in the morning, under guard of her relations, the object of these precautions of time being that the affair might not be bruited abroad, and excite impertinent curiosity in the neighbourhood. She and the bridegroom exchanged cups of sake (rice beer), after which she was at once led home again. This brief ceremony was repeated three nights running, after which she remained three days with her parents, while the bridegroom was carried off by his friends to hold high revel. The object of this step, so far as the man was concerned,*

Plate 27. An Okinawan from Naha

was that he might, on the very threshold of matrimony, prove his independence of wifely leading-strings, while to the woman it gave an opportunity to display freedom from jealousy, which was considered the worst of all female vices. After three days spent in this manner, the bridegroom went home, being joined by the bride, who kept house with him [or rather assisting her mother-in-law[27]] for another period of three days, at the expiration of which the bride went to her parent's home whither the bridegroom followed her. Her relations awaited his arrival with a pestle, painted and ornamented to represent a horse, on*

184

which he rode in, while all the boys of the neighbourhood greeted his advent with drums and tomtoms, and anything that would make a noise.[4a]* The source of this horse-play was probably legend. It is said that *once upon a time, an anju . . . committed polygamy to such an extent that at last the boys of the village waylaid him as he was going to the house of an additional bride and fastened on him a hobby-horse, and made him walk with a broken umbrella over his head. This made his offence so public, and so humiliated him, that he remained faithful to his last bride and sinned no more.*[27]

Plate 28. An Okinawan woman

A grand family feast then took place, after which the happy couple returned home [to the groom's house attended by both families], *and the long wedding ceremonies were at last concluded*[4a]* *by the bride and groom reclining together on a couch for a few minutes; this was known as misu-mori.*[27]*

Some of the arranged marriages, as one might have imagined, were not always agreeable unions, and divorce in the first few months was far from uncommon. However, if the couple stayed together for a year or so, then only the gravest misdemeanours of either party would induce them to separate. Generally, then, married life was *mostly harmonious, as wives yielded to their husbands in all things. Should the*

185

husband have died, the widow almost always remained true to his memory, which was an item of feminine devotion much prized in Far-Eastern lands, where, though a widower married and made himself comfortable again as a matter of course, widows were encouraged by public opinion to remain desolate.[4a*]

First cousins could marry, provided they were the children of brothers; the children of sisters could not marry.

If a married man remained childless, or his wife could bear him no male heirs – sometimes three male heirs were insisted upon[viii] – such grounds could, and did, form the basis for divorce, and the unfortunate woman would be sent back to her parents or family. Occasionally, though not strictly legal, a man of means could take a second wife, which he would house separately, if he wished to retain his first wife in his quest for children. Sometimes, when the discarded wife's *family was too poor to receive her and provide for her subsistence, a rich husband would build a little apartment or hut on the edge of his premises, in which one or more divorced wives would be doomed to live apart in loneliness and degradation.*[17*] Once children were born to a couple, however, divorce was rare. I believe that I am correct in saying that a wife at that time could only become divorced from her husband if he committed a criminal act.

Married women [of the upper classes] *were seldom allowed to see any men but their husbands, with the exception, perhaps, of very intimate friends, and even then they could not converse. If a visitor called when the husband happened to be from home, no matter how excellent the terms of intercourse might have usually been, he was not allowed to come inside the door. These precautions were adopted in order to prevent suspicions of unfaithfulness from being excited.*[14*] [ix]

For the benefit of Western readers, and Eastern one's come to that, I have a tale that may interest them. I remember once visiting the grave of William Hares, an English seaman aboard the *Alceste*, who, critically ill at the time of the ship's arrival, died aged twenty-one, on the 15th October, 1816. My great-great-grandfather had instructed one of his men skilled in masonry, under the king's personal direction, to cut the inscription that had been written by the clergyman of the *Alceste*, Mr. Taylor, upon the gravestone in India ink. Unfortunately, whilst much of the inscription was readable some seventy years later, the name of Hares has since faded and may no longer be read. I recall a conversation between the doctor of that ship and my great-great grandfather that has been handed down through the family. The ship's surgeon said: *That proud and haughty feeling of national superiority, so strongly existing among the common class of British seamen, which induced them to hold all foreigners cheap, and to treat them with contempt; often calling them outlandish lubbers in their own country, was, at this island, completely subdued and tamed, by the gentle manners and kind behaviour of the most pacific people on earth. Although completely intermixed, and often working together, both on shore and on board, not a single quarrel or complaint took place on either side, during the whole . . . stay; on the contrary, the . . . [Okinawans] were always seen in cheerful association around the sailors' mess tables, and each succeeding day added to friendship and cordiality.*[3]*

The Hares' monument, sited at that shady spot of Amikudera, near the temple, and *a spot already rendered sacred by many Okinawa tombs,*[2] which is about two-thirds of a mile from Naha and close to the sea, was striking to me at the time because it was so different to our burial monuments and the way the dead were treated. Much expense and great attention was paid to family burial sites. The turtle-back tombs made of coral blocks cemented over with calceous stucco, with their outlying walls, resemble, and are said by some to represent, a womb. I personally subscribe to this view and all that it symbolises. The Okinawan dead, in those days, as I have previously noted, were interned in a ceramic pot and shelved within the family tomb. Many generations of the same family could thus lie together, and my countrymen found comfort in that. It may be of interest to readers to learn that on Okinawa at that time, the New Year opened with ceremonies where our ancestors were worshipped. These services were conducted on the 1st, 8th and 15th of the month. On the 16th, ancestral tombs were visited and lanterns lit before the burial chambers. The tombs were visited again, two months later, and in the last month of the year ceremonies were held to ward off evil spirits. I later read that when Funakoshi went to Tokyo in 1922, and stayed, he wanted his wife to go with him, but she would not leave her duties to her ancestors. This I can understand, by leaving Okinawa, which in the end she was forced to do by the ravages of war, she left the comfort of eternity in the company of her deceased family members. Now, her ashes lie alongside those of her husband and eldest son in Kakiu. How sad for Hares then, to lie in soil so far from home, away from his loved ones. But is it not a curious irony that only his name, not the rest of the inscription, has worn? Perhaps his soul alighted back to England. If not, he lies not alone, for several other European seamen have been laid to rest in the same spot. There was also a burial ground for US citizens at Tomari, and I think Perry left nine men buried there in 1853–1854, as did the

French in 1846 and 1848.

My great-great-grandfather had attended Hares' funeral on the 17th October, 1816. He told me that *the body was carried to the grave with all the formalities usual on such occasions, Capt. Maxwell, according to custom, walking last, with the officers and crew before him.*[2] My great-great-grandfather, along with the other dignitaries present, all dressed in white robes, realising the English custom, placed themselves at the front of the cortege, thus taking up the lowest rank. The Okinawans *preserved throughout the ceremony the most profound silence.*[2] The following day, the Okinawans performed their own funeral service over the grave, and sacrificed a large hog and burned a quantity of spirits.

I also remember being told that Capt. Maxwell – who my ancestor held in very high esteem for his gentleness, forbearance and manner – was fond of riding, and had fallen with his pony on the beach, the beast being unable to bear his weight, and he had broken a finger. Captain Maxwell was attended to by an Okinawan surgeon who placed the *finger in a thick paste made of eggs, flour, and some other substance that he brought along with him. He then wrapped the whole in the skin of a newly-killed fowl. The skin dried in a short time and held the paste firm, by which the finger was kept steady.*[2]

Two days later, a party of senior officials, of which my great-great-grandfather was one, went aboard the *Alceste* for dinner. This proved to be one of my great-great-grandfather's chief topics of conversation when asked to talk about the Englishmen's visit to our shores. The dinner was served at five o'clock in a truly sumptuous manner, and my relative sat near Mr. Hickman, a lieutenant. They all ate and drank freely, and the Okinawans complained about the size of the glasses, which were much larger than ours, and the strength of the wine. All forms of spirits were served and tasted from punch to champagne – *the briskness of the last indeed surprised . . .* [the Okinawans] *not a little, and effectually muddled two or three of them for some time. Cheese was the only thing they all objected to, probably on account of its being made of milk, which they had never tasted . . . When the dessert was put on the table, and the wine decanters ranged in a line, they exclaimed in astonishment, 'Moo eeyroo noo sackee,'* [six kinds or colours of wine]; *but the sweetmeats and prepared confectionary pleased them the most.*[2]*

After sitting for about an hour and a half after dinner, the Okinawans rose to go, but it was explained to them that it was the English custom to sit a much longer time, and they resumed their seats.

They drank the health of a number of people, lit their pipes and had a wonderful time, for all were drunk. And this state of drunkenness was deepened by the games they played, where a cup of wine was the forfeit. The Okinawans had taken their own little cups, and these were used. Let me tell you two such games they played! *One person held the stalk of a tobacco-pipe between the palms of his hands, so that the pipe rolled round as he moved his hands, which he was to hold over his head, so as not to see them. After turning it round for a short time, he suddenly stopped, and the person to whom the bowl was directed had to drink a cup of wine. Another was a Chinese game: one person held his hand closed over his head, he then brought it quickly down before him with one or more fingers extended; the person he was playing with called out the number of them, and if he guessed right, he had to drink a cup of wine. These and other games caused a good deal of noisy mirth.*[2] Later they danced and sang. *The words of the dance song were, 'Sasa sangcoomah, sangcoomee ah! Kadee yooshee daw;' when they came to the last word they all joined in the chorus and clapped their hands.*[2] Captain Maxwell had had a large cake baked for the children of the families of the men present, and each took a piece home with him. The next day, my great-great-grandfather said that he had been *weetee* [drunk], and that his head ached very much indeed!

Four days later, Prince Shang Pung Fwee paid a visit to the ship, and steered clear of the wine. Naturally a silent man, he held the highest of the nine orders of chiefs and wore a pink *hatchee-matchee* with *perpendicular rows of black, yellow, blue, white, and green spots. He was clothed in a robe of light blue silk, lined with silk of a shade lighter, over which he wore a girdle richly embossed with flowers of gold and different silks.*[2 x] He was about fifty years of age at the time and his beard was full and white. My great-great-grandfather was one of the retinue of fifteen who accompanied him. The Prince was fascinated by a number of things, including Mrs. Loy, the boatswain's wife. There was an attempt to induce her to stay on the island by *some great man . . .* [and] *great offers were also made to the boatswain to induce him to comply with this bargain.*[3] Also, the ship's fire-engine, and an African negro who was on-board were of interest to the prince. *When the black man was brought before him he looked exceedingly surprised . . .* [and] *one of his people was sent to rub his face, as if to discover whether it was painted or not.*[2] On leaving the ship, the rigging was manned, and a salute of seven guns was fired, just at it was before he came aboard. *The state boat was a large flat-bottomed barge, covered with an awning of dark blue, with white stars on it, the*

Plate 29. An Okinawan prince

whole having the appearance of a hearse. It was preceded by two boats bearing flags with an inscription upon them, having in the bow an officer of justice carrying a lackered bamboo, and in the stern a man beating a gong. A vast number of boats were in attendance, and all was as it was when the prince sailed out.[2]

My great-great-grandfather had the opportunity to examine a sextant and a thermometer and was given a cut wine glass, something that I am admiring now, as I write, which is a most valued family heirloom. The ships captains were generous with their presents, the prince later being given fine cloth, *cut crystal decanters and glasses, and three dozen of wine of ten different sorts, with several books, and a number of smaller articles*,[2] in repayment for gifts received earlier. A cow and calf were given to the king.

However, and before I tire the reader with my family history, my great-great-grandfather's keenest memory was of the *Alceste* and *Lyra* dressed in colours and firing a royal salute on the anniversary of King George III's accession to the throne [25th October]. Only a single ensign had been flown aboard each ship on Sunday's until that morning, when several hundred flags were displayed, of varying colours. This had a great effect upon the many hundreds of spectators along the quayside. My people had presented a large number of coloured paper lanterns to the ship for the purpose of illuminating her at night to honour King George. The lanterns were lit after dark and were *regularly ranged along the yards and rigging, the main-deck ports illumintade, sky-rockets thrown up, and blue lights burnt at the yard-arms, bowsprit, and spanker-boom ends, with a feu-de-joie of musquetry, thrice repeated round the ship. The whole had a very brilliant effect upon the shore, where thousands of . . .* [Okinawans] *had collected to view the display.*[3]

My great-great-grandfather noted of that day, *so novel and remarkable, will often be recalled with delight by all who witnessed the pleasing scene of two people differing widely in national manners, language, and dress; distinct, in fact, in every thing that is exterior, yet so harmoniously united in hearty good-will and convivial friendship.*[3]

Captain Maxwell had wanted an audience with the king, who, incidentally, only had one wife, but twelve concubines, and seven sons. Maxwell was informed by the prince that *it was contrary to the laws and customs of Okinawa for any foreigner to see the king, unless sent by his own sovereign,*[2] and Maxwell dropped the idea, unlike others who came later. Essentially, Okinawans at that time would talk to westerns, or strangers generally, about any subject, with the exceptions

Plate 30. Okinawans on the quayside

of the royal family or the women, both of whom invited great curiosity because of their reclusive habits. If a man, especially a westerner, saw a woman, they *startled like frightened deer*,[9a] and would run off leaving behind what they were doing. I think, in reality, *the old women were driven away, or made to stoop in hiding their heads, but were, in all probability, taking a sly peep under their arms; and the young ladies in the houses were very plainly pulling the blinds aside to get a sight of the barbarians.*[11]

And that brings me back to Okinawan women. As mentioned earlier, women scarcely ever left the house, but if they did, *so strict were the rules affecting intercourse between the two sexes that an Okinawan woman of the shizoku class who met an acquaintance of the other sex in the streets was not allowed to speak to him; both passed each other as if they were strangers.*[10] Such an apparent *mark of disrespect . . .* [must have] *accorded badly with . . .* [the men's] *mild and amiable deportment when met by foreigners.*[8] Wealthy men only allowed their women to stir out of the house in a covered palanquin, and that, it was not *considered proper for a man's wife to be seen by any visitor, except it be an intimate friend. To such a pitch was this feeling carried, that persons had been known to live for years in the residence of a Okinawan without once meeting the mistress of the house.*[10] Perhaps the most descriptive, if not revealing words of Okinawan men's attitudes towards their women-folk in the nineteenth century, comes from, strange as it might be, the legendary *karateka*, Sokon Matsumura. In a translation of precepts to his pupil, Ryosei Kuwae, Matsumura wrote: *Gukushi-no-Bugei is nothing more than a technical knowledge of Bugei. Like a woman, it is just superficial and has no depth.*[xi, xii, xiii]

Times were changing. When I left for Japan, there were some ten thousand houses in Naha and neighbourhood and some forty thousand people. In Shuri, there was half that number of houses and about half the number of people. Before I left, the usual manner in which to visit the outlying parts of the island was by the use of small coastal transport. In 1885, a road across Okinawa was built.

Following on from drought and then the numerous typhoons that year, with tempests driving wind speeds up to one hundred and fifty miles an hour, it was time for the Black Current to take me from the island of by birth to a new capital and a new life. Few ventured out onto the ocean at this time for fear of engaging the sea god's wrath, when the harvest was shortly to be gathered. Fate wasn't to be tempted on so important an issue. I bid a tearful farewell to family and friends, including Itosu *Sensei* and Funakoshi. A south-westerly breeze picked up, perhaps a portent, as I was paddled through the harbour waters. I recalled, in my mind's eye, the dashing and colourful dragon boat races of my youth that were held on this spot, and the quiet, unspoilt bays I had explored in my childhood. I thought of Shuri Lake and the horse racing on the *baba* [racing grounds], with people dressed in their bright clothes under the giant pine trees.

On the three-day voyage to Japan, I remember we passed the Sho family's steamboat, the *Taiyu-maru*, which had been a gift from the emperor, but was later taken back so that it might operate commercially between Naha and Osaka. Not long afterwards, the Sho family operated a shipping line from Japan to Naha, a venture that lasted successfully for about twenty-five years.

V

A TRIP BACK HOME

After graduating, and qualifying as a physician from Tokyo University, and having spent several years engaged in hospital work, I travelled back home once again before returning to take up a new post in private practice in the capital. I had only been home once before in seven years, a visit that I've already alluded to. My parents had taken the opportunity to visit me in Tokyo a number of times during the intervening period, and as both my younger brothers later studied in Tokyo and then took up residence as engineers, my parents too moved to the Japanese capital. After my immediate family had left Okinawa, and with my marrying and having a family, alongside establishing a busy medical practice, the next forty years were spent in Japan. The year 1892 was the date of my last trip back to my homeland. As an old man, I had thought of returning one last time, but with the onset of war, and the devastation of the islands, there was little to see from my youth, and I thought it best to keep the untarnished memories.

I embarked from Kobe aboard the steamer *Mutsu Maru*, owned by the Nippon Yusen Kwaisha [Japan Steamship Company], bound for Naha, via Kagoshima and Naze. I remember passing the island of Oshima, where *a sugar refinery was erected by the Prince of Satsuma with the assistance of the Messrs. Glover of Nagasaki,*[28] the year I was born. The trip was, as usual, subject to bad weather, and the delay caused meant that the captain had to wait hours for high tide before he could enter Naha harbour and secure the ship. Shoals of porpoises, mercifully too shy to catch, could sometimes be seen, as was the occasional small whale and albatross. *On approaching the main land, a conspicuous wooded point could be seen, having rocks on its summit like the ruins of an abbey; this formed the south side of the anchorage.*[2]* The best passage into Naha harbour was to approach the port from the west, slipping in through a gap in the coral reefs and following a channel from nine to nineteen fathoms in depth to the harbour, which was in nine fathoms, and with a muddy bottom. The reefs to the north (left) as one entered the port were not visible in fine weather, being between three and twelve feet under the surface, there was little swell, and great care had to be taken not to stray. An alternative route was to enter the harbour from the north, where there was a little less depth of water, but it was more consistent. The northern entrance to the harbour was *narrow, and had several dangerous rocks in the channel, which, as they were not in general visible, were very likely to prove injurious to vessels.*[24]* When the weather was not so obliging, as on this particular day, one could see *along the whole line of coast, the surf . . . breaking on the coral reefs, which in some places extended out for miles, showing a crest of foam as beautiful as the reefs were dangerous. Within the reefs, a few fishermen could be seen, some of whom had nets suspended from poles, which they elevated and depressed.*[13]* By this latter route, one came quite close to Nami-no-ue[i], where stood a Buddhist temple known as Quan-kwo-she, and Dr. Bettelheim, the Christian missionary, lived close by, near a house that was *perched on a rocky but salubrious elevation, overhanging the sea.*[17] *A spot better adapted for exclusion from the people . . . could not have been fixed upon.*[17] The pole, where Bettelheim raised the British ensign to attract Commodore Perry's attention some thirty-five years before, and a number of other ships come to that, still stood, despite violent tempest and innumerable typhoons. The white towers of Shuri shone. Once inside the harbour, boats were very secure.

It was early morning when we steamed gently in, and as we did so the stormy weather suddenly abated, leaving a fresh serenity. Among the boats in the harbour that morning were two Okinawan junks *decorated with an eye on each bow and by a red ball on a white ground on the stern.*[28] *The first fishing boats came creeping out, their great dragon's-wing sails of yellow matting gleaming in the sun, and only lightly filled by . . .* [the now] *gentle northerly breeze, and the narrow little 'dug-outs' skipped over the waves towards us, propelled by two or three . . .* [men] *in huge straw-hats, paddling with short quick strokes . . . The boats* [in the harbour] *were more curious and picturesque than anything in Japan, being very dilapidated, and much stained with age and wear. Quantities of sun-browned men were busy amongst them, working, cleaning, and some cooking their breakfasts over fires of fir-boughs.*[15]

A number of senior-ranking Okinawans were conversing, waiting, and the bright light caught their two hair pins apiece, especially the ones that had a *star-shaped flower of five petals at the end,*[18] which

Plate 31. A view of Naha taken from the fort

glittered brilliantly, reflecting the sunlight on the water. I was reminded of a story my grandfather told me when I had been a boy, that when a western ship had called in to Naha in 1849, an immense crowd had gathered to witness the landing *and the bright sun shining on these glittering ornaments produced a curious appearance, as if many hundreds of stars had descended from their spheres to perch upon the heads of these wondering Okinawans.*[18] So, there were still individuals who, in a prolonged act of defiance, had not yet obeyed the nationwide edict, despite the passing of more than twenty years, of cutting off their topknots. It was apparent that the Obstinate Party was still very much alive!

We were taken to a flight of broad low narrow steps to land; these steps were swarming with men, women and children, all on the lookout . . . All our bags and bundles were seized by blue-tattooed hands . . . The boatman charged us [the equivalent of] *sevenpence for bringing us and all our luggage ashore from the ship, which must have been a good mile out at sea.*[15]

Cargo handlers had been up since the first light, and on the wharf all sorts of merchandise was standing, ready to be stowed and transported. Packed *in square piles, with flags upon sticks, stuck here and there upon the bales of goods, which were apparently done up with straw matting.*[24] I believe that I am correct in saying that *commerce between Japan and Okinawa was conducted entirely in Japanese vessels, which brought hemp, iron, copper, pewter, cotton, culinary utensils, lacquered furniture, excellent hones, and occasionally rice.*[24]* Also beans, rapeseed oil, tea, tobacco, vermicelli, and miscellaneous items such as dried fish, sake, seaweed, hair-oil, timber and foreign goods.[ii] Indigo, of excellent quality, Cinnabar, turmeric, Indian corn, beans, pumpkins and many others of the gourd family, were special products of the island. The exports of Okinawa for many years had been *salt, grain, tobacco, samshew spirit, rice, when sufficiently plentiful, grass hemp . . . and cotton* [also yellow dye, *awamori*, umbrellas and rope]. *In return for these, they brought from China different kinds of porcelain, glass, furniture, medicines, silver, iron, silks, nails, tiles, tools, and tea . . .* [The goods carried to Japan] *consisted of silks and other stuffs, with Chinese commodities . . . corn, rice, pulse, fruits, spirits, mother of pearl, cowries, and large flat shells, which were so transparent that they were used in Japan for windows instead of glass.*[24]* Okinawa exported probably about twice as much as she imported at the end of the nineteenth century.

Naha, however, was far from being the best harbour on Okinawa.

The best was undoubtedly Unten, *a snug little harbour*[9a] on the north-west coast, but it was *wasted, because* [it was] *situated in a hilly district remote from the centres of population and trade. For this reason the Japanese steamers and most junks repaired to Naha, in Shimajiri.*[4] Okinawa was divided into three provinces then: Kunchan, Nakagami and Shimajiri, from north to south, respectively. Each of these provinces were subdivided into districts, called *magiri, of which there were nine in Kunchan* [also popularly known as Yambara], *eleven in Nakagami, and fifteen in Shimajiri, the highly civilized central and southern provinces being thus much more minutely subdivided than the barren northern moor and forest land,*[4] which features mountains to fifteen hundred feet and is sparsely populated.

I had been to Unten only once, as a boy, with my father and a party of his colleagues, accompanied by pack-horses and bearers – who used to carry baggage hung from a pole and slung on the shoulders between two men, though sometimes women would act as bearers carrying loads on their heads – and I'd like to say a little about my memories here, for I expect that it has changed a great deal, and the purpose of this book has been to recall what I remember. Also, I suspect that in the history of karate it has, indirectly, an important place, for it was here that the Satsuma samurai landed after being repelled from landing at Naha, and their success here ensured the defeat of Okinawa. Shimazu subsequently banned all weapons, as I have already noted, and this provided the impetus to refine unarmed technique. I have always wondered, if the banning of arms had been in effect for some two hundred years under the edict of Sho Hashi, where these weapons had been stored for a time of national emergency. The Okinawans had clearly been able to put up such strong resistance against warriors known for their ferocity, so practice with the said weapons must have taken place in the intervening period. To me this is a bit of a mystery. It may have been that with Sho Shin's ban, only a portion of society were prohibited from carrying arms, I don't know, but the Shimazu ban prohibited everyone from owning weapons. Hence, as I say, what became known as karate is thought to have undergone a tremendous period of refinement as a consequence. But back to Unten!

The British Navy called it Port Melville in honour of Viscount Melville, First Lord of the Admiralty. Our party, which included some very senior officials from the *Tachi-ho* [Board of Agriculture] and *Yamabugio-sho* [Department of Woods and Forests], left Shuri stopping off at *kung-qua* towns. A *kung-qua* was a public building for the accommodation of travellers, and these towns occurred every twelve miles or so along the island's main thoroughfares. Since in Okinawa at the time there were no other travellers, *kung-qua* were used solely by government officers, and that, *being used only by persons of some consideration . . .* [they were] *far more neat and elegant in every respect,*[5] than might be expected. We travelled via Peko, Necumma, Nugah, Farnigi and Shah Bay, which, *if it had depth enough at its entrance, would be one of the finest harbours in the world.*[9a] The point I remember most about all the *kung-qua* that I visited, was the scent, for peach, plum and apricot grew in abundance in their gardens. These fruit trees were confined to the property of the more wealthy, and whilst we had them at home, as did my friends, I found it the unifying factor of all the *kung-qua* that I stayed at.

The area we transversed is composed almost entirely of precipitous hills and ravines, with the streams issuing forth water both *beautifully clear and pellucid,*[7] though the riding was made easier by the *tree-ferns, often twenty-five or thirty feet high, and from six to eight inches in diameter . . . forming, with their feathery tops, a canopy to each tree of fifteen to eighteen feet in width, of exquisite gracefulness and beauty . . .* [there was also a] *great abundance of azaleas, their heavy clusters of large red flowers sprinkled thickly among the tropical foliage.*[9a] We also saw stockade fences, probably erected to keep wild boar out from cultivated areas. I also remember staying in *kung-qua* in Vicoo, Isitza and Kannah, but that of Ching was the most memorable to me personally. *It was like* [visiting] *an elegant private residence; having a garden, enclosed by a square, clipped hedge of jessamine, and a separate establishment for servants and attendants. There were rows of chrysanthemums . . . and two peach trees in the garden, besides a stout camellia, clipped into a fanciful shape,*[5a] followed by the *kung-qua* at Un-na. The reader will appreciate that we travelled back from Uten in a most odd fashion! Why we went where we did, I forget all these years on. I remember the red roof tiles of the *kung-qua* at Un-na *glittered in the sun; the whitest and softest of mats covered the floor; the garden blazed with a profusion of scarlet flowers; and stone basins, seated on pedestals, contained fresh water for our use. Its aspect of comfort and repose was a balm to travellers as weary as ourselves,*[5a] and I fancy that was why I recall it.

The streets of Unten were *regular and clean swept; each house had a neat cane wall, as well as a screen before the door; plantain and other trees were growing so thickly in the inside of the fence that they completely shaded the house[s]. Near the beach were several large houses, in which a number of people were seated writing: on going up*

*to them they gave us tea and cakes . . . In front of the village, and par-
allel with the beach, there was a splendid avenue thirty feet wide,
formed by two rows of large trees, whose branches joined overhead,
and effectually screened the walk from the sun; here and there were
placed wooden benches, and at some places stone seats were fixed
near the trees: this space, which was about a quarter of a mile long,
was probably used as a public walk.*

*A range of hills of a semicircular form embraced the village, and
limited its extent: at most places it was steep, but at the point where
the cliff joined the harbour, there was an overhanging cliff about
eighty feet high, the upper part of which extended considerably beyond
the base; at eight or ten yards from the ground on this inclined face, a
long horizontal gallery had been hewn out of the solid rock: it communicated with a number of small square excavations still deeper in the
rock, for the reception of the vases containing the bones of the dead.*

*The trees and creepers on the edge of the precipice hung down so
as to meet the tops of those which grew below, and thus a screen was
formed which threw the gallery into deep shade: everything here being
perfectly still, the scene was very solemn and imposing. It took us
somewhat by surprise, for nothing in its external appearance indicated the purpose to which the place was appropriated: happening to discover an opening amongst the trees and brushwood, and resolving to
see what it led to, we entered by a narrow path winding through the
grove. The liveliness of the scenery without, and the various amuse-
ments of the day, had put us all into high spirits, but the unexpected
and sacred gloom of the scene in which we suddenly found ourselves
had an instantaneous effect in repressing the mirth of the whole party.*[2]

From Unten, we took a boat round Ee Island, which was named by
the British, 'Sugar Loaf Island,' as my father wished to show me this
wonderment of nature. It certainly was, and one suspects still is, an
extraordinary place. *Eegooshcoond (tower or castle) . . . can be seen
distinctly at a distance of twenty-five miles when the eye is elevated
only fifteen feet. It is a high conical mountain, varying very little in its
aspect when viewed from different quarters: as there is no other peak
like it on or near this island, it cannot be mistaken . . . The base of the
cone and one-third of the way up was covered with houses; and the
whole island had the appearance of a garden.*[2*]

We took carriers of course, mostly boys aged *from twelve to sixteen. I noticed as a curious fact that, in spite of the heavy loads they
carried, and the rough by-ways we frequently obliged them to take,
they never perspired in the least, nor partook of a drop of water, even*

in the greatest heat. They were models of cheerfulness, alacrity, and endurance, always in readiness, and never, by look or word, evincing the least dissatisfaction.[5a] I remember one labourer, a Chinese, who had become ill after drinking *sake* and eating green peaches. His load was given to other carriers, *and he obtained temporary relief by punching his throat, in three places, so violently as to produce an extravasation of blood. Counter irritation was the usual Chinese remedy for all ailments, and it was frequently very efficacious.*[5a]* My sojourn to Unten over, let us return Naha.

I remember *the causeway leading to the town was three hundred or four hundred yards long, with arches underneath, to give the water a free passage; for as the tide flowed up to the town, over the coral banks which extended from it to the pier-head, it was necessary to give the water its course without any obstruction. The town extended along the shore to the North some distance . . . Trees were interspersed among the houses; and the country rising to a moderate elevation at the back of the town, variegated with cultivations and clumps of woods, equally diversified the view from the sea . . . At the extreme of the town, to the North, was a burial ground* [as I have previously noted]. *The* [whitened] *tombstones were . . . conspicuous as you sailed into the roads.*[1]*

I recall the junks, docked, and one sailing out with its matted sails taut in the wind. Some carried small guns to defend themselves from piracy. A number of Japanese junks, not unlike the Chinese in construction, but with a different arrangement of rigging, were taking on cargo; the two great eyes inserted in the bows ready to guide them home through those treacherous waters. The large boats in dry-dock, seeking attention, were flat floored. The Okinawans chose the Chinese model for their ships, and I remember one such junk having *Shung Fung Seang Sung* [may favourable winds attend us] painted in large letters on her stern.

The sail was becoming a less frequent sight now, being superseded by steamers. These were large ships, some eighty to ninety feet in length, with a beam width of some twenty feet and a similar depth of hold. Used mostly for sugar, they normally sailed for Kagoshima, but sometimes Osaka.

On disembarking, a number of points struck me, the first of which was the nature of the streets in Naha, which were cleaner. This I believe was due to the presence of the Japanese. Naha, and for that matter other Okinawan towns, had never been as dirty as the Chinese towns, but were never as clean as the Japanese. Naha, being a busy port and the seat of Japanese administration, had an altogether more Japanese feeling about it, compared to when I left to study. Even the manners of the inhabitants had changed slightly, reflecting Japanese customs. In direct contrast, Shuri remained old-world. In Naha, there were no vehicles of any kind, and no form of public lighting. This still made the narrow bye ways of the new capital surprisingly disconcerting after Tokyo, yet I had known it that way all my life. From time to time packhorses came along, and then pedestrians had to be on the lookout; for the absence of pavements and the extreme tightness of the streets caused numerous collisions. Walking down these narrow streets of Naha, with each house's garden *divided from each other by coral walls and bristling hedges of yucca and cactus . . . the walls topped with cactus,*[5] I saw my first Okinawan pillar post box, and I was informed that there was a telephone link between Naha and Shuri.

I also remember that when I had left for Tokyo, the first prefectural hospital was being erected. When I returned, a second hospital, Wakasa Byoin, had been opened two years.

Shortly before I arrived in Naha, Japanese Christians from the American Episcopal Mission at Nagasaki were sent to Naha and Shuri, but the local people always treated the venture with great suspicion. Thirty-five years had elapsed since Moreton and his family had abandoned the Naval Mission. While these new arrivals were tolerated, rather like the round-faced, bespectacled and bow-tied Dr. Bernard Bettelheim many years before, they were, in truth, all unwanted guests.

I remember as youths, Funakoshi and I visited the old temple, *rotten with age,*[25] that Bettelheim had occupied. At the entrance to the doctor's *habitation were two colossal and very ancient idols, one on either side; they were formed of a stone resembling quartz, but were of so great an age that all tradition of their original construction was lost, and their features obliterated . . . they were carefully preserved from the further effects of the weather by a sort of cage built over each of them. On passing through the gate guarded by these formidable giants, we found ourselves in front of a tolerably comfortable building, with a space enclosed before it in which an attempt had been made to cultivate a few flowers, so as to make it resemble an English garden. In the centre* [of the garden] *stood a very ancient tree, which appeared to be a Portugal laurel, the top of which was flourishing and green while the trunk was so decayed that a wall had been partly built round it for its support.*[18]* I also recall a low wooden fence, which stood about hip height on an adult, encircling the temple. There, still, a bell

Plate 32. Dr. Bettelheim's residence on Okinawa

was hanging to the left of the building at the end of the broad verandah, which, I recall, had a very melodious tone when struck.

Everything was done to try and remove Bettelheim, including petitions sent to the British government, suggesting that force might be used. His life was made very awkward. Officials, spies really, would walk in front and behind him, calling to all to clear the way for a Hollander was coming. 'Hollander' was the term commonly used to describe any westerner. He was excluded from buying provisions from the people, and he was excluded from using the public ferry, for example. He was even *prevented from hiring any natives to help in destroying the snakes which infested his house and court.*[17] When he occupied the temple, early on, the priests still worshipped in a section that he had made his bedroom, which must have drawn *a swarm of rats to sport among the sacrifices offered* [25] to the idols therein.

The Okinawan people said that Christianity defied reason, and Bettelheim and other missionaries, certainly up to the third decade of the twentieth century, had very little success. I remember an Okinawan friend, named Anya, in 1912, telling me that only five French missionaries were present on the islands, and they were the only foreign residents. My people resented being imposed upon and being considered, 'virgin soil for sowing the seed of Truth' [Salwey].

To my utter astonishment, whilst staying in Shuri, I received an invitation from Prince Shojun, or Matsuyama, as the Japanese commonly styled him, noting that he would like to see me. I was honoured by the invitation, but I was also very puzzled, not to say a little concerned, as many thoughts, good and bad, rushed through my mind. I even had the audacity to consider, though I blush even now as I think it, that he might wish to consult an Okinawan doctor trained in the scientific method. I was wrong.

Prince Shojun was the third son of the ex-king and had been partly educated in Tokyo. I met him in a tea-house in Naha as indicated, *and found the prince attended by two of his nobles named Ie and Tama-Gusiku. There was no formality about the conversation, which was carried on in Japanese, of which language the prince . . . was a perfect master,* unlike Prince Shoten, mentioned earlier, who could speak no language but his own. *One of his attendants, too, spoke Japanese fluently; the other could only say a few words.*[4b] We spoke about Tokyo, my medical studies, but on that occasion it was never really revealed why I had been summoned.

A day or two later I paid visits at the houses of my host and his attendants. The exterior of such Okinawan mansions was not striking, and the gate remained always inhospitably shut. Once within, however, the visitor found himself in an atmosphere of courtesy nowise inferior to that of Japan. The disposition, too, of the apartments, with their mats and ornamental hanging scrolls, recalled Japan, and everyone sat on the floor . . . [crossed-legged, and not in the Japanese style with the knees under] *. . . But a curious peculiarity was the presence in the court outside the reception-rooms, which were of course open to the outer air in that delicious climate, of cages containing fighting cocks that kept up an unpleasant crowing. The charming female servants of Japan were absent, their place being taken by men, who, with deep obeisances, brought in tea and somewhat dubious cakes. Nowhere was a woman to be seen, though many were the heads of men and boys peering round corners and over screens as we passed in and out.*[4b] The prince was *ready to chat away in the most unconventional manner, and the party went off right merrily.*[4b]

I was introduced to a Scot, Professor Basil Hall Chamberlain, who was then Emeritus Professor of Japanese and Philology at my university. He was a very remarkable fellow, and I joined him along with the old Governor one day, to investigate how many people there were in the one jail that served the entire Ryukyu archipelago. Throughout this book I have referred to the civility of the people of my land, and that day, the 12th March, 1892, a day taken quite at random, will serve to illustrate my point. Three men were imprisoned for breaking prison or for concealing criminals; one woman for the avoidance of punishment; two men for forgery of private seals and documents; two females for murderous intent; six men for assault; one man for manslaughter; one woman for murder (two women had argued over a man); one man for libel; twenty men and one woman for fraud and receiving stolen goods; four men and three women for offences connected with stolen goods; five men for violation of various rules and regulations; three men and four women for incendiarism; and, one hundred and seventeen men and eleven women for theft. The total in prison therefore was one hundred and eighty-five – one hundred and sixty-two men and twenty-three women, which, when given the total population of the archipelago was infinitesimal.[iii]

Okinawa was now operating under Japanese criminal law of course. Formerly, Okinawa had based its penal code on the Chinese system and the ancient laws of Satsuma. When I was a child, these earlier laws, which were notable for their simplicity and severity, were still adhered too, though it must be said that sentences were not always carried out. *Offences in respect to parents, ancestors and relations, ranging from murder down to simple assault, were punished with crucifixion, decapitation, or banishment, according to the gravity of the crime. The murder of a husband by his wife was punished by crucifixion. Murder in other cases, forging the Government seals, opening or rifling graves, burglary, accompanied by manslaughter, and other personal violence, with decapitation. Bribery, libel, the profession of Christianity or other religion not recognised in Okinawa, adultery, theft of official money, entering the castle without permission, and gambling (second offence), were punished by banishment – in some cases to uninhabited islands.*[10]

Violence offered to people by persons under the influence of drink was punished – in the case of shizoku, by confinement in temple buildings; in the case of heimin, by flogging and imprisonment; in the case of officials, by dismissal. Taking a man's wife and children in pledge for money lent was a punishable offence, but did not come under the head[ing] of grave crimes. Those also who charged a higher rate of interest on money lent than twenty per cent per annum were punished. Two things were brought out very clearly by these laws – namely the subordination of a wife to her husband, and of the heimin to the shizoku.[10*]

Convicts were transported to the island of Yaeyama and forced to live under conditions of extreme hardship. The disease rate was high, and many died working in the fields and countryside. But on to more delicate matters.

Ladies of the upper classes, as I have recently noted, spent their lives in a retirement so absolute in those days that one only saw them very occasionally. *Rarely did a lady leave the house which was her lifelong home. Should some extraordinary occasion compel her to do so, she retired from view within a closely shut palanquin . . . The Okinawan gentlemen took refuge from the virtuous dullness of their homes by seeking the society of ladies of more facile habits, the number of whom was very considerable. These lived in special quarters, and practised the arts of singing, dancing, and conversation.*[4a*]

These women, mistresses, were astute at business and served a valuable function. I should like to quote from Mr. Ijichi, who, writing at the time, sums up the situation nicely: '*Every Japanese trader arriving in Okinawa engaged one, to whom he entrusted everything, even to the management of his mercantile affairs; and when he departed, the girl sold to best advantage the articles confided to her charge, so that when her master came back again she was able to render him a satisfactory account, in which there was never any error or prevarication to the amount of a single penny.*'[iv] These women, though unable to read or write, tied knots in cords to assist their memory in transactions that could run into tens of thousands.

Such women danced for the benefit of the public generally, on certain days. During my stay, such an occasion presented itself in Naha, and whilst I had seen numerous festivities of this kind, my new Scottish friend, had not. Thanks to Professor Hall's writings, which he was kind enough to send me upon publication, and which I still possess, I am able to present an account of that day, and what happened, that far exceeds my memory. '*Being told in the morning that a curious procession and dance were to take place, I got up early and hurried off to see it. The crowds were dense – numbers of people on the roofs of the houses, and a few even on the roofs of the funeral vaults! These crowds were composed almost exclusively of the lower classes, dirty and perspiring. I twice saw the procession pass – one as a common individual, standing in the sun and jolted by the crowd; once as an aristocrat, for whom space was cleared through the intervention of that ever-delightful individual, the Japanese policeman. The police treated the people pretty roughly, pulling and throwing them about like bundles; but the tortuous narrowness of those coral-wall-lined streets made drastic measures necessary. All the actors in the procession were women, some quite elderly – the owners or duennas of 'establishments' – some little girls, but most young women, all smiling and happy; not delicately fragile like the Japanese, but buxom and healthy-looking, and evidently enjoying to the full the amusement which their bright dresses and their dancing, or rather posturing,* *caused to the spectators. First came a figure armed with a long stick to clear, or pretend to clear, the way; for in this the Japanese police were the real agents. Then a flag with a picture of a carp swimming up-stream, the well-known symbol of successful endeavour; and immediately after this strutted a gorgeous lion with flowing mane and hair of red, black, green, and lilac, and a bright green face, attended by several dancing-girls in red and a woman with a gong, while behind came two women dressed up like men, and playing on horns which produced a sound rather like that of Scotch bagpipes.*[4a]*

'This closed the first part of the procession. The second part consisted of women pretending to ride toy horses. The third included a number of imitation Chinamen in figured silks, some – perhaps all – representing historical or legendary characters; but the only two I could identify were King Bun on foot, leading a sage Tai-ko-bo in a jinrikisha! This was the sole vehicle in the whole procession. But the most comical spectacle of all was a frail nymph of some fifty-five or sixty winters, who had got herself up like a high Japanese official of the olden time, and danced like mad. To her succeeded a long train of girls and children, each with a scarlet or purple fillet bound round the temples and hanging down behind, and this closed the procession.'*[4a]

I had a chance to visit a number people in the course of my stay, including my good friend Gichin Funakoshi, who I hadn't seen for nearly four years, though we had kept in touch by letter. I found him at home one afternoon following a tiring day's teaching at school, and his wife with their son, Yoshihide (Giei), who was, I suppose about two years old at the time. Formerly, when a male child was born, his hair was allowed to grow naturally, but towards the end of the nineteenth century, it became *the custom to shave the head until the second or third year.*[14] During the writing of this book, Yoshihide died, aged seventy. Throughout the intervening sixty-eight or sixty-nine years, I never met him, but I attended his funeral, as I did my old friend, Gichin's, on 26th April, 1957, when I read of his death in a Tokyo newspaper. Azato has been dead for fifty-six years; Itosu, forty-six years. The times we spent together seem so very distant, another world, and yet, on the other hand, they seem like only yesterday. The gods play strange tricks on human memory. My wife is dead; one of my children is dead. Why have I lived so long? I sometimes wonder – is it a blessing, or is it a torment?

Funakoshi was very poor in a financial sense, but he retained the dignity of a *shizoku*; indeed so much so, that I sometimes took him for Liu-hia Hwui.[v] At the time, he was earning the grand sum of three yen

Plate 33. Common people of Naha

a month as a teacher, paying a monthly rent of twenty-five *sen*, and keeping seven people on the remainder.[vi] I know his wife worked tirelessly, for more hours in a day than she ought to have done, and she was skilled not only in the weaving of the *kasuri* cloth, but also in the propagation of crops that kept the family going. Funakoshi's wife was a truly remarkable woman. I learned of her death[vii], from asthma, ten years after she died when reading Gichin Funakoshi's obituary in the newspaper. I was filled with a very great sadness that affected me for weeks afterwards, as I reflected back into the past. Behind every great man there is a great woman. A great man chooses a great woman; this is something that is not always appreciated, even today. Funakoshi's wife, like most women on Okinawa in the nineteenth century, led hard lives.

Funakoshi lived in a fairly humble part of Naha in a neighbourhood of tradesmen. His family had come down in the world not only because of the abolition of the Okinawan hierarchical system, but because of his father's drinking problem, and the subsequent squandering of the family fortune. Funakoshi's grandfather on his father's side, had had a house in Teira-machi, but that had already been sold. I believe that his father could not cope with the changes that had happened, and found the only solace he could in liquor. The smell of *awamori* always seemed to be about him.

Karate at this time, so I was told, was beginning to be practised more openly. Already a teacher at the Shuri Jinjo Koto Shotgakko was instructing his pupils. It would not be long before Funakoshi could practise in his garden and passers by stop and watch – how different from those clandestine training sessions only a few years before, when the art was banned by the government! Even people who didn't practise karate sometimes had *makiwara* embedded into their gardens, and would hit it for relaxation or to vent frustration, but karate was far from being popular. Unlike myself, who had trained principally with Itosu *Sensei*, though I benefited greatly from Azato *Sensei's* advice, Funakoshi, in the years I was in Tokyo, had trained under other masters, including, Kiyuna, Toonno, Niigaki, and, arguably the finest exponent of the art in the nineteenth century, Sokon Matsumura. As Funakoshi wrote in his autobiography, neither Azato nor Itosu suffered from petty jealousy, and were quite happy for their students to train with other masters.

Sokon Matsumura of Shuri was in his eighties as the time.[viii] He had learned his karate initially from the Chinese attaché, Iwah, and from Satunushi Sakugawa, in the first decades of the nineteenth century, though Iwah taught principally in Kume, and Maesato[ix], Kogusuku, and, of course, Azato, were amongst his famed students. Matsumura was a legend in his own lifetime, and the story of how he overcame an opponent without a blow being struck was famous throughout the islands, and had endured for more than fifty years. This tale is recorded by Funakoshi in two of his works and will not be repeated here. I once saw Matsumura, and only once, when he was in his eighties. He was very tall for the time, just short of six feet I should imagine, and strong, despite his age, but his most striking feature was the brilliance of his eyes, which seemed to bore holes into you. This was a natural feature of the man, I am sure, but his spirit shone through them with such profundity that a glare could stop you in your tracks. This is what happened to the Naha engraver, Uehara. He was, at least in the first instance, mesmerized. There is a line from Lao Tzu's *Tao Te Ching*,[x] that generally holds true, that reads, *One who excels as a warrior does not appear formidable* – this was not the case with Sokon Matsumura.

Karate and Kendo are related. There is a story that Matsumura studied kendo of the Jigen School when he was stationed in Satsuma. If this is so, then I feel that his kendo helped him focus his attention and his eyes helped his kendo spirit. He was not given the title *Bushi* for nothing!

Funakoshi studied under Matsumura *from time to time*.[c] Matsumura's famous students, along with Itosu and Azato of course, were Kiyuna, Kuwae, Tawada and Ishimine.

The point I remember most about Funakoshi's training with Matsumura was the old master's *kiai*. Like his eyes, Matsumura, according to Funakoshi, had perfected the *kiai-jutsu* technique, which, even with his eyes closed, could freeze you to the earth. If his eyes were ablaze, and if what Funakoshi said was true, then the combination must have been truly formidable. Imagine possessing these qualities along with the finest karate technique of the century; but then the former qualities were, I am sure, enhanced beyond all measure by the latter.

I also recall that Funakoshi said that Matsumura made little distinction between the arts and the martial arts, and that he greatly valued both the study of literature and history within a Confucian framework. Matsumura thus encouraged mind and body training, so that an individual might be well rounded. The strength and discriminating powers of the tutored mind can be used to focus technique. Too much attention these days, from what I have seen, is given to technique, without regard to the mind.

I had written to Funakoshi to let him know that I was visiting Okinawa, and he had invited me to his home that late afternoon. On the morning of that day, I walked the fine, broad paved road to Shuri – or 'Shui' as Okinawans invariably pronounced it, *as we habitually dropped the 'r' in the middle of words*[4*] – to pay my regards to Itosu *Sensei*. I remember, *en route*, diverting to Benzaiten Shrine. It had originally been constructed on an island to house early Buddhist scriptures, but these had been destroyed by Satsuma soldiers in 1609, and the temple had been rebuilt that same century. One had to cross a little bridge with low wooden railings to enter. All are memories now, for the shrine was destroyed in the Pacific War.

Itosu enquired of my studies and duties, whether I was able to find time to practise karate, and so on. I remember him saying that change was in the air. Then I returned to Naha, musing all the way.

I recall walking along *the narrow* [back] *street*[s], *or rather lane*[s], [that] *wound their tortuous way, sometimes muddy, sometimes paved with irregular stones more or less flat,*[4a] and through the maze of little low dwellings, arriving at Funakoshi's gate the same time as he, due to his being delayed at school. On meeting, great smiles came over both our faces, and it seemed to me that nothing had changed – a day could have passed since we had last met. At this time, Funakoshi was a lower-grade teacher in Naha, instructing the first and second grades, having recently passed his examination as an assistant. Later, he would pass more exams to teach older children.

We entered the grounds of his small one storey rented house. Like virtually all other houses on Okinawa it *was surrounded by a stone wall . . . which ensured privacy, but sadly obstructed ventilation.*[4a*] Once inside, he slipped off his dark jacket that buttoned to the neck with a single line of bright brass buttons embossed with a cherry blossom motif. He was obliged to wear this uniform as a teacher. His cap badge bore the same blossom design. His young wife brought refreshment and we sat down, cross-legged on the floor, and he listen attentively as I told him of my experiences in medical school, hospital, and in Tokyo generally. He said that he planned to go there one day, and I didn't doubt him, for *he was a very determined character.*[g] I recall telling my host about the cold winters in Japan. *In the winter months* [on Okinawa] *some cold days are experienced, but snow or ice are unknown,*[28] and I related to him how wondrous an experience it was to watch snow falling. We spoke of the ice-capped Mount Fuji. I remarked about Bettelheim, and he seemed to know a fair bit about him, including the name of the Christian convert, Satchi Harma, a twenty-two or twenty-three year old guard, whom Bettelheim declared a martyr, when he died in suspicious circumstances. At the time *Japanese law declared it a capital crime to preach or believe the gospel,*[20*] and Satchi Harma had, according to the missionary, been *squeezed (pressed, tortured) on hand and foot, though he added, this had been done to cure him of madness.*[20]

I also remember two other points that Funakoshi raised with regard

Plate 34. Gichin Funakoshi (sitting centre, next to man with tie) as a young teacher on Okinawa

to Bettelheim. Firstly, he noted that the authorities, upon his arrival, had instigated three *shchibang, or guard-stations, each containing five men taken from the class of literati,*[25] two stations being located in the temple grounds, the other in the lane leading up to the temple. Secondly, to attract the guards to his belief, Bettelheim *pasted large oblong slips of red paper on his door-posts, inscribed with Christian motives.*[25*]

Somehow, I recall this led to a discussion on the origin of the Okinawan people, and we both agreed that racially, the Ryukyuans had a greater proportion of Ainu and southern Mongoloid elements than the Japanese, and that within historic times, no ethnic minority of any significance had existed among them. The differences between the Japanese and Ryukyuans are most observable in the lower classes of each group, representatives of the latter country tending to have higher foreheads, less flattened faces, less deeply set eyes, arched and thick eyebrows, longer eyelashes, superior noses, less prominent cheek bones and much greater hairiness. In truth, Ryukyuans more closely resemble the people of south Kyushu than other Japanese. Later, I recall reading an academic paper that showed that Ryukyuans had a lower frequency of blood group A than the Japanese; that there was a fairly regular decrease in that blood group stretching from northern Kyushu to the southern Ryukyus; and, that the southern Ryukyuans also had a higher frequency of blood group B, and appeared quite different, serologically, to the inhabitants of islands to the north and most of Taiwan, to the west.

Above us hung a very fine piece of calligraphy by Itosu. Itosu was a wonderful calligrapher. He taught that calligraphy and karate have many feelings in common, including rhythm and *zanshin*. My host and I discussed karate and medicine, and Funakoshi wanted to know my thoughts on the subject. I was the physician with a little knowledge of karate, he was the *karateka* with an interest in medicine, and so a most agreeable conversation took place. I remember him telling me that he considered karate, apart from the strengthening of muscle (which apart from the obvious benefits, has unseen benefits, such as displacing weight on weight-bearing joints), also improved the digestive and circulatory systems.

Over dinner, I spoke of my little adventures with Prince Shojun and Prof. Chamberlain. In turn, Funakoshi told me of his teaching and his karate. He informed me of the death of a former karate pupil, Madera, who had succumbed to cholera in the epidemic of 1891. I remembered Madera well, because he had a bizarre encounter with a leper, a rare occurrence in those days. Whatever we spoke off, Funakoshi always seemed to return to karate. It was the centre of his universe.

Funakoshi's wife put on a most splendid meal, and I fancy that his extremely limited savings had gone into the dinner. I was honoured and embarrassed at the same time that my old friend should do this for me. I remember the meal as though I sat down to it yesterday: *sliced boiled eggs, which had been dyed crimson, fish made into rolls and boiled in fat, pieces of cold baked fish, slices of hog's liver, sugar candy, cucumber, mustard, salted radish tops, and fragments of lean pork, fried.*[5] It had been a cool day, and so Funakoshi, as was his custom, ate the cold dishes and a lot of vegetables in particular, as they were his favourite part of any meal. It was a wonderful reunion, and far more penetrating on my mind than my encounter with the prince. I remember, during the meal, Funakoshi and I discussed Azato's classification of three human personality types – full, contracting and penetrating, and how, if one met one type, it was only possible to overcome such an opponent by adhering to the characteristics of one of the other two types.[xi] I had never heard Azato speak of such things, so I was most interested in what Funakoshi, the master's only student, had to say on the subject. As I have said already, Funakoshi and I used to meet along the way to training, and would walk back together afterwards. I recall that, since I had left, Funakoshi telling me that he had taken to walking by himself after a hard training session, and that he had found much value in it.

Funakoshi kept me updated on what had been happening on the island, and as he did so, I could not help but think that the quiet and peaceful retirement that the geographical location had for centuries afforded us was now at an end. He said that there were nearly half a million people living on Okinawa, and over two and a half thousand Japanese residing in Naha; that there were now one hundred and seventy schools throughout the Ryukyu islands; that there was one Middle School, one Normal School, one Medical School, one Higher Female School, one Agricultural School, and one Industrial School. Good roads were being extended, and a telegraph line linked different towns, whilst a submarine cable connected the various islands, which, or course, had been largely cut-off from communication with the outside world before. Lighthouses were being built and weather bureaux had been established at Naha, on Oshima and at Yayeyama. Japan was pressing ahead with developments at last.[xii]

I also remember that after the meal, Funakoshi told me about Kanryo Higaonna[xiii], the fourth son of Kanyo Higaonna, a former student of Master Seisho Aragaki, who, through the influences and good offices of Aragaki, Kojo Taite [1837–1917] and Chomei Yoshimura, a high-ranking official, had journeyed to Fuzhou, the capital of Fukien Province, and, after studying under Master Ryu Ryuko[xiv], a teacher of Shaolin kempo of the Southern School, for fifteen years, had returned to Naha in 1882, and had gained a substantial reputation during my absence. Funakoshi told me that Higaonna, who was about forty years of age at the time[xv], was outstanding in every sphere of karate practice.[xvi]

Funakoshi also spoke of contemporaries who were later to become

Plate 35. Kanryo Higaonna

karate masters of note. I remember him speaking about Chotoku Kyan, who was about twenty-two at the time. Funakoshi said that he had trained with Itosu and showed real promise, and that he knew the *kata Chinto*, *Passai*, and *Kushanku*.[xvii]

I also recall that Funakoshi made reference to the skills of the Japanese policemen in Naha. *With their formidable and famous knowledge of the art of jujitsu, they were a powerful representative of the might of the law and a small number of police were amply sufficient to uphold its dignity,*[xviii] he said.

I should like to mention another aside here. Funakoshi changed many points in his karate, and these have been handed down to the present time. One particular point of note is the stance. Funakoshi's third son, Yoshitaka (Gigo), who I understand was a very dynamic *karateka*, developed stances that were both longer and deeper than we used to train in. Now, I have seen these deep stances, and I think they have much to recommend them for training purposes. They are good for leg strengthening, hip flexors, flexibility, and *hara*, which lead to increased speed and confidence. However, it is worth recalling that Itosu's stances were much higher for a reason, the logic being mobility, which of course is essential if training is to be conducted in a purposeful martial way. A few years ago, I received information from a friend who travelled to Okinawa and witnessed a demonstration given by one of Itosu's best students, Chosin Chibana. Chibana had, I am told, kept the old stances in his *kata*.

This question of stance is very important indeed. Please remember that Itosu taught karate in the public educational system around the turn of the twentieth century; the same time he devised the *Pinan kata*. He developed and taught a style specifically designed for school children, and this was devoid of much that Funakoshi and I originally learned. The agenda was different.

The point that I recall most vividly about my conversation with Funakoshi at that time was his telling me of another *kata* he had learned; from Itosu, I believe. He had hinted at it in his letters, and I was eager to see it performed. Funakoshi would ask to be taught a new form when he thought his teacher was prepared to impart it, but he knew the benefit of studying a *kata* deeply. As I have noted earlier in this work, Funakoshi spent many years learning *Tekki*, but I am not absolutely sure when, exactly, he had been shown *Kushanku*.[xix] It may have been before I left for Tokyo, or in my absence – I cannot remember. As this form is now widely known as *Kanku-dai*, I will refer to it as such henceforth. Funakoshi confided that he had been studying the Shorin-ryu *kata* for some years, that it contained a *Tekki* sequence, but was far longer, and that it had totally involved him.

Funakoshi demonstrated this new form for me, and I was most impressed, because he appeared to be so expert in it. The *kata* is sometimes known as the *Fighting Form Against Eight Enemies*.[a] I knew the *kiba-dachi* and *kosa-dachi* stances from *Tekki*, and the *zenkutsu-dachi* from *makiwara* practice, though I had never trained in *kokutsu-dachi*, and others, before, and Funakoshi explained to me the values of such stances. From the karate that Funakoshi and I learned, modern Shoto-kan, if I can call it that, seems to have veered noticeably with regard to these two stances.[xx] Both stances were much shorter of course, but the weight ratios were different also. Today, upon enquiring, I under-stand that the front-stance weight ratio is 60:40, front leg, back leg. In our day the ratio was more 50:50, and rather than having the feeling of going forward slightly, the feeling in the old stance was back with the front leg and forward with the back leg. This was important, for it raised the body a little and centred tension/release in the abdomen. I understand this centring is not taught today. If this is so, then it is a sad state of affairs in my opinion. The *zenkutsu-dachi* is worthy of special mention, for the toes of the back foot used to be angled much more away from the direction of the punch, and, superficially, differed only minimally from the back foot of the back-stance – the difference being that the toes of the back foot on the *zenkutsu-dachi* were pointed slightly more forward. The stance was also performed in a straight line, with the heels in line, and so our front-stance differed markedly with the modern *zenkutsu-dachi*.

Similarly, the back-stance weight ratio today, I am reliably informed, is 30:70 in favour of the back leg. In our day, the weight ratio was as close as one could get to 100% of the weight on the back leg, with the front leg virtually straight, which is impossible to achieve in today's long stance. Because both the back-stance and front-stance were performed in a straight line, the delay in switching stances was minimal and the effectiveness increased.

I should like now to include some detailed technical information and mention a few points on the *kata Kanku-dai*, for Funakoshi did teach it to me during my stay. I committed it to memory at the time, and have practised it as a form of exercise, mental and physical, when-ever possible over the past seventy years, though *Tekki* remains my favourite. I should also like to mention how the *kata* I learned differs from that which is widely practised today in Funakoshi's style. This is not a technical book, and I shall not bore the reader with too many points, though there are more [see pages 44 and 45 for an explanation of the bracketed numbers that follow].

The opening move of the *kata* was performed in the same way, but whereas [as is common practice today] it is now frequent to cover the tops of the first two fingers of the left hand with the tops of the first two fingers of the right hand {–/1b}, when I learnt it, all the right hand fingers virtually obscured all the left hand fingers {84/–}. The position of the thumbs is the same. The opening sequence continued – the hands and arms were raised, then parted and came down slowly, all the way, so that the right '*shuto*' touched the left palm, and there was no focus placed in the end of the movement [as is invariably practised today]. Also, whereas the right *shuto*, as it were, was placed in the centre of the left palm today, in my time, palms did not touch, but rather, the little finger of the right hand touched all four of the left {86/2}.[xxi] The *kaishu-haiwan-uke* {87,88/3,4} were slightly more forward from the elbow in my time.[xxii]

The move leading to the left *tate shuto-uke* {90/5} was different, as was the block. Today, a smoother move occurs where the right arm goes out in front, the left arm underneath {–/5a}, but we brought the right fist to the right hip immediately, with the left fist on top {89/–}, as I have previously described for *Tekki Shodan*. For the *tate shuto-uke*,[xxiii] we merely performed a *nukite*-like technique, palm downwards.[xxiv]

All *koshi gamae*[xxv] in our day, had the fist on top with the thumb facing the body, whereas today, the palm side of the fist faces the body.[xxvi]

When performing the two punches {91,93/6,8}, we stood very much in *hachiji-dachi*, whereas today, some *karateka* seem to prefer more of a *heiko-dachi,* but as both these come under *shizentai*, it is not a problem. Additionally, we did not punch to the solar plexus, but rather above it and to the side.[xxvii]

When we subsequently blocked *chudan uchi-uke* {92,94/7,9}, we did not twist the hips so far as to be at right angles from when we punched.

When we kicked {96/11}, we always kicked *gedan* and used the foot's instep; this we called '*kahanashi.*' The pull-up to the kick was simply to withdraw the right foot {95/10}. Nowadays, I understand, some people bring the left foot up half the length of the stance and then engage the right leg to kick. The stance is short before you start to move, and I believe the old method is best. Both the kick and *tsuki*[xxviii] were performed at *chudan*.[xxix]

On the first *kiai* point today {–/15}, the *nukite* was practised at the upper-level[xxx], whereas it is now practised *chudan*. The fingers of the spear-hand were all straight, whereas today, I have seen the centre fingers bent, braced by the first and fourth fingers.

When Funakoshi taught me *Kanku-dai*, there were no *kiai* in the *kata*.[xxxi]

The *mae-geri* today {–/17,22,37}, after the *jodan shuto-uchi*, were not performed with the ball of the foot, but rather with the whole underside of the foot {102,107, 23/–}.[xxxii]

After the *manji-gamae* {103/18}, in my time there was no left *nagashi-uke* or right *gedan shuto-uchi* {–/19}.[xxxiii] The positioning of the left arm on the pull up from the *manji-gamae* was not to form a *gedan* block or guard, but a *tsuki*.[xxxiv]

When we performed the two side-kicks, as they are today {112,116/27,30}, we kicked as I have already described. As before, the position of the hand on top of the fist on the hip was palm downward {111,114/–}. Again, what today is called *uraken*, we simply referred to as *tsuki*, with the level at *chudan*.[xxxv]

What today is called *uraken-uchi* {–/38}, after stepping forward, we used to call *urate*, and the arm was further extended.

After the *ura-zuki*[xxxvi] when one landed on the floor, we looked not forward, but in the direction we were to move in next, and our positioning was similar to a very low *kokutsu-dachi*, with the weight largely on the ball of the right foot, and with our hands on the floor, with our weight to our right, as we turned {129/–}.[xxxvii]

The move that immediately followed that mentioned above was extremely deep, resembling an excessive back-stance. The hands took up the position of a *shuto-uke* {130/–}.[xxxviii]

Before the kick {138/52} a half step was taken with the left foot.

After the *shihon-nukite* {140/54}, performed in the same manner as described for the first *kiai* point, and twist, as if one's wrist was grabbed, the modern-day *uraken* {–/55} taken through to *chudan tettsui-uchi* {–/56} was not performed. Rather, we did a *tsuki* {142/–} followed by a *jodan uraken* {143/–}[xxxix], in a movement called 'yoriashi.'[xl]

On the '*Tekki* sequence' that follows on from the point immediately described, the *koshi gamae* was not included.[xli]

The high lifting of the leg of today {–/60a} to enter *kiba-dachi* and *ryo ude mawashi-uke*, was completely absent, and we used to just step through {146/–}.

Because we did not practise in long, deep stances, we were not obliged to shorten when we performed *jodan shuto juji-uke* {148/62}.

We used to perform a quick double-kick, but we did not jump {–/64a, 64}.[xlii]

There did not used to be a *kiai* on the last technique. What today is called *uraken-uchi* {–/65}, we used to extend the arm further {153/–}.

As our stances were very straight, we never deviated very much from the *kata's embusen*.

Funakoshi was a master of *Kanku-Dai*.[xliii] He had great confidence in that form which was born out of years of daily practice. *He was a purist.*[g] I remember a senior once telling me that it takes one hundred repetitions of a *kata* to learn it; then ten thousand repetitions to understand it. I believe that Funakoshi trained in the form daily, and, if only performed once a day, he might have come to understand it in the intervening thirty years between learning it and demonstrating it when he went to Tokyo in 1922. *Kanku-Dai* was, of course, the form that he displayed before Prof. Jigaro Kano, the founder of Judo, and his senior students. Given that Funakoshi learned the *Tekki* before *Kanku-Dai*, and given Funakoshi's temperament for repetition, I have wondered why he favoured *Kanku-Dai* over *Tekki*.[xliv]

In the nineteenth century, it was common for karate masters of great skill to be familiar with but a few *kata*. When Itosu and his senior students began to teach in schools, more were developed. Variety may be the spice of life, but for the practice of *kata* the maxim does not hold up. During the eight years I learned karate on Okinawa, I was taught only one form by my teacher. Today, students seem to know many forms. I spoke to one black-belt recently of nine years training who knew twenty-six! I fear that depth has given way to breadth, and the tempering and polishing of the mind and body cannot be the same. I see little to be gained from a superficial understanding of many forms; and superficial it must be for it takes years to understand a *kata*, and there are no short cuts that I am aware of. I also note that sparring is practised in its own right without regard to the *kata*! This is an aberration in my view. I must quote from Funakoshi who knew well, and I think had something to regret: '*It must be emphasized that sparring does not exist apart from the kata but for the practice of kata, so naturally there should be no corrupting influence on one's kata from sparring practice. When one becomes enthusiastic about sparring, there is a tendency for his kata to become bad. Karate, to the very end, should be practiced with kata as the principal method and sparring as a supporting method.*'[a] I was told that Funakoshi lost respect from many karate masters on Okinawa when he introduced *kumite* and changed the names of the *kata*, and this I can well understand.

But back to the meal! I was determined to repay my host for the expense he had gone to for my benefit, and a week or so later the opportunity arose. My father knew an old nobleman by the name of

Yonabara, who still feasted in the Chinese style, and arranged for me to attend a meal in the old manner. I believe he had worked for the *Monobugiosho*, or Home and Finance Departments. I asked my father if it would be convenient for me to bring my very dear friend along, and he said that it would. I knew Gichin would appreciate what was to follow.

There was *no more squatting on mats this time, but stiff backed chairs . . . No more of the familiar Japanese fish and rice and seaweed soup, but richer and more complicated Celestial dishes served in twelve courses with an elaborate menu in Chinese. This feast was intended to be an exact counterpart of that which it was the custom to offer to the Chinese ambassadors who used to come and present their congratulations of the court of Peking on the accession of each new Okinawan sovereign. Some of the robes then worn were brought out – gorgeous red and green silks. But as it was only play this time and not reality, our hosts did not don these robes themselves. Some extremely bewitching singing-girls were present to help on the feast with native music, and* [with] *these the son of the house playfully dressed up in the gorgeous Chinese robes, producing a charming effect.*[4b]

After dinner we took a long walk among the hills and groves of this delightful island. We saw several women working very hard in the field; and the peasantry [still] *appeared to be poorly clad and in poor condition, yet they were as polite as the most accomplished mandarins.*[6] Funakoshi's wife would arise early in the morning to attend the family allotment more than a mile away, and as he walked in grand company, I knew what my companion was thinking.

Funakoshi and I chatted with the old nobleman, and I told him about my encounter with the prince and the meal, as I had Funakoshi. He then told me about when he had feasted aboard the *Susquehanna* in 1854, at the time when the regent was invited to dine. His father had been a treasurer, and wore a robe of yellow, which contrasted with the regent's, who wore dark purple and a cap of crimson. *Turtle soup, goose, kid curry, and various other delicacies formed part of the feast which was spread with bountiful profusion.*[5] Part of the dessert, melons and bananas, had come from the Bonin Islands, which Perry had just visited. The old nobleman spoke of the toasts and, laughing, that the Okinawans '*showed but a very sorry appreciation of the virtue of temperance,*'[5] to use an American's words, and that *the tide of wine and wassail was fast gaining on the dry land of sober judgement . . . The regent alone preserved his silent, anxious demeanor, and all he drank was neutralized in its effects by his excessive dignity.*[5] None of

Plate 36. Regent of Okinawa

Plate 37. Dinner aboard the *Susquehanna*

the Okinawans enjoyed the 'American tea,' which was actually coffee. Our host roared with laughter as he recalled that *the Commodore* [had] *ordered down some of the more expert performers* [of the band] *to play solos on the flageolet, hautboy, clarinet, and cornet-a-piston. The regent listened attentively, but the mayor and treasurers were too busy stowing away the epular fragments to be moved by any 'concord of sweet sounds.'*[5]

That evening at the nobleman's was the last occasion I ever saw Funakoshi. If two friends had to part forever in this world, then a finer evening could not have been wished for. When it was time for Funakoshi to take up residence in Tokyo, thirty years had elapsed. My medical practice was very local and engrossed me, and Tokyo is a very large city. In fact, a further twenty years elapsed before I first learned that karate was being taught in the capital. As an *alumnus* of the Imperial University, I attended an annual dinner, and on one of these occasions, just before the outbreak of the Pacific War, I caught sight of a poster on the students' notice board. I acquired copies of Funakoshi's books, *Ryukyu Kempo: Tode* and *Rentan Goshi Tode-jitsu*, which were out of print, and I bought *Karate-Do Kyohan*. I read them eagerly, and had intended making a re-acquaintance with my old training colleague, but somehow it wasn't to be. An incurable romantic, the nobleman's feast could not be bettered, and I suppose I didn't want to spoil that, for in fifty years people are said to change greatly. I don't know if Funakoshi ever tried to track me down; perhaps not, for I fancy he was a romantic as well.

And so, my brief sojourn back to Okinawa was over. It was now back to the capital to pursue my chosen career and to fight the common enemy – disease. Master Funakoshi, as he rightly became, believed that karate was *a defence against illness and disease.*[c] He may be partly correct, I don't know, but it is well worth listening to someone who, having suffered poor digestion and attended the doctor's daily to acquire medicine[xlv], never once consulted a doctor during the following seventy-six years! I think that with Funakoshi, it was state of mind, for he had an unswerving purpose from which he was not to be distracted. He loved his karate and was forward-thinking, and it is only right that he is credited with introducing the noble art to Japan.

My last memory of *terra firma* on Okinawa was travelling to the ship from the family home and passing a beautifully manicured garden, which had seemingly just appeared in my absence, for I had no recollection of it. Surrounded by beech trees, a neatly clipped hazelnut hedge acted as a border for the most glorious japonica I had ever seen. It truly took my breath away.

The inner harbour of Naha was as pretty a spot as one could well imagine [in those days], *though from a seaman's point of view it was of little value, owing to the shallowness of the water. The greater part of it, indeed, was almost dry at low tide; and as we floated lazily over the surface of the clear, still water* [in a shallow dug-out, on the way back to the ship], *the endless beauties of coral-land lay revealed beneath us with the prodigality of form and colouring so characteristic of Nature in warmer climes; beauties to which no naturalist, however enthusiastic, no writer however gifted, has yet succeeded in doing justice . . .*

Passing the wooded islet at the harbour's entrance on our return, we came upon [what would nowadays be regarded as] *a curious scene. A party of half a dozen natives had gathered on the bare summit, and, facing towards the west, were occupied in some sort of festal or religious ceremonial. The sun was just setting, but the thick banks of cloud gathered above our heads portended a heavy storm. Bathed in a flood of hard light, a solitary figure stood out against the evening sky, slowly waving his arms and dancing an adieu to the day. Behind him* *sat the others with . . . samisen, chanting the weird, yet not unpleasing, discords of some Okinawan song. Presently the music ceased, and another stepped forward to take the dancer's place. We floated slowly on, half unconsciously under the spell of the mournful music and the strangeness of the scene we were watching, until both had vanished into the distance.*[23]*

On board the steamer, *the deck was crowded with friends come to say farewell; and as we rounded Nammin point, this castle-like coral rock was seen to be alive with* [silhouetted] *people waving adieux to us with their green parasols, after the peculiar Okinawan fashion. The last impression I received of Okinawa was from its white, glistening grave-vaults* [catching the last rays of the sun] *on the green hillsides. Then night fell, and in the brilliant moonlight, island after island rose up in clear-cut outline as we sped rapidly northward over a sea of glass.*[4b]

THE END

REFERENCES

INTRODUCTION

i. And later re-published in 1967 by N. Israel/Da Capo Press/Frank Cass.

ii. In Vol. II, Chapter VI, pp. 459–460.

iii. *The Diary of Richard Cocks, Cape Merchant in the English Factory in Japan, 1615–1622* (Hakluyt Society, London, 1883).

iv. Adams, W. *The Logbook of William Adams, 1614–1619, and Related Documents* (J. Purnell, ed., 1915).

v. 1916 ed., Chapter IV, *Likeyskiye Ostrova*, (or, *Visit to the Ryukyus*).

vi. Such as those given in *Commodore Perry on Okinawa: From the Unpublished Diary of a British Missionary* (Schwartz, W.L. ed., *American History Review*, Vol. 51, 2, pp. 262–276, {1946}).

vii. At the time, Thomas Maretzki was a postgraduate student in the Anthropology Department of Yale University (later he became an associate professor of that university), and his wife, a graduate of the University of Hawaii, a teacher.

viii. Cook, H. *Shotokan Karate: A Precise History* (Dragon Books, Los Angeles, 2001), p. 10.

ix. Cook (*ibid*), pp. 10–11, quotes from *Okinawan Karate-do* (published under the auspices of Uechi-ryu Karate-do Kyokai), pp. 395-397, by Uechi and Takamiyagi, and *Nihon Budo Taikei*, Vol. 8 (Tokyo, 1982), p. 60.

x. Layton, C. *Kanazawa, 10th Dan* (Shoto Publishing, 2001), p. 83.

xi. In an article that appeared in the July 1935 Japanese magazine, *Kaizo* (Vol. 17, pp. 56–72), entitled, 'Speaking About Karate' (translated by Patrick and Yuriko McCarthy (*Budo Karate*, 1st Quart. 2004, pp. 19–28), Funakoshi relates how *Ryukyo Kempo: Tode* was actually written as a result of a misunderstanding between Hoan Kosugi and himself.

xii. In the *Kaizo* article (*ibid*, p. 25), Funakoshi notes that Kosugi 'had actually been studying karate seriously for more than ten years,' which means that he had begun training before 1912. It is a complete mystery as to what the inspiration for this may have been, but it is possible that someone was instructing in karate in Tokyo before Funakoshi's arrival, though as Funakoshi notes that Kosugi 'was a closet exercise buff,' it suggests that he may have seen it somewhere and was privately practising what he saw.

xiii. In the *Kaizo* article (*ibid*), Funakoshi mentions that he taught for twenty-three years. If this is so, then what he did with the remaining ten years is unknown.

xiv. Hanratty, J. *Nishiyama: The 'Master' Interview (Fighting Arts International*, 51, 39–47).

xv. Warrener, D. *Nishiyama Hidetaka: A Karate-ka's Karate-ka (Bugeisha Magazine*, 3, 50–52).

CHAPTER I

i. The number given by Okinawans at the time.

ii. Along with the Sho family, the Nakijin and Ie were the most influential on Okinawa at that time. When Gichin Funakoshi took up residence in Tokyo in 1922, Baron Chosuke Ie was one of his patrons.

iii. One of his arrows was housed in a temple near Naha.

iv. Grant served as Republican President from 1869–1877.

v. Sometimes written '*Uekata*,' or *Oyakata* in Japanese.

vi. By 1912, Salwey estimated that there were between four and five thousand Japanese living on the Ryukyu islands – approximately 1 in 200 of the Ryukyu population at the time.

vii. Satow comments that the belt was six to seven inches wide and had a length of fourteen to fifteen feet.

viii. A number of writers, such as Beechey, Abeel, and Gutzlaff, noted the effeminate nature of the Okinawan men.

ix. *Xanthoxylon piperitum.*

x. This may be *encephalitis lethargica*.

xi. Doctor Peter Parker tried to introduce vaccination in 1837.

xii. An Okinawan king of the 13th century, and great-grandson of Tametomo.

xiii. This description is of a lake in the palace grounds.

xiv. According to Brunton[28], the walks were paved 'with different coloured tiles.'

xv. The author has been unable to locate this island, though it appears, on early nineteenth century English charts, to be just East of Amami-Oshima.

xvi. Gusukama was a schoolteacher by profession and a student of Itosu. Gusukama's favourite *kata* was *Chinto*, and he died in 1954, aged sixty-four.

xvii. Sho means 'venerable.'

xviii. Any reader wishing to know the outcome of this affair after the Japanese sent an expedition to Formosa in 1874 to punish the aborigines responsible, is given in James W. Davidson's book, *The Island of Formosa, Past and Present*.

xix. At this time on Okinawa, generations were often parted by less than twenty years.

CHAPTER II

i.   Yabu is sometimes written 'Yabe.' He was born in 1866.

ii.   The first recorded writing on karate comes from a note in 1905 made by Hanashiro.

iii.   The connection with the Middle-East is interesting, and has been a theory for many years. In his, *Historic Outline of Ryukyu Kenpo Karate-Do*, Chojun Miyagi, the founder of Goju-ryu, noted, in 1936, that, 'One opinion holds that it [karate] developed, along with the ancient cultures, in the Central Asian and Turkic areas, and gradually spread into Indo-China' (*Memories of Fighting Arts and Okinawa: Part 12 – Historical Facts, Fighting Figures*, by Mark Bishop {*Terry O'Neill's Fighting Arts International*, 93, 61–65}).

iv.   Gichin Funakoshi also used the story when he taught university students as a fundamental 'karate *koan*' for the use of the central body – hips and *hara* – that dominate and lead in technique, be it arm or leg.

v.   Though this actually refers to a rank. The source for Kushanku is Tobe Yoshihiro's, *Oshima Hikki*, a selection of interviews held with Okinawan sailors shipwrecked on Tosa Clan beaches on Shikoku. See Cook (*ibid*), p. 9, for relevant translation.

vi.   Written in 1962, this statement, of course, pre-dates subsequent investigations.

vii.   Sometimes written as 'Nawate.'

viii.   Itosu actually wrote of this classification in his *Ten Teachings*, of 1908.

ix.   It may well be that the split, Shorin and Shorei, is in fact incorrect. It is widely agreed that Shorin refers to Shaolin, but Shorei is more problematical. It may be a simple mispronunciation of Shaolin, or may refer to a temple once located in Fujian Province. Then again, it may simply be a mistake and should be Wudang. As Funakoshi noted,[b] it is more appropriate to refer to the styles as 'type' or 'manner,' and that the classification is only a rough division.

x.   In Walter Clutterbuck's 1910 article, we are given the market prices of certain foodstuffs, so: 'Eggs, per dozen, 4d; a chicken, 6d; beef (uneatable except in soup), per lb., 3d; pork (which was good), 3½d; sixteen large potatoes, 1¼d.' [15]

xi.   Some writers note left.

xii.   This is in contrast to Guillemard who noted that the extent of tattooing 'appears to vary according to the age of the individual. Thus the children have only their fingers ornamented and the whole design . . . is not completed until marriage.' [23]

xiii.   Various other designs were illustrated in the nineteenth century, and Guillemard notes, for example, 'on the wrist, or just above it, is a Maltese cross – a design which would seem to have been in vogue for a considerable period, as it is given in an illustration . . . in 1827.' [23]

xiv. Twenty-five has also been recorded.

xv. A number of western writers at the time (e.g. Williams[13]) record that the better classes were taller.

xvi. Other quotes related to this point include: 'Their stature seldom exceeded five foot, or five feet three inches;'[13] 'their average height did not exceed five feet five inches;'[24*] 'the average height being about five feet six inches,'[27] and very rarely reached above 'five feet six inches.'[2]

xvii. Sometimes the forehead is recorded.

xviii. Bayard Taylor[5b] noted that the soil was considered the property of the State and that sixth-tenths of yields were appropriated.

xix. *Naihanchi* may have previously been called '*Kiba-dachi-no-kata*' before Itosu altered it (see Noble, G., McLaren, I. and Karasawa, N. *Masters of the Shorin-ryu* (*Fighting Arts International*, 50, pp. 24–28).

CHAPTER III

i. One-toothed, dense wooden *geta* – footwear similar to very heavy flip-flops and not to be confused with the '*saba*.'[26]

ii. It is astonishing to think, given the population and size of the world, that the oldest authenticated man to have ever lived, Shigechiyo Izumi, who reached the age of one hundred and twenty years, two hundred and thirty-seven days (1865–1986), was born in the village of Asan on the island of Tokunoshima, a tiny remote island some sixty miles north-east of Okinawa, and part of the Ryukyu chain.

iii. Commodore Perry's own words.

iv. 'The price of a common slave of this kind was from two to ten dollars.'[5*]

v. The *samisen* is a three-stringed plucked instrument, the fingerboard being some two feet in length, by an inch wide, without frets. The instrument produces a sound surprisingly heavy and low-pitched for its size; the strings at the time being made from liquid extracted from the spinning sacs of silkworms. The player plucks the strings with an ivory *sume*.

vi. The *koto* is a thirteen stringed, plucked wooden instrument, hollowed out with circular sound holes underneath.

vii. The *jamising* is an instrument rather like a banjo covered with the skin of a large snake.

viii. Small flag-fish and chisel-mouth, respectively.

ix. The island is also notable in relation to this book, in that not far from Ishigaki Port is the grave of one hundred and twenty-eight Chinese who were killed in a fight aboard an American ship in 1852.

x. Sometimes this has been formalised – right foot to the left foot.

xi. The difference is absolutely minimal when compared with late 1950s/early 1960s JKA film, and any variation may be simply be attributed to individual differences. However, the difference can become quite marked when compared with what Shotokan *karateka* practice today.

xii. Funakoshi's 1925 book, *Renten Gosin Tode-Jutsu,* gives the best view, as the 1922 book, *Ryukyu Kempo: Tode,* is unclear.

xiii. In Funakoshi's 1925 book the hands are brought to the side, as practised today.

xiv. *Fumikomi* were not shown in the either the 1922 or 1925 books.

xv. This was also observable in the *Heian,* before a kick. By 1925 this seems to have been corrected for the *Heian,* conforming to today's version, but *Tekki Shodan* is indeterminate, for it shows both versions, with a weighting for the new when the other three like-moves are examined.

xvi. This comes from *Ryukyu Kempo: Tode,* where *nagashi-uke* {–/9b} is not shown, and one is merely instructed to bring the right arm to the left elbow. The left fist is directed to the front of the nose, and no explanation is given as to which counter-attack is being employed. The 1932 film shows the move straight into *jodan-nagashi-uke.* In *Renten Gosin Tode-Jutsu,* two plates for the two *kosa-uke* have been inserted in the wrong places – the ordering of photographs on pages 101 and 120 should be reversed.

xvii. 1922 book.

xviii. 1925 book.

xix. 1922 book. It is not known whether *kiai* were practised in karate on Okinawa in the nineteenth century. The earliest reference to such a *kiai* the author has unearthed comes from a Tokyo newspaper report on a demonstration given by Funakoshi to the Tabata Poplar Club, which appeared in the *Nichinichi Shinbun* on the 3rd June, 1922. The report, entitled 'Secret Martial Art of Karate', notes the *kiai* in general terms.

xx. It is important to note that Hoan Kosugi (the artist), the typesetter and/or printer, publisher, or Funakoshi, actually made three ordering mistakes in the *kata* in *Ryukyu Kempo: Tode,* which must have been very confusing for the public. The alterations are triangular: Fig. 81 replaces Fig. 64; Fig. 64 replaces Fig. 70, and, Fig. 70 replaces Fig. 81.

xxi. This is the case with the 1922 book and 1932 film. In the 1925 book, the feet do not appear to have come together – unless a photograph was missed out.

xxii. From the 1932 film.

xxiii. It is a point of considerable contention as to whether Funakoshi had a daughter. If so, it has been recorded that her name was Tsuruko, that she was born in 1900/1901, and that she took the family name Morita.

xxiv. Furness noted that doors to the vaults were but loosely walled up.[27]

xxv. By 1872, according to Satow, 'the ordinary Japanese method of burying the corpse at once followed [the death], the ceremony being conducted by a Buddhist priest . . . A man's tomb was decorated with a piece of white cloth and a hat, and a pole was stuck in the ground close by on which were hung his straw sandals and wooden clogs. On a woman's grave they placed a palm leaf fan, fresh leaves of the same and a piece of white cloth.'[14]*

CHAPTER IV

i.   Taken from reference 5b.

ii.   It seems likely that *makiwara* were in use in the nineteenth century by virtue of the illustration in Nanto Zatsuwa's 1850 work. However, their presence would have alerted the authorities to the fact that karate was being practised. Funakoshi, reflecting in the 1934 article, 'Keio Gijuku Taiiku-kai Karate Bu Kaiho' (see Patrick McCarthy, *Karate-Do Tanpenshu* {2001}, pp. 41-48, for a translation), noted that Azato's house was full of training equipment, and includes the *makiwara*.

      In early twentieth century terms, Itosu records, in number four of his, *Ten Teachings* (1908), the use of the *makiwara* (Noble, G., McClaren, I. & Karasawa, N. *Masters of the Shorin-ryu* {*Fighting Arts International*, 50, pp. 24-28}). A picture of a *makiwara* appeared in Sasaki Gogai's article, 'Secret Fighting Techniques,' which was published in the December issue (Vol. 24) of the Japanese magazine, 'Secondary School World.' McCarthy (*ibid*, pp. 22–33) dates the article to 1921. In the 3rd June 1922 edition of the *Nichinichi Shinbun* (see reference xix, Ch. III) the *makiwara* is also mentioned. There is an accompanying line drawing of a *makiwara* in Funakoshi's 1922 book, and two photographs in his 1925 work.

iii. In the nineteenth century, a pistol was sometimes called a *tane-ga-shima* in colloquial Japanese.

iv.   Satow[14] writing in 1872, and, perhaps, referring to the Japanese account of Okinawa in 1850, already mentioned, notes the age for females at the time of marriage to be fourteen or fifteen. By 1925, the average age was eighteen or nineteen for men, seventeen or eighteen for women. This rose in the 1930's and entered the twenties for both sexes.

v.   *Shotokan Newsletter*, No. 104, 13th October, 1998; and, No. 105, 5th January, 1999.

vi.   What follows is a rough guide, as writers of the late nineteenth century do not always agree as to the number or order of events.

vii. 'In the higher classes, valuable presents were made on these occasions, but the common people were not expected to go to greater expense than a bag of rice and two strings of cash,'[14]* though, in direct opposition, it was also reported that this present among the wealthy classes 'was usually a large sack of rice and one yen (a Japanese dollar) in money, but among the poorer people, who could ill afford to lose the services of their daughter, the present had to be much larger, and ten or twenty yen was the usual price paid to the parents of the bride.'[27]*

viii. Note that Funakoshi and his wife had at least three, possibly four sons.

ix. Western authors seem to have very contrary points to make about weddings and faithful attachment. Clutterbuck, for example, noted: 'The idea of a wedding ring struck them as a great joke, for they have evidently little respect for married life . . . [and on asking a noble how many children he had] he immediately left the room to consult with someone outside. When he had been absent a minute he returned and said 'Ten.' It seemed difficult at first to know why he had quitted the apartment after such a simple question had been asked, but we had heard him in the distance evidently talking it over with someone. Our Japanese friend told us privately that he had a great many children, so that the query confused him for the moment, and it was necessary to calculate just which were his wife's children and which were not!'[15]

x. M'Leod wrote: 'He was above the usual size of the Okinawans, and [had] rather more of the European cast of countenance. His robe was of a dark pink-coloured silk; the cap rather of a lighter hue, with bright yellow lozenges on it. In his mien and deportment there was much dignified similarity; for, although his carriage was that of a man of high rank, it was totally unmixed with the least appearance of hauteur; and his demeanour was, altogether, extremely engaging.'[3]

xi. G. Noble, I. McLaren, & N. Karasawa. *The History of Japanese Masters: The Masters of Shorin-ryu (Fighting Arts International*, 50, 24–28).

xii. However, for *shizuko* women, this was not always the case, even with foreigners. McLeod noted an incident concerning Mrs. Loy that is in direct contrast to that quoted in the text, when he wrote: 'A young lady of high rank who had a great curiosity to see this *Inago-Engelee*, or Englishwoman, was brought to her one day when she was quite alone, by some of the gentlemen who were in the habit of visiting the ship. She walked around her for a considerable time, eyeing her with great appearance of surprise. On Mrs. Loy advancing to shake hands with her, she at first timorously shrunk behind her own countrymen, who smiled at her alarm, and seemed to explain to her the meaning of this ceremony.'[3]

This 'meeting of women' was repeated in 1837 when Mrs. King, travelling aboard the Morrison, walked around Naha: 'The crowd, constantly increasing in fresh recruits, now stood gazing at us, especially Mrs. King, who in this and all our subsequent walks attracted much notice, yet who never experienced any incivility from the multitudes around her. The messenger returned, bringing some water, and followed by a female from the house, who approached with timid steps. To encourage her, Mrs. King went forward and took her by the hand . . . This scene was observed by the by-standers with great attention, and evident pleasure.'[13]

On one such walk, Williamson noted, 'Many females, some of them grey-haired old dames, were collected in entrances of the dwelling-yards and on the tops of the walls, in order to catch a glimpse of us; and there were a number following in the crowd.'[13]

Reporting in 1910, but referring to an earlier visit, Clutterbuck noted: 'Then we had our first experience of walking about the town [of Naha]; everyone stared very hard at us, and hundreds of children crowded round, peering into our faces, shouting and skipping. They had never ['never' being italicised] before set eyes on a woman in European dress. The one missionary lady, who at the time of our visit was known to have visited these islands, having worn Japanese costume entirely.'[15] Presumably, the woman referred to was Mrs. Bettelheim in the 1850s. It seems unlikely that Mrs. Loy and Mrs. King would have worn Japanese dress.

McLeod wrote: 'When they were uncertain of our designs on our first arrival, it appeared that some order was given to keep the women in the background; but, the fears which occasioned that measure were daily subsiding, for, on walking through the invisible village the day before we left the island, there seemed to be no appearance of timidity or concealment. Among themselves, from all we could learn, they are under as few restrictions as any other women in the world; and if the kind manner in which the men treated their children be any criterion whereby to judge of their conduct to their wives, it indicated the full enjoyment of domestic bliss.'[3] Perhaps this concealment of women was a feature of mid to late nineteenth century Okinawa, for the picture painted by McLeod from his experiences in 1816, and Samuel Wells Williamson in 1837, are marked in comparison.

xiii. On another track, when seen, however, a number of writers commented upon the Okinawan women, from common stock, as being, to use Hawks's chosen words, 'strikingly unhandsome.'[5] Bishop Smith noted that, 'in both sexes there was a remarkable absence of everything associated in a European mind with the idea of beauty.'[17] Adams noted in a brief description of a market square scene in Po-tsang, on the outskirts of Naha, in 1845, that 'the old hags . . . were about the most hideous objects I have seen in the course of all my travels . . . [and noted] an occasional exception to this ungracious and not-at-all-gallant picture, might be found in the person of a young girl or marriageable maiden.'[11a] Capain Beechey noted that the women of the labouring classes were not the most attractive specimens of their sex, 'but [that] they were equally good-looking with the men.'[24]

Clutterbuck, saw something else, when, comparing Okinawan and Japanese women, he wrote the Okinawan women seemed, 'much bigger and stronger, and many of the young girls were very pretty, with their big, soft, brown eyes . . . The women in fact often reminded us of southern Europeans.'[15] He continued: 'We were introduced to our host's mother, aunts, and his family of four generations. They all squatted on the boards outside, and we had to step back out of the matted room to make the acquaintance of the Omura ladies . . . The two aunts were remarkably handsome women, with such beautiful regular features and prominent chins. They all had black hair, there was not a grey-haired person among these four generations who were before us . . . the ladies had beautiful hair, like girls of twenty and their teeth were wonderful compared with those of Europeans . . . Suddenly, Omura *San* asked if the English lady would mind showing them how she did up her hair. So she pulled out her many hairpins, and instantly the females present ran round to the open balcony behind her, and felt her hair in turn; they said that they thought it very soft, like silk.'[15] Halloran noted that: 'Twice only had I the good fortune to catch sight of some females, whose tasteful dresses, fine figures, bright eyes, and pretty faces, made me wish for a better acquaintance,'[18] and Habersham wrote that 'some of the women were very pretty.'[22]* Beechey found that 'a few of them were pretty, notwithstanding the assertion of An-yah [an Okinawan] that 'Loo Choo womans ugly womans.'[24] Perhaps, it was a simple case of being 'in the eye of the beholder?'

CHAPTER V

i.   A headland known as False Capstan on old English Admiralty charts.

ii.   The list of imports has been taken from Gubbins[10], from figures provided by the Japanese Home Office authorities in Naha.

iii.   Figures from Chamberlain.[4a]

iv.   Translation taken from 4a* of *Ryukyu Enkaku Chiri*.

v.   This comparison refers to Funakoshi's strict adherence to propriety. 'Liu-hia Hwui was one of the seventy-two worthies, who were disciples, and many of them contemporaries of, Confucius. His family name was Chen, and his name Hwoh; he received the title of Liu-hia, or Under the Willow, from the place where he ruled. He belonged to the same country and age as Confucius, and enjoyed the confidence of his sovereign. He was very strict in the observance of the forms of etiquette, and is chiefly known for his not noticing a young girl of eight or ten years of age who was once seated in his lap by a relative. He is also styled Chi-ching the Just, from his regard to equity and veracity.[25]

vi.   Later, Funakoshi kept himself, his wife, four children, two parents and two grandparents – a total of ten – on the salary of a teacher. As he noted, 'the fact that we were able to do this was due entirely to the diligence of my wife.'[c]

vii. 4th August, 1947.

viii. There is much dispute about when Matsumura was born, with dates ranging from 1796 to 1809, and when he died. He may of possibly have just lived into the twentieth century. The current evidence suggests that his dates are 1809–1901, which augur with the belief that he lived to the age of ninety-two.

ix. This is sometimes written as 'Miyazato,' and presumably refers to the same individual.

x. The classic of Taoism.

xi. Taken from *b*.

xii. These figures are taken from Leavenworth (1904), and as such are likely to be inflated for 1892. There were two hospitals in Naha by 1903, for example.

xiii. Sometimes written as 'Higashionna.'

xiv. Sometimes written as 'Ryuruko.' Colin Whitehead, in an excellent and most informative interview with karate historian, Patrick McCarthy, (*The Black Ship of Karate-Do: Patrick McCarthy – Part 1* {*Fighting Arts International*, 86, 16–22}), quotes McCarthy as having researched that Ryuruko is likely to be Xie Chongxiang (1852–1930), a shoemaker and outstanding exponent of the White Crane method, though this has been disputed.

xv. Higaonna was born in 1853 and died in 1915.

xvi. Later, Higaonna was to be given the title of *Kensei* (Sacred fists) by the people of Naha. Among Higaonna's later top students was Chojun Miyagi, who went on to form Goju-ryu karate based on the teachings of his master. Higaonna taught Naha-te. Shuri-te and Tomari-te merged in a sense, the outcome being Shorin-ryu and Shotokan. However, it is said that Itosu learned *Seisan* or *Seishan*, nowadays referred to as *Hangetsu* in Shotokan (after the principal stance's arcing motion {half-moon}), from Higaonna, the *kata* being taken, it is believed, from the Wutang School, before entering Naha-te.

xvii. Chotoku Kyan was born in 1870, the son of Chofu Kyan, a retainer to King Sho Tai. It is believed that he trained mostly under Kokan Oyadomari and Kosaku Matsumura, the two most famous teachers of Tomari karate, and with Chirikata Yara and Sokon Matsumura. Kyan, a colourful character, had a number of unorthodox methods of instruction, including, it is believed, taking students to local brothels. It is unknown what sort of instruction was given there! Later, in 1914 or 1915, Kyan, along with Funakoshi, Kenwa Mabuni, Choki Motobu, 'Gusukuma, Ogusuku, Tokumura, Ishikawa, Yahiku,'[a] amongst others, gave many demonstrations in Shuri, Naha and local towns to promote the art. Kyan died in 1945.

xviii. Leavenworth* (1904).

xix. Changed to *Kwanku* in Okinawan by Funakoshi, but 'derives from a form originally called Koshukon'[f] – an envoy of the Ming emperor of China.

xx. Much of what follows comes from Funakoshi's writings, and it is assumed that what is said in this regard is from what he was taught on Okinawa.

xxi. Master Hirokazu Kanazawa recalled: 'I only ever saw Funakoshi *Sensei* perform a *kata* once, and that was *Kanku-dai*, which was his favourite form . . . One point I noticed was the opening move. We in the JKA had always been told to bring the arms up slowly, break suddenly, and then bring the hands to the front, just as you see today. Funakoshi *Sensei*, however, didn't perform the movement this way. He brought his hands up, but when the hands were split there was no sudden break, and instead of bending his arms, they were straight. Yes, I remember that distinctly.'[e]

xxii. In *Ryukyu Kempo: Tode* (1922), plates 87 and 88 should be reversed.

xxiii. Which was more like *jodan* in the 1922 book.

xxiv. *Rentan Goshi Tode-jutsu* (1925).

xxv. These moves refer to the position of the hands just before one side-kicks in the *kata*, before the *uraken*, for example.

xxvi. In the 1925 book we see that *koshi gamae* before the *tate-shuto-uke* is not the same as that performed, at least for the first of the moves with a side-kick (the other two are obscured), where the fists are placed one on top of the other in the modern way.

xxvii. In the 1922 work the right punch is nearly at *jodan* level, whereas the left punch is *jodan*. In the 1925 work, both punches are a wide *chudan*.

xxviii. No back-fist strike is illustrated in the 1922 work.

xxix. Though no mention of level is recorded in the 1922 work.

xxx. The 1925 work shows the positioning of this technique to be neck height.

xxxi. There are none in the 1922 and 1925 books, but there is one, located on the first *nukite*, in *Karate-Do Kyohan* (1935).

xxxii. This seems to be confirmed in the1925 work.

xxxiii. This is confirmed in the 1925 work.

xxxiv. No explanation is given in the 1922 book, and the level in both that and the 1925 work seem intermediate between *jodan* and *chudan* {105/–}. This move is repeated {110/–}.

xxxv. The twist of the wrist to form *uraken* is clearly shown in both the 1922 and 1925 books.

xxxvi. {–/42} assuming one was actually performed, though a knee attack is mentioned {128/–}.

xxxvii. This had been corrected/changed by 1925. Funakoshi is to be seen, essentially, in the modern position {–/43}, but looking the other way – that is, behind him.

xxxviii.The 1925 book shows Funakoshi in a very deep stance, quite unlike his, or the modern *kokutsu-dachi*, and reflecting very much a Chinese influence. The left arm and hand, in contrast to the 1922 work, are shown performing the *gedan shuto-uke* we see today {–/44}, though the palm of the right *shuto* is on the solar plexus, and not further forward.

xxxix. Though no name is given in 1922.

xl.   In the 1925 work, the final technique of this move is a sidewards *uraken*.

xli.   This is noticeable in both the 1922 and 1925 books.

xlii.   Both the 1922 {151,152/–} and 1925 books show the absence of a jump and the foot movements clearly show a *ren-geri* technique with the supporting foot on the floor. Whereas the fists in *juji-uke* mode are kept on the chest {150/63}, and on the jump {151,152/64a} they are kept high, as though performing a *jodan* block, when kicking, in the 1925 work.

xliii. Master Kanazawa, on Funakoshi's *Kanaku-dai*, noted: 'The *kata* was not obviously strong, not fast, but it was very tasteful. There was something different about it that's hard to put into words – strange, yet highly polished timing.'[e]

xliv.   This is an assumption, for it is widely believed that Itosu taught *Tekki* initially, then other forms. It may well have been that Funakoshi learned *Kanku-Dai* from Azato, and learned that form first, but he might have equally been taught *Tekki* or *Bassai-dai*. On Okinawa in those days, *kata* was the formal practice, and as Funakoshi started training with Azato, it must be assumed he learned a *kata*. Funakoshi noted that he spent ten years learning the three *Tekki* under Itosu, but unfortunately neglects to mention which ten years. The years may have been in a single block, or in two or three blocks, for *Tekki Nidan* and *Tekki Sandan* were created for school children, with the earlier *Tekki Shodan* acting as the model. When *Tekki Nidan* and *Tekki Sandan* were created is also unclear, though probably somewhere between 1890–1910. It has also been suggested that when Funakoshi settled in Tokyo in 1922, he only 'knew' one *kata*, *Kanku-dai*, for he let an Okinawan junior, Shinken Gima, demonstrate *Tekki* for Jigaro Kano. The author finds this suggestion possible, but most unlikely.

xlv.   See Funakoshi's *Kaizo* article (Introduction reference xi, p. 26).

PLATE CREDITS

Plate 1. Kerr, B. (1958) *Okinawa: The History of an Island People* (Tuttle), Plate 26.

Plate 2. Smith, G. (1853) *Lewchew and the Lewchewans: Being a Narrative of a Visit to Lewchew or Loo Choo, in October, 1850* (T. Hatchard, London). From a sketch by Capt. P. Cracroft, R.N.

Plate 3. Hawks, F.L. (1856) *Narrative of the Expedition of an American Squadron to the China Seas and Japan, Performed in the Years 1852, 1853, and 1854, Under the Command of Commodore M.G. Perry, United States Navy, by Order of the Government of the United States*, p.168. Credited to W. Heine.

Plate 4. Habersham, A.W. (1857) *The North Pacific Surveying and Exploring Expedition: or My Last Cruise, Where We Went and What We Saw: Being an Account of Visits to the Malay and Loo-Choo Islands, the Coasts of China, Formosa, Japan, Kamtschatka, Siberia and the Mouth of the Amoor River* (J.B. Lippincott, Philadelphia). Plate facing p. 182.

Plate 5. Hawks, F.L. (1856) *Ibid* – plate facing p. 219. From a Daguerreotype by Brown.

Plate 6. Beechey, F.W. (1831) *Narrative of a Voyage to the Pacific and Beerings Strait to Co-operate with the Polar Expeditions: Performed in His Majesty's Ship Blossom under the Command of Captain F. W. Beechey R.N., F.R.S., etc, in the Years 1825, 26, 27, 28* (Henry Colburn and Richard Bentley, Vol. II). Plate facing p.171. Drawn by William Smyth, engraved by Edward Finden.

Plate 7. Kerr, B. (1958) *Ibid* – Plate 27.

Plate 8. Kerr, B. (1958) *Ibid* – Plate 4.

Plate 9. Hawks, F.L. (1856) *Ibid* – plate facing p. 189. Credited to W. Heine.

Plate 10. Chamberlain, B.H. (1895) *The Luchu Islands and Their Inhabitants* (*Geographical Journal*, Vol. V), photograph on p. 305.

Plate 11. Guillemard, F.H.H. (1886) *The Cruise of the Marchesa to Kamschatka and New Guinea with Notices of Formosa, Liu-Kiu, and Various Islands of the Malay Archipelago* (John Murray, London, Vol. I), p. 33. Engraving by Edward Whymper.

Plate 12. Guillemard, F.H.H. (1886) *Ibid* – p. 59. Engraving by Edward Whymper.

Plate 13. Hawks, F.L. (1856) *Ibid* – p. 161.

Plate 14. Hawks, F.L. (1856) *Ibid* – p. 157.

Plate 15. Hawks, F.L. (1856) *Ibid* – plate facing p. 184. Credited to W. Heine, figures by Brown.

Plate 16. Guillemard, F.H.H. (1886) *Ibid* – p. 60. Engraving by Edward Whymper.

Plate 17. Hawks, F.L. (1856) *Ibid* – p. 182. Credited to W. Heine, figures by Brown.

Plate 18. Hawks, F.L. (1856) *Ibid* – plate facing p. 164. Credited to W. Heine.

Plate 19. Hawks, F.L. (1856) *Ibid* – p. 178. Credited to W. Heine.

Plate 20. Chamberlain, B.H. (1895) *Ibid* – photograph, p. 318.

Plate 21. Beechey, F.W. (1831) *Ibid* – p. 167. Drawn by William Smyth, engraved by Edward Finden.

Plate 22. Beechey, F.W. (1831) *Ibid* – p. 162.

Plate 23. Guillemard, F.H.H. (1886) *Ibid* – p. 40. Engraving by Edward Whymper.

Plate 24. Hawks, F.L. (1856) *Ibid* – p. 172.

Plate 25. Nagoshi, S. (1850) *Nanto Zatsuwa*.

Plate 26. Habersham, A.W. (1857) *Ibid* – plate facing p. 184.

Plate 27. Guillemard, F.H.H. (1886) *Ibid* – p. 37. Engraving by Edward Whymper.

Plate 28. Beechey, F.W. (1831) *Ibid* – plate facing p. 167. Drawn by William Smyth, engraved by Edward Finden.

Plate 29. Kerr, B. (1958) *Ibid* – Plate 5. [Taken from Basil Hall's book].

Plate 30. Hall, B. (1818) *Account of a Voyage of Discovery to the West Coast of Corea and the Great Loo-Choo Island* (John Murray). Plate facing p. 196. From a sketch by C.W. Browne, R.N., drawn by William Havell, engraved by Robert Havell & Son.

Plate 31. Beechey, F. W. (1831) *Ibid* – plate facing p. 144. Drawn by William Smyth.

Plate 32. Hawks, F.L. (1856) *Ibid* – p. 161.

Plate 33. Chamberlain, B.H. (1895) *Ibid* – photograph p. 312.

Plate 34. Kirby Publishing.

Plate 35. Kirby Publishing.

Plate 36. Hawks, F.L. (1856) *Ibid* – plate facing p. 215. Drawn by Brown.

Plate 37. Hawks, F.L. (1856) *Ibid* – p. 216. Credited to W. Heine.

GLOSSARY OF KARATE TERMS

Bassai-dai – a Shotokan *kata* (to penetrate a fortress – major)

Bo – stick (staff)

Bujutsu – martial skill

Bushi – warrior

Bushi no te – warrior's hands

Chinto – the original name for the *kata Gankaku*

Chudan – middle-level (chest height)

Chudan tettsui-uchi – middle-level hammer-fist

Chudan uchi-uke – middle-level inside block

Do – Way

Dojo – Place of the Way (training hall)

Embusen – *a kata's* line of movement

Enpi – a Shotokan *kata* (flying swallow)

Enoi – relax

Fumikomi – stamping-kick

Gamae – guard

Gankaku – a Shotokan *kata* (crane on a rock)

Gedan – lower-level

Gedan shuto-uchi – lower-level knife-hand strike

Gedan shuto-uke – lower-level knife-hand block

Geta – wooden or iron clogs

Gi – outfit worn by *karateka*

Gyaku-zuki – reverse-punch

Hachiji-dachi – Open-leg stance

Haishu-uke – back-hand block

Hangetsu – a Shotokan *kata* (half-moon)

Hanmi – half-front-facing position

Hara – lower abdomen

Heian – peace (customarily translated as 'peaceful mind' when referring to *kata*)

Heiko-dachi – parallel-stance

Ippon-ken – one-knuckle fist

Jodan – upper-level (head height)

Jodan nagashi-uke – upper-level sweeping-block

Jodan oi-zuki – upper-level lunge punch

Jodan shuto juji-uke – upper-level knife-hand X-block

Jodan shuto-uchi – upper-level knife-hand strike
Jodan uraken – upper-level back-fist
Jujitsu – gentle science/skill (unarmed combat system utilizing opponent's strength to his disadvantage
Juji-uke – X-block
Jutsu – craft (distinct from *Do*)
Kagi-zuki – hook-punch
Kahanashi – instep
Kaishu-haiwan-uke – open-hand back-arm block
Kanji – Japanese calligraphy
Kanku-dai – a Shotokan *kata* (to view the sky – major)
Karate – empty-hand
Karate-Do – Way of the empty-hand
Karateka – one who practises karate
Kata – forms (set movements in set sequences)
Keito – chicken-head wrist
Kiai – expression of vital spirit; a special type of yell
Kiai-jutsu – vital spirit (yell) skill
Kiba-dachi – straggle-leg stance
Kihon – basics
Kime – focus of vital spirit
Kobudo – classical weapons
Kokutsu-dachi – back-stance
Kosa-dachi – cross-over stance
Kosa-uke – cross-over block
Koshi-gamae – hip posture
Kumite – sparring
Kushanku – early name for the *kata Kanku-dai*
Kwanku – Okinawan for *Kanku (dai)*
Mae-geri – front-kick
Makiwara – punching board
Manji-gamae – Swastika-guard (the Swastika features in Buddhist iconography)
Morote-uke – augmented-block
Morote-zuki – augmented-punch
Nagashi-uke – sweeping-block
Naha-te – the style of karate practised in Naha
Naihanchi – original name for *Tekki*
Naihanchi-dachi – *naihanchi* stance
Name-ashi – return-wave kick
Nukite – spear-hand

Nunchaku – flail

Okinawa-te – Okinawa-hand (the name is a forerunner to 'karate')

Passai – original name for *Bassai-dai*

Pinan – the original name for the *Heian kata*

Ren-geri – consecutive kicking

Ryo ude mawashi-uke – double forearm roundhouse-block

Ryu – school or style

Sai – Chinese/Okinawan hooked metal truncheon

Sake – rice wine

Seiken – fore-fist

Seisan – a Goju-ryu *kata* (thirteen)

Sempai – senior

Sensei – teacher

Shihon-nukite – four-fingered spear-hand

Shiko-dachi – square-stance

Shizentai – natural position

Shuri-te – the style of karate practised in Shuri

Shuto – knife-hand

Shuto-uke – knife-hand block

Tameshiwari – trial by wood (wood breaking)

Tanden – navel

Tate-shuto-uke – vertical knife-hand block

Tegumi – wrestling

Tekki – iron horse (generic name – formerly called *naihanchi*)

Tekki Nidan – a Shotokan *kata* (iron horse – 2nd level)

Tekki Sandan – a Shotokan *kata* (iron horse – 3rd level)

Tekki Shodan – a Shotokan *kata* (iron horse – 1st level)

Tode – (the name is a forerunner to 'karate')

Tou – bamboo bundle

Tsuki – this may be a strike or a punch – Funakoshi is not always clear

Tsumasaki mae-geri – front-kick delivered with the tips of the toes

Ura-zuki – close-punch

Ura-te – back-hand

Uraken – back-fist

Uraken-uchi – back-fist strike

Wanshu – original name for the *kata Enpi*

Yamae – stop

Yoi – ready

Yori-ashi – sliding-step

Zanshi – remaining mind

Zenkutsu-dachi – front-stance

ABOUT THE AUTHOR

Clive Layton was born in Hertfordshire in 1952, the son of an architect. He began his martial arts training with judo in 1960 under Terry Wingrove, and started Shotokan karate in 1973 under Michael Randall and the Adamou brothers, Nick and Chris, gaining his black-belt from Hirokazu Kanazawa in 1977. Originally studying environmental design, he later read for M.A and Ph.D degrees from the University of London, and is a Chartered Psychologist and teacher. Doctor Layton has appeared on both BBC television and radio in connection with his academic work. A prolific writer, with ninety publications, including eighteen books on karate, and numerous learned research notes, including those co-authored with famed Goju-ryu master, Morio Higaonna, and Kyokushinkai master, Steve Arneil, to his credit, he has emerged not only as one of the most productive, but, arguably, the finest writer on the Way of Shoto in the world. His biography of the early years in the life of Master Hirokazu Kanazawa has recently been published to much acclaim, as has his two volume work, *Shotokan Dawn*, which charts the first ten years of Shotokan karate in Great Britain. He has also acted for many years as a consultant reader to the journal, *Perceptual and Motor Skills*, on experimentation into the martial arts. Any spare time is taken up researching new books, pursuing his love of archaeology, film and fine clarets, and enjoying the peace of rural life, by the sea, with his wife, daughter and labrador. A highly innovative and deep-thinking *karateka*, in 1997 he was awarded the rank of 6th Dan.

About the Publishers

Left to right: Master Michael Randall, Sensei Anthony Kirby and
Grandmaster Hirokazu Kanazawa Kancho – Windsor England 1999

Anthony Kirby was born in London in May 1964.
He started training in Shotokan Karate at the famous Winchmore Hill Dojo in
1979 under Michael Randall.
He has also been privileged to train with Master Hirokazu Kanazawa Kancho
10th Dan, during his many visits to England. He has developed a great interest
in the history of Karate, especially Shotokan, which has progressed further
with his involvement in publishing books on the subject.
Living and working in North London with his wife and two young children
he currently holds the rank of 3rd Dan.

Michael Randall was born in London during the second Blitz of World War
Two, in April 1944. On January 7th 1964, he began practicing Shotokan
Karate under The Founding Father of British Karate, Dr. Vernon Bell. He is
one of the few people to have been taught by Masters Tetsuji Murakami and
Hiroo Mochizuki. An original disciple of the world famous Shotokan Master,
Hirokazu Kanazawa Kancho 10th Dan. On January 6th 1967, he became one
of the first in Great Britain to be graded to black belt under the Japan Karate
Association. A staunch traditionalist and much respected for his kata,
nevertheless, he represented Great Britain for kumite in 1970 (Great Britain
v Japan Karate Association). In 1976, he was British Team Coach for the
Shotokan Karate International team that visited Japan. He has researched
and co-authored various books on Shotokan Karate-do, for further details
see: www.shoto.org. His story is told in: 'The Kanazawa Years' by
Dr. Clive Layton. Currently he holds the rank of 8th Dan, and on November
13th 2003, he was awarded the MBE for "Services to Karate" by Her Majesty
Queen Elizabeth II.

The Publishers Karate Genealogy

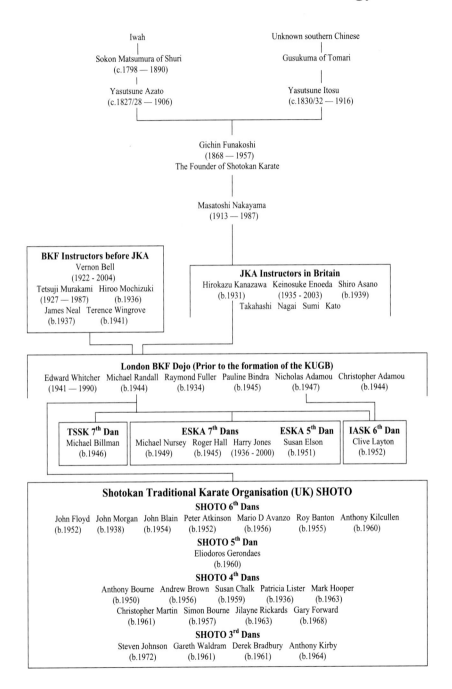

Iwah
|
Sokon Matsumura of Shuri
(c.1798 — 1890)
|
Yasutsune Azato
(c.1827/28 — 1906)

Unknown southern Chinese
|
Gusukuma of Tomari
|
Yasutsune Itosu
(c.1830/32 — 1916)

Gichin Funakoshi
(1868 — 1957)
The Founder of Shotokan Karate

Masatoshi Nakayama
(1913 — 1987)

BKF Instructors before JKA
Vernon Bell
(1922 - 2004)
Tetsuji Murakami   Hiroo Mochizuki
(1927 — 1987)   (b.1936)
James Neal   Terence Wingrove
(b.1937)   (b.1941)

JKA Instructors in Britain
Hirokazu Kanazawa   Keinosuke Enoeda   Shiro Asano
(b.1931)   (1935 - 2003)   (b.1939)
Takahashi   Nagai   Sumi   Kato

London BKF Dojo (Prior to the formation of the KUGB)
Edward Whitcher   Michael Randall   Raymond Fuller   Pauline Bindra   Nicholas Adamou   Christopher Adamou
(1941 — 1990)   (b.1944)   (b.1934)   (b.1945)   (b.1947)   (b.1944)

TSSK 7ᵗʰ Dan
Michael Billman
(b.1946)

ESKA 7ᵗʰ Dans
Michael Nursey   Roger Hall   Harry Jones
(b.1949)   (b.1945)   (1936 - 2000)

ESKA 5ᵗʰ Dan
Susan Elson
(b.1951)

IASK 6ᵗʰ Dan
Clive Layton
(b.1952)

Shotokan Traditional Karate Organisation (UK) SHOTO
SHOTO 6ᵗʰ Dans
John Floyd   John Morgan   John Blain   Peter Atkinson   Mario D Avanzo   Roy Banton   Anthony Kilcullen
(b.1952)   (b.1938)   (b.1954)   (b.1952)   (b.1956)   (b.1955)   (b.1960)
SHOTO 5ᵗʰ Dan
Eliodoros Gerondaes
(b.1960)
SHOTO 4ᵗʰ Dans
Anthony Bourne   Andrew Brown   Susan Chalk   Patricia Lister   Mark Hooper
(b.1950)   (b.1956)   (b.1959)   (b.1936)   (b.1963)
Christopher Martin   Simon Bourne   Jilayne Rickards   Gary Forward
(b.1961)   (b.1957)   (b.1963)   (b.1968)
SHOTO 3ʳᵈ Dans
Steven Johnson   Gareth Waldram   Derek Bradbury   Anthony Kirby
(b.1972)   (b.1961)   (b.1961)   (b.1964)

OTHER BOOKS AVAILABLE FROM KIRBY PUBLISHING

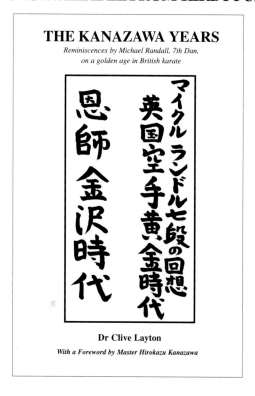

THE KANAZAWA YEARS

Reminiscences by Michael Randall, 7th Dan,
on a golden age in British karate

Dr Clive Layton

With a Foreword by Master Hirokazu Kanazawa

It is, perhaps, difficult for students of Shotokan karate today, to appreciate what training was like in Britain before the coming of the Japan Karate Association. Using the Murakami based British Karate Federation training as a starting point, Michael Randall reflects on the arrival of the JKA's Hirokazu Kanazawa, and the tremendous impact his presence had on the British Shotokan movement.

THE KANAZAWA YEARS thus mainly focuses on the period 1965 to 1968, when the master resided in this country. During this time, Michael became a close disciple of Kanazawa's – one of the Seven Samurai – and was amongst the very first in Britain to gain a JKA karate black-belt. He is, therefore, exceptionally well qualified to speak authoritively on the subject, and the book is subsequently packed full of stories, often very funny, not only about Kanazawa and the rigorous training, but also of other famous JKA instructors that Michael practised under. The work concludes with a brief "Kanazawa Legacy", a personal account detailing the following three decades of Michael's training, which is seen as a product of those three highly influential years.

THE KANAZAWA YEARS, which contains over one hundred historical photographs, is destined to become a classic, and will forever keep alive a period in British Shotokan history that was perilously close to being lost.

Hardback Edition ISBN 0 9530287 2 0
Paperback Edition ISBN 0 9530287 3 9

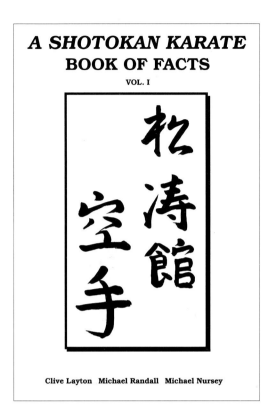

A SHOTOKAN KARATE
BOOK OF FACTS

VOL. I

松涛館
空手

Clive Layton   Michael Randall   Michael Nursey

A SHOTOKAN KARATE BOOK OF FACTS is a valuable, easy to access reference work, on general, historical and technical matters. The authors, all respected senior karateka of long standing, have collaborated to produce a much needed and well-researched quality book, which is considered essential reading for students and instructors alike, who wish to acquire a deeper understanding of their art.

Adopting a question and answer format, Layton, Randall and Nursey have explored a tremendously diverse range of material within their remit. The facts and figures presented, together with the accompanying photographs, allow this unique book to stand proud among the classics in karate publications.

ISBN 0 9530287 0 4

A SHOTOKAN KARATE
BOOK OF FACTS
VOL. II

Clive Layton and Michael Randall

In the wake of the success of Volume I of **A SHOTOKAN KARATE BOOK OF FACTS**, this book continues the tradition of providing a valuable reference work for students of Shotokan, irrespective of grade, who wish to acquire a deeper appreciation of their art.

Once again, general, historical and technical information is presented in a friendly question and answer format, and authors' opinions add much where interpretation is required. Also included in this volume are signatures of karateka and budoka important in the development of Shotokan in Great Britain, before the official coming of the Japan Karate Association. Carefully worked out kata embusen are additionally provided, which readers are advised to consult. Historical and detailed photographs accompany the text.

This sequel is one of those rare books that equals the original. **A SHOTOKAN KARATE BOOK OF FACTS** is therefore now, rightly, in two volumes. Layton and Randall have not only made a valuable contribution to Shotokan by producing this work, they are also to be commended for making the information accessible to a wide audience.

ISBN 0 9530287 1 2

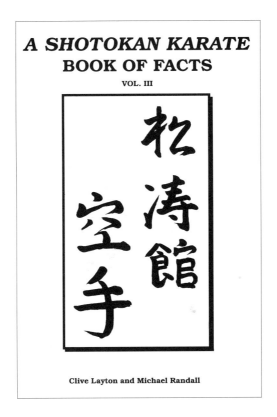

A SHOTOKAN KARATE
BOOK OF FACTS
VOL. III

松涛館
空手

Clive Layton and Michael Randall

A SHOTOKAN KARATE BOOK OF FACTS: Vol. III brings this exceptional and much appreciated reference work to an end. In all, over five hundred questions – general, historical and technical in nature – have been answered.

Features of the present volume include signatures from selected senior British Shotokan karate-ka holding the rank of sixth Dan and above, rare photographs from Japan, the earliest photographs of karate ever published in this country, and Japanese calligraphy. Of course, a whole range of fascinating questions, some quite bizarre, are answered in the same friendly manner that proved so successful in the previous two books. In a few cases, newly acquired information has allowed old gaps in knowledge to be filled, or corrected, and interesting research by the authors, published here for the first time, will open up thoughtful debate. Volume III concludes with a valuable three-volume index and terminology section.

Layton, Randall and Nursey (Vol. I only) have written a series of books that are in a sense, timeless. **A SHOTOKAN KARATE BOOK OF FACTS** really must be considered essential reading for any thoughtful Shotokan karate-ka. One magazine critic wrote of Vol. I, "A 10/10 must buy," and Volumes II and III may also be said to fall into this elite category.

ISBN 0 9530287 4 7

A SHOTOKAN KARATE
BOOK OF DATES

Clive Layton and Michael Randall

A SHOTOKAN KARATE BOOK OF DATES is an invaluable, easy to read reference work, written for both students and instructors alike. Five hundred chronologically presented date entries are included, generally following an Okinawa-Japan-Great Britain line. Dates commence with the mid 14th century and conclude at 1972, shortly after which came a proliferation of Shotokan karate associations and competitions in Britain, making recording, in the opinion of the authors, often a confusing and not wholly worthwhile affair.

A SHOTOKAN KARATE BOOK OF DATES is another *essential* work from two of Britain's most senior grades, whose collaboration in the past has resulted in the classic three volume, *A Shotokan Karate Book of Facts*, and the much praised, *The Kanazawa Years*.

ISBN 0 9539338 0 6

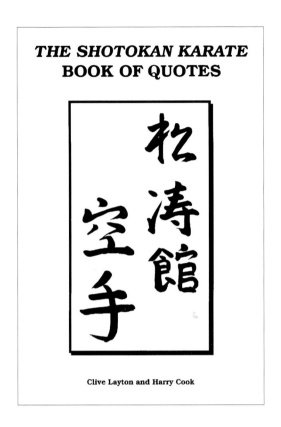

THE SHOTOKAN KARATE BOOK OF QUOTES

松涛館
空手

Clive Layton and Harry Cook

The image of Shotokan karateka sharing identical views about the nature of their art is a popular but inaccurate myth. **THE SHOTOKAN KARATE BOOK OF QUOTES** is a unique collection of the thoughts and ideas of many leading Shotokan teachers and practitioners about the essentials of Shotokan karate-do. Using the widest possible range of sources to illustrate the some-times opposing yet provocative opinions of senior Shotokan karateka of many nationalities, **THE SHOTOKAN KARATE BOOK OF QUOTES** is an in-valuable guide for anyone who genuinely wants to understand the art of Shotokan karate-do as it really is.

Hardback Edition   ISBN 0 9539338 3 0
Paperback Edition ISBN 0 9539338 2 2

KANAZAWA, 10th DAN
Recollections of a Living Karate Legend
The early years (1931-1964)

Dr. Clive Layton

Arrange for the world's finest writer on Shotokan to meet the world's most famous karate master prepared to reveal a largely untold story, then something special is in the air. Often humorous, sometimes sad, but always inspirational, **KANAZAWA, 10th DAN** is a compelling read. A shotokan classic from the first day of publication

Hardback Edition ISBN 0 9530287 2 0
Paperback Edition ISBN 0 9530287 3 9